MW00718772

The Bus Driver's Mother

The
Bus
Driver's
Mother

BEVERLY PRIDGEN

IZZARD INK
PUBLISHING

IZZARD INK PUBLISHING
PO Box 522251
Salt Lake City, Utah 84152
www.izzardink.com

Copyright © 2021 by Beverly Pridgen
All rights reserved. Except as permitted under the U.S. Copyright Act of 1976, no
part of this publication may be reproduced, distributed, or transmitted in any form
or by any means, or stored in a database or retrieval system, electronically or
otherwise, or by use of a technology or retrieval system now known or to be
invented, without the prior written permission of the author and publisher.

Library of Congress Cataloging-in-Publication Data
Names: Pridgen, Beverly, author.
Title: The bus driver's mother / Beverly Pridgen.
Description: First edition. | Salt Lake City, Utah : Izzard Ink Publishing, [2021]
Identifiers: LCCN 2021054401 (print) | LCCN 2021054402 (ebook) |
ISBN 9781642280753 (hardback) | ISBN 9781642280746 (paperback) |
ISBN 9781642280739 (ebook)
Subjects: LCGFT: Domestic fiction. | Novels.
Classification: LCC PS3616.R53548 B87 2021 (print) | LCC PS3616.R53548
(ebook) | DDC 813/.6—dc23/eng/20211105
LC record available at https://lccn.loc.gov/2021054401
LC ebook record available at https://lccn.loc.gov/2021054402

Designed by Andrea Ho
Cover Design by Meighan Cavanaugh

First Edition

Contact the author at info@izzardink.com

Hardback ISBN: 978-1-64228-075-3

Paperback ISBN: 978-1-64228-074-6

eBook ISBN: 978-1-64228-073-9

*To my father who taught me
to love words.*

To Randy, of course.

And to my own bus driver.

1

Andy

A ndy made a quick appraisal of his brand-new toy. It was shining like a black diamond in the sunlight, its windows sparkling, the tires blacked, and the rims polished. The massive gray and black body was poised powerfully, like an elephant ready to charge. Andy still felt like it was Christmas several months after receiving the gift. The routine of caring for it was never wearisome. It was like caring for a child. The black swooshes on the exterior were outlined in brown like carefully applied eyeliner and insinuated the notion of speed, efficacy, agility, and most of all, drama. He checked the long-lashed windshield wipers, admired the gleaming chrome grill and bumpers, and scrutinized the broad sleek automated door from top to bottom. It opened with a whisper. He especially admired the large chrome lettering on the massive flat face. The font was unpretentious yet unabashedly large, proclaiming the bus's elite heritage as a touring coach: "Prevost." No flies on this beauty, he thought smugly.

He was still amazed that he was one of a chosen few, one of 150 employees, to "sort of" own one of the new beasts. It was an outright privilege. He took vicarious ownership, knowing full well, of course, that it belonged to Jan and Rory, the owners of the Salt City Bus Company. For all intents and purposes, however, it was his to drive, maintain, and control. It was his baby, his to oversee and his to enjoy day in and day out, come rain or shine. The weather was never really an issue to Andy anyway. He had complete confidence in his ability to maneuver this mean animal in snow, sleet, or slamming rain, and he looked forward to the challenge of each. He was determined to be the best caretaker of this new creature, like an expert zookeeper with an exotic animal.

What an amazing day it had been when he was couriered clear across the country, via another employee's rig, to the doorstep of the illustrious Minnesota factory to retrieve it, brand spankin' new. It was a dream come true.

The tour bus sported new black pebbled leather seats padded to luxurious perfection, clean, sleek wood-grained floors (albeit laminate), and immense picture windows spanning the entire length of the interior. Even the lavatory discreetly tucked into the rear was contemporary, clean, surprisingly ample, and comfortable. His favorite part of the interior had to be his own home office: the cockpit. It had virtually all the technical bells and whistles on the market, which he proudly knew all about and how to expertly employ. There was a substantial bucket seat fit for a king, a padded perforated-leather steering wheel, and two generous mirrors with smaller bubbled ones attached. They tilted with the touch of a button to a myriad of different angles, which allowed him to see the whole kingdom behind at a glance. In another generous mirror situated between the windshields, he could appraise what was going on down the aisle to the back, and in the last overhead reflection, he could clearly see each and every passenger. One of his favorite phrases, one he often repeated, was "Your mirrors are your best friends."

He planned out a detailed schedule for upkeep and tried to adhere to it strictly. After all, how worthwhile was a trip in a grimy pedestrian bus, trying to see the sights through a dirty window? Not on his watch, he doggedly decided. He cleaned the massive outside windshield several times a day. He made certain to point the bus away from the sun, so that the windows wouldn't dry too fast and become streaked. Splattered bugs were absolutely unacceptable, though usually difficult to remove and required a scraper. He also cleaned the inside of the passenger windows every single day of each trip using Windex™. He found this product to leave the fewest spots; he certainly didn't want his passengers to have watermarks marring the pictures they snapped along the road.

Every evening as he closed up the bus for the night, he'd begin at the back as if curating a fine museum. He'd check the lavatory and spiff it up carefully, just like his mother had taught him to clean the bathroom at home. When that was spic and span, he'd move up the aisle, looking both ways, checking every surface for trash. Then he used Marque Multipurpose to wipe the columns between the windows. It was Andy's policy to wipe down all the seats every two weeks with Meguiars Gold Class leather conditioner, whether they needed it or not. As for the outside, he soaped, rinsed, and polished the behemoth body to perfection. He made certain the tires were blackened for every trip. He found that Armor-All foam worked best, and Black Magic was just a touch too greasy. Last of all, he made certain the bottled water supply was adequate for the next day.

Sometimes Andy reached down and pinched himself just above the elbow of his uniform to make sure he wasn't dreaming. It was short sleeved now for summer. The uniform was a clean, freshly ironed taupe shirt with black cargo pants and black belt, finished off with polished black shoes. Of course, he wore a thin black tie for professionalism. He caressed the embroidered red and blue logo on his chest pocket. Very official, he thought. His hair was always crisply trimmed, his cheeks freshly shaved, and his fingernails neatly clipped. It was important work he had, and he knew darn well it was crucial to look the part. He realized how significant it was to his clients, the people in his charge, that he was ready, capable, willing, and most importantly, happy to take responsibility for their very important vacations. It goes without saying that it's the driver that makes the difference. It's the driver who makes people comfortable, happy, welcome, and most of all safe as they embark upon these long-awaited trips. These were often all-important trips, saved up for months or even years, at least for the older folks. They were journeys across America to see sights only glimpsed in magazines or on TV, and oftentimes dreamed about for a lifetime. His customers would set eyes on things they'd never seen before and would likely never see again. They paid good money to zoom down the highways in luxury, not having to worry about potholes and danger, drunk drivers, or unexpected trouble. Not in one of these fine buses. And not on his watch. Not with a driver like Andy.

2

Ella

I propped myself on the edge of the bed and continued my silent incessant blubbering. My pillows were squashed, wrinkled, and damp. The quilted blue bedspread appliqued with ridiculously cheerful trailing roses was rumpled and disheveled, uncharacteristically grimy. I'm usually inordinately compulsive about such things and would have remedied it immediately, but today I didn't care a whit about anything but my grief. I had been lying with my knees pulled into my chest, tears filling up the little basins of my ears, and my brown hair uncomfortably damp. It was already dirty and stringy after several days of neglect. Usually that would be unacceptable. I was aware that my despair was augmented and intensified by the residual hormones streaming through my body, but that fact alluded me at the moment. All I could think, round and round in my brain, was that my baby was gone. The precious tenant I had been landlording for nine full months. The shock and isolation of having him gone was more torment than I could bear. The void in my belly was flaccid and flabby, making an exclamation point to the emptiness. Just a few days earlier, it had been as full and solid as a gigantic watermelon. Yes, it was obvious to everyone that my baby had not perished, and though appreciative of that, gratitude was not an emotion I could muster. I was home while he remained imprisoned in the hospital. You'd have thought he was my first child, the way I was carrying on. Contrary to what one might assume, the bonds are not weaker if it's number five or number 10. I was home where we both belonged, and he was still stuck at the hospital. Although he was healthy and large, there was some sort of serious infection. What had I done wrong? Had I caused his problems? Though I couldn't pinpoint anything, I felt like somehow I had failed him. Paint fumes, not enough green and leafy vegetables? I was acutely aware my thoughts were a jumble, but I didn't care.

Sitting in a chair across the room, my husband continued to cut his eyes at me with raised eyebrows. I knew he thought I was being crazier than usual. He probably felt that an attempt at reason would do no good, so he simply looked at me with resignation and went back to his newspaper. He could at least attempt to be sympathetic, I thought resentfully, or pretend, but then again, I didn't reach out to him either. Our long-term pattern of remoteness and silence was indelibly set now, and I knew he would rather avoid me and my muddle of emotions and hope for the respite, which would likely come later. Our mutual isolation had become almost comfortable, at least more so than entering the mine fields of undetermined interface, and I resented it more as each year passed. It was its own brand of loneliness. There were so many times, this one in the offing, that I desperately needed to cry out loud, speak freely and uncensored, puddle on the floor if necessary, and display blatant driveling pity for myself. It would have actually been a perfect time for him to accuse me of blowing everything outrageously out of proportion or to say that I was being shockingly impractical. Even simpering platitudes would have been music to my ears, and I would have fallen on my face to hear the words, even if untrue, "Everything is going to be okay." At this moment, I felt like a twelve-year-old, incapable of managing out-of-control thoughts and emotions. What I really wanted was a sturdy backboard to slam mental balls against and not be punished. But that was not part of our wheelhouse of couple comfort. What I absolutely did not want was to be looked at as mentally unstable, and worse, not worth the effort. I was well aware that I was not thinking in a straight line, but that's precisely why I needed the freedom and encouragement to fall down and let loose.

I guess I couldn't expect him to understand. Realistically, only one who has carried a child ceaselessly through nine tedious and oftentimes excruciating months can possibly relate. Only one who has had countless intervals of bone-leaching fatigue or who has felt alarmingly wretched, as her body has become so whale-like and cumbrous that she can't bend down to tie her own shoes. One who has not slept well for nights on end because of having to pee every hour or vomiting up burning acid because a large stone has compressed her innards. Or one whose back aches all day from hauling around a large garbage bag-sized load of bricks. Only one who has finally shed that burdensome load by rafting down a river of fear, pain, and labor can possibly be sympathetic. But the startling crescendo comes as she finally cradles the expelled burden in her exhausted arms, suckles him contentedly at her breast, counts the tiny perfect toes, and gazes into the odd little velvet face. It is then she realizes that every single second of the ordeal is absolutely worth the price, and that the burden of carrying the child has not come to an end, but is simply transferred to the outside of her body.

Further, only a person who has given birth can comprehend the wrenching pain of having the new being she has sustained for 280 continuous days being abruptly separated from her. It is impossible to comprehend the notion that this appendage could actually be sovereign. It will continue to occupy a sizeable chunk of her mind, body, and soul, even when she cannot see it. Disengagement after delivery is not reality. At least for a time.

When an unnatural separation occurs, short or long, no one but a new mother can grasp the disorientation and panic of leaving him behind. More to the point, she is not whole. Uncoupling is unnatural and unthinkable. It should not be. It is a mountain too cruel and impossible to traverse. This day, I felt impossibly fractured, mentally and physically.

I had no comprehension of time at all. Although some sort of length-ened out soothing or logic may have done much to assuage my misery, there was no one I could turn to. I was alone, and I was alone in it. Perhaps, in a mother's whole lifetime – at least one with a modicum of maternal instinct – she cannot completely disengage from her child. Even if that child absconds with someone else's money or burns some-one's house to the ground. When her newborn is finally separated with a clean crisp slash, she is left with a terrifyingly gaping hole, and the only hope of healing it is shifting her focus to the bundle in her arms.

"Oh, he'll be fine," the nursing staff had assured me patronizingly, but they seemed to have forgotten the delicate balance between a new mother, her newborn, and lucidity. Logic all but ceases for the first few hours and days. The flaxen cords, which have bound the two, are not stretched out by an influx of reason. They snap back. The bonds are sopping with intensity and ambiguity, not to mention actual blood. The blood ties are too fresh to be undermined. That part might take a lifetime.

I brushed my tears aside, wiped my ears and eyes, and smoothed down my droopy hair. I should bathe. I would really love a hot bath. Bathing was a major coping routine. My mind wandered back to the previous weeks when the baby was still inside my body, and I was im-mersed in a deliciously warm foamy bath. In a balmy bath, even bor-dering on scorching, my mind lets go and unstrings itself. Momentarily, I can ignore needs and duties, shut my eyes, and let my frazzled body release the tensions of the day. I remembered, and it made me smile a little through the tears to remember how when I let out a little water to add more hot, I would tip the drain closed with a toe. At that moment, the baby would inevitably startle and lurch as he heard the sound of the metal clanking and reverberating through the water. It was astonishing that the baby reacted so suddenly. It was a renewed awareness that I was carrying a completely separate life. Yet, at this moment, a bath was impossible.

I had to get myself together, get dressed, and tend to the other four children. They'd been playing alone too long while I'd been obsessing. They were the other appendages I could never detach from. They had to be fed, bathed, assessed, and attended to. It wasn't as if I could afford to indulge my heartache indefinitely and retreat from my duties. No. Doing that would just make everything worse. I wiped the drear from my face and practiced an adult expression, one more stoic and controlled. I ran my fingers over my saggy, unoccupied abdomen apartment, smoothed out my unkempt denim maternity dress, and trudged down the stairs.

My husband was within his rights to be perturbed with me, even though that was the norm. I was being pathetic. I slapped my own face mentally. Come now, Ella, get a grip. The baby is doing pretty well. He's in the hospital, yes, but not dying. At least not now. I repeated that three times. You are being an idiot and blowing things out of proportion. I went to find the children.

The baby hadn't been vigorous enough to latch on to nurse. Heaven knows I spent a lot of time trying, pinching his little bow lips, stroking his cheeks, and squeezing myself into his mouth. Now I must hook myself up to an electric breast pump and take some bottles of my precious elixir to the hospital. He was able to gulp the priceless watery liquid from a bottle quite happily. He still had a few tubes and monitors dangling from his little squishy body, but he was progressing. My emotions were trussed up a bit, and I was dealing. I tried to smile, just for effect, though my heart wasn't in it. I noticed that my husband was not watching me like a mad woman ready to implode at any moment. Progress, I suppose. I was making good progress.

The children seemed to be all right. Obviously, they were relieved to have me home and functioning. Jenny, ten and the oldest, was surveilling me surreptitiously; David, seven, was pretending to be nonchalant; Beth, the five-year-old, was openly clingy; and three-year-old Luke was doing what he always does when things are not going well. He was picking on everyone else.

Children can take many things in their stride, but are rarely comfortable being roped to a fearful or fragile mother. If their mother is terrified, their world takes a nosedive. If she's unstable, then so are they. She is tethered to them, of course, but they are more so to her. For a long time, they are an integral part of her, inextricably linked. I know this to be true instinctively, to the very soles of my feet, and long ago determined to go to any length to keep their lives in balance. That, of course, is why I brought them into the world in the first place. I refuse to shirk or be a victim. I have few illusions about my many weaknesses, but those strengths are worth a lot, I think.

3

Ella

S tay in your bed! my mother barked, and I wondered what reason she had to be so mean. I was sure I hadn't done anything wrong. She wasn't usually this ornery. Well, she did yell a lot, but mostly at my little sister. I was only getting off the big bed to wander around. Well, maybe to run around a little. I wanted so badly to sneak outside and play. No harm in that. My mother usually told me to run outside and get out from under her feet. Something was different. I suspected I had caught something. Probably a bad cold or the flu. I didn't feel bad all the time. I was kind of chilled, and a little tired, but that was all. That is until the red spots began to appear all over my stomach and legs and my throat began to burn. Now I was being told I must stay in bed. I was trapped in my parents' bedroom, and all the curtains were drawn. The heavy draperies were dark brown with a silver metallic fleck running through them, and they had a profuse white lining. I never liked them because they reminded me of huge muddy dresses. Before she left the room, my mother pulled them tightly across the windows and commanded me to stay put. It was dark and boring. I had a pile of books but couldn't see them clearly in the darkness. I soon became disinterested as well. The little table light on the dresser was on, but it was so dim that it was hard to see even the

cereal or sandwiches my mother kept leaving there. I supposed I must
be quite sick because everyone was whispering about it, and I thought
I heard the doctor telling my mother to be sure that I stayed down.
Queer. I've always heard grownups say that sunlight and fresh air are
supposed to make kids more healthy, not less. He also told them to
keep me in darkness, which I could not understand for the life of me.
I didn't think the dark helped anything one iota. You can't see in the
dark. Yes, my head had ached so badly at times that it felt like a hammer was pounding a nail into my eardrum. But the chalky white
pills – I know they're called aspirin – always made it feel tons better.
It seems like my mother always gives aspirin to everybody for everything from headaches to the flu, or for the many leg aches we seemed
to get. I admit that in between the aspirin tablets, I didn't feel well at
all. In fact, I felt a terrible dark feeling throbbing back and forth inside my body like a big black snake, but that was only when my head
got so hot it felt like my hair might catch fire. The hotter my head, the
colder my toes felt. But when my mom gave me a glass of water and
another aspirin, I was okay again soon. So, to not waste good time
between pills, I'd jump out of the big bed and sneak out the back
door and run in the cool grass or feel the heat of the pavement on my
cold bare feet.

This went on for two weeks or so, and finally I was released from the
prison I never really stayed in at all. Everything went right back to normal. I didn't give it a second thought after that, but when it came time
for my kindergarten check-up, I suspected there was some sort of com-
plication. While the doctor put his stethoscope over my chest, I studied
the pretty, framed photographs on the wall of red balloons and clowns,
jars of brightly colored gumballs, and blue bicycles. They all had blue
skies and puffy white clouds in the background. I think that was to reassure sick kids that life would soon be bright and happy again.
Dr. Richards listened, then listened some more, and then became very
quiet. His face looked stern at first, and I wondered if I had annoyed
him by wiggling around while he was listening. After that, his dark

bushy eyebrows began to rise up and down like furry caterpillars dancing a jig. He looked at my mother and gravely uttered something about "heart murmur." He said other things I couldn't understand or keep track of, but I always remember thinking that my heart was mumbling or complaining about something. I always wondered what.

4

Ella

I washed the counter, twice in fact, and polished the faucet, moving across the kitchen to the bulky white refrigerator, making certain to wipe the hundreds of fingerprints from the previous day. Loved the fingers, hated the fingerprints. I folded the rag and towel and hung them neatly on the hooks underneath the sink. I quickly assessed the rest of the kitchen, amazed at how much enjoyment I derived from the cleanliness and order. Most likely an inherited tendency, I figured. But not from my mother, as her messiness was always a conundrum and an annoyance. Yet I'd come to see this trait as more of a flaw than a strength, mostly because of the reaction I got from my sisters, who seemed to think I didn't fit in. Regardless, I really enjoyed domesticity. My mantra was "order first, details next." I've often been criticized for being a little obsessive-compulsive, and though I fold within myself self-consciously at this negative labeling, I have found it useless to resist what must be hidden deep inside my DNA. "To each his own" has always been a comforting platitude.

I had begun taking it a little further as of late, by actually focusing more on the design aspect. This added a different dimension to the constant mothering I had to do. A little burst of creativity here and there had become habit forming, giving me a bit more pleasure and something more substantive. I decided I must be visually oriented because I was constantly moving things around to look more pleasant and pretty. The process seemed to calm me like warm baths. Wherever I went, I was always studying the aesthetics. The details of this and that. Judging, thinking about what looked good, what didn't, and what I would do a little differently if given the chance.

Compulsive orderliness and many children are not necessarily compatible. The juggling, sorting, the careful attention to who was hungry or tired, or who needed a little correction, could be very tiring and tedious, not to mention overwhelming. Though I loved these little creatures as much as my own life, and I was determined not to fail them, it was a complicated two-step for someone who required more control than was natural. Definitely not for the faint of heart. Yes, it could be energizing or exhausting, but oftentimes I found it could drain the person right out of the person, if you know what I mean. Becoming invisible was terrifying. Yet, in my opinion, becoming irrelevant was much worse.

As I brushed the crumbs from the table onto my lap, the tightness of my skirt frightened me. I couldn't handle the thought of more chaos, confusion, and work that another baby would bring. I arched my eyebrows a little, knowing full well I was adding more wrinkles to my forehead as I did. Oh well. My fears were not possible yet. I could not be pregnant again so soon, although I knew it did happen. I pushed it from my mind.

Daydreaming is like escaping into the pages of a good book. I studied the gleaming burner trays on the little stovetop and glanced at the metal bucket perched on the countertop, which I painted pale pink just the other day. It was overflowing with white daisies and pink fuchsias from the yard. So cheerful and pretty, always vying for my attention away from the drudgery of cleaning toilets and scrubbing floors. More and more, small details and touches of art went a long way in softening my workload. I wiped a little fruit fly out of the rim of the chipped grey and white Limoges gravy boat in the windowsill. The elegant Parisian china was a relatively luxurious passion I had recently and guiltily acquired. Of course, I bought the few pieces I owned by carefully combing through second-hand, antique stores, or garage sales. I paid so little, I felt like I had stolen the pieces in my collections, but it made me love them even more. I noticed with delight the delicate pink and white flowers hand-painted on the little French teapot and the small blue nosegays ambling around the cup and saucer. I observed a tiny chip on the cup's handle, but it didn't bother me. Small but poignant pleasures, and worth it. Perhaps more grocery money foolishly spent, but I was not sorry. I looked past them through the gleaming wood-paned windows into the backyard and watched the wind dancing delicate Norway maple leaf shadows across the deck floor like a silent symphony in motion. My prized rose-pink geraniums nodded their heavy heads in the breeze and the sky-blue lobelia twinkled like little stars in the sunshine. Somewhat silly, I admitted. Other times I wondered if there was something a bit little wrong with me. Yet my heart skipped a fleeting beat, and I registered "happy" for a moment or ten. Oftentimes, I thought, a few moments of contentment were enough.

It was July, and baby Andrew had been home several weeks. He seemed to be doing fine, though he still hadn't the strength to nurse. He latched on but seemed to tire quickly, then he would stop and look up at me as if I should realize he just could not do it. I glared at the rented demon perched close to my bed on a stool, which every few hours I allowed to grab onto my breasts like an alien and suck the life out of them. The watery white substance was deposited into a basin attached by tubing, and I transferred it into a baby bottle. I allowed this beast to drain me many times a day, so I could feed Andrew what he desperately needed. That was a significant comfort, at least. He was still taking antibiotics and seemed much thinner than the other babies did at that age. His little thighs seemed to have become a bit flaccid and concave. He was as beautiful as ever, though. His bright round head was feathered with downy white fluff, and his perky round eyes were blue as the azure sky. His lashes were long and dark, though a bit thin, I thought with a smile. I also wondered if I saw an almost imperceptible smile spreading across his little face. Perhaps just the beginnings of one. Or not. His little legs kicked back and forth, and his chubby toes wiggled around like little peanuts. He certainly looked perfect. But no matter. I had already taken the plunge deeply and fully into the sea of love with this baby. I was immersed in his velvety down-covered apricot cheeks and his full little lips. The minute his eyes fixated upon mine, the merging was complete. I could no more be aloof to this baby than fly off to Mars. He was, in fact, the moon and all the planets to me already.

I heard fussing, so I ran up to the bedroom. The baby squirmed in his bassinet, which was growing visibly smaller every week. His little body was getting bigger, and that made me happy. His chubby little fists grazed the sides as he waved his arms wildly. Sometimes I was afraid his puffy little feet would kick a hole in the wicker. I finally gave up trying to get him to nurse. He did not have the strength for nursing, and the pediatrician recommended that it was so much easier to mix formula in a bottle. I was not sorry to return the monster milk pump taking up so much space in my bedroom, not to mention the monotony and violation of my personal space. But formula was not a viable option. One morning there was an angry red rash spreading across his stomach and thighs. His little cheeks were blazing as a sunburn. I resorted to running to the dairy farm twenty-five miles down the road for fresh raw goat's milk. Thankfully, he was thriving on the goat's milk, growing rapidly and putting back on all the weight he seemed to have lost. I hated the commute to the farm with all the other things I had to do during the day, but I was just grateful for a solution. Just a small pothole in the road, I reasoned. One I could easily navigate and adapt to.

The August sunshine beckoned the children outdoors for most of the day, but they paused between activities to spend a few seconds with Andrew. He'd begun to lift his head and smile at them as he lay on his stomach on the floor. His curious eyes followed every move they made. He was beginning to giggle aloud, and his charm was bewitching. His little cheeks folded into dimples when he smiled. I toted him around the house under one arm on a hip. My body was almost, but not quite, back to its svelte self. I was enamored by his robust little body, his round face, and its constant happy grin. His eyes were just as blue as before, but maybe a touch lighter now, and his tufted hair was growing out thickly. It reminded me of the fields of sun-bleached white straw in early summer. His cheeks were constantly flushed, and I often wondered if he were running a slight temperature or if he were just super plump and pink. Though babies are fairly resilient little creatures, not as fragile as one would think, I stressed about their routines, their comfort, their hunger, and anything else which might make a tiny person uncomfortable. Now that he seemed to be recovering from his initial difficulties, I was on guard for new ones. I admit to being a glass-half-empty kind of girl and tend to imagine the worst-case scenarios. I attempted to brush off the fear like a fly on my shirtsleeve.

One scorching summer afternoon when the kids were particularly bored and restless, I decided to load everyone in the car. Heading up State Street towards the Arctic Circle for soft-serve chocolate-dipped cones, I glanced over at Jenny bouncing Andrew on her knee in the front seat next to me. The thought crossed my mind that he might bump his head. We had no rules against such dangerous practices, and of course, we had no car seats or belts. Impulsively, I diverted by making up a little ditty about Andrew, and one by one, the children began to join in. By the time we got to the drive-through window, they were singing at the tops of their lungs, tapping their feet, or bobbing their heads. The car was almost swaying. It became a family song of sorts, one they sang often. It was a lame and silly little song, but apt, I think. And it distracted me from the file marked "things to worry about" tucked in the back cabinet drawer of my mind. "There's sunshine in my boy, there's sunshine in my boy .... There's sunshine in his big blue eyes, he is my greatest joy ...."

5

Ella

I was the oldest of seven children – six girls and one boy. There were four freckly but beautiful true redheads, ranging from light strawberry to intense firebrick, and two bright, sunny blondes. I was the only unremarkable brunette. I'm not really certain why, but my father flagrantly favored me. It was embarrassing, but I won't say it was unpleasant. What child doesn't like to be the apple of her father's eye? And who in their right mind would think of giving that up? Perhaps it was only because I was the oldest, and the only boy came much further down the line, or maybe he thought I needed the extra attention, because the redheads got most of it. Or it may have been that it was pretty obvious I was not preferred by my mother. She and my maternal grandmother seemed to prattle on endlessly about the rare and special recessive gene making its appearance so richly in their offspring. They bragged about it often to their friends. Sometimes I wondered if I had been adopted before my sisters had had a chance to be born. I recall watching my grandma comb, braid, and embellish with satin ribbons the beautiful copper and russet tresses. I don't remember her even once offering to run a comb through mine. My father, I think, figured I should be somebody's favorite. I'm not sure that was the reason, but it's as good as any. His attention was blatant and awkward, but if I were honest, I basked in every minute of it.

My dad was an educated, handsome, and gregarious dark-haired man who worked as a teller at the bank on Main Street. It was a venerable and respectable white-block building, a landmark. It wasn't a large bank, but it was formal, elegant, and imposing, and when he drove us past it, I was duly impressed. Every weekday morning, he put on his dark blue suit, white starched shirt, and a tie and headed off to the city. I adored him and accepted what he dished out as doctrine without questioning. It didn't matter if he was talking about the way to apply toothpaste on your brush or what not to say to Aunt Mickey. The way he treated me, along with my perception of him, made me want to swallow anything he said. But over the years, I came to learn that he was far more complicated than he appeared.

My mother was a good woman who toiled at home tirelessly and relentlessly, and in my estimation, a little aimlessly. I tried my hardest not to be critical, which has always been my nature, as she was so diligent in her work, and there was obviously no one else to do it. Yet I had a hard time understanding how she could not desire more from her life. More time for her own interests, hobbies, or pastimes. She was a conundrum. I admired her exemplary work ethic and selfless sacrifice, and had no doubt it was worth emulation. There was nothing at all to criticize except, perhaps, her disinterest in order, which felt like a cheese grater to my nerves. I suppose I also wished for a bit more of her attention and genuine interest, aside from her hard work. But what I really yearned for, what I really needed, was to see her be a little more selfish. Not in a destructive or narcissistic way, but a way that would give me the permission or blessing to be a little of the same in my future life. I wanted to see her want a few things. Not unhealthy or extravagant things, just some of the things we didn't have or could possibly enjoy. I wanted to see her have dreams and aspirations. I needed that to be okay. I yearned for that to be a positive thing, not a fault or wrongdoing. I would have clapped my hands for joy to see her bring home a pretty dress or pair of unthrifty shoes she couldn't really afford. At least once in a blue moon. I suppose I pined to see that it was okay to wish and hope for things you don't yet have or to be ambitious for what you have not yet achieved. I didn't want that to be wrong. Although her life was extremely righteous and above reproach, all I saw her do was ceaselessly cook, wash, and iron. I recall thinking that if I were consigned to do only that for the rest of my life, I'd simply rather not marry. I'd have much preferred going into the city to work at the bank. I wondered if her only claim to fame might end up being her excellent laundry skills and the effort she put into it. I'd like to say that made me very sad, but it really just made me resentful. And I did know that was wrong.

My mother would hang out all the bedding and clothing on the line to dry in the backyard. Just by virtue of the process, it rendered them ever so wrinkly and stiff and caused them to require more ironing. It seemed a tiring and fruitless cycle. She labored valiantly from sunup to sundown, always appearing to be exhausted and drained. The washing and ironing took second fiddle only to the meals she prepared. She completed it all, collapsed into bed, and started over the next day, because apparently, I suppose, with such a large family, the washing and cooking is never really finished. The first time she came over to tend to my little ones, she immediately pulled out the ironing board and proceeded to iron every wrinkled item in my household. It was her way of helping, contributing, and her way of smoothing out things that were out of her control. I can appreciate that.

I still see her in my mind's eye, usually in a shroud of gray skies, out behind the house with her apron blowing in the wind or the snow falling softly on her short brown hair. There, she seemed to be in another world. I remember the faraway look and confusing contentment that washed over her face. It was almost as if she didn't live inside the house at all, just out in the backyard under the heavens.

Now I see it was her way of jumping into a hot bath and locking the door behind her, or escaping to some far-off pleasant destination while not neglecting her duties. It took me years to see the crucial constant she provided for the family. For her, the constant was that the wash would never be neglected. What we didn't understand as children, but felt on some deep subconscious level, was the fact that because we were her children, we would never be neglected if she never neglected her wash. When I came to suspect that, her monochromatic and passionless routine became quite comforting. I realized that if the wash didn't progress, the family probably wouldn't move forward either. I see now, as well, that it was her way of being a good mother with the scanty resources she had in her control. It's taken me years to understand that we each have our different methods of being successful at mothering. Some design, run businesses, clean, sew, work at the bank, or garden their hearts out. Perhaps others take a little drink now and again to get through it all, an option my mother would never have considered. My mother washed, and she did it in an excellent way. Clean, fresh laundry still brings a modicum of serenity to my days. As it turns out, I'm a little obsessive-compulsive about it as well. I love the feel and smell of crisp sun-dried cotton sheets, though mine are always machine dried now. When I was young, they used to smell like honeysuckle and light rain, and I remember wriggling down into them happily, when it was dark and cold outside. I still beg Sam from time to time to build me an outside clothesline, although I'd most likely never use it. To this day, I prefer low-count cotton sheets over the more luxurious ones.

6

Ella

I watch Jenny interacting with her friends and think about the girl I used to be. She seems so stridently assured. She runs here and there, bossing everyone around as much as she can get away with. Her yellow ponytail is in constant motion as she flies through her days, and at times, I wonder if the tail has a spirit of its own and is really taking the lead. She's smart as a whip and as courageous as heck, and I can't help but admire her strength and sassiness, especially when it isn't directed at me. Was I similar, I wonder?

My grade school days glided along quite placidly. Like most children, there was at least one grade when I had no friends and was the only one to not be invited to a birthday party, and of course, I thought I'd just as soon die. There were a couple of years when my legs and arms seemed to shoot obtusely from my clothes like toothpicks, and I had no need for a bra when all my friends seemed so curvy. For the most part, though, the days were uneventful. They were bursting with night games on the lawn, dodgeball, tetherball championships, school work, 4-H, softball, sewing classes, piano, and singing lessons taught by my own grandmother. And of course, church.

I was enthralled with scorching summer days, running through a rusty lawn sprinkler in my one-piece bathing suit, or riding my pale blue Schwinn bicycle with its wicker basket wired haphazardly to the handlebars. About once a week, my best friend, Jan, and I were driven by one of our mothers to the library, where we'd scour the shelves for every Nancy Drew book we could find. It was my goal that summer to read every single one written. Then, we'd pile our trove of mystery novels, along with bags of carrots and apples, into our bike baskets, and spread blankets on the grass to loll away the afternoons in the sweltering heat. There was no air conditioning inside the house, so it always seemed cooler and more comfortable out under the shade of a large sugar maple. And I could get away from the annoyance of my younger siblings. The sky was cobalt blue, and the puffy clouds appeared to be dolphins or elephants leisurely ambling across heaven's terrain. I lay on my back thinking thoughts and feeling feelings that only freedom, sunshine, warm breezes, innocence, and youthful optimism can conjure. I thought heaven itself must be made up of such afternoons.

When school started up again, I often played "horse" in the field in the back of our house. I pretended to be a white mare named Snowball. I galloped nimbly across the plains and imagined fascinating equine adventures. Or I'd climb the giant Russian olive on the fence line and while away the hours pretending to be one of the Little Women, usually Jo. Other days I'd hone my significant Hula-Hoop skills or scrawl a hopscotch on the driveway, hopping and skipping over chalk lines for hours on end with a friend, sister, or alone. I was discovering that I rather enjoyed my own company, a gift that has continued through the years.

Sam says I am an outlaw to the core. In my estimation, it is he who's honest to a fault. He blurts out the most inconsequential facts that would be much better left out altogether, and he often brings needless attention to himself or us. I, on the other hand, keep my lip zipped unless it's immoral or illegal. Even if it's not altogether forthcoming. I don't call that dishonest. Of course, I have glided through many a stop sign and let my vehicle speed to whatever I can get away with. Breaking rules like that rarely bothers me, and I think Sam wonders what small piece of wiring has been kinked in my brain. I admit, I don't hesitate to steal lilacs from a yard if they are hanging over the sidewalk side of the fence. Or to go home and get a shovel to dig up an iris from the side of the road, even though I always look in every direction before I do. Admittedly, a few of the rule lines are a bit blurry.

In elementary school, however, I did actually out and out steal something, an item that did not belong to me. Every once in a while, even as an adult, I look back and wonder how I could possibly have done it. Perhaps a few hours behind bars would have helped to assuage my guilt. Back then, I think I would have willingly gone to jail.

I was in the sixth grade and my friends and I played hopscotch like it was going out of style the next year. It was the one sport I was any good at. I loved dodgeball and tetherball, but no one ever asked me to be on their teams if there was an alternative. I'd drift around the schoolyard yearning to be asked, and if I was lucky, there'd be a vacant position. So, this hopscotch thing was a really big deal. Each recess and every night after school, I couldn't wait to get out to practice or play. I'd watch the big clock on the wall of my classroom and count the minutes. I'd dash home from school and immediately switch my skirt for jeans. I was rather gifted, I humbly believed. It wasn't just a pastime, it was a full-blown obsession. To my delight, I was winning many, if not the majority, of the games I played. I felt in demand or first choice as an opponent, and that was a new feeling for me. It was becoming my claim to fame and put a bit of luster on my adolescent self-esteem, something most sixth grade girls can relate to.

There was just one small problem. I didn't own a hoppy taw. Most of my friends had at least one. I was desperate to possess my own, with special colors swirling through the rubber. I actually daydreamed incessantly about the red and blue one I'd choose. It would have just a fleck of green whorling through it. It would be unique. Like me. It would be my trademark. I would definitely win more games because of it, and I would get more and more popular. I used to study the taws belonging to my friends and note the thinning edges from constant use. Those were the best kind. They were the proof you were a practiced contender. It was like having the heels of your tennis shoes worn down from many dodgeball games. I borrowed my friends' taws at school, but at home I made do with a used metal pickle jar lid. I glued little scraps of my mother's nubby wool fabric onto the bottom, so it wouldn't slide around so much.

One day after school I was at a friend's house, and we happily played hopscotch in her driveway all afternoon. She didn't seem abnormally well off to me, but with only one little brother, she didn't lack for much. More importantly, she had three hoppy taws of her very own. I couldn't begin to wrap my brain around that. Just before my mother came to retrieve me for dinner, without considering the consequences for even a second, I quickly slipped one of her taws into my jacket pocket. She'd never miss it. I jumped into the car and almost immediately, it began to burn like a hot coal, and I kept touching my pocket to see if there was an actual hole where it may have flamed through. Once at home, I tucked it safely into my underwear drawer and piled lots of socks on top of it. I obsessed all evening, hardly eating a bite of my supper. Another hole was now smoldering just as hotly in my conscience. I didn't take the taw out for two full days, but I went in often to look at it. I hadn't heard a word from my friend. I would open the drawer, pick it up, and roll it over and over in my palm. I studied the swirls in the rubber and ran my fingers over it hungrily. After a couple days, however, I began to notice that it didn't feel the same. Something had changed and I wasn't quite sure what. It wasn't even as pretty. And after all that, I wasn't excited to get it out. It kind of felt like I'd been hiding a pistol from the police.

Finally, I got up the courage to try it. I carefully slipped it into my pants pocket and carried it out to my chalked hopscotch on the driveway. I tossed it deftly onto the first square. I jumped and hopped, then threw it onto the second. I was just beginning to feel a little bit comfortable holding it in my hands when I spotted my father's car rounding the corner and coming down the street. Before I could even run and pick it up off the cement, he jumped out of his car and strode over to where I was playing. "Hi, Ella, how was your day? Playing yourself a little game of hopscotch, it looks like." He said it tongue-in-cheek and mockingly, as of course, he knew I ate and slept hopscotch. He had a big grin on his face and seemed happy to see me. Before I could reply his eyes drifted towards square number two. They stopped and rested on the taw. Silence. All he had heard from me for the past few weeks was, "Dad, why can't I buy a hoppy taw?" His answer had always been the same. "Ella, all you have to do is pull all the weeds out of the four o'clock garden by the back door, and you will have earned the money, and I will drive you to the store myself." I had been procrastinating. That garden was chock full of noxious bindweed and dandelions. It would take hours. I knew I'd have had to use the hose to soak the ground before they'd come up, and all I had time for these days was hopscotch.

He looked over at me wordlessly and then back at the hoppy taw on the pavement. His dark eyebrows arched just slightly, his lips puckered into a tight circle, and he thrust his hands into his front suit pockets. But he didn't say a word. He didn't yell or scold like I expected, or even wanted. I was actually used to that from him if I did something wrong. This day, he simply turned on his shiny black heels and walked into the house. The suspense of having the secret locked away in my drawer and now being caught red-handed by my dad was more than I could bear. I threw both hands over my eyes and plopped down on the grass next to my hopscotch. I sobbed for what seemed like hours. I have no doubt that my father was watching through the kitchen window. I was mortified. I had disappointed him beyond belief. I had broken one of the Ten Commandments he had always drilled us on. Blatantly. Thou shalt not steal.

After my face had dried and lost its innumerable blotchy red spots, he quietly drove me over to my friend's house, stayed in the car, and watched somberly, while I walked meekly, head down, to the front door.

7

Ella

I felt like I had cooked for an army. I didn't even enjoy cooking. It had always been a necessity, not a pleasure. And I'd never been good at it. Obviously, I knew how to follow a recipe. And of course, I was careful. Some of my friends pored over recipes as if they were creating masterpieces and bragged about their culinary ingenuity, but I couldn't relate. In fact, I preferred cleaning toilets than figuring out how to fill all those hungry mouths day after day. Food money was sparse, so I resorted to the same five or six simple humdrum meals every week. Boring. And exhausting. I suspected that my energy level was at its very lowest when I was standing in one place, and I guessed, probably accurately, that it might have been my unstable heart. But I couldn't quite give into that excuse. By the time I set the table, cooked the meal, made sure everyone got their fair share, and cleaned up the mess, I felt like taking a couple of Tylenol and going straight to bed.

My mother's cooking was the single plentiful commodity in our household, as everything else was pretty darn meager. She had been taught by her own mother to cook and she excelled at it, like doing the wash. She made good, hearty, home-cooked fare, deliciously and simply prepared, even if predictably repetitive. Mashed potatoes, smooth brown or white gravy, depending on which meat was being cooked, melt-in-your-mouth fried chicken, spaghetti and meatballs, a heavy moist meatloaf, a good round roast slow-cooked by braising until all the toughness was simmered out, and canned salmon smashed into crispy patties pan-fried to brown and salty and flaky perfection. Yes, my mother was a good cook and what she served made the world go 'round. It made up for a lot. There was always something to look forward to, no matter how dull the day or difficult the schoolwork. And the baking – well, the baking was literally the frosting on the cake. The baked goods made the tiny drab kitchen into a palace fit for the six princesses and the prince. Cakes, fluffy cornbread, white bread and rolls, light-as-air muffins, deep-fried scones, chocolate chip cookies that melted as they touched the tongue. And our favorite – flaky pies – picture perfect and always scrumptious. Rhubarb, fresh from the garden, sweet-tart apple with a thick sugared crust, or coconut cream with bananas. My siblings and I, if we learned anything, was that you were never, ever late to the table and you always took as ample a portion first time around as you could get away with. You couldn't always eat what you took or get away with what you wanted, but you'd have a go at it, knowing that whatever you got, you got, and that leftovers were nonexistent. Even with my own grown children nowadays, I unconsciously jerk away or slap a wrist if one tries to jab a morsel from my plate. My intentions are to be generous, but those habits are so ingrained as to be permanent grooves tooled into my brain to protect me from starvation. Those were the jungle rules if you wanted to enjoy the best part of living in that home.

The furniture was sparse, and worse in my opinion, thoroughly uninspired and haphazard. Bless my mother's heart, decorating was the last thought in her head. She simply didn't have a moment left over from her daily duties to worry about such trivial pursuits. The towels were tattered, the facilities adequate but simple, and the niceties limited to the bare necessities, and nothing – no, not anything – was ever squandered. That was clearly high on the wicked list. We accepted it as life in a big family on a meager income. Probably normal for most people, or so I thought. I had no doubt my parents did their best to provide, and I never really felt deprived. I never even looked around much. Life was not to be questioned or complained about, just accepted. There's a lot to be said about normal being the only normal you know. We were told the stories of starving children in Africa who went to bed with distended and hungry tummies, and no niceties at all. Thus, we were pretty content and happy. What more could a kid ask for? It had not yet begun to dawn on me.

Looking back now, I realize my mother had a particular challenge at Christmastime. I didn't have a clue how much effort was involved until I had my own children and my own complexities. I never thought about the pressure that they must have endured to provide an adequate Christmas for those seven children. We were never disappointed. The presents seemed to spill out from the Christmas tree by the hundreds. Our eyes would be as big as saucers. There were dolls, home-sewn doll clothes, socks, underwear, nail polish, and small drugstore toys, as well as candy, unshelled nuts, and fruit. We didn't hang up our stockings like our friends did, and after a few years I realized it was because those items were needed to expand the volume of presents under the tree. Each was wrapped separately, carefully, and thoughtfully as to maximize the importance of each small gift. I recall with some emotion that often there was not enough scotch tape to finish the wrapping, and the paper was held together with straight pins. They were happy times, if not bounteous. One year I got a bit of a reality check. I was invited to a friend's house to see her Christmas stash, and my jaw actually dropped to realize that someone just up the street could be given such lavish gifts as a necklace and small brooch, an actual dress or blouse, or even a pair of pajamas or shoes. In our household, those items only appeared when the shoes had holes or the clothes were too small. Dresses, skirts, and blouses were usually handmade or hand-me-down, and doled out only at the beginning of a school year, especially when you grew four inches in one summer as I did a time or two. Those were the only Christmases I ever felt the pangs of envy or deprivation, and those feelings seemed to fade quickly and be forgotten.

8

Ella

I often wonder if I'd had more courage or gumption (or perhaps, maturity) to attain my first choice of career, I wouldn't be grappling with the underwhelming dilemmas I face every day due to my tendency to obsessive order. Most likely, I wouldn't be making beds or doing laundry in the first place. I'd be paying someone else to do it for me and feel perfectly fine about it. I wouldn't be preoccupied with color and design. I wouldn't waste time worrying about what goes where or how I could transform this room or that. No. I would simply be a highly skilled, fastidious surgeon with an impressive reputation. No one would care if I were particularly eccentric. My services and skills would be sought out. People would admire my gifts and exacting abilities to mend bodies with precision. My peculiar tendencies would be perceived in an entirely different light. By others, and mostly by me. This leads me to wonder why I have allowed "my intense environmental focus" to continually predominate my thoughts and perhaps dictate my emotions. The genesis, I suppose, can be found in my girlhood recollections.

My father sent me to visit his mother, my grandmother, for about a month every summer in Levan, Utah. He was a dutiful son, and I'm sure he thought it would be good for her to have a visitor. He probably thought it wouldn't do me any harm either. Occasionally, he drove the three-hour trip to take me there, and I loved that option because it gave us three full hours to ride together and talk about everything. But most of the time, one or both of my parents walked me to the corner of State and Vine, a few blocks from our home, to meet the bus. One carried the old tattered tweed suitcase and stood with me until the big Greyhound arrived. The bus stop was in front of the corner grocery store where we shopped. I remember the dread churning in my stomach as we waited for it to arrive. This, I believe, was the genesis of my lifelong pre-trip blues. I wanted to go, but I didn't. I could see the bus approaching from a distance, tiny then larger and larger until it appeared as a square building at the side of the road. I tried to will it to turn off in another direction. But of course, it always came, and mostly on schedule. It stopped and opened its big mouth for me to board and made an air whooshing sound as it did. It made another loud sound, too, like it was dropping something heavy on the opposite side to make room for me. I could picture someone else's luggage being bounced onto the road. I looked soberly at my dad and then at my mother, hugged them stiffly and awkwardly, and wiped away the tears, which wouldn't stay put inside my eyes, no matter how hard I tried to sniff and swallow them down. Displays of affection in general, especially in public, were always scarce in our family. Then I'd steel myself and reluctantly ascend the accordion-like metal steps leading into the hollow of the giant. They were high and hard to climb. I didn't want the people on the bus to think I was upset, so I held my head high and didn't make eye contact. I couldn't understand my swings of emotions, as I was always anxious to go until the time arrived, and then I wanted desperately to run back home. Stoic and unwilling to disappoint my father, I would have never backed out.

For some reason, I was always relieved when the bus driver smiled at me. If he had a kind face, I felt much more at ease. The buses were generally crowded, and when it started to move forward, I wobbled and jerked down the aisle, almost toppling over, looking for a friendly, benign, or clean face to share a seat with. The trip seemed very long, but the padded black bench seats were quite comfortable, and the windows were wide enough to watch the landscapes flying by. My introverted nature didn't lend itself to chatting, so I turned my face away from those who might consider prying. I preferred to sit quietly and read or look out the window. I didn't feel safe with strangers coming and going from who knows where. It all seemed very mysterious and a little dangerous, though I trusted my parents' judgment. It was towns and farmland all the way, a pastoral and pleasant journey, taking over three hours with all the getting on and off. Levan seemed a continent away. Looking back, riding the bus was when I felt the most homesick. On it, I was all alone. I was away from my parents, but not within reach of my grandmother.

When we finally arrived at the old gas station on the single curve in Levan's tiny frontage road, the driver seemed to know I needed to get off, and he always stopped. I was more than grateful. There was a thin string running along the top of the windows and made a little tinkling sound when pulled, signaling that someone wanted to disembark at the next stop. Most of the time I got anxious, watched, and waited nervously, afraid I would not pull the string in just the right place and miss Levan altogether. The thought of missing my stop scared me to death. I could end up in Scranton, Ohio (a place I had heard mentioned somewhere) with an ax murderer or all alone in a far-off city with no one I knew. When I finally got off, I dragged my suitcase through the dry powdery dirt up the road. I walked the four blocks up and one block over to my grandmother's house. I always paused for a moment or two before crossing the little wooden bridge and striding up the dirt walk to the door. I enjoyed gazing at the house and mentally getting prepared for the weeks ahead.

As much as I liked to be home in the summertime, I had to admit to being beckoned in the southern direction almost as powerfully. I longed for the little farm town and my grandmother's quiet, unassuming, and accepting demeanor. I think I would describe her as completely even tempered. Smooth and colorful as white flat paint. Never ruffled, not with anger or discontent, but lacking expression and gaiety at the same time. She was not particularly affectionate or animated either, but clearly, she was happy to see me. I was her oldest granddaughter, and I had no doubt that she loved me. She was never unpleasant in the least. I suppose I would say she was just plain placid. She was a woman of few words, and calm seemed to ooze from her body and permeate the space, speaking volumes without sound. My biggest challenge was to figure out what was locked inside those volumes so I could please and understand her.

With so much commotion at home, both positive and negative, there was a stillness here, found in no other place. The two places contrasted starkly. Yes, I was lonely a lot, unless my cousin happened to come, but there was something quiet, serene, and safe here. No parents bickering, no noisy siblings, no stern expectations, chaos, or busy streets. It was still, uncomplicated, and clean like a fresh, clear stream gurgling down the mountainside. That's the only way I can describe it.

My grandmother's white adobe house was tiny and peeling in places, its plaster a little more crumbled every time I saw it. It was simple but storybook-like, and the steep gables added romance to the otherwise boxy house. It was topped with an old, dark green shingled roof. Its windows were white and paned, and some of the glass was a little wavy. Most months, even in the winter, there were bright red geraniums perched in the sills, frilly and cheerful. The house was so small you could take one step inside the front door and see every room at a glance, while barely turning your head from side to side. Each space was di-minutive yet inviting and interesting. I can't quite describe the feelings the house evoked in me. It was like stepping through time, past and present, and as if all the previous spirits were embedded there in the walls, watching, listening, and silently expecting. If that was true, they were undoubtedly good spirits with lots of stories to tell if they had had utterance. The rooms were bright and white with lots of painted woodwork and stained unpolished pine floors. The light seemed to vault itself through the chipped, white, divided-light windows, up and down the walls, around the furniture, and across the floors as it frolicked. Each room was detailed in an austere yet artful way, and by necessity, a simple one. There was not, nor had there ever been, any money to speak of except for a meager monthly Social Security check. Yet my grandmother had cleverly and carefully saved and gathered her treasures, placing them in a homey, masterful manner. I could never understand how she had squirreled away enough to buy the sweet little chiffonnier made with honey colored quarter-sawn oak and ornamented with her own hand-crocheted doilies. Or the little graceful dark cherry china cabinet, which cradled her few but precious pieces of collectables. It displayed a delicate pink-flowered gravy boat from Austria, a couple of lovely violet-covered teacups and saucers, two blue Copenhagen pitchers, and my favorite piece of all – a single dark green dinner plate. It had a hand-painted scene of blue sky, two large red apples smack dab in the center, and little sprays of white baby's breath circling them. I was told this was once cherished by her mother, my great-grandmother. It always stunned me a little to realize that my father and his brothers were raised in this very house.

9

Andy

Truth be told, driving the bus wasn't Andy's first career choice. It really wasn't even a close second. From the time he was just a little kid, his real dream was to become a police officer. He was certain that was his purpose in life. He dreamt about it at night, daydreamed during the day, role-played, pretended, and imagined. Everywhere he went, he looked for a police officer doing his job. He hungered for the chance to watch them in action. He remembered going to kindergarten one day and being mesmerized by the blue uniform on the street corner. The officer was carrying a nightstick and a gun, smiling and directing traffic. He seemed so dedicated. Andy watched for others, bravely and swiftly sweeping the freeway in their cruisers while heading to the scene of an accident. He could picture the blue and red lights suddenly blazing dramatically from a patrol car covertly parked at the side of the road before racing to pull over a speeding vehicle. He recalled the dignity of the uniformed man striding to the driver's side door and leaning gracefully into the window as he issued a ticket or a warning. Andy was certain he saw a smile on his face as he did. He was simply keeping the roads safe for everyone else.

Andy collected Matchbox police cars as a child, in various models and colors. He had several highway patrol, sheriff, and police vehicles in his collection. In fact, he often had two of each make and model. They were his favorites. Those guys were the real deal. In his book, they were the heroes. They were the ultimate public servants. Not only did they keep the peace, but they put their lives on the line every single day. They went bravely and willingly into the paths of danger. How could you not admire them? They made people feel safe and secure, especially the little people of the world.

Andy had a crystal-clear third-grade recollection. While he was running across the playground during afternoon recess, an older and bigger boy threw a heavy parking lot chain across his path, which ended up slicing his knee open clean to the bone. Blood was gushing everywhere, soaking through his Levis, and pooling onto the cement. The slimy pinkish-white gristle of the underside of his kneecap flapped over and shimmered in the sunlight. It was absolutely terrifying, and he felt like throwing up. His breathing was becoming faster and faster until he felt lightheaded. Certainly, he thought, this was going to be the day he went to heaven. Just before he felt the lights would go out forever, he looked up. His father had miraculously appeared at his side, kneeling down, putting pressure on his wound with his wadded-up plaid work shirt. All he knew was that he immediately felt a little better. As Andy looked up through the tears and pain, he spotted the blue uniform casting a large shadow over his father. Inside the blue was a police officer looking down at Andy soberly. He had brown eyes and a bushy black mustache. His mouth curled up in a grin, revealing even white teeth. As he smiled, the corners of his eyes crinkled like wadded tissue paper. The officer's hand patted his father's shoulder. He bent down and picked Andy up in his strong blue arms. He cradled him gently and carried him to the open back of the ambulance. As he set him down, he smiled again widely and declared firmly that everything was going to be just fine and dandy. Andy's knee still bears the scars of more than a hundred stitches.

So, that's what he always thought he'd do when he grew up, but things didn't quite go as planned. As hard as he tried, he simply could not pass the entrance exams for the police academy. But the special uniform, the position of leadership, and the opportunity to help people made driving a tour bus squeeze into the category, if only a little. It also helped that he could wield a bus around like nobody's business. He kept a large blue and white poster hanging in his apartment captioned "The Thin Blue Line." He picked up police mementos in every state he drove the bus through. Each time the news carried the sad story of an officer's death in the line of duty anywhere in the country, Andy felt the pain and loss as if it was one of his own brothers. Yes, in Andy's opinion, they were definitely heroes.

Bryan, one of Andy's friends and coworkers, often asked after a long trip, "How much in tips, buddy?" This always put Andy off a bit, but he didn't say anything. That kind of thinking was just plain wrong. You were not a bus driver to make tips. You were there for people, just like the police officers. You were there for the service, and most of all, there for the safety. Not that he didn't make good tips. He usually made more than any of his coworkers. His clients were so satisfied and happy with his performance that they usually reflected it in a generous tip and continued to request him for subsequent trips. Now that, Andy reasoned, was the best tip of all.

Andy was frugal with his earnings. A large portion of each paycheck went to pay child support for Mandy, six, and Adam, four. He had not seen his young children in a few years. It wasn't because he hadn't wanted to. He ached every single day to see them and he thought of them constantly. Heaven knows he had tried. He made appointment after appointment to be there for them. But his ex was always mysteriously MIA when he showed up to take them for a few hours. He'd sit on the front porch for an hour or more, hoping they were just around the corner and on their way. After ten or fifteen times like that, he just quit bothering.

Andy gave up because he felt he had no other option. The state court systems were not super sympathetic to fathers' rights. He had done his best to navigate the twisted paths of the legal system, but found it so complicated that it made his head spin. He had already accrued an unbelievably large debt to his lawyer, which he knew he would probably never repay. When he did muster up the courage to appear in court, he became overwhelmed and confused. So, to keep from stammering or saying something stupid, which he thought might get him in further trouble, he resorted to being silent and staring at the floor.

He didn't really understand his rights anyway, and though his ex-wife's allegations were blatantly unfounded, the judge seemed to believe and favor her in his rulings. So, instead of trying to do what he really didn't have any idea how to do, he just kept paying his child support month after month, year after year, hoping his children would know that he loved them and, of course, was always supporting them. That hope kept him going most days. He yearned for the time when they might see how hard he had worked for them and come to know and love him on their own accord. A day never passed when he didn't picture their sweet faces as he followed the white lines along the road through his bus windshield.

His personal needs were minimal, and he never felt deprived. He ate well, often at the gratuity of his tour groups. He slept well, often in the same hotels they stayed in on their dime, and except for a fairly reliable car, he needed very little to be happy. A small studio apartment for between trips was more than adequate. Most of his contentment lay in doing his job well, being appreciated for it, and having the privilege to drive the bus he loved. He found he could save a little extra money here and there if he was careful. One of the company bus protocols was that each driver must personally purchase and sell bottled water to the passengers. Another bus rule was that each bottle of water must be sold for exactly one dollar – no more, no less, and that there should be no limit per customer. One thing was for certain; people always required a lot of water on a bus trip. Andy found he could actually buy a case of two dozen for three dollars. He felt guilty making that kind of a killing selling water to his people.

10

Ella

A ndrew had been doing so well that I was settling down to being more peaceful and hopeful every day. I was optimistic that his fragile beginnings were behind us.

One average run-of-the-mill weekday morning, I was making certain each child had finished their oatmeal and gulped down the allotment of orange juice before I shuffled them off to school. As usual, I needed to assess the clothing choices of the younger ones to make sure they had the same color socks on both feet before herding them out the door. Homework? Book bags? Notebooks and number 2 pencils? Oh, and lunch money. I snatched my shabby brown, albeit real leather, purse from the hallway hook and scribbled out a check for Jenny to deliver to the school office. She was the oldest and therefore in charge. I tried desperately to keep my checkbook balanced but didn't have time to subtract the debit just now, so all I could do was hope that the darn thing would clear. More often than I would like to admit, it would not.

Fussing and fidgeting almost done, I glanced at Andrew and noticed he hadn't been as alert or demanding in the last hour or so. He just lay there in his little padded plastic seat with the rotating handle. It was always perched on the countertop during the morning hubbub. I had used it for the last two babies, and the garish orange and yellow daisy chain fabric was beginning to wear thin, the edges of the binding fraying. Andrew wasn't kicking or bouncing as usual. His skin had a sallow gray hue rather than the rosy-cheeked creaminess, and his eyelids were sagging a bit unevenly. I ran the back of my hand across his forehead and was startled by the heat. Oh, no. Now what? I bustled my band of ragtag soldiers through the front door and up the street the few blocks to the elementary school. Everyone, that is, except little Luke, who was two years older than Andrew, and not old enough for kindergarten. When they were out of sight, I bundled him up, buckled the baby in his car seat, and raced into town.

After a quick assessment by Dr. Rosquist, my trusted pediatrician, I did as I was told and headed straight to the children's hospital for a few more specific tests. The doctor acted nonchalant and relaxed, but I knew his facial expressions well enough to know that he had concerns. At this point Andrew was downright lethargic, almost dangling listlessly from his little chair, his eyes closed. I half ran up the stairs to the emergency room of the century-old institution, lugging the chair over one arm with my baby strapped to it. With the other hand, I held a tight grip on Luke's small wrist. He whimpered, pulled, and struggled to let his weight drop to the floor. I was practically dragging him. Every chance he got, he straggled behind, intently fascinated with the rolling beds in the hallway. Given half a chance, I knew he would lie down under one of them and study the mechanisms of its underbelly. That was Luke for you.

The hospital's substantially long but boxy body had been erected from ancient barn-red brick. Its eyes were the many rows of small, white-gridded windows, which looked as if they had peeling painted eyeliner around each. The glass was so old it appeared to have heat waves running through it like the highway on a sweltering day. Inside, it had long, narrow, drably painted hallways and old chipped linoleum floors laid in a large black and aged-to-yellow checkerboard pattern. As I walked along the corridor, I peered into the rooms I passed. I couldn't help but notice that each was stuffed with several tiny patient beds in close proximity. The parents sat in metal chairs bunched closely around each bed or crib. Some were staring ahead zombie-like, and others were cordially chatting with one another. The smell was both antiseptic and sour, a bit like old bleached but mildewed tennis shoes. The ancient cavernous hospital was downright dreary. It also felt a little scary. It reminded me of a scene from *The Shining*. As I opened the door to my assigned room, I felt a scorching panic rise in my chest.

The nurses and doctors were cordial, concerned, and kind, but it was as if they were cardboard props that didn't really belong in this old set. They smiled vacantly, conferred, and ordered tests and more tests. They whisked my baby away for a spinal tap to check for infection, but not far enough out of earshot to not hear perfectly and clearly his pathetic wailing. My heart was in my throat, and it was all I could do to sit still and hang onto the metal arms of my own chair with both hands. I wanted to leap up and run to the sound of my child's voice, and rescue him from the brutes who were torturing him.

I dutifully called my husband at work, but he told me that while he was extremely sympathetic and worried, he could not leave his morning meetings just now.

Alone was what I felt most often in life, and I was fairly accustomed to it, but right now I had an imminent and draining burden to shoulder. I needed to share it with someone. It felt like acid was gnawing a hole in my stomach lining. I was usually pretty capable and stoic, but at this moment, I didn't think I could navigate flying solo. Not to mention, I desperately needed someone to hang on to and watch Luke, who was wandering around touching everything in sight. I was agitated, anxious, and afraid of becoming unstrung. I resorted to doing what I had done my whole life. I called the only person I knew would come without question. I called my dad. Of course, he'd be there, he told me, and as usual, I began to relax. I released my grip on the arms of the chair, and released a gigantic cleansing sigh, letting the air out of my constricted lungs.

Dad took Luke home after a few hours, but Andrew and I spent three never-ending days in that drab little room before the doctors could calculate an outcome. They were long, frightening, and lonely days, but I could hold him almost all the time, which made it tolerable. In the end, the tests were inconclusive, and thankfully, Andrew's color and vigor returned. I took him home happily, hoping against hope that this was yet only another temporary jog in the journey I was reluctantly becoming accustomed to.

11

Ella

W hen I was a child, the Sabbath, as my father called it, always rolled around too often. I had mixed feelings about its arrival. It was supposed to be the proverbial day of rest, but that meant restricted activity and staying in our church clothes, which I didn't much like. It was also the day we had a large, wonderful, midday meal cooked by my mother, with hot rolls and a decent dessert. I remember rolling out of bed and running to the front steps to see if I would be first to pick up the big rolled newspaper. It was about three times larger than the weekday ones. There were many store advertisements, from which my mother always cut the coupons for the week's groceries. But in addition, there were two or three full-size pages of full-color comics. We always called them the "funnies." During the week, there was only a half-page or so of black and white ones. It was so much fun to flip off the fat red rubber band and begin the search. I spread them out across the floor and hungrily read every one. I liked "Blondie and Dagwood," "Lil' Abner," "Peanuts," "Dennis the Menace," "Calvin and Hobbes," and "Little Orphan Annie," where all the characters had round hollow eyes. And of course, there was "Prince Valiant." I really didn't like "Prince Valiant" at all, but it was my father's favorite, so I made sure to keep up on it in case he wanted to discuss it. There were numerous fights over who got which page first. Sometimes we had to tear the pages apart and share.

Also on the Sabbath, there was always and ever, church. Oftentimes one or two of us would say we weren't feeling well, or out and out say that we would really rather stay home. My father used to tell us we could go willingly or that we could go and be mad about it, but that in our house, we go and worship the Lord.

I remember as if it were yesterday, sitting on a bench on the right side of the chapel, swinging my skinny legs back and forth under the brown wooden pew with the high back and generous seat. I remember admiring my black patent leather Mary Janes and short, white, ruffled ankle socks. I was in love with those shoes. I recall belting out the hymns I knew mostly by heart and the feelings they evoked. I liked gazing up at the massive silver organ pipes above the pulpit – they were in everybody's line of sight. Sometimes I spent the entire meeting counting them over and over until it was time to go home. I was pretty sure there were 172, counting all the little ones, but the next week I'd start all over again and the count would be off. I enjoyed studying the large chandeliers suspended in rows down each side of the chapel. Each was hung from the ceiling on six brass rods and looked to me like large open, upside-down umbrellas. They were shaped like that, I surmised, to catch the dewdrops falling from heaven. The glass in each section was opaque and creamy yellow, and lightly veined like a nautilus shell. I used to wonder if they had been gathered up from the beach. Invariably, the organ itself was played by a fat-bottomed lady with a helmet of curly hair. Her thick bare feet glided across the wooden foot pedals as if they were frosted with butter. Occasionally, she would fiddle with the buttons on the upper part of the organ, which resulted in ear-splitting chiming or deep booming base sounds that punctuated her music like exclamation points. I watched sleeping parishioners jolt awake when she did. Some Sundays, my attention was caught up by the lady who conducted the music. She waved both arms quite gracefully, but her hands flopped like trout as they came down on the beat.

The sun glimmered through the tall windows in the afternoon and spread across the congregation like large splayed fingers. Perhaps they were the fingers of the Lord Himself, I conjectured. I recalled the sermons. Not specific words or messages themselves, but the feelings they evoked, even in me, a child. The gospel was preached week after week, and the tender feelings of emotion and reverence grew within my young chest. I loved to sing "A wintery day descending to its close, invites all wearied nature to repose. And shades of night are falling dense and fast like silver curtains closing o'er the past." It felt warm and inspiring to look outside at the gray skies shedding soft sheets of snow like white blankets over the peaceful earth. Sometimes I felt such intensity that I wondered if the Father had placed a tiny microphone inside my ears and was transmitting directly to my spirit. Other times it was like a crystal goblet was being struck ever so gently with a heavenly fork, causing a tinkling reverberation back and forth, round and round inside the chambers of my heart, resonating louder and louder until I was certain I might burst. My father used to tell me I was feeling the spirit. It took some time to understand what he meant by that.

I suppose I always believed. At least I knew my father always believed, and if he did, I should, too. More accurately, I think I never remember not believing. Even later when life got uncertain, foggy, and downright painful, and I was absolutely certain I had no use for faith anymore, and that it was doing me absolutely no good, I kept believing. When I read the scriptures, they felt like clear, clean water you could actually drink into your heart to heal it. I knew in my whole body at a tender age that God was in everything. He loves everything, He gives everything, and somehow, some way – I was never quite sure how – He will make everything not fair be fair again and the bad things right and good. Maybe not now, but someday. Even if someday is a long way off. I was taught that He is unchangeable and constant, and that He keeps His promises. I learned that life does not end with today, and because of that, it is somewhat bearable. And mostly, I learned that God is good. Good to the point you want to cry and cry for hours, but then you stop before you have to get up out of your bench and walk past other people to go home.

I know what I know. And in the same indiscernible way, I will always know. That's what believing is to me. And I know now that faith is not only a choice but a gift.

12

Ella

My grandmother's story was poignant and astonishing, no matter how many times I begged her to recite it to me. Sometimes she blatantly refused, and other times, she relented and doled out a snippet or two at a time. She told the stories mechanically and without emotion, leaving out many details, as0 if they were just some old articles in a long-forgotten newspaper. Sometimes she seemed to wander through her memories like she was living in them, and she had an abandoned far-away look in her old blue eyes. When she was in this mode, I was wary to interrupt or ask questions. Her eyes swam in pools of moisture and her sparse grey eyelashes were flat and wet. In spite of the tears, her words came forth with no sentiment whatsoever. It was in these moments that I discovered the most, and where the real stories were spun into richly layered chapters, vibrantly and lucidly coming to life. I was spellbound and learned to listen as silently as a mouse in the corner.

I knew the story of her childhood well. Her young shoulders had borne a heavy burden, as she was the oldest in a large poverty-stricken farm family. Her father was diabetic, which eventually led to the loss of both his legs. Her mother suffered dementia and at one point almost burned their house down. Despite my grandmother's mass of chestnut hair, the old snapshots reveal a fairly plain face. Unfortunately, her beautiful blue eyes were obscured by dark-rimmed spectacles with coke-bottle lenses.

I knew she had been a spinster until the age of thirty-five. I also knew she had watched stoically and silently, and obviously with some envy, as her brothers and sisters procured jobs, courted, married, and began to rear families of their own. She had been in charge of protecting her aging parents and seeing to the household duties they could not shoulder, leaving very little time and freedom for her own sociality. When her parents had finally been safely situated, she journeyed up north to Salt Lake City and acquired a bachelor's degree in education, unusual for a young woman in her day.

After graduation, she returned to teach at the little Levan schoolhouse. She was reconciled to spending the remainder of her days alone. Happily, destiny felt to deal her an additional hand, and at age thirty-five, she serendipitously ran into an old school chum by the name of John. He was tall and dark, as well as handsome. He thought she was beautiful. They fell instantly and madly in love. They married and took over his parent's little house and five-acre farm on the upper east outskirts of town. This is where the real drama began to play out.

As I listened raptly to her stories on those shadowy evenings, it was the first suggestion I had that life's deep longings and bone-searing disappointments are never, ever expunged as the days and years march on. The hardhearted calendar doesn't care about or even acknowledge the wounds etched upon the soul. Bursts of unrelenting despair splashed across my grandmother's face as she related her stories, but she quickly autocorrected and reverted back to the stoic and disciplined bearing I had become accustomed to. I could understand that the scabs covering her wounds were being dislodged as she deep dived beneath them back in time. Those crusty layers, I think, are the insurance that we will go on living, even against our will. She did go on to live a long and solitary life of courage and dignity, while eking out a solid and rich existence for her boys, no matter how paltry the subsistence or profound the wounds.

I perched on a weathered forest green stool, which sat next to her bedside. I recall it had twisted wire crisscrossing the underside of the round seat, from leg to leg, to keep it steady. She colored in for me the romantic snapshots of the couple's five short but blissful years together. The evening skies and the fatigue of the day seemed to bring her melancholy to the surface. She smiled faintly with faraway eyes as she recounted their long walks and his bedtime brushing of her long heavy brown hair. The corners of her mouth crinkled as she spoke of laughter, sunny days, three little babies born just a year or so apart, and the flowering of hope and dreams after so much loneliness and toil. But five years is a very short time to be married. Shortly after their fifth anniversary, her beloved John passed away with the complications of a bleeding ulcer.

She recounted bits and pieces of their final days together. They were confined to the dreary white-walled hospital room with the black and white linoleum floors. She seldom spoke of the burning fevers or the anguish of their knowing he was soon to leave his beloved little family. Once, when uncharacteristically off her guard, she distractedly reminisced about hearing the clacking of the doctor's leather shoes as he approached in the hallway, while she braced herself for the news she was not remotely prepared to hear. Only one time did she tell me about watching the snow fall softly outside the hospital window as she sat by his bedside in the final hours. She would never admit that she had been weeping, but it wasn't hard to surmise. And only once did she describe the bleak charcoal skies folding in like a shadowy cape over the distant white fields. She spoke of it once, and when she did, it was as if I wasn't even in the room.

It was in increments that I learned about the rainy overcast day in the little Levan cemetery on the outskirts of town. They had been huddled together, reverently and silently, standing over his freshly manicured grave. It had a blank space adjacent, for her to lie with him, in the hopefully distant future. Her two little boys had been bundled up tightly and the baby had been cradled in her arms. She unflinchingly recounted the raising of three rambunctious growing boys with little or no sustenance. I knew about shirts sewn from flour sacks, government welfare, and nickels and pennies saved in a jar by the sink. She seemed proud to tell me about the black-faced sheep, the light brown jersey cow, and the endless bottles of green beans, peaches, apples, and beets she canned every autumn from her own garden and stored in the cellar for the long winter months ahead.

I always enjoyed revisiting a little poem hanging over her curvaceous brass bed. It was daintily scrawled in the center of timeworn paper, set in a narrow carved wooden frame, and coarsely matted in cream. I wasn't certain if it had been carefully cut from an old magazine or book, but the flowery cursive script was fading, and the pale gray and brown water-colored parchment was darkening with age. Each of the top corners cradled a tiny diamond-shaped cluster of flowers. Yellow sego lily, a white daisy, and two small bluebells. Above the lettering was a sparkling golden archway of sky, dotted with tiny stars. Under the sky was a small sketch of a woman in a yellow hat sitting prettily on a beach, white puffy clouds overhead. The poem, which I painstakingly memorized as a girl went, I think, exactly like this:

> I was thinking of you, and my dreaming was sweet and was
> kind and was glad;
> And though you were far, yet in seeming, you smiled – and the
> dream that I had
> Was by that smile joyous and splendid, illumined with
> wonderful light,
> And somehow the dream, when it ended,
> Left all of my day the more bright.

She used to tell me, trance-like, that in the early years she would pray fervently before going to bed that she might dream about her beloved John. But instead of sweet dreams, she usually awoke with a terrible nightmare. So, she told me matter-of-factly, she had long since given up the prayers to dream. Nevertheless, she continued to take comfort in the poem.

13

Ella

J unior high was only a gentle fork in the road. Nothing too different. I was beginning to think I could find a comfortable rhythm within my burgeoning social life. Girls actually seemed to be interested in being my friends, and the real surprise was that boys were the real epicenter of everything. All of a sudden, they were interesting and intriguing. I was also beginning to notice how smart I was becoming in a short time, and how average my parents were getting in the same amount of time. Adolescent normal, I suppose. So many highs and lows, so many new independent thoughts with no real context or reference, no position to solidly rest upon. But I wasn't in touch with all of that, of course. I just wanted to find a safe and comfortable place in which to find myself.

It dawns on me that even early on, the perceptions of my parents, their interactions with one another, and how they dealt with me play a crucial role in my own ability to parent, and how I navigate my adult life.

I attended the same school where my father taught business and English. Truth be told, I had mixed emotions about that. He was one of the more popular teachers at the school, which didn't surprise me, but I hadn't expected his notoriety, which was unwelcomely blowing in my direction. I adored him, but it was a little awkward to run into him in the hallways when I was busily flaunting my newfound "coolness," messing around, or feeling my oats. It may have been my imagination, but I often thought his expression was a little skewed. I couldn't discern what it might be conveying., but I knew him well enough to know it was something. It felt like a smattering of amusement with a touch of disappointment dragging behind it. I hoped I was wrong about that. I had always tried so hard to please him. He had been the heart of my life for as long as I could remember, and this scenario seemed to be throwing a wrench in things.

Home was a little different story. As I was the oldest, my mother, for the most part, expected me to be the watchdog. If my youngest sisters got dirty, wandered off, or were scuffling, I usually sensed her disdain for the way I handled things. It was not clear why, but her disappointment in me seemed palpable. I tried hard not to let her down, but the younger ones were always acting like little kids do, and I felt my mother expected more than I could deliver. Clearly, she counted on me to make her own frazzled life a little easier. She was always overworked, overwhelmed, stressed, and fatigued, and I couldn't help but feel I was to blame for some of that.

Later on, when I could look at things through a more mature lens, I wondered if my mother might have assumed a different position if my father had treated her more gently. Yet, he had been raised by a single mother, as his father died when he was just three years old. I wondered if that lopsided upbringing afforded him little or no patience for weakness in women. His only role model had been one who was capable and in charge. As for my mother, she was coddled. Her mother rode the bus to our bus stop every Friday and walked the several blocks to our house, in spite of her crippling arthritis, to take charge of the cleaning, cooking, tending, and piano lessons. In my mother's defense, however, a little forbearance and tenderness from her husband would have gone a long way in lubricating the mechanisms of family accord. In his defense, he seemed ill equipped and unable to give it. I have often considered that when two such different individuals from very different backgrounds merge their complex lives, it's quite amazing they make it at all.

I think back to my parents' interactions often as I traverse my own. I found it difficult to navigate the nuances of my mother's disparagement and her instability. She seemed highly daunted by her austere life and numerous children, which resulted in a flare for the dramatic and an inclination to victimhood. Her emotional bouts were confusing and disorienting. I couldn't say her attitude towards me was ever hateful, but it somehow transmitted the notion that I was not as important or relevant as the younger ones. Grasping, I even wondered if it was because I was not graced with the distinctive ginger hair, which I now think is absurd. Oh, the meanderings and errors of childish conclusions, and their consequences. There was little doubt in my mind that my mother loved all her children, and she unwaveringly worked her fingers to the bone to prove it, but she exhibited an inexplicable air of indifference to me as a person. Perhaps it was because I was groomed to be more of a partner and caretaker than a child. She, in turn, was more of a child than I needed her to be.

My father, on the other hand, made practically no attempt to hide the fact that I was his favorite. Even my siblings perceived and acknowledged it. In my mind, he was trying to make up for the lack of affection my mother displayed. He took over the role of predominant parent; fulfilling duties such as taking me to buy my allotment of school clothes, quizzing me on my homework, sorting out my angsts, or helping me paint my bedroom furniture. It seemed he was making up for what my mother couldn't or wouldn't do. He was strict with all of his children, me included, but rarely unfair. He insisted we eat our sweet potatoes and macaroni and cheese before leaving the table, even if it meant having to sit alone for an hour, cry till our eyes were swollen, and the food was gone. He tolerated no bickering whatsoever (except, of course, between my mother and himself). He insisted we toe the line and "strive for excellence." Study, achieve, work hard, do your chores, and help your mother. He had little tolerance for mediocrity. There was not much leeway there. We deferred to him respectfully and knew if he were crossed, it would likely result in disappointment we couldn't tolerate, consternation, or an occasional smack on the rear. He never hurt us, he just put us in our place. To be fair, I'm not sure he had much of an inkling how to be the leader of a large family, but it didn't mean he wouldn't die trying. We knew he considered us worth the effort. Though we were a bit afraid of him, we loved him dearly and vied for his attention.

Inexperience aside, he was a wonderful father. Kind, thoughtful, listening, and talkative. I believe he found it impossible to not be constantly teaching us one finer point or another. As an English teacher, he loved literature. During breakfast each morning, he'd pull out our book of the month and begin to read while we'd eat. He read us many of the classics – *A Tale of Two Cities, To Kill a Mockingbird, Moby Dick*, and even *Les Misérables*. His aim was to bestow a love for reading and fine writing upon his children.

14

Ella

Christmas was quickly approaching, and I felt the familiar mix of excitement and dread. I was up and down, happy and melancholy. It has been this way for as long as I remember. I still swing between mildly depressed and hopefully beguiled by the season's charms and beckoning spirits. It has a clever way of enticing and teasing me into getting my act together, only to become overwhelmed. The allure of lights in the city, snowflakes skating across gray skies, Christmas carols, and mugs of steaming hot chocolate is always irresistible. Who can put aside these romantic recollections? They gesture enticingly towards toasty fires and snow-encrusted Christmas tree lots, gingerbread houses and holly wreaths. They elicit years of enticing childhood memories, yet they also dredge up nagging feelings of insecurity and doubt that worm their way in to muddle it up. Holidays have a poignant way of reminding me of loss, the dysfunction of my relationships, and the disparity between what should be and what is. It is also a dark demarcation of the previous year's failures, which plays directly into my glass-half-empty mentality. It always feels like the end of "comfort and joy" is just around the corner, making the deliberate sentimentality of the season just plain contrived. Whether it's my inherent negativity bearing down or not, all the merriness tends to underscore the futility and falseness of the season.

In contrast, the children were abuzz with optimism, excitement, and never-ending impossible plans. Their enthusiasm was irresistible, and the last thing in the world I wanted to do was throw cold water on their magical expectations. I, myself, admitted to looking forward to augmenting the ever-growing yet inexpensive little Christmas village while the kids fluttered around my feet dizzily with anticipation. I also loved to put up the tree with its collected and homemade ornaments, which had been carefully scavenged and overspent for over the years. As well, I took pleasure in lighting up the outside of the house and watching the children ooh, ahh, and clap while their hands and faces turned red, and they saw their breath in the frigid air. I actually couldn't wait to get out the carefully packed and labeled boxes of extra decorations, which I only allowed myself to do after Thanksgiving had been adequately observed.

Christmas was, indeed, a conundrum for me, and there were several reasons why, I conjected. Perhaps it's because my childhood was so complicated (whose wasn't?) that I felt such angst about the holidays. Or maybe it was that my marriage was convoluted and disappointing, and I felt like a failure. Or it might have simply been that Christmas, with all it's beautiful promises of love, peace, and perfection, made real life seem a little shabby.

I completed my plans for the baking – sugar cookies for tree decorating and traditional deep-fried Danish klejner, which my mother and grandmother always made. The children loved to participate in the tradition, but that meant a huge happy mess of flour splayed all over the kitchen, and I had to grit my teeth to begin. I watched vigilantly so no one got splattered with hot grease, but someone inevitably sustained a minor burn, which I simply slathered with Neosporin and kisses. Before it was over, there were pools of oil all over the floor that little feet and paws skated around in gleefully. When we were finished, the carefully knotted and deep-fried cookies were tucked away in metal tins to be doled out generously on special nights during the month.

I completed the inexpensive neighbor gifts, which I stressed about for months and felt obliged to give. I whined a lot, but the process secretly allowed me to impress the neighbors and show off my creativity. I felt a tiny bit of guilt about such vanity, but it was never enough to impede me. That year I filled small red and green poinsettia-printed boxes with homemade fudge and penuche, trimmed and embellished with several strands of silver satin ribbon and hand-cut glittered snowflake tags.

I was not so humbly smug about the beauty of the house and tree I had decorated. I had labored for hours to perfect the magic, which, ironically, only added to my feelings of futility and superficiality. I always asked myself throughout the process if it was really worth it, and I answered with a resounding "no"; but I kept on doing it anyway. After all, the season would be over in a blink and I would recover from the angst. Strange psychological game I kept playing with myself. It was a beautiful exhibition, and the children were appropriately enthralled. I swallowed down every feeling that threatened to put a damper on my mood.

I had shopped as much as was possible with the little money allotted. There were presents for each child – simple, practical, inexpensive, personal, and, of course, fun. I hoped it was enough. They were hidden away under the stairs in a very large cardboard box, where I prayed they wouldn't be discovered. As usual, I would procrastinate the wrapping until after the kids were tucked into bed on Christmas Eve. It was just another strange and curious part of my Christmas ritual.

I had the gingerbread houses almost ready to decorate. I had spread the dollops of clear-colored homemade candy on waxed paper to dry and then glued them with stiff frosting into the carefully cut windows of the artfully formed slabs of baked gingerbread. Proudly, I thought that year's house looked a lot like an English farmhouse. I had perused magazines all year to find a pattern for the upcoming masterpiece.

House design was something I could not resist, whether for brick and mortar or for gingerbread. It was as if I got one more chance to build a new house every year. As often as not they fell flat, were burned on the edges, or were a little too soft to stand up. Then I had to start all over. I scoured the stores for sale candy to decorate with. That year I had squirreled away bags of licorice, peppermints, chocolate kisses, and orange sticks for the rooftops and railings.

The children were anxious, sneaking bits of this and that from the bags, and begging to start the elaborate, if disorderly, construction process.

Little Andrew was sitting quite solidly now, toppling over every now and again. His fat little bottom kept him fairly stable on his "blankie" on the floor. I was content with his overall progress. I was relieved that I wouldn't have to worry about him crawling to the Christmas tree to pluck off ornaments. He was a round little Humpty Dumpty, and his plump rosy cheeks tucked back toward his ears in a continual grin. His blue eyes ratcheted upon me as I busied myself about the kitchen. *He's amazingly patient*, I thought adoringly. I wiped my hands on a towel and walked over to pick him up. The macaroni and cheese, made a little fancier with slices of hot dogs, had heated through. The kids seemed to consider it gourmet. Andrew was able to sit erect in his highchair now. He picked up a few pieces of sticky macaroni in his fat little fists and stuffed them into his mouth, though I wouldn't dream of giving him a hot dog. Too much of a choking risk. I grabbed him from the chair, washed his grimy little face, and settled down in the rocker to feed him a bottle before calling the rest of the brood to dinner. As I tipped him back, I took a moment to enjoy my little cherub. With a little spit on my finger, I flattened down his short thick hair. He contoured into the crook of my arm and smiled up into my face. Just before I stuck the rubber nipple into his mouth, my hand swept lightly down the back of his head. I was startled to feel a pronounced protrusion on the lower right side. It was just behind his ear, and I had definitely never noticed it before.

15

Ella

Grandma recounted the period of family history when the Second World War was threatening to bring down the whole nation. Its spidery black fingers reached and darkened their sheltered little world as well. My father, who was the middle child and a senior in high school, had been elected student body president. In spite of the honor, he felt obliged to leave school to enlist in the navy, albeit without his mother's permission. Having recently turned eighteen, he didn't need or ask for it. Grandma admitted she had been angry and heartbroken, and had pled for him to reconsider, which he did not. Subsequently, all three boys ended up serving their country on different warships in the vast distant oceans, leaving her alone again, to pray and to hope there would be no portentous knocking at her door. She knew what the blue stars pasted in the neighboring windows signified. More poignantly, she knew that the gold ones, which replaced them from time to time, declared, not so subtly, that the unimaginable had happened. The time her boys were gone was an eternity to her, and she was alone again for the first time in twenty years. Thankfully, all three sons were honorably released and returned home safely, though only briefly. Each married or left home to embark upon their own life paths.

I recalled her dispassionate and matter-of-factly recited account of a night in the little house several years after the war. She had retired at her usual time, and around midnight the jangling of the phone in the parlor awakened her with a start. At that time of night, a phone call was always a harbinger of something unexpected. Disconcerted, she made her way through the darkness to answer it. Della, the telephone operator who manually connected practically the whole county to one another, intrepidly told her someone was waiting on the line to speak to her.

"Hello," she responded warily and a little irritably, considering the unearthly hour. After ascertaining it was my grandmother to whom he was speaking, a man's voice said gently, clearly, and calmly, "Ma'am, I'm very sorry to bother you like this. My name is Hartley Forbush, and I am a police officer in the Daggett County Sheriff's Department. I am sorry to inform you that about an hour ago, your son Alvin passed away from injuries sustained in a truck accident."

Grandma related this calmly, as if it were just a story in a book, but I could see the tiny black specks swimming around faster in her watery old blue eyes. She said she heard only the last sentence before dropping the phone with a clatter. She had grasped the edge of the phone table with both hands, clinging to it for a few seconds before crumpling to the floor in a heap. Impassively, she related that she had grabbed a crocheted cotton tablecloth she had been working on the previous night from a nearby chair. It was painfully cold in the house, so she wrapped it around her shoulders and lay there exactly where she had collapsed, throughout the remainder of the night. When she could see the pink shades of sunlight peeping through the lace curtains on the front door windows, she got up and went about her morning routine. "Red skies at morning, sailors take warning," she mused rotely, as if she were reciting a poem. My eyebrows raised indiscreetly in unease, but I said nothing.

Alvin was her oldest son. He was only twenty-six-years old. He left behind a wife, a toddler, and a newborn baby girl. The story was one of the most uncharacteristically descriptive ones I ever heard her tell.

I reiterate my grandmother never bothered to toss around platitudes or blabber about perspectives. Clearly, she did not favor pontification of any sort. But having observed her life, I know clearly what she would have told me had she elected. I know because her life was a manifest and unmistakable articulation of what she believed. These are my words, not hers, of course, but I think she would have expressed that life is just one big bucket of tears dumped out gradually and oftentimes forcefully over the head of every person born upon the earth. And that if it's not one trial, it's going to be another. She would say that there are so many different sorrows we can't begin to guess which one we might need at any given moment. She would probably emphasize the word *need*, as if someone is standing in the wings to make certain our weaknesses are forged into strengths, even if by firing squad. I think she might say that no matter which hardship is doled out, we must not stay in the puddle for too long. We must get up, wipe our eyes and our noses, and keep on trudging through to dry ground. I'm pretty sure she'd say there's no room for victims in the arena of heroes. And I know for certain she'd tell me that we won't get too far without finding someone with more courage, harsher trials, or one who will bear them better. She would emphasize that stretching is what we're here for in the first place, and that life is too short to float comfortably in the sunshine for too long a stretch. Yes, I think that's what Grandma would have told me, had she been inclined.

16

Ella

After consulting with the pediatrician about the bump on Andrew's head, I am referred to a neurosurgeon by the name of Dr. Whitehouse, whose office is in the same ancient children's hospital I have reluctantly become quite familiar with. I deem this as only a nitpicking precaution to cover all the bases. I trudge down the hospital's haunted halls again to search out the Department of Neurosurgery.

When I meet the doctor for the first time, he genially holds out a large thick hand, but when he shakes mine, it is less vigorously than I would have expected for such a large man. I always assumed neurosurgeons would have long, thin, agile fingers, but not this one. He is a kindly and very confident man – tall, burly, and middle-aged. The pocket on his open white lab coat declares his name and credentials in red and blue cursive, and belies a bit of a belly protruding over his expensive brown belt. His hair is thinning, blonde, and graying at the temples, and his forehead seems to roam miles up and over his prominent round head. His form is rather imposing, but his manner, thankfully, is far from it. His blue eyes crinkle when he smiles, and I am about to find out that he smiles a lot.

After reading the x-rays, Dr. Whitehouse informs me matter-of-factly, though a bit delicately, "I note that Andrew's suture line is impenetrable." What this means, he explains, is that normally the ridgeline on the top of an infant head is open and will close gradually after several months of life, but that is not the case here. Andrew's suture has in fact, been sealed tightly since sometime before birth. The bump I discovered at the base of his skull is where the bones are attempting to expand to make room for the growing brain. I recall being told from the time I was a little girl that when you hold a newborn, you must be very careful not to put pressure on the top of the head with your fingers. Now, for the first time ever, the light begins to dawn as to why. Dr. Whitehouse proceeds, matter-of-factly, to explain the dilemma "we" have. I suppose the "we" is so I don't feel so alone in it.

He tells me there will be scheduled visits every two weeks until Andrew is around two years old. At each visit there will be regular scans to ascertain that the space within the skull is adequate for the growing brain. If the time comes when there is reason to believe there is not, there will be surgery, where the skull will be chopped into small pieces and fit together loosely, ensuring adequate space over time. Next, he would be fitted with a contoured helmet, which he would wear until the healing of the bone was complete. The doctor is so soothingly calm and seemingly unconcerned, I almost believe this is a routine occurrence. But just as I begin to give way to his relaxed stance and explanation, I stop myself. I feel panic rising into my throat like vomit. I have never heard of this phenomenon except peripherally, and the thought of such an extreme surgery on my sweet little baby seems major, cruel, and dangerous, not to mention the hassle and inconvenience of the upcoming two-week visits and scans. My heart leaps around wildly in my chest, and I feel the tears begin to pop up into my eyelids and sting my eyes. Get a grip, Ella, I sternly command. I begin to blink rapidly and take deep breaths, because as unnerved as I feel, I have no intention of falling apart in front of this confident and kindly physician. At least not now and not today. I bundle my baby tightly in his little coat and blankets without making eye contact with Dr. W. Looking out the window and at the baby's things, I thank him cordially, nod my head affirmatively, and wave goodbye. I know without seeing that he is smiling. As I carefully descend the steps of this old chicken coop of a hospital with clouded eyes, the tears fall steadily onto my coat collar all the way to the car.

The visits are scheduled, and I adhere to them like clockwork. No excuses or exceptions. I am nothing if not reliable and consistent, especially where my children are concerned. When they get older, they will chafe at the hovering and teaching I do and try to break free from the grip they think I have imposed upon them. They will be wrong, however. It's not been something I have a choice over anyway. It's just the kind of mother I was destined to be, I believe wholeheartedly.

I have adjusted to the disagreeable hospital by now, with its narrow corridors and unpleasant smells, as we have been coming for months. Each time I come, I climb the two dozen shallow and creaky wooden stairs on the north of the building, which lead directly to an outside door of the second floor. But when they have fresh snow on them and I'm afraid I will slip and fall with the baby, then I come through the double front doors on the east. It's less direct and much farther to walk, but safer. I make my way down the gloomy hallway to the laboratory. When the prescribed scans have been done, I am to meet Dr. Whitehouse in his office for consultation. Even this illustrious neurosurgeon has a small dingy office painted a monotonous off-white and fitted with a somber gray metal desk and chair. His credentials are framed simply and unobtrusively in plain black metal and are hung too high in the center of the wall above the desk. They look out of place and lonely. The only other accoutrements in the room are a pretty brass pharmacy light, a definite disparity with the desk, and a somewhat rumpled gray flannel loveseat with a couple of slightly soiled blue and white striped throw pillows. It's pretty clear that ambience is not in his wheelhouse or interest. His blue eyes crinkle with the familiar kindly smile, and he reassures me that all is well for now. Apparently, he thinks I need a little cordial chatting, so he asks how things have been and comments on the weather. I am appreciative, as it makes my visits almost comfortable. Then I gather up Andrew and leave the same way I came. The relief when the doctor's decision is to watch and wait for the present, allowing me to take Andrew home to normalcy after each visit, is incalculable and washes over me like spring water. On the way home in the car, I am aware that I am deeply sighing repeatedly. I slump back in my seat, my hands relax on the steering wheel, and I cut my eyes gratefully over to my happy little baby. He hasn't a worry in the world.

17

Ella

When I was in junior high school, my father, to make ends meet, got the notion he could become a real estate magnate. He was convinced that by becoming a landlord he would be able to double his meager income as a schoolteacher. He proceeded to scour the newspaper for foreclosures and buy up inexpensive low-end apartments in several especially run-down areas of town. Then he would try to rejuvenate them. He'd do all the plumbing, electrical, painting, cleaning, and repair work. "Saves a lot of money to do things yourself," he always said.

I remember many a school night and Saturday being "recruited" to "help." I learned to paint, defrost freezers, unplug drains, plunge toilets, and most of all, clean up terrible messes left by people my father called "slugs" or "yardbirds." It was mostly filthy work, scraping blackened bathtubs with two dozen greasy rings ground into them, or putting my hands into rusty fetid toilets and trying my darnedest to bring them back to some sort of white life, which was often impossible. I regularly cleaned an inch of crud off baseboards and scrubbed crusty and cracked old linoleum floors on my hands and knees with a bucket of soapy water and a brush. It was apparent to me that most of the apartments had not been cleaned in years.

Painting was my forte and favorite duty. I was always quick to volunteer for the job, if only because I found it to be clean, renewing, and reviving. It somehow magically erased a grimy and unsavory past right before my eyes. White was always my favorite color, if only because it seemed to immediately revive the dingy, dark, and dirty rooms and let the light bounce around so gloriously. There were always mouse droppings, centipedes, silverfish, and most dreaded, cockroaches. I will never forget swallowing down my stomach contents as I emptied cupboards bursting with spoiled and foul-smelling food, teeming with weevils. I have clear memories of scooping swollen and rusting cans of green beans and Spam into garbage sacks. Not a few times did I sweep up soiled diapers piled high into the corners of a room. My dad always tried to scoop up the stacks of pornography strewn among the messes and toss them out quickly before I had a chance to see them. But I knew what it was, though I pretended not to.

It was not always such terrible work at the apartments, but it was terrible often enough to make me hate going and assisting my father, who I knew was so in need of help. When my part was finished, I'd sit out on a porch stoop or in the corner of an empty or disassembled room and wait for him to get tired enough to go home, which was never early. He was always determined to accomplish more than humanly possible, perhaps to lighten the workload for the next day. I often brought my schoolbooks and tried to study. At times, I was so tired, I'd bunch up my coat, lay my head on it, and fall asleep. Other times, it was so frightfully cold, I couldn't doze off. The floors were often so grimy, I'd have to spread out a few layers of old newspaper to sit on. Too chilled to sleep, I'd tuck my coat around my legs and wait as patiently as I knew how.

After all, I reasoned, my poor father was probably just as cold, and at least as weary after a full day of teaching and working on the apartments. So, I waited as patiently as I could while he toiled to fix another toilet or coax another ancient boiler back to life, deep in the belly of a foul-smelling building.

18

Ella

My maternal grandmother's old house, which my mother had fortuitously inherited, was situated close to the gravel road. There was supposedly something advantageous about that positioning back in the day, but there were at least five more acres of beautiful meadowland sprawling across the sides and back.

Concealed discreetly just north of the porch was a large patch of bright yellow buttercups mounded in clumps. Their leaves were multi-layered, scalloped, deeply green, and pretty enough to stand on their own. Each tiny, vibrant, butter-yellow flower springing from them was an individual marvel. There were layer upon layer of fragile wafer-thin waxy petals melded at the core, creating a miniature masterpiece. I was obsessed with them. I picked one after another, staring at them intently, carefully tearing the petals from the center and letting them cascade like silken confetti onto the lawn. I sat there until my bare legs began to itch from the grass.

To the east and behind the house there were at least a thousand purple bearded irises, their knife-like leaves pointing straight towards the sun, their yellow whiskered tongues chattering about something or another, their bright heads waving in the warm breeze. I often stood out in the center of them just because no one ever said I couldn't. I felt like the queen of the flowers. There were patches of pink and blue delphin-ium swaying to a soundless melody in the wind, and numberless tall stems of Virginia bluebells vying for attention among the weeds. They were sky blue and delicately hanging in columns from graceful stems. They looked as if you might actually be able to ring them.

Grandma's cache of prize burgundy peonies – she said 'pe-own-ies,' not 'pe-an-ies' – were spaced formally and evenly in the perimeters of the front gardens and were sprinkled with violets, violas, and pansies. She told me these were just cousins in different shapes and sizes. As she pointed them out, she unconsciously polished the buttons on her sweater, as if they were children she was proud of . As she walked among the pansies, she always said they had their own faces. I looked at them differently after that and decided she was right. I could pick out the eyes and the mouths. I have four or five of the treasured blood-red peonies spotlighting my own garden, dug from the remnants of the now weed-strewn Levan yard. With them, I have an unexpected bur-geoning collection of the bluebells as well, which were stealthily em-bedded in the roots of the peonies.

Another of my favorite haunts in the yard was a large, round, dirt root cellar sticking up out of the ground like the hump of a whale, mostly hidden. I imagined it could be a gigantic hobbit hill with a little weathered side door, practically invisible. Over the years, the cellar had ingeniously disguised itself with masses of thickly tufted, dusky, elliptical-shape-leaved myrtle. It was growing lush, layer upon layer, and was peppered generously with lovely black-eyed periwinkle flowers. This very color has remained my favorite shade of blue. Large butterflies continually hovered over the blossoms, their bright wings opening in delicately stained-glass yellow and black. I used to call them monarchs but later came to learn they were actually Tiger Swallowtails. Exploring the yard was like thumbing through a book of fairy tales, filling up my senses with enchantment. I was often con-tent to sit on a nearby stump for a half hour or so and soak up the magic.

Then there was the ancient granary. It was a small but perpetual two-story structure, constructed of random-width boards stacked and nailed horizontally, one upon the other. They were blackened and a little mossy from age and inclement weather. A dilapidated door hung precariously from rusty old hinges and was wedged shut. The padlock wasn't really locked but looked as if it was. With the aid of a pointed stick you could get inside easily, if you weren't afraid of what you'd encounter. The first thing you noticed when you entered was the labyrinth of cobwebs and hundreds of capsule-like moth larvae embedded in the wood. They looked like seed pods but much more sinister; I kept my distance from them just in case. The inner walls consisted of lodgepoles. I used to venture in quite often, hoping and imagining that I might uncover a treasure. Perhaps something that would make my family wealthy. It smelled strongly ancient, or what I imagined "ancient" to smell like. In reality, I'm pretty sure it was just the scent of rotten oil and rust, mingled with mold, but maybe that is the smell of "ancient." On one side of the building, there were dog-eared, mildewed, and weathered boxes of old junk piled almost to the ceiling. As I carefully lifted them down (not all in one visit) and pulled the lids off one by one, I found old books, piles of letters tied with coarse twine, old magazines, and crates of dirty tools. There were shovels, pickaxes, old trowels, and what seemed like an inordinate assortment of wooden-handled dandelion diggers. I wondered about all the past gardening days of my grandmother or great-grandmother or their offspring. It was fun to imagine the activity and bustle of their country days. One tale I had heard so many times that I knew it must be true was that of one of my grandmother's uncles. He hid bootleg liquor there under bales of hay during Prohibition times. It was said that a rival had snuck over in the dead of night to light the granary on fire to squelch the competition. You could still see where the wood had been repaired, and a remaining section of charred and pitted boards.

As for gardening, Levan was the place I where found my passion for it. I would awake to the sun teasing and beckoning "good morning" to me through the little windows. I would find rice pudding and raisins sprinkled with cinnamon and sugar waiting for me on the old coal stove. I used to think wryly how good the pudding would taste if it didn't have rice in it, but I never said that to grandma. It took only a moment for me to spy her in a wheelchair these days, out in the front garden, hoe in hand, leaning out precariously into the dirt. The red peonies hung their heavy heads in glory, and I think, in dire dread of the upcoming Memorial Day, when everyone wanted some for their loved one's graves. The pansies' little faces smiled sweetly as they preened their pastel heads in the sunshine.

Those sweet, humble gardening experiences in my grandmother's yard stayed with me my entire life. When we had the opportunity to travel to distant places, even other countries, the first thing to attract my attention was the gardens. I recall standing mesmerized at a hotel window in Bruges, Belgium, while accompanying Sam on a work trip. I looked out at a patch of deep green, fluted pachysandra leaves dappled with sunlight. I felt what I now recognize as pure wonder. I have entered a statue garden amidst a sumptuous bed of pink larkspur and Shasta daisies, columbine and violets, and literally felt like weeping. I'd pilfer (I never did consider it stealing) tiny starts of black cherry and fuchsia hollyhock from the grounds of the library and stuff them in an empty soda cup. Or I'd take a shovel from the back of my station wagon to an abandoned bed of yellow irises at the side of the road. Plants, flowers, and gardens became one of my fixations. It was always an absolute necessity to have my own significant plot of earth to work, tend, and make alive. To me it was as fundamental as breathing clean, fresh air into my lungs. It still makes my chest swell in reverent gratitude.

19

Ella

Our last visit to the children's hospital came on a Monday morning, and I had become pretty complacent and calm about the regular CAT scans and the occasional lumbar punctures, which had now become routine. I didn't dread the trips nearly as much; I was fairly certain that after all the time that had lapsed uneventfully, Andrew was out of the woods. I was confident we had escaped the dreaded unthinkable. I was actually enjoying my little meetings with Dr. Whitehouse now. We had become all but fast friends. His easy affability made these trips as pleasant as they could have been. This day, he invited me to sit down on his little crumpled loveseat, and we chatted benignly for about five minutes about the weather and such. Then, without fanfare, he enthusiastically heralded the conclusion I had already come to hope for and suspect.

His eyes crinkled and flashed even more brightly than usual as he told me that it was his opinion that the bullet had been dodged. His eyebrows were doing a happy dance, and I knew he was as pleased as I was at this outcome. Then he paused, looked me in the eye, and cautioned a little somberly. This was not something anyone could say with absolute certainty. The skull appeared to have reached the bulk of its maturity, he told me, so we will hope for the best. Subsequently, there would be no more visits.

He took both my hands in one of his very large and sturdy ones and smiled. I thanked him profusely, shook his hand again, and probably smiled a little too brightly. We were now allies of sorts. I felt much gratitude towards him, and I almost felt – only almost – a little sadness at the prospect of not visiting him anymore. Yet, the final good news made me feel especially happy, relieved, and good natured. When this happens, as is usual, I begin to babble. He seemed slightly amused and winked as I turned to leave.

As I began to walk down that dreary but now seemingly brighter hallway, there was a small random thought buzzing around in my head like a fruit fly, and impulsively, I decided it might be wise to run it past Dr. Whitehouse before I might never see him again. It was only a random thought. Can't hurt to ask. If only to remove it from my overflowing mind files. Especially now that we are out of the woods. Turning around, I retraced my steps across the black and white tiled linoleum back to his office. He was standing in the doorway writing on a yellow notepad. Perhaps notes about our visit, I guessed. He looked up at me quizzically. I vaulted into my monologue. "Uhm ... I thought I should mention that Andrew's not really talking." I stated it rapidly and matter-of-factly. "It's later than for the other children. He's not even saying 'mama' clearly. He's happy and normal," I assured him a little too cheerily, "but he's not really speaking." He stopped, pursed his lips, took a couple steps backwards towards his metal desk, and carefully regarded little Andrew hanging sideways on my hip. He deliberated a moment before saying anything. His eyebrows were now tightly knitted together instead of dancing. I felt like sucking the words back through the air and into my throat. I wanted to run back down the hallway before he had a chance to say something I might not want to hear. What in the world was I thinking by voicing my uneasiness? Just when things were righting themselves after so long. But it was too late. It was obvious I had pushed a button.

In a couple of weeks, I found myself back at this same old dismal institution with an appointment to see an audiologist. As kindly and cordial as Dr. Whitehouse had been, this man was a horse of a different color. He was tall and gangly, with a thousand large pores on his narrow nose and moist, clammy-looking skin. He wore topstitched beige polyester jeans which directed the eye downward to unusually long, pointed tan loafers. He was, in my opinion, milk toast burnt around the edges. He delivered his assessment straight-faced, sans kindness or sensitivity. He made it crystal clear that his diagnosis was absolute. Clearly, there would be no questions in this office. To heck with the fact that I was a mother of a toddler with a disturbing and complex history. Forget that I was alarmed, fearful, and apprehensive about what this new diagnosis could mean. Obviously, this doctor was "the man" in this department, and his word was the gold standard. I had better get on board with the plan and do it right away.

The news was swift and certain, at least in his "professional" opinion. Not rocket science, I supposed, but fairly run-of-the-mill, out-of-my-housewife-league kind of data. The tests disclosed that Andrew had scarcely any hearing in one ear and only about twenty-five percent in the other. Nerve damage, he declared ostensibly. Not only that; categorically irreversible. Who was I to doubt? He should be fitted with serious hearing aids immediately and scheduled for regular speech therapy to recoup some of the language lost in two years' time.

I was downcast, discouraged, and mostly disappointed that my zig-zagging journey had yet more lengthy legs tacked onto it, and unpleasant ones. I felt a flare of anger and unreasonable resentment towards the message bearer. I had the audacity to argue with the esteemed audiologist. "I am his mother, for heaven's sake. Wouldn't I, of all people, be able to tell if he had a serious hearing loss? Impossible. I am certain he can hear. At least pretty well." (I was beginning to question my judgment and becoming a little less emphatic.)

"And how could you possibly know that?" he demanded condescendingly.

Now I wanted to hit back. "I just do," I said as snarkily as I dared. "There has to be some mistake."

Obviously, I had lost this battle. I didn't really have a leg to stand on. In a couple of weeks, he was fitted with large flesh-colored upside-down slug-shaped apparatuses, with tails that hovered over his little head and twined down into his ears. As I studied the new monstrosities, I questioned impulsively as to whether or not the sound might be distorted or perhaps merely terribly annoying to such a small boy. The audiologist tilted his clammy hairless chin towards the ceiling and looked down his long, crooked nose at me with impatience, resignation, and a not a little disdain. He grabbed the hearing aids out of little Andrew's ears and shoved them, not so gently, into my own. "See for yourself what a difference it will make to him. I'm sorry," he said haughtily, "but you need to settle down and face reality. You need to adjust your attitude if you expect him to wear them and benefit from them." I felt toppled.

20

Andy

I t was 84 degrees outside the comfort of the super-duper cooled bus – not so hot, really, most likely a perfect summer temperature for most folks. But as many of Andy's passengers tended to be elderly, they were relatively more fragile, at least in ways younger people weren't. He was always looking out for their comfort, and temperature was one of his most basic concerns. Yellowstone was a high point for most people, and definitely on the majority of bucket lists. They had heard so many stories of the mountain grandeur, wildlife, geysers, and the wide-open rugged beauty. Yellowstone National Park was famous all around the world. As he listened to the chatter, he realized a lot of them were finally attaining a long-awaited goal, and the tension on the bus was positive and high. They were standing up and craning their necks out the windows they had opened from the top, and some were even cupping their hands on the glass to get a bird's-eye view. There was a camera around every craggy neck. Again, Andy enjoyed being the one privileged to present this stunning marvel of nature to his passengers.

Yellowstone was unusually warm this month. The temperatures usually stayed relatively cool all summer long. Compared to Salt Lake City, however, this was a dream, thought Andy, which was at this moment approaching 103 degrees. It was fresh, mild, serene, and majestically beautiful. But having seen everything in this place a thousand times, Andy was just a tad bit bored. It seemed that he had seen Old Faithful erupt 500 times. Today was low-key and routine, as these trips go. He was rolling along at a contented pace, focused on the pleasure of these first-time visitors.

Andy had to admit he always enjoyed getting to know his new bus families. It was a challenge at times, but he tried to focus on each person individually, listen to, and absorb what they were putting out there about themselves. He tried to imagine what their lives had been like. This group was no different. He tried to make friends with each, except maybe the old curmudgeon, Louis, who had quickly taken up permanent occupancy in the very back window seat. He had fanned his belongings out in a way that declared he owned the area. Lou wasn't rude but was pretty off-putting, letting anyone know who smiled at him or dared to be openly friendly that he was just not interested. 'Keep your darn distance and don't attempt to speak to me' was the obvious message spread across his weather-beaten face.

Andy was familiar with the Louis types. There were often one or two of them on every trip. Not always, but often enough to recognize them right away. A little surly and a lot grouchy. As usual, Andy studied Louis and tried to discern what had made him so grouchy. In the first place, his appearance had probably not drawn many people. His head was shaped like a very large grapefruit and had tufts of short, white, curly hair sporadically sprouting from the top. His glasses were thick and black, and his hearing aids were melded to them without a gap. His face was not so much wrinkled as it was pitted and hardened. There were clumps of white hair under his nose and on his chin, sparsely spread in patches, not heavy. His nose was bulbous and red-veined, probably from years of sunshine and buckets of beer. His body was ox-like, though rounded like his head. His arms looked like thick rubber cylinders continuing from his curved shoulders in one ongoing line. It reminded Andy of a stretchy rubber doll he had played with as a child.

His paunch dripped over his stretched out, skinny-in-places leather belt. Andy had learned to cut a wide berth for the Louis's. Let them be, give them their space, be respectful and politely aloof, but still smile kindheartedly as often as you can. He was beginning to understand how life and time could wear a person down to such sourness. He didn't let it bother him much, but he felt sorry for such folks.

It was easy for Andy to feel affection for people. It was as natural as the sunlight glistening on the trees in Yellowstone Park. He rarely met someone he didn't like or couldn't be interested in. His simplicity, guilelessness, and honest courtesy put people immediately at ease. At first meeting, he stuck out his hand in an easy gesture of acceptance. He didn't have the slightest inclination to hold back or be remote. It wasn't in him to be anything *but* friendly and open. He lacked the capability, and thus the desire, to learn the finer points of reserve, aloofness, or feigned sophistication. He didn't even realize there were such strategies to grasp. He spoke openly and without reserve, just as easily as he breathed in and out. He couldn't have been any different if he tried. Life was just life, straightforward and clear. There were no nuances to master, no processes to use in conversation, and no subtle tricks to appear more knowledgeable or more interesting. All those little gaming attributes were simply and inextricably beyond him. It made no sense to hold back or appear to be different than one was. You are what you are, end of story. That made his interaction with people simple, clean, straight, and much easier for everyone.

He made it a practice to learn each name in the group, which usually only took the better part of a day. He made it a point to exchange pleasantries, asking about their lives and families, and of course, their health issues. It hadn't taken him long to figure out that aches and pains were a very important part of life for older people. The result of his interest was that they dropped their guards and became his dear friends. When they did, he became their leader and their protector, which gave his work great meaning. He was, he often thought, much like the father of each family. He watched over; gave direction; provided stability, comfort, and information; and most importantly, he parceled out security and safety. Most likely it was because he was not able to see his own children that he relished the opportunity to be a good caretaker.

Yellowstone was famous for its bears, wolves, moose, buffalo, elk, bison, badgers, and otters. Very occasionally, one might spot a wolverine or lynx. Andy actually had seen them all. Yes, he was so accustomed to seeing wildlife it was practically commonplace, except for maybe the two wolverines and the lynx he had encountered. Now the high point was showing his bus family the stunning animals, most of which they had never seen. He'd pull over, often in the middle of the road, to allow them to look out the windows or disembark for an up close and personal look at a leggy, woolly moose, large black bear, or menacing bison. He cautioned them, of course, to keep a healthy distance. Yes, you can snap a picture or two, he admonished, but do it and then retreat quickly to the safety of the bus. They were always entranced and excited, which gratified Andy to the core. He was excited to provide these experiences. Most of the time it was totally safe and predictable, but he had encountered the occasional passenger who thought he was indestructible or perhaps unbreakable, who had darted out into the road and right into the face of a dangerous animal for a close-up. Some had even attempted a petting zoo maneuver. Too close for comfort. Andy hated those occasions and felt a fever-pitch panic until he could corral the person back to the safety and shelter of the bus. In his mind, it would be akin to the alarm of losing a child in a department store, or the terror of a perceived abduction. Things Andy could simply not fathom.

This day was like most others until the passengers spotted a mother moose and her baby off in a clearing at the side of the road. Andy was well aware of the dangers of this scenario. It had the potential to be deadly, as mama moose are not afraid of anything and tend to be viciously protective. He steered the bus to the side of the road, leaving a lot of space between the bus and the moose duet. He cautioned vehemently, as usual, and allowed those who desired, to exit the bus to stand a safe distance away to snap a picture or two. All went well at first. Andy always offered a hand to everyone who got off the bus, whether it be a man or woman. He'd joke with the married couples by saying, "Joe, hope you're okay with me holding your lovely wife's hand."

Donna was next in line to exit, seemingly excited to see a real moose in the flesh. Andy had struck up a pleasant conversation with her previously, as he usually tried to do, and had asked the usual questions about her life and family, as well as covertly configured inquiries about her health. She was closing in on eighty and lived in Indiana. It was obvious Donna had been saving up for this trip for a long time. She was unusually tall and wispy, not quite boney, but graceful and well-groomed for her age. Her skin was lightly creped, and her eyes receded into her high cheekbones, giving her a slightly ethereal but skeleton-like look. Her thin arms dangled from her body like chopsticks, and her sparse yellow-gray hair hung loosely on her shoulders. Such a nice lady, Andy thought. She was one who clung firmly to her dignity while inevitably losing the bloom of her youth.

Donna had been sitting in the middle section of the bus, and when her turn came, she gingerly descended the bus steps, smiling appreciatively as Andy took one of her hands to steady her. She had taken no more than one step forward when without warning, she fainted. Andy reached out to catch her, but she was almost a foot taller than he was, and her body caught his shoulder blade as her dead weight dropped four feet to the ground. Her face hit the gravel with a sharp thud, and her glasses crumbled under the weight of her head. Andy could see that a shard of glass was embedded in her eye, and she had road rash on both forearms. She became conscious very quickly and was so startled that she raised her hands and promptly jerked the piece of glass from her eye, causing it to spurt blood. No one was paying any attention now to the moose family, and everyone gathered around Donna worriedly. Andy stood up without bothering to brush himself off or take stock of any injuries he might have sustained. He rushed to Donna's side, stooped down, and cradled her bloody head in his hands. "Oh, let's call the paramedics!" he exclaimed. "You're going to be alright," he said at least three times, before reason kicked in. He grabbed his phone and dialed 911.

Donna was checked out at a local hospital and deemed in good enough condition to continue her trip if she wished, though she sported a pirate-like bandage over one eye and several large ones on her arms. The hotel shuttle returned her to the bus. Her eye was going to be all right. The medical personnel explained the reason for the fall to Andy. Donna was diabetic and had consumed four cups of coffee for breakfast, no food whatsoever. She apologized repeatedly for being so silly. She should have known better. Old age and such, she explained. In her excitement to see the moose, she had gotten up too quickly from her seat, she reasoned. She thanked Andy profusely for protecting her from added injury and for saving her life. He thought she just might be right about that part.

It was just such an occasion, which made Andy question his profession. He had a difficult time seeing anyone suffer, especially an elderly person. He knew he wasn't at fault, but it was something he would walk a mile to avoid.

A day or two later, Donna found she had misplaced her wallet, most likely in the emergency room. It held the remainder of her trip money, which was now gone. She was terribly upset, even though she had insurance to help her cover the remainder of the costs. She had tears in her lashless grey eyes when she told him that what bothered her most was that she had no tip money to give him now. This made Andy sad. The last thing he cared about was a tip from Donna, poor gentle lady. It was beginning to dawn on Andy that this job as a bus driver was impacting others in a very meaningful way, much like the police officers he had always admired.

21

Ella

A few weeks after my sophomore year, life took an unexpected turn. I had been enjoying my life more than I ever thought possible. I had some good friends. I got decent grades. I had done reasonably well at navigating the confusing nuances of high school. I had even been invited to the homecoming dance by, of all people, the senior class president. He was a great-looking guy, and a very popular one, though I couldn't begin to fathom why he would ask me. My father had taken me to JCPenney to buy my first nice dress. It had been a floating amethyst chiffon with an empire waist and puffy sleeves. It was, of course, on clearance, but the dance was a dream come true. We began to date sporadically, and I was really beginning to like him. At this phase of my life, I felt like my fairy godmother was waving her glittery magic wand all around me. Yes, things had been going well.

School had been out only a couple of weeks, and I was excited to see what the summer would bring. I had high expectations. One balmy June evening, everyone in our household retreated hastily inside, as a storm was quickly approaching. Portentous skies enveloped us, when normally they would still be bright and sunny. Like a giant whip, a robust squall blew in the first rain. Before long, the drops were so large and fast, they pounded the pavement like stones. I looked out the front window and watched them splatter the concrete and splash into small fountains. Thunder grumbled, and then bellowed, as lightning slashed the skies like varicose veins on an old woman's leg. It wasn't more than ten minutes before the rain turned to hail, large as nickels and then quarters. It bounced around the grass like popcorn and made a racket on the windows. It was eerie but also exciting. It was a fun and interesting change of pace. I kept my nose plastered to the window, mesmerized by the drama. I have always loved a good storm. Inside, I feel protected and sheltered from the spectacle outside. Little did I suspect that for our family, on this night, a storm of greater magnitude would shortly erupt and alter the perimeters of my safe little existence.

Lightning continued to entertain us with its impressive lightshow, and the rain quickly turned into a heavy steady drenching, thoroughly soaking everything. It puddled on the lawns and streets. My father gathered our motley little crew into the kitchen around the gray metal-edged melamine table, which was reflected in the dark corner windows. It was so black outside I could see my reflection as clearly as if I were sitting in front of a mirror. The gray vinyl-covered metal chairs were scooted closely together so we could all fit around the table. Everyone watched the skies light up intermittently as my father began to speak. We weren't paying too much attention to him, as none of us had a clue what was about to happen. He spoke authoritatively, as usual, but meekly. His countenance seemed distant and sad, and I thought of the strange yellow light that had hovered over the sky just before the storm. It was also quiet and ominous, giving no hint of what was to come.

He gently but somberly explained there had been an unexpected turn of events concerning the apartments he had been working on so long and hard. Stunned, we turned to him with our full attention. He neglected to explain the exact nature of the catastrophe, probably because we would not have understood. All we really wanted to know, anyway, was how it would impact us. He said, without elaboration, it meant we could lose our house. It must be sold as quickly as possible to save us from some sort of vague, inexplicable, but terrible ruin. In simple terms, we must move before summer's end.

To say I was upset would not do justice to the tumult of fear and disappointment flashing through my brain like lightning. I saw myself in the dark mirrored window in front of me and did my best to blank out any expression. Yet I felt I had been slapped in the face. The storm had quieted now, but it was still raining steadily. My heartbeat began to take on the rhythm of the raindrops drumming relentlessly on the windowpane.

22

Ella

Grandma had her own brand of "industrious." If anyone knew her at all, they would know she felt that productivity is paramount to a meaningful life. Her routine didn't have much space for "fiddling around," even if there wasn't really much to be done in the first place, I thought sardonically.

Get up, get dressed properly, wash up, eat breakfast, do the dishes, time for a spot of gardening, and so on. Grandma said washing up is when you wash your face, never forgetting to wash your neck as well. "Just look at Emmy's dirty old wrinkly neck, bless her heart," she'd say with a grin about her old friend down the block. "Never leave a dirty dish in the sink and don't leave the kitchen until it's as clean as when you started. Fold the towels so they dry nicely and hang the dishrag over the edge of the sink." Then it was time for a bit of news on the old humpbacked wooden radio, and then a small space for chatting – but only a little. Like I said, she didn't have too many words to share.

Then it was time for lunch. That was usually home-bottled fruit, a little bread and butter with some homemade peach jam, and a slice or two of cheese. The plates, glasses, and napkins were always neatly set at the table. "No eating on the run," she said. Sometimes lunch was a tuna sandwich, with her own bottled dill pickles chopped into the mayonnaise, along with a splash of mustard. Then it was time for a little nap. If I couldn't sleep, resting quietly was enough. An hour was sufficient, she'd say. Then it was time for a little handwork. This was when we'd go to the sewing machine to piece quilt blocks or get out our thread and crochet hooks. To be fair, if she sensed I wasn't in the mood, she'd sit in her chair and embroider or tatt while I'd lie on the floor at her feet with a book. It became clear only years later that the somewhat stringent, albeit simple, routine was what made her austere and solitary life hum along. Broken into segments, her days had purpose. I try very hard to remember this on dull or downcast days. I never, ever remember her being despondent or down. Sometimes she'd say she couldn't understand what they call "depression," because she'd never had any time for it.

One of the first and most dreaded duties I had each time I visited Grandma was that of taking care of her feet. She seemed almost jubilantly anxious to get this done as quickly as possible after my arrival. She probably thought I might find a reason to avoid it. Once I had naively volunteered, and after that, it became my specified personal task. I felt bad because she so looked forward to it, and I hated it so much. I used to cross my fingers behind my back and pray fervently at the same time that she would forget. She rarely did. She wore her black lace-up shoes and nylons from the moment she stepped onto the floor in the morning until the time she peeled off the moist stockings and swung her feet back into the bed at night, so her feet never got a breather from those sturdy shoes the whole day. She did a bit of hand washing in the bathroom sink, but she didn't own a washer and dryer, so I couldn't hold that against her.

The particular job I inadvertently landed myself was to clip the hardened yellowed toenails onto a piece of newspaper, and then take a single-edged razor blade and scrape her corns and callouses onto the paper as well. Her heels were particularly thick and crusty. She was as meticulous a person as I ever knew hygienically, but when I stripped off her stockings, the smell of her feet about knocked me on my head.

I tried to hold my breath, but it was still as unpleasant a task as I have ever had. Yet how could I say no? I loved her dearly, I felt sorry for her lot in life, and I knew it was something that needed to be done. I became quite proficient at hiding my revulsion and just sped through it as quickly as I could. Then I'd race to the bathroom and scrub my hands with a bar of Dial soap and a brush.

23

Ella

Speech therapy was an entirely different experience than with the audiologist; it was surprisingly pleasant. The therapist, Miss Jensen, was not what I expected. She was petite, pretty, young, easy going, and extremely charismatic. She was almost sappily sweet with Andrew, and it took me a little while to adjust to that. His reaction was classic fly-to-honey. Although he usually went eagerly to anyone, even strangers, he took to her in a big way. Clearly, this was going to be an advantageous match.

I was curious in every respect about Miss Jensen. She was not your run-of-the-mill educator. She didn't fit the stereotype. No spectacles or poofy hair. Her wardrobe was considerable, probably expensive as well, chic, and expertly put together. In comparison, my jeans, worn blouses, and T-shirts made me feel dowdy, unpolished, and old. My brown hair was usually tied back haphazardly in a ponytail, while hers was dark, perky, thick, shiny, and bobbed to below her collarbones. Her makeup was not exactly conservative, either, but expertly applied and attractively effective. I found myself feeling anxious to return each session, if only to see what Miss Jensen was wearing that particular day. I find envy to be a strange and complicated sort of emotion. Her presence elicited feelings of inferiority and frumpiness, which I did not like, along with a sort of compulsive curiosity and appreciation, which was motivating.

Her perfectly lipsticked mouth seemed to involuntarily curve into a smile, as if any other expression would be physically impossible. I admit I liked her at once in spite of the intimidation factor. I immediately trusted her and felt comfortable asking her any question; and I had many. She wasn't self-absorbed, as her appearance might suggest. She was open, friendly, and genuine. She seemed sincerely interested in me and how I was coping with Andrew's problems, which put me at ease. I quickly perceived that Miss Jensen had that uncanny ability to put everyone at ease, especially the mothers of her students. As for the little ones, she showed immense tenderness, animated interest, and real empathy.

Andrew's lessons were conducted in a cheerful eight-by-ten-foot cubicle that had been painted vibrant peach. He was perched on a small apple-green stool in front of a child-sized tangerine-colored table, making the whole scheme brightly coordinated. The table was lined with a continually fluctuating assortment of toys, which kept his attention. A large plate-glass window constituted one whole side of the room and showed through to the waiting area, where we watched. The speakers were turned just high enough that I could hear clearly every word spoken inside. Because of that, I always felt part of the process and was grateful to be able to keep track of his development. I was certain Andrew had no interest in the window, or any clue that others were watching.

Miss Jensen faced him at his level on a small fuchsia-colored chair and patiently taught him the words for different toys and items, enunciating the syllables of each carefully and clearly. She praised him lavishly when he repeated them even slightly correctly, and if he didn't say them at all, she patiently repeated the process. At first, he watched her lips carefully, trying to mimic her sounds. Though determined, he usually spit them out with too much emphasis on one consonant or vowel. She would gently repeat the word, emphasizing it more slowly and loudly. One day she held up a colorful toy train while enunciating the word. Clearly, he loved trains, and seemed very excited. First, he bounced up and down, saying, "rain, rain, rain," looking ever so pleased with himself. She brushed her tongue across her white teeth and articulated an exaggerated "t" sound. His eyes blinked questioningly, and he looked a little bit lost. She repeated the sound several times. All of the sudden his little eyes got big and round, and a definite light flashed across his countenance. He very gingerly repeated the "t" sound a couple of times and then loudly yelled "train!" Miss Jensen clapped her hands delightedly and reached over to pat his cheeks. He lit up like a lantern. It was a distinct milestone.

Andrew was bright-eyed and anxious to please his adoring teacher. His vocabulary multiplied rapidly every single week. It was emotionally gratifying to see him overjoyed to be let into a world he had not clearly known existed. I was often moved to tears at his jubilant attempt to please Miss Jensen, but at the same time, I was terribly sad to understand how severe his hearing loss had actually been. I had to choke down a mountain of guilt for allowing myself to languish in denial and not recognize his deficit sooner. I tried to rationalize my position, even though clearly, my oversight had not helped my child. I told myself I had been so engrossed in the neurological problems and potential ramifications that I hadn't had time to conceive of something else being wrong. This excuse generated a vinegary sting of self-reproach. Most days, however, I succeed pretty well in letting myself off the hook for what was possibly blatant neglect.

I sat behind the glass with little Jeddie, who was just a year old at the time, three times a week. He sat at my feet quietly or toddled about the room, playing happily with his allotment of toys. This child was calm, healthy, large for his age, and pliably good natured. His natural personality traits at this difficult juncture with Andrew could not have been a better fit if I had ordered him out of a catalogue. However, every week Jed was becoming more like Andrew's twin in size, movement, intelligence, and language ability. He was advanced, I would tell people, to minimize Andrew's deficit, and it was mostly true. They were pretty much on the same level and advancing at a parallel pace, at least for the time being. This twin phenomenon was mushrooming into a huge handful, especially with Andrew's multiple challenges.

I carefully positioned the hearing aids into Andrew's ears every morning after changing his diaper and dressing him. He would look up at me with his innocent blue eyes, as if to assure me he was intent on pleasing me and doing exactly what I wanted him to do. He was charming and lovable, good natured and adorable. I knew he meant well, but I also knew that it was beyond his ability to follow through. Before breakfast most days, the aids had vanished. They were hidden somewhere in a different place every time. He wasn't stupid, but not so smart, either. He clearly knew I would demand to know the whereabouts of the aids, but he couldn't deduce that anyone would possibly suspect he had anything to do with their disappearance. I'd ask him sternly where they were, and he'd shrug his little shoulders innocently and dodge. He'd look me straight in the eye and shake his head as if he hadn't the slightest idea where they had gone. His language was minimal, but his face said plainly, "I don't know, Mom. They just disappeared." I blustered a little or a lot and pretended to be outraged. Then I resorted to hunting. Sometimes my patience was exhausted after a few minutes, and sometimes I hunted a long while. I'd find them in the toy box, behind the cereal boxes in the cupboard, stuffed behind the television set, or down the laundry shoot mingled with dirty clothes. Once I found them floating on top of the diaper pail. It turned into a little game he and I played, and it was rapidly wearing thin. One day, I couldn't find them the whole day or the next, and I became downright frantic. Then, one of the other kids playing in the street spotted them wedged in the sewer grate.

After six months of paltry attempts to force Andrew to keep the hearing aids in for more than an hour, and rarely, if ever, being successful, I decided I must try a different tactic. Admittedly, my patience had worn thin. More importantly, the most crucial factor was that he was not acquiring the skills he desperately needed and that the aids would facilitate. I was at a critical crossroads without a plan. I was losing the war in a big way, but I couldn't just give up. I had run out of solutions. So, I began to pray day and night to know what I should do. I could never exactly put my finger on what the answer was, but I began to have a nagging impression, which surfaced constantly. It was a feeling so strong when it did surface, that it rose from the pit of my stomach into my chest and caused my heart to pound. It was quietly shouting at me. But what, if anything, was it urging me to do? I had no idea. Still, a soft nagging voice in my head kept insisting there was something more to be done.

One autumn morning, I scraped myself out of bed when the alarm went off, sat up, and rested resolutely upon the edge of it. Wearily, I stretched and straightened my spine, sitting erect and tall. This has to be the day I take action, I determined. I will do something today. I think most people would have frowned on my drama and impetuosity. Audiologists usually know their business pretty well. Who did I think I was, and what did I think I could do better?

My husband and I had been separated for six months now. He was pretty much out of the loop, as he had been for the most part before the split, so I didn't even think to consult him. Unless I had something of consequence to report, he rarely asked about the goings on in the household. After the kids went off to school, I opened a kitchen drawer and took out the big thick phone book we always kept. I opened it up to the "Ear, Nose, and Throat" section of the yellow pages. I ran my index finger up and down the page, closed my eyes, and stabbed the tip of my finger stubbornly onto a line. I had no clue as to whom to call. Any line, any doctor. I opened my eyes and looked at the name I was touching. It was, of course, one I had never heard; a random name. It took all the courage I could muster, but I quickly dialed the number. An appointment was set up for Andrew.

After an initial cursory, then meticulous, examination by the new specialist, a surgical date was set to separate the tiny bones in Andrew's inner ears. The new doctor ascertained that those small skeletal appendages had been fused by the long-term infection during the first months as an infant. In his opinion, there was a high likelihood his hearing would be vastly improved with the surgery. After the first audiologist's absolute and unequivocal stance and diagnosis, I assumed the second opinion would likely be the same. But I had decided to get the second opinion for my own comfort and reassurance. To my great surprise, without disparaging the other doctor outright, he pretty much scoffed at the other assessment. Within two short weeks, my little boy had much, if not most, of his hearing restored.

24

Ella

The move from our little red brick house went more smoothly than I could ever imagine. Not that I had any experience in these matters. What I wanted was for it to take forever. I really hoped that the process would be long and drawn out, and perhaps so much so, that we would be forced to stay there no matter what. I used to kneel by the side of my iron bed and plead for something unforeseen to alter the course and change the bleak equation. After all, isn't that what faith is for? But the house sold very quickly, and we packed up everything we owned and left.

The obvious and logical solution was to move north into my mother's childhood home. She really never told us how many years her mother's mother had lived there, but I surmised by the stories that the house had likely been around since the early 1900s. It seemed to me in a serendipitous way that my grandmother had chosen to take her last breath in the hospital just in time for the family to take up residence in her house.

Grandma's house made our previous home seem palatial. It was situated close to the road on Highway 89, which was a well-travelled thoroughfare. A stream of traffic zoomed by nonstop, often bumper to bumper, and it included large semitrailers and tankers. The upcoming interstate was only a dream in someone's mind, and this was the only direct route through the state and into Idaho. You could hear the traffic more than you could see it. It had a continual rhythmic whoosh as the vehicles flew by. If you closed your eyes, you might believe you were standing in a train yard. You practically had to scream to be heard if you were near the street. It was so unlike our secluded little subdivision. There was a gas station situated directly across from the house. It had two bays of pumps painted bell-pepper green, embellished with several wide, horizontal white stripes. Its garishly painted facade seemed to be hollering at the traffic and infringing on our peace. In my mind, this was a very odd place for a family dwelling.

The house was situated between two others built in the same era. They were the three musketeers or the three stooges, depending on how you wanted to see it. In any case, they were three small frame boxes in a row, making worthless, unintimidating threats to the traffic. For some odd reason, unfathomable to me, the houses had been built very close to the road, but more likely, the road had later been built close to them. The ample acreage behind them loomed emptily up the backside. The house on the left was painstakingly painted pale green and the house on the right, not so meticulously, dirty tan. The middle one, ours now, was faded and dingy white and had been painted so many times the sun had worn foregone blotches in the wood here and there. Except for the colors and the upkeep, the houses were pretty much indistinguishable. They were all clapboard, all small, and all old.

As for ours, there were several chipped and crumbling cement steps gesturing halfheartedly to the sad little front door. A mismatched metal screen, obviously added much later, accosted at first glance, failing miserably to add even a speck of charm. The house had matching picture windows on either side of the door, not large but symmetrical. The roofline was only slightly pitched, but the small gable was a saving grace. The shingles were aged and crumbling, and they incessantly tossed miniscule grains of black and brown roofing sand all over the porch. It reminded me of coarse ground pepper and crunched when stepped on.

The front door opened into a very small living room, adjacent to a miniscule kitchen. This room was spanned by a disintegrating plaster archway. I used to track one of a dozen meandering cracks in the ceiling from the first to the second room, pretending it was a map to buried treasure. In front of the window perched our grandmother's bulky, albeit almost threadbare, mauve sofa. It had seen grander days, but I couldn't remember it not being in exactly the same place. It had a five-inch rope fringe sewed along the bottom. The little ones used to sit on the floor and comb through it with their fingers. There was chunky avocado armchair across from the sofa. It was in okay condition but very itchy on the legs, even in skirts or pants. Hovering haughtily against the wall between the two pieces was my grandmother's midcentury honey-brown stereo cabinet, which always seemed to be putting on airs.

On the other side of the archway was an old mahogany upright Baldwin piano with a worn silky patina. I had often watched my grandmother caress it lovingly with her Lemon Pledge. She was an accomplished organist and pianist and played by ear. I couldn't comprehend such a gift. It seemed more like magic than talent. I remember her playing anything asked without sheet music at all. At Christmas, she played and sang simultaneously, "Bless this house, O Lord, we pray, make it safe by night and day ...." She never once looked down at the keys but threw back her head and crooned as she gazed around the room. The last thing in this tight little space was a squatty but massive black and white Zenith television set. None of us was excited about that; we had so hoped for color.

Behind the piano, there was a short pathway of doors. The first led to the only bedroom, the next into the laundry room, and the third opened out to the back yard. The last door still makes numerous appearances in my nightmares. I am forever latching this rickety door with its small hook-and-eye bolt. It never closes without effort, and more importantly, it never really closes securely at all. There was heat wafting through it in the summer and a frigid wind whistling in the winter. I knew if there was that much space around the door, other scary things might easily break through or creep in. I have slammed and feverishly latched that door a thousand times in my dreams.

A small slice of the little back bedroom eventually became my sanctuary, as it was the only available spot left in the house. It wasn't private because I shared it with two of my sisters. My single bed had no head or footboard and was jammed between the back of the door and the little window. The short walls were stiflingly papered with green and white vines twining on a wine-red background, peppered with large, faded cabbage roses. I suppose it was pretty in an old-fashioned way, but it was suffocating in the small space. What the little room needed was a bit of airflow. The tiny domed opaque fixture in the ceiling cast mostly shadows and light. There were about two feet between my bed and my sisters' bunk beds, which were crunched next to the back wall. There was a tiny closet between the back door and the bed, which my sisters now shared. My clothes and shoes were stashed in a narrow mud-brown metal cupboard, about a foot and a half deep and five feet tall. It was situated at the head of my bed behind the door. I guess it doubled as my headboard. The bedroom door clanked against it when anyone entered. I resolutely placed a little gold-framed picture of my family, a couple of favorite books, and a little yellow jewelry box on top of it. A paltry attempt at personal expression. The cupboard fit my few clothes easily, and I stacked my shoes on the floor of it. One afternoon after returning from a girls' camp, I left my suitcase open on the bed. At dusk, I returned to find an adolescent skunk sauntering around my things, sniffing and scratching. Quietly and desperately, I ran to call my father.

As the days drifted by in this strange little house, I began to have a recurring pressure in my chest. It felt like a weight on my diaphragm. Sometimes it was hard to breathe. At first, I thought something was very wrong and considered telling my parents. Then I began to suspect it was only homesickness for my former life and my lavender bedroom back home. I regretted having taken it all for granted. I think we tend to take most of what we have for granted. That bedroom seemed like the Taj Mahal compared to this tiny closet I had to share with my sisters. I missed the double bed, the old metal vanity, and the little matching dresser, all painted heliotrope purple. I missed the two large street-facing windows with the lilac floral curtains my dad had bought at Sears. Now just a memory, it became the bedroom of my dreams. I missed being able to close the door for a bit of privacy. I missed having a place to bring a friend. That would definitely not be happening in the foreseeable future. I missed being able to play my radio or portable record player and daydream about teenage-girl things. Now I could only pile the covers up around my face and try to shut out the noises of the household.

The little kitchen was about half the size of the living room. A small free-standing stove and oven were tucked against the back wall. Behind them, the wallpaper was peeling up towards the low ceiling. It had the texture of old dry construction paper, and was printed in a dizzy pattern of red cherries floating on a mint green background. It was bubbled, scorched, and faded, forming a wide pale blue halo around the stove.

Our melamine table and padded gray chairs were positioned under the front window adjacent to the stove. It was so cramped that the table leaves had to be removed, and the chairs were bunched against the wall. Even the skinny kids had to shimmy between the sink and table to take a seat. The short counter was narrow, and cradled a deeply scratched cast iron sink with loose and leaky faucets. There was heavy rust around the connections and a wide circle around the drain. The countertop was not modern laminate as we were accustomed to, but merely a thick slab of marled black and white cracked linoleum bound with metal edges. The original caramel-colored cupboards were chipped and peeling. Nothing had been abused; it was just ancient and shabby. The chubby Frigidaire stood back alone as if it had misbehaved, crammed into an alcove next to an outside door. We had to shut the fridge to get out the door.

I often think about the saying "Every cloud has a silver lining" and have come to think that while true, perhaps the reverse is often more so; "Every silver lining conceals a dark cloud." As I look back, I think fortune, destiny, or God smiled upon our stricken family by giving us just enough extra to make it through this trial. Just sufficient to persevere, even if uncomfortably. Ironically, the silver lining or saving grace of the little box house turned out to be a little addition that stood five feet away from it. A few years back, our grandmother had hired a handyman on the cheap to build a tiny studio apartment to rent out, which would augment her meager social security check. This little addition reminded me of an odd-shaped puzzle piece dropped randomly onto the side of a totally different puzzle. It did not fit, in any sense. It was about ten by fifteen feet, or one-hundred-fifty square feet. It suited Grandma just fine, but in order to make it work as extra space for us, my father built a diminutive tunnel leading from our little bedroom into the apartment. He cut a hole through each end, just large enough for one person to pass through at a time. He crafted the walls from fiberboard, not even bothering to paint them, and roofed the outside top with brown shingles. This way everyone could stay out of the elements while passing through to utilize the other space. The tunnel he crudely built ended up being only five feet high as well; this meant everyone but the little kids had to bend over as they passed through.

The apartment space was mostly used as a bunkhouse for the rest of the family. It contained a tiny bathroom boxed into one corner with a small shower, sink, and toilet. Thus, we were now upgraded to be a two-bathroom household. I remember another tiny sink, a miniature fridge, and hot plate tucked to one side of the main area, but we never used them. We needed absolutely all the space to contain the rest of the beds. My parents' double bed sat next to the wall at the entrance to the tunnel. There was a bassinet tucked into a corner adjacent for whomever the current baby happened to be. The sides of the small infant bed flared up and out like beaches rising from a lake. I remember seeing my parents stacking layers of newspaper under the little mattress for more space at the top. So as the baby grew larger, so did the pile of newspapers under it. Sometimes the baby perched so high, I worried it might topple out onto the floor. Another double and single bed were evenly arranged in the remainder of the space. Without that extra room, our family could never have existed in that house at all. So, decidedly, I thought, this apartment had to be a silver lining.

25

Ella

After the handwork part of our daily routine, it was time for one, and absolutely only one, soap opera. We turned on the old black and white TV set, which was squashed to one side of the living room, at exactly one o'clock. As far as I could surmise, Grandma's single life indulgence was "Days of Our Lives." I was a little surprised that even this was allowed, as she was so conservative and proper. Her opinions were crystal clear about trashy TV or anything remotely worldly or superfluous. I was okay with it and quite looked forward to it. I used to wait for the oversized hourglass to appear on the screen with sand pouring through its tiny waist. That concept of life, however, was incongruent for me, because as young as I was, life ahead seemed like an eternity.

After watching, it was time to sit out on the front porch. Apparently, this too, was on the chore list. Its chubby wooden turned posts were peeling mint green paint and showing flecks of old olive underneath. There was only room on the porch for two small chairs, and often our knees would touch. As we stared out on the pastoral expanse, she spoke sparingly, as was expected, but our time together was quietly warm and companionable. In those afternoons, I was mesmerized by the winds teasing or blustering at the gate. When the gusts kicked up, there could be swirls of dry leaves turning somersaults in the air. I always hoped for a spontaneous summer storm to blow through the little valley, if only for variety. I loved the drama of low-hanging dark clouds, skies with knives of lightning slashing through them, followed by startling cracks of thunder. I always counted "one-thousand-one" and so on, to gauge the distances. Enormous cottonwood trees at the edge of the road tossed their massive heads in the wind, making a surprisingly loud whishing sound only they knew how to make.

After porch time, when Grandma retreated to her bedroom for an hour or so of napping, I was free to sleep, read, or roam wherever I wished. I usually walked around the yard or ambled down the little road a block or two. Near the small shed at the side of the house was a red-handled water pump sticking up out of the ground about a foot. Grandma said it came from a pure, clear underground well. Oftentimes she sent me out with a large bucket to fill. She liked keeping some in the refrigerator for drinking. There was a large Red Delicious apple tree, a tart Granny Smith, and a sweet purple plum. I often ate four apples at a time, knowing full well I'd pay the price with a stomachache later on. Sometimes I'd pick the soft dark plums and fold them into the front of my blouse like a bowl to carry around and eat at my leisure.

Some of my happiest times were sitting on the little wood-slatted bridge over the small cement culvert between the gate and the street. I'd sit for what seemed like hours in the bright sunlight, the heat soaking into my brown ponytail, my legs swinging over the water as it rolled on by. I didn't have a single care in the world, at least for a little while. I would cup my hands just low enough into the water to catch a few water-skeeters to corral in a paper cup.

My attachment to the little Levan house was deeply embedded in my soul, to the point of not being able to detach. I came very close to procuring a loan to purchase it. Sam's unremittingly patient posture stopped short of my impractical passion. He raised his eyebrows, didn't say a whole lot, but basically put his foot down. We had too much debt of our own. Many years later, after Grandma passed, some crotchety old curmudgeon purchased her property from my dad and uncle. I was feverishly angry. I couldn't stand the thought of someone else inhabiting her property, much less not being able to own it myself. I heard he was going to burn the house and pull a ratty trailer onto the lot. Disgusting. It may have been my very first panic attack. I schemed and fretted about scraping up enough to buy it myself, but it was impossible.

One heavy-hearted morning, I begged Sam to unhinge the beautiful new oval-windowed door from our new home. He kindly obliged and boarded up the open doorway with the cardboard box from our new refrigerator. I bungeed it onto my mommy van, piled a couple of the children into the car, and headed off to Levan. When I knocked at the door, the weathered old fool who had so rudely invaded my hallowed territory eyed me suspiciously. I felt like hauling off and decking him, then running. But I merely gestured towards the new door atop my car, and said condescendingly, "I'll trade you for the old one," motioning to Grandma's front door. He looked at me as if I had lost my marbles, but quickly agreed. Cynically I thought, he was adding up how much he could get for it. He knew the old one was worth nothing. Without too much trouble, I talked him into giving me the old chipped porch posts as well. I secured them all to the top of my van and drove home singing.

26

Ella

I was sixteen, and the first scorching summer on the highway was nearly over. My sisters and I sunbathed on the roof of the old house, climbing it easily from the little room in the back. We watched as our mother hung the many loads of wet laundry day in and day out, rain or shine, on clotheslines strung from metal poles across the yard. We watched the little kids run through and around the masses of weeds in back, playing quite contentedly while our mother snapped the clothespins to the wire.

It was quite a beautiful little acre we lived on. From my perch on the roof, I had a good vantage point. The meadow was green and grassy, and the hills in the background were verdant and pretty. I climbed up often when I felt suffocated or blue, or needed a bit of solitude. There were fruit trees dotting the acreage. A couple of Bartlett pear, two Elberta peach, a Golden Delicious and Jonathan apple, and three run-of-the-mill apricot, whose names I can't recall. It was always a pleasure to follow my father out to prune the trees or pick the fruit. He was usually in a hurry to get somewhere or to get something done, so these times were rare. He was always going or coming from school, hurrying to his janitor job at a different school, or running off to the church assignments he took so seriously. He didn't sit still for long, but for some reason, when he was doing these arborist chores, he rarely seemed rushed and retreated into some sort of peaceful state. I liked that. On these early evenings by his side in the orchard, time stretched out like a gossamer thread. I loved standing out in the sunshine above the little house while he puttered. Later on, I suspected that the root of his pleasure had come from similar memories of his boyhood.

I treasured time with him as he continued to teach me this fact or that, this "correct principle" or another. One day he reached into his pants pocket and pulled out a rusty flat round weight, about the size of a silver dollar. He pressed it into my palm and told me that it weighed an ounce. He looked me in the eye soberly and told me that I would do well to remember that "an ounce of prevention equals a pound of cure." That was all he said about that, but I knew he was teaching about choices. Though I wasn't always appreciative of his lessons, he never seemed able to stop teaching. His messages were peppered with kindness, though sometimes sparsely dispersed, depending on how busy he was. These days when the family was crammed into this odd little house, his attention felt like manna to my soul. As much as I loved the delicious peaches and apples, I gobbled up the time spent with him more hungrily.

It seemed we turned around and it was August, and the first day of school was quickly approaching. I was definitely not ready to embark on the precarious journey of navigating a new school. I had made no friends at all, and going to a school I had never even laid eyes upon made me downright queasy. I hated having to live in this dilapidated house, even though it was situated on an acre I loved. The house was like a bumpy old wart on a lovely peach. I wondered how it would affect my new relationships – that is, if I made any. I was deeply embarrassed by it, and at the same time, I felt guilty about being embarrassed. Clearly, there was no money for anything this year, as my parents had not begun to recover from the apartment debacle, whatever that had been, and which I still was not privy to. All I did know was that I desperately needed some new clothes for school. In fact, I had grown three and a half inches during the summer months, and almost nothing fit.

Everything I owned was too short or too tight. My shoe size was the only thing that hadn't changed. The lack of a few decent clothes would be a big angst for any high school girl, let alone one traversing foreign territory. I knew better than to ask my parents for money, so I just didn't. It would have been futile anyway, not to mention inconsiderate. I was feeling desperately sorry for myself, but I also felt very badly for my parents. Plainly, they were as uncomfortable in this little old house on the highway as I was. They were doing the best they could under the circumstances, and I would not dream of demanding anything from them.

One stiflingly hot August afternoon, I lay on the lawn under the trees close to the highway, knees up, feet flat. The trees overhead had rows of small, dark, oval leaves running up and down large fronds. They swayed and nodded in the wind, making spaces between the branches so I could watch the puffy clouds above. I wasn't sure what kind of trees they were, but I had listened to my grandmother complain about their ugliness and constant messy droppings for years. They released large flat brown crescent pods with little bean-like seeds, which we liked to pry apart with our fingernails. They had been there as long as I had been alive, and I had acquired a sort of affinity for them. Although she called them trash trees, she obviously held some sort of sentiment for them as well, to have allowed them to stand for so many decades. They were grouped together in three clumps close to the road.

As I studied the clouds skating across the pond blue sky, dressed in my usual cut-off jeans and tee shirt, I felt as desperate as I had in my life. It wasn't that I needed clothes, it was that I simply couldn't live without them. I needed them immediately, and there was no resolution in sight. I felt like slapping the ground, screaming, and refusing to go to school at all. But how could I? I occasionally considered running away. But to where? So, I just lay there under those trees, daydreaming about exact outfits that would characterize and distinguish my nonexistent image. I'd plan skirts and blouses, dresses and sweaters down to minute detail, and I'd picture myself walking casually and confidently around the school as I wore them.

27

Ella

Every Wednesday morning in the summer months, all the women "of a certain age," and a few privileged younger ones like me, met at one of the larger homes in Levan for what they called a quilting bee. I never quite understood how the "bee" part was relevant. At least twenty-five women showed up, and that was a lot for a tiny town. For many, it was the highlight event of the summer months. The women, including my grandmother, worked all year long to finish their masterpieces. Almost everyone got a turn to bring one of her own handmade quilt tops, expertly pieced, to be stretched out on the large wooden frame. It was then hand-quilted with small-gauge needles by the whole group all at one time. There were chairs brought in and bunched tightly in every possible space around the quilt. Typically, one was completed in an afternoon. If not, a few of the stalwarts finished it in a few more days.

No one ever came a hair's breadth to admitting it, but there was no question that there was an ongoing, yet silent, competition for the most creative and beautiful top. Even at the tender age of seventeen, I could sense the tension of the contest. The room whirred with pride and more than that, mock humility. This seemed funny to me at the time, and I was not too young to pick up the irony. No matter how self-satisfied each woman was with her own work, the lavishly piled praise for her neighbor's billowed forth expansively through the room, wider than the span of fabric which filled it.

I was fascinated with the variety of quilt tops presented. I was duly surprised at the expert work almost every woman had accomplished. I rarely saw puckered corners, uneven stitching, or crooked designs. Obviously, it was a genuine art form for the serious quilters. It was what set them apart from the amateurs.

It was here I began to covet my favorite quilt patterns for future reference. There was the popular "Double Wedding Ring." It consisted of rows of large circles cut from many different fabrics, twining through one another like coupled wedding rings. I was fascinated with the "Old Maid's Puzzle," which had many different brightly colored triangles arranged into blocks. The "Honeycomb" was very trendy at the time and looked exactly as it sounds – many tiny hexagonal pieces bricked onto each other to make a large, impressive honeycomb. The "Flower Basket," also a preference; it was triangle-shaped pots with small triangular flowers heaped on top. One of my very favorites was the "Texas Star," which had colorful stars with bright round centers, swirling around six-sided pastel blocks. There were denim quilts, too, cut from everybody's favorite jeans or husband's overalls, which had become quite the rage. (Frankly, I thought they were silly, unattractive, and quite unrefined. To each his own, of course.) Some tops were appliqued, intricately hand sewn, and expertly embroidered. These were the ones I most admired and considered to be among the more beautiful and imaginative. But the quilt top I really wanted to someday create for myself was the one with rows of little girls in sundresses and hats. It was so quaint and pretty.

There had to be hundreds of hours of piecing in each top. As I shimmied behind the chairs and around the frame, I watched for the tiny pin dots of blood here and there and spotted more than I could count. They were the proud evidence of countless hours of toil, sacrifice, and ingenuity. It was explained to me that one could easily remove the blood with one's own spit, but I doubt anyone was interested in erasing those little spots of effortful creativity. It felt wonderful to be among the artists, designs, and beautifully colored fabrics. Some of the fabrics were soft and pastel; others were vibrant and pretty. A few, I thought, were garish and juvenile, but I kept that to myself. And as with all good cooks in the kitchen, each was arguably convinced that her own concoction was the best.

The bee was a party I looked forward to. I was usually one of the youngest, and sometimes, if no one was paying attention, I'd crawl under the quilt canopy tacked to the frames with large white tacks. I'd sit cross-legged in the very center. It was my private fort. I listened to the congenial chatter, peppered with a little banter and sprinkled heavily with the local gossip, which was sometimes a little shocking. Clearly, though, it was a celebration of sorts, and I was a happy guest. In my hiding place, I could study the long and short, skinny, veiny legs, the chunky dimpled knees, the swollen ankles, the running nylon stockings, and all the shoes. They were almost exactly the same except for the sizes and colors. To me, they looked precisely like my grandmother's. They were sturdy black or brown leather, stitched neatly around the oval toe. All had laces and most had one and a half inch heels, which I mentally measured as I gazed around the merry-go-round of feet. And, I thought petulantly, they were all really ugly.

With nimble fingers, each quilt was stitched quickly and expertly in between and across the designs in the intricate patterns the artist had chosen. They were marked in washable blue ink. I was amazed they would care so much about white thread running through white fabric.

After a couple of focused hours, everyone looked forward to the fun part. The luncheon. When all the needles had been set aside, the plates of food began to appear. There were freshly baked cinnamon rolls smothered in sweet, runny white frosting. Yum. There were green salads loaded with garden tomatoes, carrots, onions, and turnips, which always ruined them for me. There were yellow and green Jell-O concoctions hiding floating bananas or pineapple wedges, heaped with whipping cream and neon-red maraschino cherries. There were mouth-watering cakes, often from prized and top-secret recipes, which the ladies argued genially about, and homemade cookies. There were carrot and walnut, chocolate chip (of course), and oatmeal and raisin. And often, to my delight, there would be an apple or cherry pie. To wash it all down, there was plenty of fresh-squeezed lemonade with ice cubes, served in a variety of tall glasses borrowed from everyone, since no one had that many in a set.

Eventually, I learned to piece quilt patterns on the sewing machine and hand quilt with tiny, short, even stitches. While shutting one eye, I could proudly thread my needle in one swift pass. As the summers floated by, I was finally invited to sit around the frame with the regulars and actually help do the quilting. It was an honor to be accepted into the inner circle, and a privilege to have a seat of my own around the table of the experts. In time, I learned to set up the large wooden quilting frames all by myself, cinching the edges of the fabric with the large metal screw-clamps, pushing the fat white tacks into the edges ever so evenly, while making certain the quilt was taut and straight. Though I became fairly skilled at the craft, I have made only two quilts of my own. I was easily bored, not to mention the fact that clearly, my work could never hold a candle to my grandmother's. But I wouldn't trade those magical summer days at the quilting bee for art classes in Paris. The memory of those days still conjures bottled sunshine.

Thanks to Grandma, in addition to quilting, I became quite proficient at crocheting. Holding the crochet hook correctly was my biggest obstacle. With rapt attention, I studied her knobby knuckles and gnarly fingers, which looked a bit like talons as they flew through the thread or yarn, one end of it wound loosely around her crooked little finger for stability. I watched her heavily ridged fingernails pull the thread into perfect little knots. I never quite mastered tatting, which in my opinion, was akin to web-spinning, and just as impossible. I kept that to myself. It didn't take long to apprehend that grandma was snobbish about knitting. She considered it beneath her skillset and her dignity.

She made it clear that she'd rather leave that decidedly easy and inferior endeavor to those who couldn't crochet, tat, quilt, or embroider. Needless to say, I didn't learn to knit. Many afternoon hours, I settled willingly in front of the sunny geranium-filled front window at Grandma's old treadle sewing machine, learning to sew straight regular stiches, put in a zipper, or follow a Simplicity or Butterick pattern. Often, I found it profoundly boring and was impossibly impatient, but I would never have admitted that to her. Years later, as a young mother on an extremely tight budget, I took in sewing for extra cash. I sewed prom dresses, trousers, blouses, and even a couple simple wedding dresses. I knew Grandma would have been delighted.

28

Ella

On the highway, just two doors down from our small house, there was a little café. One day as I passed it, I spotted a "help wanted" sign in the front window. It took all the courage I could muster to walk the few steps to the store. I meekly ducked inside to ask if I might fill out an application. Another teenager, probably a year or two older than I, was slumped against the cash register. She was wearing a lime green, geometric patterned circle skirt, a pin-tucked white blouse, heavy blue eye shadow, lots of blush, and bright coral lipstick. She looked at me as if I were a homeless urchin or someone from another planet, or maybe just a fly who had buzzed through the open door. After sizing me up, she half-heartedly handed me an application and went back to her work.

I took my pen and paper and walked over to a red-padded, round metal stool at the counter, and began to self-consciously scribble down the information requested. None of your darn business, I thought. I had to focus to keep my hand steady, as I this was my very first experience applying for a real job, and I felt everyone in the whole place was watching me, though probably very few even noticed I had come in. Working in the real world seemed mysterious, frightening, and uncertain. I wasn't confident I could function well with people I didn't know.

I wasn't sure I could learn and perform ambiguous new duties, and more specifically, deal with paying customers. I had always been intrinsically introverted. I felt more like a child, and one with very few qualifications or skills.

The only job I had previously held was that of babysitter. I had done plenty of that in the previous neighborhood for my parents' friends, mostly. I had to admit, they always seemed to prefer me over my friends. It was a rare weekend when I wasn't booked solid. But I considered that to be understandable, as I was the oldest of a large family. Obviously, they knew I'd had experience with kids of different ages. In addition to being a favorite with most of the children, it seemed I had another rather strange qualification. After attending to the children, I felt obliged to straighten up the homes as well, especially the messy ones. After the kids were played with, read to, and put to bed, I'd start in on the dishes, picking up and cleaning the counters. Then I'd move on to the living room, putting things away and vacuuming, if necessary. It quickly became apparent that I had been hired as much for my cleaning abilities as for the tending of their children. I did feel a little odd about that but continued to do it. After all, as paltry as the hourly wage was, I was earning a lot more than any of my competition.

Where it asked for previous experience on the application, I thought about writing "babysitting." Considering for a moment, I left it blank. For some reason, the white empty space on the paper brought to mind the salt flats of the Great Salt Lake, almost as barren. I finished, got off the stool, and diffidently walked over and handed the paper to the condescending girl who had given it to me. She tossed it under the counter without even a glance. I stood there a second or two waiting for her to say something, but she didn't even look up. So, I turned and skulked out the door. It was a genuine surprise when the very next day, someone called and asked for an interview.

The owner of the little business was a genial but brusque little woman by the name of Lois Piggles. She owned another restaurant in the city center, which was said to be very successful and the preferred eating establishment for locals. Smiling but business-like, she explained the duties, hours, and expectations of the job. Her eyes loitered upon me, moving up and down and side to side, which brought the familiar flaming to my cheeks. I half expected her to ask me to turn around, so she could inspect my backside. Mrs. Piggles was short, sturdily built, and as round as one of the donuts under the glass dome on the counter. Her appearance brought to mind the phrase "bibbidy bobbidy boo." The most prominent characteristic I noticed, however, was the energy which seemed to exude from her short little body like invisible puffs of smoke. When I came to know her better, I called her "the little steam engine who could." She waddled briskly, rolling her hips as she strode, and I calculated there would be no waste in her steps. I kept pace determinedly. She moved from counter to tables to cashier stand, waving her plump, efficient hands quickly, gesturing about this and that. She reiterated how crucial it was to be quick, efficient, clean, polite, and especially accurate. While pinpointing the importance of honesty, she cast a brief, barely discernable glance over at the cash register. I got the message. Also, she cautioned, one must take care to never, ever spill hot coffee on a patron, hinting that it would be the kiss of death to the job. When she finished her dissertation, she stuck out her short arm and small hand, and I instinctively put mine into hers. I had not shaken many hands in my life. I was taken back by the strength of her grip, and she pumped my hand up and down enthusiastically. She ended the interview by saying I would start work the next day. My schedule was for every other day at four o'clock sharp, as well as Saturday mornings at ten. At that point, she smiled widely but briefly, turned and waddled into the back room, and shut the door. I attempted a poker face but couldn't keep the exultant smile from spreading across my cheeks.

I must interject at this point that the day came, indeed, when I did spill the coffee. And I wasn't fired. In fact, I don't believe Mrs. Piggles ever found out. One average winter afternoon, the actor Jack Palance sauntered smoothly into our little café. He was doing musical theater nearby and stopped in for a bite. We all knew who he was, and I admit to being bowled over by his celebrity and rugged good looks. After taking his order for a club sandwich and coffee, I went into the back room and fanned my red cheeks while the other employees laughed their heads off. The notable part of the story came when I delivered it to him. I had carried trays of sandwiches and coffee dozens of times uneventfully. This time I was desperately trying to be efficient, cool, and a little aloof. My toe caught the edge of the table leg, and I tipped the saucer holding the hot coffee right into his lap. He leapt out of his seat in alarm and pain but quickly recovered his suavity. He grabbed a few napkins, wiped down his trousers, smoothed them out elegantly, and looked up at me. My heart was in my throat. With a charming, toothy grin, he looked me in the eye and winked. The corners of his eyes crinkled good-naturedly. He grinned and said, "Sweeheart, don't worry, it is going to be a-okay."

29

Ella

With approximately 650 residents, the town of Levan was tiny, the lack of amenities was predictable. Its only real claim to fame was being the bellybutton of the state. Right smack dab in the center, so to speak. Someone told me that some wise guy decided it would be appropriate and funny to spell the word "navel" backwards and call it good. Apparently, everyone enjoyed a good laugh and agreed. There was a part-time gas station, a small chapel, a miniature market, a tiny post office, and a very small cemetery on the south side of town. Of course, there were no paved roads. There were also no streetlights, so when it got dark on a cloudy night, you couldn't see your hand in front of your face. Even so, it was the antithesis of dangerous. I don't think anyone ever thought to lock their doors. I admit, though, to having my doubts about nightfall. When the sun sank slowly behind the horizon, the blackness began to creep in and spread like a dense heavy cloak over the little valley. It was not just dark; it was pitch black, unless there was a full moon.

One moonless night while Grandma was in the back bedroom getting ready for bed, I dared myself to venture out onto the front porch. Just for a minute. Dressed in my light cotton nightgown, I cracked the screen door a skitch, stuck one bare toe out gingerly and silently into the darkness, and then as if jumping off at the deep end, I took the full plunge outside. Afraid of what might be hiding in the bushes, I stood as still as a statue. Slowly, I tilted my head upward. I was stunned. It appeared that a giant saltshaker had been tossed in the sky and that every tiny white granule had been frozen in space. Never had I realized there were so many stars. It was astonishing, exquisite, and a little scary. Of course, I had learned about the universe at school, and of course there were stars where I lived, but because of the city lights, I had never really seen them like this. It was a sight I never imagined. The grains of salt shimmered and shone like the sands of the sea in sunlight, sparkling and twinkling wildly, as if in competition for the moon's grand prize. It was so very still; almost silent. I realized a bird was flying nearby. While I couldn't see it, I could hear and feel the whirring of its wings as it passed. The large cottonwoods at the street were barely whispering now, as their round leaves quivered softly. As my eyes adjusted to the blackness, I began to see shapes here and there around the yard and across the road. The herd of black-faced sheep, formerly huddled together in the field, had morphed into one enormous black monster looming out there by itself. I could hear strange movement around the dark creature. All of a sudden, my imagination got the best of me. Spooking myself, I slipped inside and threw the lock across the old fir door. Grandma was almost at her bed now, moving slowly behind her walker. I hurried to the bedside to attend to my nightly duty, which was to carefully lift her old white legs up and into the bed while causing as little pain as possible.

Helping Grandma into her bed was a painful routine. Painful for her and painful for me. Many times, she had described what made her hurt, and there were several images in my young mind. It made me sad to picture her poor hipbones deep inside the flesh, grinding back and forth together in the sockets as she moved. I could almost imagine the sounds they made as they collided. The first picture that flashed into my mind was one I had seen of a pharmacist's mortar and pestle, pulverizing limestone into powder.

I watched her wrinkled, yet lovely face, contort as she slowly lifted her legs onto the bed. She was really only comfortable in her wheelchair or when her limbs could be still. I often thought about my own childish narrow calves and thighs, and how, without taking any thought, I could run and dart from side to side. Like most children, it never occurred to me that one day I might lose this youthful ability. Paradoxically, now that I've had a plate implanted into a foot, a total knee replacement, and a triple spinal fusion, I refer back to those unrestricted and naive days.

On this particular summer evening, I decided I must take matters into my own hands. It was my obligation. I was her oldest granddaughter, for heaven sakes, and who, if not me, had greater responsibility to take action? I pondered for days as to how, and it always came down to higher powers and the faith I had been taught from my childhood. I referenced back to the stories of Jesus healing the blind and the lame. I thought about the poor bleeding woman who thought only to touch the hem of His robe to be healed. I believed it all, and my ostentatious idea began to make perfect sense. If I could, I must affect a healing for my grandmother. Why not? We were believers. I had been taught to pray every single day of my life and usually did. I prayed about every little detail as a child, believing my prayers would be heard. As I grew older, I still prayed regularly, albeit with a little less hope and intensity. But never did I not believe, and as an adult, it is more relevant than ever. I knew that not only had Grandma centered her life around these principles, she was the very person who had taught my father.

One night as Grandma and I lay in the pitch-blackness of her bedroom, tucked cozily into her saggy-springed old iron bed, under a handful of her hand-stitched quilts, I bravely broached the subject. I took some deep breaths and swallowed hard before venturing to reveal my presumptuous plan. It didn't occur to me at that moment that obviously she would have come up with a plan of her own long before now, given her many years of living and her store of substantial faith. And of course, I should have realized that this flash of brilliance would not have come only to me. But I plowed ahead bravely and humbly, or at least I thought I did.

"Grandma," I waded in, soberly and heroically, "I believe we can end your pain altogether and make your hips well again. Wouldn't that be wonderful? I believe in miracles, and I know you do, too. I think with enough faith and some really strong praying, we can make you better. Clearly, it's the right thing to do. Why wouldn't Heavenly Father want to heal you? Why would He sit by and let you keep suffering for no good reason? He sent Jesus as the example of what can be. He healed lots of people, so why not you? Together, you and I have enough faith. I'm sure that by morning you will be all better. Just wait and see." She didn't say anything, so I advanced boldly.

I took another deep breath and began to pray aloud. My fervent prayer began quietly, and to my way of thinking, it expanded quite maturely. I pleaded shamelessly for the healing of my grandmother, demarcating all the obvious positive rationales. I went on and on, intentionally protracting my prayer. It was loquacious, specific, and implicit. I imagined that the more words used and the more time it took, the better the chances for a positive heavenly response. As I continued, I began to feel such emotion and certainty that the tears began to spill steadily from the outer corners of my eyes onto my grandmother's hand-embroidered pillowcase. When I finally closed my petition to the heavens, I felt emptied and exhausted. I lay there anxiously awaiting her reaction.

She was silent for a very long time. She didn't fidget or move a muscle. She didn't shift her weight in any direction. I held my breath and waited patiently for her to speak. The minutes ticked by and I realized there might be no response, as disappointing as that would be. She didn't minimize my childish faith, throw a wet blanket on my naivety, or toss out platitudes. She didn't take the opportunity to expound on an important life lesson. She didn't argue or seem the least bit disappointed or agitated. She didn't preach or pull out any imperceptible pins to pop my childish bubbles. She was simply as still as the darkness around us. I knew she wasn't asleep because of her breathing. I could almost feel tranquility seeping through her nightgown into mine. I had no idea what she thought or felt. Had I hit the nail on the head? Was she pleased, in agreement, or was she trying to let me down easy? After what seemed like a long time, she simply reached over and placed her knobby-fingered hand on top of mine. It felt smooth and warm. Then she patted it affirmatively a half a dozen times or so, leaving it tenderly on top until I could hear the deep rhythmic breathing of her sleep.

The next morning, the sun was up earlier than I, and was shining gloriously through the rippled glass in the old paned windows. I felt several emotions at the same time; fear, expectation, dread, and a splash of hope. I threw off the heavy covers, swung my thin legs onto the floor, and ran to the kitchen to find, as usual, the regular rice and raisins barely simmering on the old wood stove. The nickel-plated, curly-handled iron was secured to the round, flat burner, and was glinting in the sunlight. I spun to the window apprehensively to locate Grandma, afraid and excited at the same time. I took a deep breath and forced myself to look. There she was, out across the lawn at the edge of the garden. Her white head was bent over a hoe, and she was loosening the soil around a bleeding heart, which was loaded with heavy hanging red valentines. I could see her face clearly. She was not smiling, but there was a definite an air of peaceful contentment in her expression. She was enjoying the familiar morning sunlight and her gardening. She was, also as usual, firmly anchored to her wheelchair.

When I grew older, I was embarrassed by the memory. I felt foolish, childish, and silly. Grandma and I never spoke of it, as if it had never happened. I often wondered if she had been a little more like my dad, more open and vocal, what she may have offered. Would she have lectured in the classroom of affliction? Would she have stated rain falls on the just and the unjust? Or discussed passage on the mortal cruise ship? My children were not so fortunate, because I was more like my father and compulsively taught at every juncture. But my restrained sagacious grandmother knew, through her own grief and hardship, that the greedy schoolmarm named Life would teach me the lessons at her own pace. What were Grandma's thoughts about that awkward night? I'll never know. I can only remember the light shining on her calm, serene face that morning in the garden.

30

Andy

Today Andy began a tour he had driven more than a dozen times. It was comfortably familiar, and he fell easily into the pleasant routine cadence. It was to begin in Rapid City, South Dakota. He was to drive the bus from the Salt Lake City headquarters to Denver, where the passengers who chose could board and enjoy the extra six hours from Denver to Rapid City. Typically, about half the group opted to do that for a few extra sights. Today was no exception, and as the people handed in their registration forms, Andy could see the bus was going to be about half full. As usual, the majority of his passengers were quite elderly, albeit in good enough shape to travel. There were a few middle-agers, but the seniors had generally been saving up for a while. They were also in that segment of the population who were not obsessed with airplanes and fast travel. They loved the long, laid-back bus rides. At this point in their lives, they were used to ambling along and had quit expecting lightning-speed gratification.

Andy was pleased again to see that his new bus family enjoyed seeing Cheyenne, the capital of Wyoming, and were anxious to pour through the Welcome Center at Torrington. They stopped for a leisurely lunch at a quirky little diner, then proceeded to head down Highway 85 to Rapid City. Andy was eager for the next stop. The response would be predictably gratifying, and he always looked forward to it. The bus sashayed effort-lessly to a stop in Deadwood, directly in front of the home of Kevin Costner. Andy proudly announced that this was the home Kevin had built for his own parents. Of course, most appreciated mulling over the gallant gift from a famous son. In telling the story, Andy almost felt he was bequeathing a gift to his enthralled clients. Later, at the Midnight Hotel in the same town, they got an out-of-the-ordinary look at every costume Costner wore in his movies. They were dizzy with delight, and Andy felt proud to be the presenter of such a moment.

Andy had a distinct fascination with Deadwood. He never tired of seeing Costner's parents' home or visiting the Midnight Hotel. He thought it very noble of the acclaimed actor to take such tender care of his parents, something Andy would do in a heartbeat, given half a chance. He was always loving and respectful to his own parents. His appreciation and fixation on Kevin had grown through these trips, and he concluded that if he could ever meet just one actor, it would be Costner. He yearned for an inadvertent glimpse of him every time the bus wheeled into town. He had daydreams of snapping a selfie with the actor. Now wouldn't that be a mind-blowing Instagram post? His sec-ond favorite actor was Harrison Ford, but he couldn't exactly tell you why. Probably because he seemed to have some of the same qualities as Costner. They were equally dashing and undaunted, yet both had a definite air of humility. What he wouldn't give to meet them both.

The tour bus ambled along pleasantly to the Woolly Mammoth Mu-seum, which was always a hit, and then on to the School of Mines in Rapid City. After enjoying those sights, they moseyed through the Black Hills and Badlands, which were rich in Western history. Andy never tired of this leg. It was never boring to envision the colorful sto-ries, which had only been read in the pages of a book, not to mention the always interesting stop at the Crazy Horse Memorial. It was usually one of the pinnacles of the trip for most folks, and was yet another gift Andy could give. The granite and iron portrait of the Lakota leader seemed to rise up from the ground triumphantly, always thrilling those dwarfed in its substantial shadow.

Often the bus company sent along a tour guide, who sat in the front of the bus, microphone in hand, explaining the details of the various sights to the enthralled passengers. There were times, however, when Andy had to be prepared to present the information himself. He considered this a duty of great importance and prepared the best he knew how by practicing in front of a mirror. Secretly, he was happy when the role fell to him, and was honored to be the key player in their portrayal. It was like being the first to talk about a movie nobody else had seen. It reminded him of the feeling he had as a kid when given the job of passing out treats to his siblings.

The passengers were buzzing like a swarm of bumblebees about what they were certain would be the apex of the journey, up next on the docket. It was, of course, Keystone, the birthplace of Mount Rushmore. Andy braced for the noise, which would predictably fill the bus like an explosion. It was the typical response, never varying, and he was never disappointed. As they rounded the bend, there was the sound of absolute awe. It was, indeed, startling to catch a glimpse of the amazing, colossal, six-story stone sculptures, which arose seemingly from the dust. Andy had become accustomed to the oohing, ahhing, and low whistling, but for some reason, he had never quite seen it the way they seemed to. He considered it a bit too much hype and build up, and he inevitably felt the thump of anticlimax. Maybe, he thought, it was because he'd been here too many times.

He much preferred the drama of Crazy Horse. He could recite the history of the famous Native American by heart now, and rehearsed often in his mind just in case. The story felt very important somehow, but he wasn't exactly sure why. He kept his partiality to himself, however, because even if he could have, he wouldn't dream of diminishing a drop of the thrill for his passengers.

The most significant facts about Mount Rushmore, in Andy's opinion, centered on the man who was responsible for it. Andy had learned that his name was Gutzon Borglum, and that he was a mountain sculptor and Danish immigrant from Idaho. Perhaps because his mom always made a big deal of her own Danish heritage, he felt a bit of kinship. Andy's grandmother and grandfather had been born in Copenhagen, and that may well have been the root of his captivation.

At the visitors' center, he had painstakingly memorized as much as necessary to explain the story. He knew a little about the artist and couldn't, for the likes of himself, fathom how all this chiseling had been accomplished. He tried to imagine it in his mind but couldn't. His story related that 90% of the sculptures had been done by dynamite and had involved four hundred men. Borglum had presculpted each head in his studio and then used a massive projector to cast the images of the presidents' faces on the mountain after dark, while his men outlined them in white chalk. After carefully dynamiting the rock in specific places, the gifted men chosen for the job would hang precariously on ropes and chisel with forged tools and drill bits. Andy finished off his dialogue with what he considered a fun fact. At the current rate, Mount Rushmore only erodes one inch every 10,000 years. Perhaps Andy's carefully prepared recitation wasn't 100% accurate in every respect, but he knew it was pretty darn close.

The Avenue of Flags, where all fifty state flags wave, was another highlight, and most considered it extremely inspirational to see pictures of all the presidents lining the streets.

Yes, this was an important component of being a bus driver, Andy thought, and he took it very seriously. Not only did he get to see the sights his own parents and siblings had yet to see, he was really learning things. Important things. Things he'd had no idea would ever become part of his experience. He who had slipped through high school by a whisker and the help of many, especially his mother. And to put a cherry on top, he was teaching other people. He watched them learn, smile, relax, and realize a few of their own dreams. What more could one ask of a profession, he often wondered, with a grateful swelling in his chest. This is an important uniform, he thought, as he patted his logoed pocket. A badge of honor, you might say. Almost as good, but not quite, of course, as those of his beloved compadres in blue.

31

Ella

My new job at the café gave me fresh hope. Having been taught to sew by my grandmother and refining those skills in the 4-H program, I was equipped with a few resources and a plan. I could use my wages for fabric to sew new clothes. I had a couple weeks' pay saved now, and I carefully folded it into my old leather coin purse. Luckily, the city bus stop was just across the street from my house, and before long I became adept at hopping on it, riding into the city, and returning before dark. It turned out to be very liberating. The bus drivers were usually accommodating, and I felt comfortable dropping my dimes and nickels into the large slot machine next to their seats. I tried to take the same bus as often as I could, craving the familiarity of drivers who seemed to recognize me.

I was definitely venturing out of my comfort zone. I became familiar, and even comfortable to a degree, inside Walgreens. If I had enough money, and usually I had barely enough, I would buy a small chocolate ice cream cone at the metal-edged counter. I sat by myself on the round metal stools with flat, round bottoms, bolted securely to the black and white checkerboard floors. Or I'd head straight to Auerbach's Department Store, which was an uncomfortable venture for such a country mouse. But the store was an exciting, posh icon of the bustling city, and

I couldn't resist checking it out. I covertly studied the older and better-off young women who wore nice clothes and good shoes, and carried expensive bags. Some seemed extremely snobbish and walked with their heads and noses lifted. I decided then and there that for sure, I never wanted to be that wealthy. To be prosperous enough to buy a few nice things would be sufficiently wonderful. I knew wealth was never really in my sights anyway. It seemed like a pipedream for my sort, and I was content to dream about dressing well enough to simply not feel self-conscious at my new school.

I began to relish my time alone. I wandered the aisles, daydreaming and imagining. I spent hours poring over the endless choices of makeup in the never-ending rows of glass-topped counters. It was a lot like studying the rows of fine chocolates two floors up. I tried on blushers and powder, and picked up every sample in every dish. I eyed the fashionable new eyeliners and mascaras, the mauve lipsticks and even the new pale white ones, which were becoming so trendy. I sniffed the perfumes, dabbing them sophisticatedly behind my ears, wrists, and in the hollow of my neck. White Shoulders was becoming my favorite, but I liked Evening in Paris, Chanel No. 5, Chantilly, and even Shalimar. Last, I tried on all the new face foundations, making sure to grab a few extra samples.

Lerner's was for clothes and shoes, quite reasonably priced, and the Yardstick was strictly for fabric and notions – zippers, thread, buttons, pins, and the like. There, I would sit at the table and study the newest Butterick and Simplicity pattern books from beginning to end. They were more interesting than novels.

Sometimes I'd look up, surprised to see that an hour or more had evaporated into thin air. The best days were when I could actually buy a pattern and fabric to create with. There were bolts and bolts of delicious fabric to linger over and touch. Linen, cotton, velvet, chiffon, and crepe. You name it, I loved them all. I caressed them with my fingertips, savoring the different textures, picturing the outfits I could fashion from them. Textiles were a delight and passion from an early age, and the penchant has remained. I have sewn clothing, drapery, pillows, and even upholstery. Even when I couldn't afford to buy what I wanted, I considered the fixation a compensating blessing. It was a pure pleasure.

By far, my favorite store in the city was The Chalk Garden. Not to spend money in, of course, but to window shop until I was pretty much dizzy. I went hungrily from rack to rack, drooling over the beautiful skirts, blouses, and dresses. Then I'd saunter, ever so casually, over to the shoe department where I'd plop myself down on an elegantly upholstered tuffet and try on a half dozen pairs of the most sumptuous pumps or flats. I longed to own a pair of pale pink suede kitten heels. I sensed the clerks immediately discerned that was not a serious mark, and I tried not to look them in the eye. They pretty much ignored me or watched to see if I might stuff something into my bag. I loved shoes like an addict craves drugs, so despite my pride, I kept showing up at their store. Never to buy, just to dream. If nothing else, it was one of my biggest diversions and best adventures.

If I could have kept the school year at bay indefinitely, I certainly would have, but trying would have been like spitting into the wind. The so-called privilege of rising first to bathe each morning was mine because I was the oldest, but it was really because there was only one bathtub and everyone needed a turn. Although I've always adored taking a bath, this became a dreaded ritual. When the little metal alarm clock I kept close to my pillow went off, I slid out of bed and quietly closed the door to keep from waking my sisters. I tiptoed into the living room and kitchen area to turn on the lights. To say this was my least favorite part of the day was gross understatement. I can't begin to describe my dread for it.

When I flipped the switch, light was instantaneously flung into the rooms. It was then that a thousand cockroaches, ranging in size and age, scattered like rats in a dance hall-sized cellar. It was as if I was walking in on shameful and dishonorable acts being committed under the cloak of darkness by terrible ghoulish creatures.

Their hard black shells were large, shiny, and oval. Their antennae frantically swept every surface like hungry monsters on a rampage. Others were smaller adolescents but flew like mischievous teenagers on scooters of greased lightning. The majority seemed to be toddlers or infants with their milky, transparent, and filthy little bodies, skimming the walls. They made my skin crawl and the acid slide up into my throat. I was often afraid I'd actually throw up before I could get a bath. They scuttled over the counters and stove, and scrambled up and down the cabinets. In a minute or two, they literally all magically vanished into the woodwork, behind the appliances, or under the floors. It was as if they had never been there at all.

So, to me the most eerie part of living in that house was the deceptive reality of sharing it with vile and filthy cockroaches, and who knows what else. They were the most horrible creatures I had ever seen, and the fact that they scuttled all night while I was sleeping was something I cannot ever get out of my mind. I had to will myself not to think about them in order to fall asleep at night. To this day, I cannot look at one without revulsion and the hair raising on the back of my neck. Most mornings I stooped quickly through the tunnel to my parents' sleeping quarters, where I pleaded with my father to come and dispose of the one or two giants trapped in the bathtub.

The big yellow school bus came every morning, sunshine or snow, stopping just a house away from mine, which made things easy. Once ready, family prayers and reading done, and a hearty breakfast eaten, I ran out the door to board the bus. My mother always cooked oatmeal, cheesy eggs, or pancakes, and plenty of each. That kind of a breakfast made up for a lot. We never once complained that we had to leave the house hungry.

Once again, I latched on to my fondness for bus drivers. This time they took me to school. Most were cordial and seemed genuinely to enjoy their jobs. Usually there were one or two assigned for the whole school year, and it was comforting after a long, complicated day, to climb the stairs of the big bus and see a kind and familiar face. This was especially true in the early days when every other face on the bus was an alien one. For the first few weeks, every expression seemed frosty, aloof, indifferent, or, perhaps only in my imagination, hostile. I was probably oversensitive, I reasoned, but I wasn't ready to risk being too friendly. As well, it just wasn't my nature. For me, making friends generally takes time. On the other hand, I could count on the regular school bus driver, whose name I learned was Roy, to deliver a welcoming expression, which to me said, "Good morning, Ella, I'm so happy you came today," and then see to it that I arrived at school safely and on time. He was quite a bit older than my father, perhaps retired. His uniforms were clean and starched, his full head of butterscotch hair was stick-straight and unruly. It was apparent that he was happy to have this job. He seemed to have too many teeth for his mouth, and they protruded as he kindly smiled. His presence seemed to exude "reliable." When the day was over, his facial expression would crinkle, "Have a nice evening, nice girl," as he deposited me securely in front of my house.

My first day was terrifying. I actually did not recognize even one face. There were pretty girls, handsome boys, and the opposite. There were rich, poor, shy, and outgoing kids. There were mean boys, reckless girls, and a mixture of all kinds, which I wasn't good at discerning. Truthfully, at this juncture, I wasn't certain which category I fit into. I began to wonder how I came across to other kids. Certainly, they would see me as anxious, fearful, introverted, underprivileged, and maybe a little prideful. I wasn't at all certain I belonged here in the first place. No one knew I had come from a place better. Better house, better friends who actually liked me, and a better neighborhood. It seemed that as the bus navigated northward towards the new school, the houses increased in rank and stature. Ground zero began as pitiful and poor, like my area, and went on to small, unattractive, sort of nice, conservative, larger, nicer, and on up to really nice, as the school building came into view. Clearly, the wealthier kids lived nearer the high school, but I soon realized that most of them did not attend it at all. Apparently, when carving out the boundaries, the district jumped a whole section of town whose students had, for decades, attended the illustrious central high school. Clearly, those parents had no intention of letting anyone interfere with their longstanding distinguished traditions. So, to fill up the brand-new school, they were grabbing up students from the less affluent perimeters of town. The reason for the disparity of incomes, I surmised. Oh well, at this point, I had already learned a few things about that.

The classes themselves were more comfortable. I was familiar with the drills of curriculums, textbooks, homerooms, students, and teachers. I had a game plan; I usually positioned myself on one side of the room or a little towards the middle to be unobtrusive and unnoticed. I knew I had the wherewithal to be a good student, and that made class doable. If nothing else, I could focus my attention on the teacher, the subject, and the lessons, and get by just fine. I secretly studied the students on either side to see if there was someone who might smile or be a potential friend. I had no high hopes or expectations. Finding my locker, maneuvering the halls, locating the bathroom, and tracking down the correct classrooms were my first priority. Whatever else came later could be dealt with later. I got through the first few days unnoticed, which I found to be a great relief. But I was excited to gather my belongings, board the big yellow bus, see the bus driver smile, and get home.

The first couple of weeks, lunchtime was agony, but before long I began to get the hang of it. I brought my lunch in a brown paper bag, grabbed a carton of milk from the wire basket at the lunch counter, and self-consciously slid to the end of a perimeter bench table. I surreptitiously surveyed the room while I ate my sandwich and chips, careful to keep my expression impassive, while guardedly scouring the tables for someone who might be my kind of people. In a new high school, that was difficult to ascertain.

During the third week, a large boy with yellow hair, straight teeth, and pudgy fingers by the name of Jared carried a lunch tray to my table and unabashedly plopped it down next to mine. He unreservedly began to make chirpy small talk as he blew through his food, obviously relishing every bite. He asked me a dozen questions, barely stopping to let me answer. How were my classes going? How did I like the new school? Was I making new friends? And anything else relevant or irrelevant that seemed to pop into his head full of blonde hair. He was good-natured and friendly, and I soon realized I was actually relieved to have someone to share lunch with. It meant that I didn't stick out like a sore thumb. The pattern continued for a couple more weeks, and one by one, other kids, mostly friends of Jared, sat down to join us. With absolutely no effort on my part, at least five people had been added to my list of acquaintances. I was happily relieved of the burden of being alone.

For a couple weeks, I had been watching a large group of girls eating at a central table. They seemed to be the bustling hive of the school. One or two of them looked, possibly, to be the queen bee, but it was hard to say for certain. Maybe the hive had more than one. They swarmed around each other gleefully and breezily, talking loudly, gesturing wildly with their hands, laughing, and sharing secrets. Most of them were stylishly dressed and had decent haircuts, mostly shiny shoulder-length bobs in an assortment of blondes, browns, and reds. The dos were smartly adorned with bobby pins or tortoiseshell clips. A few wore jauntily bouncing ponytails. On certain days of the week, a couple of the girls wore short, pleated, yellow wool skirts and dark red sweaters. The emblemed uniforms not-so-subtly announced their membership on the school cheerleading squad, which was ever so intimidating. After watching them carefully, I thought most of the girls appeared to be quite nice. Not inordinately snobby or stand-offish. What was all too apparent, and not remotely in question, was that they were generally accepted and admired. That's exactly what unnerved me. They were the popular girls.

One day, as I was crumpling up my brown paper bag, having finished my tuna sandwich with pickles and my small bag of chips, I got up and walked to the back of the lunchroom. I was dumping my trash into the large communal can when I felt a light tap on the shoulder blade. I turned on my heels quickly and almost collided with a tall, dark, and very handsome boy wearing a crimson letter jacket. He had slicked back brown hair, wide-set brown eyes, heavy eyebrows, and an unassuming but sophisticated swagger. He casually asked how I liked the new school and proffered his name. "Don Stoddard," he said. He commenced with some brief small talk about the new school, while I stood there awkwardly silent. I wanted so badly to be the object of his attention, but I couldn't quite believe it. I felt the heat rise from my neck, and seep into my cheeks. I hoped they weren't on fire, but he didn't seem to be looking at them. Then, without warning, he simply asked if I'd like to go to a movie the following weekend. Just like that. A movie? A date? I forced myself to suck in the breath through my nose and blow it out slowly through my teeth, to control my expression of shock and conceal my incredulity, and my awkward delight. As he asked the question, I found myself glancing over my shoulder to see if he was actually speaking to someone standing behind me. He wasn't. I caught myself before the words came out in a sputter. I swallowed hard and smiled as brightly as I knew how, just to kill a second or two before answering. When I was fairly certain I could speak without stammering, I said, with amazing poise, "Yeah, sure. That would be great." Although this would not be my first date, it was the most exciting prospect I had ever had, especially after being thrust into this new school. "Thanks." Then he asked where I lived so he could pick me up. With that question, my stomach began to tie itself into a bowknot. Yet if I was going to go out with him, I had no choice but to tell him. He said he'd see me at six-thirty.

I put on the blue wool skirt, then the green dress with the sweetheart neckline, then the blue skirt again with the thin white cardigan. I changed flats several times before deciding on the first pair I had tried. I was afraid to wear my kitten heels because I couldn't remember exactly how tall he was. I ratted my hair a little on the top and then combed it smooth again, before heating up the curling iron. I applied eyeliner a little too thick and had to wipe it all off. My mascara clumped, and my cheeks seemed too rosy already for any of my powdered blush. I was so nervous that I had to remove my sweater to put on more deodorant. Yet there was a palpable excitement running through my body like a pulse. This has got to go well, I pleaded with I have no idea who.

The date did not go as I had hoped. I was nervously tongue-tied all evening long, thinking perhaps the sight of the dingy little house had changed his mind about me. How could it not? During the movie, my stomach made loud gurgling noises, and I had no doubt that he could hear them. I was too nervous to eat popcorn, and the soda made bubbles in my stomach. The more anxious I was about the house and the stomach acid, the more tongue-tied I became. I could barely carry on a conversation. He'd make an offhand comment about the movie plot and I'd open my mouth and try to say something witty or deep, but nothing came out. I could not for the life of me relax and be myself. It felt like an alien had inhabited my body. He took me straight home, walked me to the door, and quickly departed back to his spiffy little car.

I was not at all surprised when he did not ask me out on a second date. Who could blame him? But one date was, in fact, all it took. Don was the student body president of my new high school. The date with him, albeit a dismal failure, changed my status at the school in one fell swoop. Word spread like wildfire that the awkward new girl had gone out with him. Before long, I had a regular place at the center lunch table with the hive and soon became one of them, buzzing about with newfound wings.

Truth be told, I never fit in very well at that school, except superficially, though I thoroughly enjoyed my easy new status. I learned to blend in without standing out, as was my intention. I was never confident enough to feel at ease in the spotlight anyway, but I was overjoyed to find a somewhat solid standing.

I was never terribly close to any of them individually but rather affable with them all. As time went on, I did make a few good friends here and there, which made my life so much easier and pleasant.

In short, my high school experience was the typical whirlwind – full of excitement, insecurity, ups, downs, and all sorts of in-betweens. Even in the best of circumstances, high school is a not a smooth ride. There's not enough stability emotionally, physically, or otherwise to do anything but hold on to your seat and get through the ride.

There were parties and proms, dates, and girl nights. I was asked out quite a few times, but never with anyone I would have chosen. I literally never invited anyone over to my house – girls or boys – and I ran out the door quickly when someone honked to pick me up. I grew my hair into a shiny shoulder-length bob and learned to apply eyeliner like a pro. I curled my eyelashes and wore pale pink lipstick. I became a pretty proficient waitress at the restaurant. I settled down into my new life. All in all, I suppose it was better than I expected.

32

Ella

As a girl, I was torn between the two houses. The house where my parents lived and the little house in Levan, a couple hours away, which may as well have been a thousand miles.

To waste away the time at Grandma's during one of my monthly summer visits, I watched the black-faced sheep huddle under the trees across the gravel street in front of the house, their bodies squished together tightly to grab up all the shade. Only the lambs languished in the sun, their little forms shaded by the tall grasses. As often as Grandma would let me, I'd scrounge up a little change, usually a couple dimes, nickels, and pennies and walk down to the post office to retrieve the mail (there was none most days) and buy penny candy at the little grocery store next to it.

When the Sabbath came – Grandma always said "Sabbath" like my father – I couldn't wait to put on my Sunday dress and black patent leather shoes. What I did not look forward to was having her French-braid my long hair. I knew it had to be done because she insisted on it every morning I was there. I had no doubt it would be evenly and perfectly plaited, but she pulled and tugged very firmly, and I always had to bite my tongue or put my knuckles into my mouth to keep from crying out. When I was ready, I walked the four blocks down and two over, to the old pioneer chapel. I was careful not to kick up the street gravel and scuff my shoes. She didn't make me go when it rained. For the most part, though, I wanted to go and visit what I assumed was the most ancient of buildings. Even as a girl, I was enthralled with anything vintage. The church stood across from the post office and grocery mart. It was built of old orange brick and was stately gabled. It was narrow, not large, but very tall.

Massive darkly stained double doors opened grandly into the surprisingly simple setting. It always took my breath when I stepped up the stairs, through the doors, and into the chapel. The raw pine floor was worn, patinaed, and bleached silvery gray from many decades of stalwart churchgoers. I imagined my father and his brothers as little boys running unruly up the stairs, along with my faceless great-grandparents; that made it all the more intriguing. The floorboards were elevated gradually from the back to the front of the chapel, a bit of a climb for old folks and toddlers, but the rise succeeded in making the pulpit taller than it would have been on a flat surface. Everyone could see, even if they could not hear. There was no microphone. The orators were forced to sort of yell out their sermons. They were a lot like the speeches I heard at home. The hymns were bellowed out loudly and with fervor, echoing through the high space, and were often a little out of pitch.

The old wooden organ was strikingly handsome with its elaborate carvings. They tracked up through its honey brown flanks and laced through the attached music stand. They were so intricate that I couldn't see a distinct pattern. The hymn that got my blood running was the one that went, "True to the faith that our parents have cherished; true to the faith for which martyrs have perished." I always wondered what a true disciple might look like, but when I sang that song in that chapel, I thought I might really be one of them. The song still makes me feel extra valiant. As I belted it out, I vowed that I would "never, no never" let go of my faith.

The pews were also rough-hewn, worn, and greyed, but shone as if they had been hand waxed. There were scratches here and there on the backs, and the wood showed years of wear from human frames. The seats were narrow, and the backs were short and straight, making it impossible to slump without sliding off, and difficult not to pay attention. The planked walls were whitewashed the color of snow. A single chandelier perched front and center like a bejeweled headdress; each of its aged brass arms was curved, holding what appeared to be a dish of murky glass. The vintage glass pooled the light in large circles on the vaulted ceiling, which brought the word *halos* to mind.

My favorite element of the chapel, however, was the continuous rows of windows on either side. I had never seen anything like them before, and nothing since. They were comprised of innumerable white, wooden-framed panes of glass, which sparkled like diamonds in the sunlight, casting so much light at noonday I could scarcely take a breath. They peaked at the top like cathedrals, soaring up both sides of the walls, stretching themselves from just above the floorboards to the top of the twenty-foot ceilings. They were as close to "celestial" as I had ever seen. It was as if their calling was to open the chapel to many sources of light so as to inspire its parishioners. It poured through them like gold, brilliant and shimmering, illuminating the simple little church with a grandeur it could never have aspired to. Sometimes I gazed out through them to the grassy churchyard and imagined the trees were swaying to the organ in the breeze.

Every so often, I got so homesick that I thought I might die. I've come to believe that children who must adapt to a lot at home tend to cling more fiercely to their discomfort because they know nothing else. But Levan became a temporary sanctuary, not unlike that little chapel. It was a respite, a timeout from life, and a soupçon of peace. My whole life long, I will never forget standing in the side yard at dusk looking northward towards home. The farmers' carefully planted fields created a patchwork of green, brown, yellow, and amber, stretching out many miles before my eyes. They appeared to roll gently up and over the ground like a quilt. As the sun began to set, the edges caught the salmon glow of the sun and cast pink shadows. The clear crisp air cleared my head, while the golden shafts of light burnished the mountains to the east and kissed the fields to the north. As I stood, I wondered what my parents were doing. I hoped they were having a nice evening and weren't fighting. I hoped they were eating a good dinner. I missed them terribly. I missed my stoic and strong father. I missed my mother's cooking and her wash waving in the afternoon breeze. I even missed the little kids. At the same time, I felt remarkably content with my grandmother. Though the two worlds were so different, I think I felt a little disloyal to my family by being happy away from it.

Again, I was torn between the two important places in my life. I wondered how much of the genetic material that made up my family – especially my father and grandmother – would be an integral part of my own being. They being so different, who was better? Who would I most resemble? Maybe the real question was who should I emulate? Did I even have a choice? Would I inherit their habits, flaws, gifts, intensity, or lack thereof? Is it in the blood, and will it remain there to be passed to my posterity through me? Or is it more complicated than that?

When I look back to those summer days, I wonder how it came to be that my grandmother was who she was. Was she inherently stoic, quiet, and self-contained, or did someone pass it on to her? When I endure the hard knocks of my own life, I realize that though my grandmother's sermons were not vocal, they were poignant. They were etched in her face, her posture, her character, and her life. I had only to recall the stories to know exactly what she thought, why, and how she overcame. She was her own homily.

That said, I couldn't fault my father for being the opposite. He seemed incapable of not giving a protracted discourse. He shared his experiences, observations, and sentiments in detail, hoping, I would imagine, to vicariously inculcate them into his children. He didn't want them to take all life's lumps themselves. I'm not certain it works that way, but you had to admire his motives and tenacity. The benefit was that I knew someone was there to chew over things to death with.

33

Ella

As high school progressed, I continued to be embarrassed to bring anyone home, and never did. I couldn't quite jump that hurdle. Yet, I was developing a confusing peaceful stability I never expected. I had to admit my point of reference was evolving, and my paradigm was shifting. I felt a sort of swelling pride, which was perplexingly calming. Pride about what? It seemed paradoxical, but I had begun to question the notion I had always embraced, which was that being well off is synonymous with being accomplished and successful. Perhaps, it became necessary to adopt that point of view to be okay with our station. I was proud of my parents, especially my father. I adored him, and I knew without a doubt that he was doing the best he knew how. I began to suspect there were just some things he was not very good at, and that making money might well be one of them. For the first time, I was considering that people are given a variety of gifts, not just a set of the predictable. I had no doubts as to his strength, his wisdom, and his goodness. He embraced his beliefs, lived them the best he knew how, and tried to instill them in his children. It was his driving aspiration. If I truly respected him and my mother, and I did, it would be incongruent to be critical or to blame them for our predicament, as well as to think less of them because of it. This turning point in my thinking caused me to expand my definition of achievement, even in our desperate circumstances. I suppose that was the pride part.

I never did embrace the pitiful little house as our home and never really lost the shame, but I was beginning to feel a burgeoning dignity. If I could have put it into words, I was feeling a smidgeon of smugness regarding our humble circumstances. I was beginning to understand what people mean when they say, "proud to be poor."

I sewed my school clothes on my mother's old Singer. I was quite proficient, and proud of it. My goal was to have four or five outfits hanging in my little metal closet to choose from every day. I made two A-line skirts, one in green and white cotton paisley, and the other in pale blue linen. I loved them both, especially since I handpicked the patterns and fabrics myself. I sewed a yellow quilted blazer, which had small royal blue arrows running through the cloth. I made a navy skirt, which fell just above the knee and boasted straight, even pleats. I saved up and bought one decent gray cardigan sweater, which I could wear with almost everything. In spite of that, I often daydreamed away my algebra class, letting my mind wander to the outfits my classmates were wearing, wondering what it would be like to have real store-bought dresses, skirts, and sweaters.

Every year, there was a popular promotional contest in one of the prominent downtown department stores. Its aim was to recruit stylish junior girls from every high school in the valley to represent the store for the upcoming school year. It was, of course, a tricky and effective marketing ploy. The winners would get their pictures prominently displayed in the clothing area of the store for an entire school year and model the clothing. I studied the portraits carefully many times as I wandered the store, dreaming, envying, and thinking how amazing it would be to be one of those girls whose polished faces stared down at everybody else's. But I would have never dreamt of entering the contest. It was simply not in the realm of possibility for me; that was very clear.

It was, of course, open to any high school junior. As misfortune would have it, three of my popular and pretty friends asked if I would be interested in going downtown to audition with them. A debilitating dread surged immediately, yet I tepidly agreed, if only to be part of the group and the excitement. The questions "What if you embarrass yourself?" and "Shouldn't you at least try?" hammered like opposing bullets to the brain. It was the kind of outrageous thing you might let wander around in your head for a little while, just for fun, but deep down, you knew it could never work. I tried on every outfit I owned several times before deciding on one I considered most flattering.

One of the girls with a classic BMW drove us downtown. I think we were all feeling quite chic, at least in attitude. As we parked and waited at the light to cross the street, we chatted expectantly and excitedly. It was surreal. I could actually feel a tiny bubble of hope bobbing around in my chest. As we dillydallied at the light, the eminent storefront was visible up ahead. I smoothed out my skirt, straightened my blouse, and swiped under my eyes in case a little mascara had run. Out of the blue, and before the light changed, one of my so-called friends abruptly stopped her chattering. She was not one of my closest girlfriends in the group, and I had always tried to ignore her penchant for meanness and arrogance. Inevitably, there are always one or two of those types in every group. But this day, I was caught off guard when she turned those attributes in my direction. It took years for me to realize she was just narrowing the competition in the only way she knew how. She turned on a pale blue leather kitten heel with raised eyebrows to study me. With an upturned nose and heavily blue-shadowed eyes, she examined me critically from head to toe. With a haughty smirk and wave of her meticulously manicured pink fingertip, she asked how in heaven's name I could ever expect to go in wearing what I had on. Stunned and caught off guard, I looked down at my hand-sewn quilted jacket and well-worn but cherished blue A-line skirt. I absently smoothed out the linen again. Deflated, my confidence collapsed like a boulder, plummeted to the sidewalk, and shattered into a thousand pieces. The sound in my head was as thundering as if one of the large skyscrapers had crumbled in front of us. The other girls looked startled and embarrassed but said nothing. There were no words forming in my mouth either.

As we crossed the street and walked the half block to the storefront, I was nonplussed but pretended to be unaffected. When they entered the building, I hovered in the adjoining alcove and watched silently. My decision had been set in stone back on the street corner. I watched as they promenaded happily in front of a line of genial judging faces. I don't think they even noticed that I did not go in. Paradoxically that day, two of my friends won spots in the promotional contest. Their pictures were prominently displayed for a full year above the "juniors" section of the department store. I tried as hard as I could not to look up when I went shopping.

34

Ella

I graduated high school and was somehow, incredibly and magically, awarded a four-year, full-ride scholarship. At least it seemed unlikely that it should be awarded to me, not that I hadn't worked very hard at my schoolwork. It just felt like things like that happened to other kids, not me. In any case, I trotted off to college in Southern Utah. I figured leaving our little bungalow for a little while would do me some good. I had no idea how debilitating and downright awful the homesickness would be, even more so than in the past. I almost couldn't function for two solid months. I was sick to my stomach all the time and missed my family. As in the past, I couldn't deal with leaving them behind. Perhaps I felt guilty for being able to step out of what seemed such difficult circumstances for us all. Sam always says I should have been a Catholic, for all the guilt I sustain about anything and everything. I made extensive plans to hop a Greyhound bus and give it all up for good, but I finally got my sea legs, as Dad would say, and stayed put.

As I learned to navigate college life, I discovered it to be amazingly enjoyable. I went to class, studied, worked, and dated. The campus was small, which made it very navigable without transportation. I found my classes and professors engaging and fascinating, and I was shocked to learn that I had an aptitude and interest in physics. I dated only sporadically, never with any serious attraction, but the sociality was significantly agreeable. With the exception of one girl (another mean, spiteful type who tends to pop up regularly in flocks of girls), my roommates were pleasant and friendly. At this juncture, I had learned to ignore those petty souls who seem to put others down to prop themselves up. I particularly enjoyed my roommate, and we spent many hours getting to know one another. She quickly became my best and trusted friend. I found her only flaws to be a tall, curvaceous body and beautiful long, blond hair, which rendered me almost invisible when I was with her in a group. She was so engaging and kind, however, that I had no choice but to forgive her.

Almost immediately upon arrival at the school, I was invited by the class presidency to be their candidate in the annual homecoming queen contest. I embarrassingly accepted and tried my best but withered like a fading wallflower in the competition, as my confidence was so low. I will never forget, however, the fun of waving at people on a float in my evening gown, through the center of town.

My employer was a kindly English professor, and I helped him several hours every day after class. Even so, I could barely make ends meet and often couldn't buy books – or food, if I decided to spend my money on the books. That didn't throw me too terribly. I found that the advantage of not having things is that you don't expect to have them. And not having them doesn't tip your world upside-down.

I met a boy the second year and got married three days after turning twenty, like many of the girls in my sphere. It was the logical and expected thing to do in the conservative and religious community I had grown up in; move forward with a husband and then children, as quickly as possible. A career? Well, I didn't exactly want to give that up either. I'd just go with the flow and worry about it later. As it turned out, there were many aspects of life I was extremely ignorant about, and "going with the flow" didn't really help things work out perfectly. Less than a year later, I gave birth to a beautiful baby girl. I named her Jenny.

My husband was a very nice fellow and got along well with most people. He was tall, blonde, and handsome, and his family was extremely well off. On the surface, it seemed to me like they had figured out everything that my family had endlessly struggled with. They lived in a magazine-worthy home in an upscale neighborhood, in the best city in the state. His father was an attorney with deep ties to the political community, and his mother was a prominent women's rights advocate. As for as the religion I had grown up fully immersed in, his family only dabbled in it. Clearly, it was not an issue for them. My husband's intentions were to finish college and go on to dental school, which seemed like a dream to me, or a happy ending in a movie plot. It almost didn't seem real that he would want to marry me. The contrast between my early life and his was pitch black and bright white. He had grown up with a credit card in his wallet and a shot at any opportunity he could choose. Yet we didn't really connect, even in the dating phase. He was fun to be with but distant and unaffectionate, even then. He loved hanging with his guy friends more than with me. I couldn't understand it and refused to consider any of several red flags, though a few of my friends made it a point to challenge me. All I could picture was a more pleasant and less stringent life for myself. Perhaps a small medium-sized house with a garden. Yes, I willingly attached my own blinders. No one forced me, and after all, I was still a babe in the woods.

Life was quite pleasant. Marriage, only slightly pleasant. Actually, I found it to be empty, strained, and melancholy, but I accepted it as the bed I had foolishly, impulsively, and prematurely, made for myself. I had no choice now but to dig my heels in and make the best of it. I had hope for better days where the marriage was concerned, but I absolutely adored my little girl. She was the very sun, moon, and stars my life revolved around. That was something I hadn't really planned on.

We moved from apartment to apartment, then house to house. My husband took a job to get himself through college but decided against dental school. He seemed to be at loose ends where a vocation was concerned, and though he had every intention to create stability for us, it was a zigzagging course. I really didn't blame him, as we had baby after baby, and I couldn't really blame him for that. The children came like pumpkins laid out in a field, and I contentedly made room for each. His parents, however, were not happy. They had hoped for more for their son, and much less in the way of grandchildren. The children were the brightest spots in my life, and I discovered that this journey with infants and small children was a delight I could never have conjured. Being a mother was now my vocation by default, and I threw myself into it with appetite, exuberance, and ferocity. These little individuals provided purpose, focus, and genuine joy, though there was no question as to the arduousness of the work.

I often felt like the woman who lived in a shoe, overflowing with busywork and mountains of stuff. But as I put my shoulder to the wheel, I made a surprising discovery. It dawned on me that if I could learn to love the shoe as well, I could love the children who spilled from its windows even more. By attempting to do that, I found immense pleasure in homemaking and domesticity. I cooked, cleaned, ordered, planned, nurtured, tended, gardened, and designed. I was pleasantly surprised to realize I was enjoying the entire process.

Money was not plentiful, probably not unusual for a growing young family, and because of that, I was forced to learn a fair amount of frugality and ingenuity. Necessity is the best teacher, and so on. Each home or apartment became my castle, and I genuinely enjoyed the process of feathering it with creativity, a spattering of flare, and of course, order.

Obviously, I was far from a perfect mother. I did try, but with no written instructions, I made many mistakes, though I think just small ones. My biggest fault was being, at times, more exacting and harsher than I intended, and perhaps yelling more than I thought wonderful. I was, as well, loving and attentive, I think in pretty fair measure. However, I did expect a great deal from my children. They were, after all, my stewardship, my life's work, and my priority, and I had no choice but to take this job very seriously. Like most parents, I felt I owed them enough stability, guidance, and affection to be happy and successful in their future lives. I remember thinking they were the arrows in my quiver, and I was determined to be a good archer.

35

Ella

Although I was not as social as I once was in high school or even college, I always had friends, even if not as many as others'. I took pleasure in female companionship and conversation. I had morphed into a different person, and I berated myself for not having or making friends more easily. I entertained the thought that somehow I was not as interesting or engaging as I once was. It's probably just motherhood, I assumed. Perhaps I had taken it a bit too seriously.

When the first two children, sweet and saucy little Jenny and quiet and thoughtful little David, were small, we lived in a large apartment complex adjacent to a busy road. It was a long row of fourplexes situated close together, two units on each side, one perched on top of the other. They were homely brown-brick boxes with flat roofs. The doors on each level opened to face one another. We lived on the top, which in my mind, was most favorable.

In the morning hours, beginning around nine, it was typical for most of the mothers to begin gathering (in mild-weather months, obviously) on the steps of each building. They dragged their children out to play and wander about while they sunned, lounged, and chatted. In this period, I became very certain I was not socially adept, and maybe a bit more odd than I had imagined. Instead of joining the others, I intentionally shied away from the group. I came up with lots of excuses. I had to nurse my baby, feed my toddler, eat my breakfast, and begin a rather stringent daily routine, which made lolling about the front steps quite superfluous.

As my apparent appointed life's work, I had no choice but to take mothering and domestic duties very seriously, even in this tiny apartment. I reasoned that because now it would be implausible to become a doctor, accountant, or fashion designer, I must excel where I was stationed. Even though I had dreams, just like with the homecoming queen pageant – I allowed them to wither in my lack of confidence and hope. Realistically, these options had no chance the minute I became pregnant with Jenny.

I did stay the course as a mother; I couldn't picture a dentist not doing a good job or not finishing his or her work, or a business owner not tending carefully to her store. That would be tantamount to recklessness and imprudence. So, I bathed the children, put the baby down for his morning nap, began the wash, and commenced in making the beds, doing the dishes, wiping down the kitchen, and tidying up everything else. Even in this two-bedroom apartment, it seemed like important work. And if it wasn't worth the effort, I worried it would translate into "my life is pretty worthless." So, I leaped into productivity.

When I peered out the window at the other women on the stoop, I felt even more peculiar. I sensed they considered me aloof, inflexible, eccentric, and even a little uppity. Yet my children and my little domain were quickly becoming my center of gravity. What could be more important than making your children a proper lunch, even if it was usually no more than a peanut butter and jam sandwich and milk? (I fed little David rice cereal, fruit, and an uncooked egg yolk, because I had read that raw vitamin-filled protein was good for babies.)

After lunch, it was time to settle them down in front of the TV to watch one episode each of *Sesame Street*, *Mr. Rogers*, and *Electric Company*. As they'd sit and watch, I'd watch with them, rehearsing the letters and numbers audibly, as if it could possibly make a difference. Then it was nap time. I nursed the baby to sleep while lying in bed with my daughter, reading two or three stories before we both slept. I usually slept more than she did. When afternoon was over, it was time to start thinking about dinner. Poof, day over. Thus, hanging out with the moms was rarely an option for me, though through the years I have regretted not making more friends and taking life a little less seriously.

As for the little austere apartment, it was there that my creative inclination to design began to surface. The perplexing fastidious and meticulous ways also began to emerge. I think now they were simply an intrinsic part of me. I have come to believe you are what you are, even in the most particular or peculiar things, unless you break your neck to change. Fighting is usually a waste of effort. For a long time, I was dismayed at what seems to be my integral tidiness. I chafed at the freaky part of being different. I suppose in the long run, however, I have grown to rather enjoy it and just go with the flow.

As a girl, I was extremely interested in medicine. I compulsively read everything about it I could get my hands on. Only a handful of times was I audacious enough to imagine I could really become a doctor. Even in college, I gave up and majored in English because it seemed more practical. In my provincial little world, it would have been fairly preposterous, but I still dream about it on a regular basis. I often wonder now, but didn't then, why I couldn't have done both. A husband and babies rounded out the world I had grown up in. I often watched people with successful careers and noted with interest that most are built around excellence, precision, and discipline. I never heard anyone criticize an efficacious businessperson, surgeon, or attorney for being too focused or too good at their jobs. Where homemaking and child rearing were concerned, I suppose I decided that because I had ended up with them, I owed them my best.

In any case, the little apartment became an important focus. It kept my attention away from anxiety and boredom. I was constrained to keep it organized and discovered that interesting details make things a little more interesting. I spent three hundred dollars on a clearance sofa, which we still couldn't afford. It was long, low, and upholstered in cotton velvet with orange and brown stripes jettisoning across a yellow field. I begged a few more pieces of furniture from my father's basement – a decent upholstered brown chair that had come from my grandmother's house in Levan and a vintage wooden rocker. I even ventured to apply orange and yellow plaid wallpaper on one wall in the little kitchen nook. Other tenants who saw it were horrified that I would have the impudence and audacity to do so, and they told me I'd be sorry and lose my deposit. We couldn't afford to lose even a dollar, and I had signed on the dotted line to not paint or alter anything, but I could not constrain myself from embellishing those two walls behind the table. The colors matched the sofa perfectly and gave me no end of pleasure. I went on to sew a straight little yellow blind for the small single kitchen window and embellish it with loopy fringe. My washer and dryer, hidden in the back nook, were polished and clean at all times, as if anyone would ever see them, or care. Looking back, I understand it appeared a little neurotic or even pretentious to my apartment friends, using the word *friends* loosely. I think now, I was just trying to find a way to feel unique, creative, and a little successful at the career I was stuck with.

In the afternoons or early evenings, I was often profoundly weary. Boredom always seemed to be hovering, waiting to catch me off guard and ensnare me in a blue net of melancholy. It fools me into thinking I am depressed, anxious, or unstable, but I have come to realize it's just the old trickster attempting to get me down. I have learned to avoid long intervals of unoccupied time.

After a routine day in the tiny apartment, I often secured Jenny and David into a makeshift double stroller that had been inexpensively adapted to fit them both. They were always excited to take a walk, and we headed anxiously up the street to explore. Their father attended the university and worked evenings until midnight, so I most often got the kids up in the morning and put them to bed at night. We could barely afford one vehicle, so the stroller was our only option. I relished the long leisurely walks, and at the same time, my children were getting a break from the small apartment. I waited until the other women had gone in for the day. I didn't want to call attention to myself, or worse, have them think I was snooty by preferring my solitude to their company.

I hiked as long as their patience would bear. The skies were often dark before we returned to the apartment. We walked up and down West Temple and Main in the city. We looked at buildings and gardens, and peered into shops, windows, and restaurants. I always ventured back to my favorite streets, gazing longingly at the real houses, no matter how humble. I desperately longed for a home of my own, which, I reasoned, would be the next logical step in my "career." An infeasibility, no doubt. I kept returning to Beatrix Avenue. It reminded me of a miniature town from somewhere in time and had a protected space for my kids to run and play. It was two rows of charming little houses, which faced each other with no street in between. There was a large expanse of lawn in front of each row, and a narrow sidewalk ribboning through the center. The backs of the houses lapped up against the roads on either side.

Decidedly, this was where I would choose to live, if given half a chance. Quaint, well-kept, quiet, domestic, and sweet. Though the houses were small and squarish, they were painted in soft colors. The dark green and black rooftops were pleasantly pitched. The polished windows and brightly painted doors reminded me of cheerful faces smiling at me, as if to say I would be very welcome there. And that life would be happy if I lived there.

36

Ella

The stress of not having an income was testing my limits. For the past two years, there had literally been no salary. Yes, of course, he was working. Very hard, in fact, each and every day, as well as traveling on weekends. But the company he was in bed with was not remotely profitable. Yet, they asserted "it was just a matter of time" and "patience" was of the essence. The six principals in the mix were convinced they had a good thing going and unanimously agreed to roll the dice. Some of their wives had jobs, some didn't, like us. I simply had too many children to find a decent job I was qualified for and pay a full-time babysitter. It didn't make any sense, and he adamantly argued that it wasn't necessary. They'd hit the jackpot very soon, he'd say. We had taken a second mortgage on the house to keep some of the creditors at bay for a little while. My patience was running thin with his attitude about it all. It was one thing to pinch pennies, entirely another to not have any to pinch.

I was accustomed to squeezing blood out of turnips and going without, but something I couldn't wrap my head around was not being able to provide Christmas for my children, even a meager one. Clearly, there was no money in the forecast this year. It had reached a place where there was no longer any point in keeping a budget. It had been stretched and diluted past the point of surplus. We were so far in the red, catching up wasn't in the realm of possibility. The rubber band of optimism had snapped and broken. Christmas had been a struggle ever since the older children had become aware of it, but when it did come, we usually managed to scrape up enough for Santa to make a stop.

Christmas, fickle as it tends to be, is deceptively merry, especially for children. They have no clue that Santa has parameters. I often reference the Christmases of my childhood and try to take a leaf from my mother's playbook. Whatever her failings, she was undeniably a holiday aficionado. She slaved at the sewing machine for months making doll clothes. She wrapped every little gift separately, from socks to lip gloss to toothbrushes. Sometimes there was not enough Scotch tape to finish the wrapping, and it was not unusual to get our fingers pricked from the straight pins holding the paper together. An abundance of tiny presents was her recipe for a successful Christmas morning. Another was to put only fruit and candy in the stockings, saving every little dollar doodad for maximum impact under the tree. I admired her for that. As modest as they were, my own Christmas mornings were magical.

These days the prospects were so bleak, I couldn't allow myself to think past the day at hand. I began to feel as drained as our checking account. I had learned to trudge through the days numbly and acquiescently, but after the stress of the past couple of years, it was almost impossible to dredge a speck of holiday hope. I couldn't fathom a Christmas more grim than the last. If only I could rip the December page off the calendar and make it January. There was no way I would think to ask anyone in the family for help, and I certainly wouldn't go outside of it. Between my father, sister, and friends, I'd used up my handout and hand-me-down allotments. The past couple of years had been so parched, the well was dust-dry.

I pasted on a nondescript expression and plodded through every day, trying to keep the children from sensing my despair. I didn't speak of the holidays, and I didn't mention our traditions. Despite rhetoric to the contrary, denial can be the wisest and most peaceful state of mind, and often the only avenue. Was I hoping a check would float down from the sky or that an unnamed benefactor would stuff a wad of cash into our mailbox? I had no such illusions. I had reached the point where hinting and begging were no longer feasible, even if I had been predisposed to it. Sadly, I learned for myself that there is a limit to goodwill, even from the most charitable of people.

There's actually a point when most individuals become weary of giving repeatedly, especially when they see no sign of reversal. It may be cynical, but I have learned there's actually a place where the exhilaration and satisfaction of benevolence and generosity flame out and crumble to ashes, or die on the giving vine. Being on the receiving end when that point is reached is downright humiliating, and I knew it had arrived for me. My pride had taken a thrashing and was scarred to the point of futility. What wasn't available to us just wasn't going to be, and probably would never be. That was my frame of mind.

David was nine and still pretty oblivious to the particulars of family finances. As long as his stomach was filled four or five times a day and he could play basketball or be taken to practice, he had no complaints whatsoever. In fact, his spirits seemed unusually buoyant where the upcoming holiday was concerned. He speculated several times a day as to what Santa might bring – a basketball, new sneakers, or one of the new Transformer toys. This expectation made me cringe and smile at the same time, because I knew he no longer believed in Santa at all.

Jenny was a different story. Three years older than David, and tall for her age, no one had to tell her what was up. She questioned me often as to what Christmas was going to look like this year, and so on. Lights on the house? A Christmas tree? Of course, I spread it on thick, and shamelessly reassured her. "We have that artificial tree in the attic – you remember the one. And we'll make some fun new bread dough ornaments like in the new *Better Homes and Gardens*. It will be so fun." Beyond the tree, I just sidestepped, pretending to be preoccupied. Or I simply dodged. I knew darn well this wouldn't placate her for long. She was becoming too savvy for that. One day a couple weeks before the holidays, she grabbed my arm and drew me into her bed-room, shutting the door secretively behind us. She proudly told me she had things for Christmas all figured out. Her blue eyes sparkled, and her long yellow ponytail swayed in excitement. She presented her well-thought-out plan. My heart quit beating as I turned my full attention to my young, naive, and expectant daughter. As the firstborn, Jenny had great maturity as well as experience. She was an excellent babysit-ter, very much in demand in our circles. She proudly revealed that she had been carefully setting aside her earnings. She had close to fifty dol-lars saved in her little gray boondoggled leather wallet, the one she had made at girls' camp, and it was now secreted away in her sock drawer. Her solution, she purported, was that she would be in charge of the shopping this year. She would purchase one nice gift for each of her siblings, one that she and I would plan carefully. I was deeply moved and hugged her as I gave her my blessing. When Jenny and I finished discussing her covert little scheme, I retreated to my own bedroom and shut the door. I plastered myself across the bed and shed tears at her thoughtful generosity. I was amazed at the budding character of my growing daughter, but I shed a few more with an aching in my heart.

Fifty dollars was quite a large sum – not enough to fill the tree skirt with gifts, of course, but it would be something rather than nothing. I had to keep telling myself that. I noticed, too, that after outlining her proposition, Jenny was walking a little taller, and her shoulders seemed a little broader. Her demeanor was calm and purposeful. Always confi-dent and intelligent, never wanting for friends, and flourishing at school, she even seemed a little perkier. I couldn't help being proud, in spite of my trepidation. In a short few days, it seemed Jenny had stepped confidently through the portal from child to young woman. She had calculated her way through a tough dilemma and was trium-phantly preparing to save Christmas for her struggling family.

Jenny and I left David home to watch the others and drove over to the mall, it wasn't far from our house. It was a rare occurrence that we went there nowadays – we hadn't been in ages – but with Christmas so close, it turned out to be a fun treat. This time of year, the mall is like walking through Disneyland, although none of us had ever actually been to Disneyland. The mall abounded in silver snowflakes, blue glitter balls, and red bows at every juncture. There were sky-high Christmas trees with long shimmering icicles dangling from their branches. They glimmered with flashing blue lights, and were adorned with large white organza bows, tied carefully into bunches. Bouquets of holly and ivy cascaded from their centers. The bottoms of the trees were skirted in yards and yards of sky-blue taffeta, which billowed out like puffy clouds. Each was laden with elaborate, yet obviously empty, silver packages tied with sparkly red bows. Everywhere you looked, all you saw was blue and silver, and a splash of red.

I'm always amazed how well the blatant commercial circus actually works. We all want to breathe in the enchanting spirit that attaches itself to the blaring intercom carols, which permeate the entire several-block area. It's so magically festive, we all but toss our better judgment to the wind. We're willing to throw our money into the air and say yes to every offering, because we feel hypnotized by the alchemy. Today the atmosphere was, indeed, glorious and infectious, and Jenny skipped, then galloped up and down the wide hallways, peering into almost every store window, leaving me breathless in the dust of her enthusiasm.

I stood back as best as I could, coaching every so often. I let Jenny pick out and pay for all the gifts. She chose a red, green, yellow, and blue Simon Says game for David. It was a little out of her budget range, but she knew he would be the most difficult to please and the quickest to be disappointed. For Beth, she carefully poured over the Barbie dolls, finally settling on one with a peaches n' cream dress, feather boa, and long blonde hair you could actually wash and comb. She bought a ten-inch red, white, and black Jetfire Autobot transformer for Luke. She just knew he would love it because he's drawn to anything he can take apart and put back together. She chose a Mister Potato Head for Andrew, complete with pink ears, black glasses, googly eyes, mustache, red nose, and hat. She could picture him pulling out the pieces and putting them back again for hours on end. She was right about that. For baby Jed, she bought a big red Hoppity Hop bouncy ball almost as big as he was, with a Mickey Mouse head for handles. She wasn't quite sure he'd be able to climb it to bounce, but she argued he was tall for his age. The money was all but gone, and Jenny had purchased nothing for herself. I watched her pick up and study a snow cone machine, but she put it back quickly and moved on stoically. I made a mental note; I would sell my fairly new electric curlers, if I have to. Jenny seemed self-satisfied and upbeat. She sauntered resolutely over to a bin of Silly Putty eggs and dropped two into the cart for herself. It's what I've been wanting, she said, with a grin.

I held to my promise and mixed up a large batch of ornament dough – basically a mixture of flour, salt, and water. I kneaded the dough and shaped it into soldiers, Raggedy Ann and Andy dolls, and snowmen. I admit, it was fairly artistic work, which I enjoyed. With the leftovers, I used a small heart-shaped cookie cutter and punched out about thirty small hearts. The dough was baked in a slow oven and cooled. I painted them carefully with different colors of craft paint. The children helped, but mostly watched, and were gratifyingly delighted with the new tree ornaments. The small hearts were painted red or white and decorated with pin dots in the opposite color. Andrew took only a few bites out of three of them, which was a Christmas miracle, in and of itself. The tree was magnificent, and it brightened my spirits each time I passed it. I was actually very thankful it turned out to be such a sunny spot for us all. Before bedtime, the children turned out all the lights but those on the tree, laid out their blankets or pillows, and sprawled under it for a little while, just looking up into it, or quietly reading their library books. Pure magic, I said to myself, and felt a surprising surge of cheerfulness. And a tiny spatter of hope.

Jenny's gifts had been carefully wrapped and hidden under the stairway in a large cardboard box. She had done all the wrapping herself and had used a large quantity of masking tape to go round and round the large box so it would be safe from prying little fingers and eyes. "Just to make sure," she said with a sly smile. She could hardly restrain her excitement, but I had no fears she would spill any beans. She was too intensely invested. I noted an interesting new smugness about her, and an added spring in her step. She was brimming with anticipation and counting down the hours until the day arrived. That is, until two evenings before it finally did.

It was Christmas Eve eve, and darkness crept across our windows like chestnut curtains. We had just finished a dinner of meatloaf, baked potatoes, and frozen peas. Andrew and Jeddie weaponized the peas with their spoons, and there were little green balls all over the floor, some of them smashed flat. I was scolding them and warning that they'd better pick up every pea or I'd send them to bed without reading their precious library books under the Christmas tree. The older kids made themselves scarce to avoid doing the dishes.

There was a hard racking at the front door, and one of the children ran and threw it open, despite my many admonitions to the contrary about that. We all turned our attention to the gaping doorway. There stood the infamous red suited, white bearded, rosy-cheeked guy himself. He was dressed from head to toe in a sort of shabby red velour suit. He had a long fake white beard that hung loosely from his jowls. His belly was authentically voluminous and bulging. He was holding an enormous black garbage sack in his large Home Depot gardening-gloved hand. I could see an unsubtle dusting of rouge on the apples of his cheeks and a little red lipstick smudged across his mouth. The eyebrows were uncharacteristically dark for Santa, but overall, he was a pretty good facsimile. All the blue eyes in the room got big and round, and gasping sounds emerged from every mouth. As for me, I was reeling with a couple of emotions. First, having a sub for Santa was not on my bucket list in any lifetime. As a kid, we lived through many times of scarcity, and never once did my parents ask anyone for anything. Second, I had absolutely no idea who this Santa was in real life. I studied his face, his features, and the nuances of his voice, but he was unrecognizable. I wracked my brain to figure out who would do this for our family and could come up with nothing but embarrassment.

Beth let out a scream from somewhere in the deepest depths of her little body. Her long curly blonde hair went flying, and she ran upstairs as fast as her legs could carry her. I found her huddled under one of the beds. Santa ho-hoed as realistically as he could, sounding a little like a congested frog. He scooped up the small children nearby into his bulky arms and held the older ones on his ponderous knee, after thunderously flopping down onto my sofa. I couldn't help but cringe. He explained the premature Eve's eve visit by saying his world gift-load was larger than usual this year, and he'd been forced to make a few early deliveries to ensure that everyone was taken care of. He hoped they'd understand. He reached into his scanty snug pockets and brought out large candy canes for each child. With a lopsided wink, he sternly instructed me in everyone's earshot, to keep the black garbage bag full of toys securely tied until after the children went to bed the next night. Then he ho-hoed a bit more. By now Beth was hiding behind me in the doorway, the trails of tears streaking her smooth little cheeks. I took her by the shoulders and gently nudged her forward. She reluctantly advanced and then willingly proceeded to perch on Santa's knee. She stared wide-eyed into his full, salt and pepper mustache, and studied his appropriately portly cheeks, which were smattered with the peony-colored blush.

Out of the corner of my eye, I spotted Jenny hovering in the kitchen, not joining the raucous laughter and excitement surrounding the Santa in the living room. She was standing with her back to the oven, her white-knuckled fingers gripping its long black handle from behind. It looked like she was trying to either shove it backwards into the wall or force it to hold her upright. Her jaw was clenched, and her face ashen. I sensed tears were being squelched, and anger swallowed down. My first thought was a question. Then it hit me like a ton of bricks. Duh. Why hadn't I realized it instantly? Santa and his clandestine helpers, in their generosity and charity towards our destitute family, were not resuscitating Christmas. They were out and out ruining it. At least for Jenny. Her carefully executed plan to save our Christmas had been foiled and stolen out from under her nose. She had no interest in the bulging bag of gifts, only in what it was doing to eclipse what she had so lovingly executed for her brothers and sisters.

One of the first random thoughts that bubbled up in my head was this: When you step into a more enlightened stage of life, as Jenny had recently done so gracefully, you become subject to the risks inherent and attached to the advanced state. Betrayal, disappointment, disenchantment, failure, and disillusionment are a few of the integral realities of moving away from innocence. It's a sad day when these intellectual concepts become actualities. They are worse than monsters in the closet any day of the week. I could see a dismal trail of disappointment marching darkly across Jenny's face as she stood against the stove.

I had no choice but to leave her there for the moment and continue my overly animated gestures of humility and gratitude for the gifts given in our destitution. It was something I had practiced a lot lately and had become very good at. Nowadays I was accustomed to smiling widely, being appropriately emotional (genuinely or feigningly), and acquiescing with appreciation when faced with a munificent offering. It was, of course, the acceptable expected response from one who requires handouts. Sometimes I wonder if the givers ever grant a second thought to the shame or humiliation it may cause the recipient. Probably not. I felt guilty being cynical when I should have been more genuinely meek and humble. But charity always trumps everything else, or so they say. Not always the case, perhaps, but now my understanding was much clearer as to Christ's admonition to not let the left hand know what the right was doing. Humble pie rarely slides smoothly and often gets caught in the gullet as it's choked down. Don't get me wrong; I was truly grateful. Really, I was. These people absolutely had the best intentions, and I appreciated it. I was just becoming so weary of being grateful.

After the hullabaloo subsided, Santa made a dramatic and sweeping departure. The big bag of gifts was stashed properly, and the children went to shower and get ready for bed. I decided it was time to go upstairs to check on Jenny. She lay curled in the fetal position on her white rose-vined bedspread. Her ankles were crossed and her pink painted toenails stuck out of an old woolly blanket. She wasn't crying or making any sort of fuss. She was just lying very still. I felt a knot pull itself tightly in my chest. The thought crossed my mind that less than a dozen years before, I used to watch her lie in a similar position with a calloused baby thumb in her mouth. A few dried tear tracks caked her still-velvet cheeks. I sat down by her side and gently laid a hand upon her back. I moved it up and down and back and forth lightly, as I had when she was little. As thought tumbled upon thought, I ventured to speak, hoping I might say something comforting and meaningful.

"I'm so sorry, Jenny. I understand how you feel. I do. You must be angry and disappointed. I don't blame you in the least. I'd feel the same. You need to know that you are not selfish and wrong for feeling that way. It's absolutely understandable. I get it. You're upset and annoyed by all that show of benevolence. I am so familiar with those feelings. We must not forget, though, that those people, whoever they are, mean well. They have goodness in their hearts, and we must try to appreciate that, at least. We would do the same for someone else in our position if given the chance. Especially now that we know what it's like to go without. You would be the first to step up, I know you would. This will turn out okay, I promise."

As much as I hate making promises to my children, which I know very well may come to naught, I do it without hesitation. That's what mothers do. They outright lie all the time, if there's a ghost of a chance it will make their children feel better or not be sad. We don't tell dangerous or damaging lies, nor do we lie just for the sake of lying. But we tell huge white whales when we need to. I went on. "Jenny, I need you to realize something I'll bet you haven't even thought of. I know what you did at great expense and generosity for your brothers and sisters, and for me. I'll never forget your unselfish act as long as I live, and I'm not the only one. You need to know that heaven keeps perfect records about these things as well. There are people who love you who do not live in this realm anymore. Unseen eyes have watched and recorded your lovely generous spirit and your sacrifice. I know it's not going to be the same Christmas as you and I expected, but it will be just as good or better. No one can take away from what you did. Please think about that, dear girl."

The dreaded and also much-anticipated Christmas Day made its grand entrance, as it always has before and ever will again. It seems it will never arrive soon enough to suit the children, and the adults will continue to hope it takes its sweet time. It's one of the chief mileposts in our lives, no matter what stage we find ourselves in; but it remains as certain as the sun's setting and rising.

This complicated year, it made its dramatic entrance on a clear, frost-shrouded morning, picture-perfect for a memory. It was still dark, but I could feel a little body stealthily squirming in close to mine under the covers I was cozily nestled in. It was Beth, and she couldn't wait even one more second for the jingle bells to start ringing. My bedside clock said a quarter to six. I pretended to be asleep, but she wasn't having it. She wrapped her little flannelled legs around mine and wiggled annoyingly until I gave up my pretense of unconsciousness. I shushed her a couple times and told her we should let the others sleep a little longer, that they'd be less grumpy, but before long I could hear shuffling noises in the hall. Other sleepy bodies were making their way, one by one, or two by two, to my bedroom. I knew it was all over now. No more catching any winks for me, though I'd been up till all hours. The excitement in the room was spreading like a rash. The giggles and whispers evolved rapidly into laughs and shouts. Okay, okay, I told them to wait a second while I went to the bathroom and brushed my teeth. I was stalling as long as I was able. I ran a quick comb through the tangles in the back of my hair. They all knew the Christmas morning drill, and when I came out, they were already lining up on the stairwell, one on each step, from youngest to oldest. It had been one of our longest-standing rituals on Christmas morning. "Merry Christmas everyone!"

I mock-chirped in my froggy voice. I pasted on my brightest smile, raised my eyebrows, and they all echoed back the salutation. The excitement was palpable, and when you think about it, it does add a context to 'it was like Christmas Morning.' As I pushed in front of them to lead from the lower stair, I could see skinny little legs sticking out of tight short pajamas, some were frayed at the bottom over ragged toenails. It was a rag tag bunch at this point in time, but who the heck cared on this day? Christmas was busily casting its enchanting spell over the entire household. Not the tiniest bit of gloom nor reticence would have half a chance. I admit I even felt quite cheerful. As Christmas dictates – no, commands – we began to indulge in its extreme merriment and over-the-top gaiety. Even if for only a morning. As soon as I took a downward step, they all stampeded like a herd of elephants down the stairs.

When we reached the living room, I slipped behind the chair to plug in the tree lights. I went to the Christmas village and lit that up, as well. I'd been looking at it all for several weeks now, but in the morning revelry, everything seemed to be ablaze. I could almost feel the electricity from all the lights pulsating through my veins. Indeed, it had to be the legendary magic of the ages taking over.

The kids surrounded the tree, plopping down here and there, awaiting the next ritual of the morning, the long-awaited opening of the presents. I admit the tree did seem overloaded with wrapped treasures, as usual. I was pleasantly surprised to sense that the children had all but forgotten the events of the strange previous evening. If some had not, they were doing a good job of faking it. Even Jenny seemed expectant. It was as if Santa, the real Santa, had wriggled his way down the chimney and scattered presents galore, all while the impatient reindeer waited on the rooftop. To make the excitement last longer, we had long since adopted another tradition. It was to open one gift at a time, while everyone else watched, employing anxious, but requisite patience, and a little feigned interest in the others. That has to be a good thing. Of course, a few of the younger ones made the occasional attempt to cheat and open two at a time, but they were censured sternly by the hard-liners. This definitely prolonged the crescendo of anticipation, and the older children had learned it was well worth the wait.

Obviously, no one had any idea which gifts had come from the big black garbage bag attached to the sloppily-gloved hand of the rouged faux Santa and the other more meager offerings, which must be there, as well. At this point, it simply didn't matter, because this was the real Christmas morning. I watched as each gift was opened, and I was closely observing Jenny as they were. She was mostly taciturn and silent as she looked on, except for a comment or two while opening a gift of her own. It became blatantly apparent as each child opened Jenny's personal gifts, however, that she had spectacularly hit each nail on the head.

David ripped open his Simon Says game and studied it for a few seconds. Then his face was awash with smug satisfaction just as if he had splashed it with water. We all knew he was thinking. He was looking forward to displaying his genius, later on in the day. As for Beth, she jumped to her feet, held her Barbie high in the air, and twirled in a circle, while shrieking her excitement. Luke immediately scrambled off to a corner by the fireplace and began engaging his new Transformer in a gun battle. Someone reminded him that he still had a couple presents to open. Andrew tore into his wrapping, pried open the box with Mr. Potato Head in it, and began poking the facial pieces into every hole, willy-nilly. The nose on the head, an ear on the mouth, and the mustache in one eye. Little Jeddie simply drug his deflated rubber Hoppity Hop over to me and demanded that I blow it up forthwith.

Jenny had kept her cool amazingly well all morning, not saying a word about her choices or her contributions. That is, until she unwrapped her Snowcone Machine. She had only a section of the paper torn off when she just stopped short and placed her hands back into her lap. She didn't move a muscle for a couple of seconds, and then she cut her eyes over at me like a knife blade. They were unreadable. Oh, no. Was she upset? Had I stolen her thunder or crossed an uncrossable line? She brushed a strand of blonde bang from her forehead and wrinkled her brow. Her lips tightened into a straight thin line and her teeth clamped down over her bottom lip. Just when I thought to be worried, her mouth eased into a knowing smile before opening to a full-blown grin. "Oh, Mom," she said, "how did you ever know? It's just what I've been wanting!"

I glanced around the room at the now-contented faces, engrossed in the enjoyment of their fun new gifts. Christmas, you crafty old fool. You always somehow get your way, don't you? You bring out the best in us. There was no doubt in my mind that Jenny's Christmas morning was a remarkable success. As was my own.

37

Ella

I t became clear that for a long time my marriage had been hanging by a thread, and I had not been able to hold on to the tiny slippery filament slipping faster and faster through my fingers. For many months I had been distraught, confused, and depressed about what was right or what was wrong. I believe the last little tattered piece of straw was pitched with the imminent devolution of my husband's company. He and the five other principal players in the struggling software company had held on hopefully and stubbornly for several years. At this point, I was way past being hopeful or sympathetic. All that mattered to me now was that they were not successful enough to feed, clothe, and sustain my family.

As a last-ditch effort, the principals decided the way to propel the dismal red numbers into the black was to obtain more capital. Conventional methods had failed, so they considered the most expedient way to achieve it was to acquire the equity from each family-owned home. It was strategically sound, they said, to "borrow" the cumulative sum for the greater good of the company, and the good of the families as well. They pronounced it brilliant, surefire, and righteous. Almost every single person involved agreed. That is, except me. I considered the reason to be my vulnerable indecisive state of mind. I stewed until my head throbbed. My heart hammered until I could literally look down and watch my blouse flutter. My stomach was queasy and inside-out most of the time. I tumbled through a dozen emotions as I went back and forth with the possible outcomes. I felt selfish, guilty, angry, self-pitying, defiant, and futile. I felt angry disdain for those who had put us in this precarious position. I was exhausted after the years of pinching poverty, on top of what we had been through with little Andrew. I felt like my brain was bleeding, and with that, I was being drained of clarity. On rare good days, I acknowledged that the proposal could be a positive thing to pull us out of the hole and give us a new beginning, both financially and in our marriage. Both had become critical. On the flip side, we could lose virtually everything we owned, and make it all significantly worse. I was doubting my husband's loyalty to me and the children. I was also doubting myself. If I were a better wife, wouldn't I muster one last leap of faith, a little more trust in my husband, and jump, as I had watched the other wives do, seemingly without question?

One warm, blustery day, as I was contemplating my purview of bleak choices, my husband appeared in the doorway in the early afternoon, which was a rarity. He said we had an appointment and we shouldn't be late. Surprised, because we rarely ever went anywhere together anymore except for church, I questioned him about why and where. He looked a little chagrined but remained silent. Okay, I shrugged, and got into the car. Perhaps it meant we were going to get money somewhere – a bank loan or such, as his demeanor seemed a little more confident. To my surprise, he drove just a short distance away to the home of the president of his company. Several years before, this man had been a trusted ecclesiastical leader in our church, one whom I had respected and admired. Upon reaching his home, I jumped from the car, ready to go in. The door shut behind me and I looked back, but he remained decisively in the car. He told me matter-of-factly he would return in a little while to pick me up. To say I was dumbfounded and confused would be an understatement. "You're not coming with me?" I bellowed, and not quietly. "He's your boss, not mine. I'm not going in there alone. Why would I possibly want to go in there? What's this unusual summit about?" I demanded with hostility. He smiled vaguely but assuredly, rolled up his window part way, put the car into gear, and drove away. I wasn't quite sure what I was supposed to do now, but I did know that walking up to the house in front of me was the only alternative, since I couldn't walk all the way home. So, I wiped the windblown strands of hair from my face, smoothed down my rumpled dress, squared and shrugged my shoulders, and marched up to the front door. I didn't know what else to do but ring the bell.

Our friend and bedfellow in debtor's prison answered the door with a wide grin as if he hadn't laid eyes on me in years. He was a wide, squarish man, but not pudgy. He had thick, obstinate, dark hair, which stuck up like a bristled brush, in spite of his little dab of Brylcreme. He had a face to match his body in profile. It was wide and fleshy, yet handsomely angled. He wore wide-legged jeans a little too high above his worn-out white sneakers. His eyes were wide-set and dark brown, and his brows looked to have a smidgen of Brylcreem in them as well. He gave me a swift little one-armed half hug and welcomed me heartily inside. "How nice to see you, Ella. You're looking so well. The wife and I speak of you and your family often. We miss you guys. How are the kiddos?" How compassionate of you, I thought sarcastically, not saying a word. I wanted to rage and confront, but of course, I would not have. I wanted to ask what business it was of his how we were doing. He knew darn well we were stretched beyond any sort of reasonable limit and had been for years. He was aware we couldn't buy groceries without being humiliated, pay our bills, or even think of buying the basic school clothes for the upcoming year. We were always in need of all sorts of essentials, which I had simply quit expecting to have. I was watering down the dish soap and the shampoo, and every single towel was frayed. Why in the world was he asking the questions he obviously knew the answers to? I was certain his family was living the same austere life we were. He deserved no answer, but I didn't say that, either, so

I kept my mouth buttoned. He led me to a couple of blue velvet wing-back chairs grouped closely together so you could speak and see eye to eye. I wasn't comfortable in this position with him. With my hands folded in my lap, I began picking at my fingernails while surreptitiously glancing around the room at the same time, looking for signs of impoverishment.

I looked at him directly, my eyebrows raised, as if to shriek, "Go ahead, tell me what you really want!" I suspected the point of this strange meeting was to tell me something earthshaking that couldn't be conveyed by my own husband. He continued the prattle about our families for a short time and then stopped for what seemed like an entire minute. Without any more chitchat, he looked me in the eye and launched his attack missile. It hit me broadside, and very soon into the conversation, I knew I would lose this battle and indeed become a sinking ship.

He spoke highly about everyone involved in the company. He spoke of character and integrity, selflessness, sacrifice, investment, hopes and dreams, diligence and focus, and of course, the beloved families. He spoke of the company's lofty goals and that when it did succeed – he reiterated when, not if – it would be a boon to the community and to technology in general. It was a brilliant scheme just waiting for the right application. It was, veritably, a sure thing. It would take just a little more time, a little more patience, and a lot more faith from us all. Faith in the dutiful husbands, faith in the process, and just plain old faith in the highest of powers.

By the time he wound down, I must admit that I had allowed him to fill my sails with much needed wind. I had been running on empty for so long. I felt like a sponge wrung dry from so many recent hardships. Little Andrew, lingering poverty and burgeoning debt, the burden of children with little or no support, continual fear, anxiety, and weariness. As I listened to his skillful and powerful pep talk, I realized I was anxiously soaking in these sure bets and positive outcomes as fast as I could gulp them down. His words were like cool water to dry, cracked desert soil. I suppose there were just too many cracks in my own life at this point. I simply couldn't resist his arguments, and more than that, I didn't want to. I had allowed him to persuasively talk me into doing what they all had asked me to do in the first place – relinquish my home equity into the hands of the company, which was literally all I had left in the world monetarily.

And so, when my husband returned to retrieve me like an errant child who had been in urgent need of some straightening out, as well as a little chastisement, I was meekly repentant. I told him I would agree to the arrangement for the home equity loan and that I had been mollified of my doubt. I actually apologized for my constant questioning of him and his motives. He was, of course, jubilantly triumphant.

Yet, in spite of my sudden change of heart, I didn't settle down like I thought I would. I continued to waffle. I procrastinated, avoided, wept, wavered, and stewed. I didn't voice my concerns to anyone, although I really should have. I was waiting, and I knew how silly it was, for a sign to drop out of heaven down onto my head. If we were to exhibit the faith our friend had schooled me on, wouldn't that be reasonable? Just a little slip of paper which had a simple "yes" or "no" written upon it. I held my tongue and continued to delay until all the documents for the loan had been prepared and everything was in place to move forward.

Then one day without any warning whatsoever, I bailed. I simply said no. "I can't and I won't do it. I cannot wager my children's home or last shred of security on this risky gamble." Something deep inside me had risen up like a titan and held fast and sure. That was that. My fears had conquered everyone else's reasoning, and I would not listen to any more from anyone. Surprisingly, my husband didn't say one word to me. He didn't argue, and he didn't get angry. For the most part, he stayed busy and absent. There was complete quiet in the house for days. Neither of us said anything at all but brushed past one another like furniture. There was only uncomfortable, unbearable, and screaming silence.

Then the pressure cooker top began to jiggle a little, and then a lot. I could never have guessed the aftermath of my defiant independent decision. It was a hailstorm of coercion and shame. First one, then another of all those involved came to visit me. The husbands and even the wives, and a couple of elderly parents. Still no word from my husband, but a whole lot of rhetoric from everyone else. First, they came to look at me pitifully, sympathetically, and supportively. They smiled and were kind and understanding. They reasoned, cajoled, tried to see my side, and so on. And when that didn't change my mind, they got nasty. They berated me and told me I would ruin things for everyone. How could I, they harangued? They had thrown their children's welfare into the pot, and a couple of them, their aging parents. I began to feel like a pariah and plain old burnt toast. I did have some second thoughts, and often I felt like the dark black villain in this drama. In the end, however, I wanted only to cover my head and bolt the door.

It took about three weeks for me to regain a bit of balance, attempt the status quo, and try to move on. Move on to where, was the question front and center. As it turned out, this had been the true turning point for me. Staying in the marriage for highfalutin and high-minded reasons, as in the past, obdurately lost its footing. The whole darn cliff fell in one loud thud. In the whole messy state of affairs following my outrageous self-centered decision, my husband had been strangely aloof and totally absent during the pressure visits from his cohorts. It was as if he had intentionally allowed everyone but himself to administer the punishment, turn the screws, and thus, I reasoned, escape culpability for all of it. Yet his position had always been crystal clear. I was alone in my martyrdom now and realized that I had been isolated for a very long time. This was the last and hardest blow, as well as the most clarifying. In the end, it was the proverbial straw that broke the back of my marriage. Clearly, I reasoned, I had been a mother on the dole with six young children for a long time now. How much worse could it get with divorce?

38

Ella

There was considerably more going on in my complicated life than just Andrew's health problems. I was separated for almost six months and divorced for six more. There had been little or no money trickling into the household for three years before the separation. I had not been able to pay the bills or buy food, clothing, or gasoline. I was weary and desperate. I tried to find a job, but with six young children, the pickings were slim. I walked the mall and filled out applications on a regular basis but found nothing that would earn enough to offset the cost of a babysitter.

I held on to the marriage as long as I could, as is so often the case, for the sake of the children. Yet, the reality was that my husband and I had been ghosts haunting the same house for a long time, walking around and through each other. We no longer had voices for quarreling.

The long journey had taken a heavy toll. The stress of managing a house full of children without income and keeping it together emotionally was difficult. I felt numb, almost zombie-like, and heaved myself through the days as if plodding through thick mud. It became difficult to keep track of time, and the days bled together in a cloud. I began to worry about my own stability and wondered if this was what having a breakdown might look like. I was ordinarily level, organized, firm, and decisive, but not these days. I had heretofore seen those qualities as my strengths. I used to move purposefully and resolutely, getting things done efficiently, even under duress. But now I'd walk into a room and completely forget why or what I had come to do. I'd stand and scratch my head and feel like an eighty-year-old battling dementia. I dragged myself though the hours with heavy limbs, often hanging on by only a fingernail. I was questioning my lifelong notion of not being in the least bit fragile.

I recall watching my mother puddle in an exhausted and over-whelmed heap at almost any bump in the road. She wasn't one to exhibit much patience or stamina when trouble came knocking at our door. She let my father shoulder the emotional burdens. I suppose that was in their contractual agreement. I always resented her lack of forti-tude. At the core, I believed she felt like a victim of her circumstances. Yet, when I look back, I'm inclined to be kinder and cut her a bit more slack. I don't think I gave her credit for the little control she had over her life. Yet, as a girl, it was distressing to watch your mother fall apart, give up the reins, and retreat, like an adult must never do. In my imma-ture assessments of things, I judged her and blamed her unhappiness on what appeared to be her weakness. Yet now I was doing exactly the same, struggling to stay on my feet. I moved ahead torpidly, not really caring whether it rained or shined. Some days I let the stress trickle out in droplets of tears as I traipsed through the hours. There was often mascara smudged across my cheeks. Other days, I just sat in a chair and wept until I could move forward. My predominant thought, how-ever, was "How can I not keep going?" My resolve was leveraged by the six other souls who were counting on me. Clearly, my stability was paramount to their well-being. That awareness actually kept me from giving up and puddling in a heap myself. There was nothing I wouldn't do for them. I had no other option than to keep engineering the train calmly down the tracks. For their well-being, I had to remain func-tional. They were mine to shepherd and mine to protect. I could not possibly let go of the ledge and let myself plummet. If I fell, they'd surely tumble with me.

Letting go of the marriage was difficult for both of us. It took years before I realized that from the very beginning, we were focused on different goals. He, on his business ventures, and I, on the children and the house. We didn't stop to assess the consequences of our separate paths in time to avoid the fatal crossroads. We both assumed the paths were leading in the same direction and were taken off-guard by the alarming fork in the road.

In three years, the income had, except sporadically, virtually ceased. In the beginning, I was hopeful things would turn around, as was he. He pledged a certain and positive outcome, and I did not doubt his intentions. He continually begged for my patience, and for a while, I succeeded in offering it.

As per my nature, I was determined to set a plan in motion to get us through. The first step was to sharply cut back on everything. I dipped into our emergency basement food storage. We had plentiful basics – buckets of wheat, rice, beans, pasta, powdered milk, sugar, and flour. I had collected those essentials for years. I pored over my recipe books and tried to come up with meals made only with those staples. I began to grind my own flour and doggedly baked a dozen loaves of whole-wheat bread every single week. The bread was moist, delicious, and perfect for toast and sandwiches. The kids didn't seem to mind in the least. What little money I could scrape up went for a few fruits and vegetables.

Store-bought diapers and wipes became a thing of the past. I resorted to cloth diapers, which I purchased in bulk at JCPenney. I kept a diaper pail in the bathroom filled with water, detergent, and a little bleach. With both Jed and Andrew in diapers – Andrew showed no signs yet at all of being potty-trained – the diaper routine was predominant. As soon as I arose, I emptied the pail into the washing machine. I rinsed and spun, washed, and carefully bleached each load before drying them. Then came the endless folding. Third by third, stacked in neat piles. I bought a few clearance towels at Fred Meyer and cut them into six- by six-inch squares, zigzagging the edges on my sewing machine. They were sanitized with the diapers. My bathroom countertop was lined with clean folded diapers and piles of terry cloth wipes. The rubber pants that kept the cloth diapers from leaking grew rigid and inflexible from the heat of the dryer, and the boys sounded as if they had candy wrappers stuffed into their pants as they toddled around the house. But all this rigmarole saved a lot of cash for where it could be used more. About once a month, I'd get up to find a giant box of Pampers on my doorstep with no mention of a benefactor. I'd look shyly from side to side, but not so long that I couldn't retreat quickly into the house, diapers in hand, happy and grateful.

When things got dire, which they did on a regular basis, I didn't even have pocket change for necessities. My dreaded and final recourse was to make a trip to the local outdoor drive-in theater, where in good weather, a regular food pantry was set up for the poor. It was open on Wednesday and Saturday afternoons.

Hesitant to resort to this, I had to work up to it. I had to think through all the reasons why it was necessary and, also, acceptable. I reassured myself that it was doubtful I would run into anyone I knew. By necessity, I took a couple of children. Not only could I not afford a babysitter, I needed the extra hands to carry the goods I would, hopefully, be given.

Smiling, charitable people accustomed to every sort of humble down-and-out folk and the occasional take-advantage type adroitly concealed any air of condescension or pity. It was difficult, however, not to detect some obfuscated glances in my direction. I knew I did not fit the profile. I appeared too well off to be here, basically begging. The children were well clothed and kempt. I, myself, was fairly well dressed and polished. Not enough time had elapsed for my clothes to get too shabby. No one spoke a word to me, and I was relieved. Everyone simply smiled kindly and appeared to be very happy I had come. No judgment; only charity and goodwill. With my children in tow, I stood patiently in the various lines. I was more than grateful to be handed a large block of cheese, a few pounds of butter, a large bag of potatoes, and several dozen eggs. Sometimes there were fresh vegetables as well, which I gathered abundantly as discreetly as I could. As I wandered through the lines behind many sorts of people, most of which I could not relate to, I did my best to withhold judgment. How could I judge? I was at a place in life I never thought in a million years to be, and yet I was. I realized that many share the same underprivileged boat, for one surprising or unimaginable reason or another. At the same time, I found it almost impossible to hold my head high and not look at the ground. My children, on the other hand, seemed totally at ease, oblivious to any negative nuance. They ran around, laughed, struck up new friendships, and played. I could almost feel the pride being sucked from my body like those distorted heat waves rising up from the hot blacktop in the afternoon. After a few trips, though, I grew accustomed to the drain, and my main emotion was humble gratitude for the generous augmentation to our scanty resources.

Each month for four or five months, my father met me at the local grocery store where he was employed and generously paid for my groceries. I took a carefully edited list, so as not to waste his money on unnecessary items. I was amazingly appreciative of his generosity. My tears dripped as I pushed my cart through the aisles. As had always been the case, he was the one who came to the rescue. He was kind, stoic, and willing to do this for me, but each time it became a little more apparent that this was not doing him any good; for his pocketbook or his pride. I could tell he was torn. On one hand, he wanted to help his grandchildren and me, but on the other, he felt he was enabling my husband's inability to step up and support his family. This was meant to be stop-gap, not indefinite. Finally, I found I could not choke down any more charity from him or anyone else, so I went to the state county building to cash in on the welfare system.

As with the food lines, it was something I never thought, in my wildest dreams, would be my lot. I had always been critical of those, in my mind, who milked the system for support and were not self-sufficient. It went against the grain. My parents would never have resorted to such an idea. But it was done, and the people there were supportive and sympathetic. After hearing my plight, they generously encouraged me to take what was allowed from the system. It solved so many problems. I could actually begin to pay my delinquent mortgage payments and in-arrears utility bills. I could put food on the table for every meal. It was such a relief, it felt like Christmas every single day. I couldn't believe the change in my well-being and state of mind. I was calm and patient with the kids. I could breathe more deeply and take longer baths. I wasn't always looking over my shoulder and avoiding phone calls from solicitors. The heavy burden I had been carrying for so long had, thankfully and drastically, been lightened. I began to understand the notion of caring for people who cannot care for themselves.

There was, however, a significant downside. I was now forced to drag my brood of children through the grocery store checkout line and plop down every single food stamp to be examined and stamped, while flanking customers looked on curiously. Some people politely turned their heads pretending not to notice, but others watched interestedly or self-righteously, as each was imprinted with the appropriate black rubber stamp of approval. It sounded to me like a gavel being pounded mercilessly onto the cash counter, dizzily reverberating arbitrary judgment. Several times the cashier rejected a certain item with a superior expression, saying it was not on the approved food stamp list. I felt my face flush crimson as I meekly and embarrassingly handed back the item, while my children looked on, perplexed. How dare I try to pull the wool over the system's munificent eyes? After all, I was in their debt. On shopping days, after all the food was safely squirreled away, I usually went to my bedroom, closed the door, threw myself across the bed, and cried my eyes out.

39

Ella

The days leading up to the divorce from my first husband were a blur. Each single step was sliding gradually and smoothly forward, however, like an elevator inescapably moving to the next floor.

One sweltering August evening, I made the usual plans to pick my husband up from the airport at the conclusion of one of his multitudinous sales trips. I couldn't understand how he could just book a flight and disappear, with the rest of us left at home with no milk in the fridge and a quarter in my wallet. He'd often depart with our old car's gas tank all but empty. When it was time for me to pick him up, I'd remind him that in order to get all the way back home, it would be necessary to stop for gas, which was never a lie. It was a regular routine, one I always dreaded, except for the forced refueling. It gave me just a drop of comfort to know I wouldn't be left completely without transportation until the next time, as it usually kept me going through the next week.

That night, like many before it, I packed all the children into the old brown Woody station wagon. I never paid much attention to the scrapes and dents, but the balding tires, inoperative air conditioning, and 120,000-mile mark on the odometer worried me every single time we loaded up. This evening, I arrived at the airport and herded all the children (there were five at the time) into the terminal like a mother duck with her ducklings toddling behind. We walked what felt like two miles to gate "Umpteen E." I had to clamp onto Andrew's wrist and drag him along as he looked hither and thither, of course waiting for the slightest chance to escape and run into oblivion. Finally, we made it to the gate, and I got them situated in five plastic seats – not together, but close enough. I was startled to hear my name booming loudly across the public intercom system. I ran to a wall booth and took the call. It was my husband letting me know that he had inadvertently missed his flight and couldn't get another until morning. Of course, I thought wryly. After I have come all this way with the ducklings. By now, though, I was in "whatever worse can happen, will" mode. Downcast and worn out, I wearily drug the wily and whiny children back through the maze of concourses and out to the old car. Even in the shade of the parking garage, its interior felt like we had stepped into an oven. We quickly rolled down every window and started for home. I must admit, I was not all that surprised when about halfway home on the interstate, the car began to glide to a stop. I knew we were unambiguously out of gas. With an acquiescent shrug, I guided the car smoothly onto the shoulder.

I left everyone but ten-year-old David in the car. I could see no other way out of this mess except to walk down off the interstate ramp to find help. I sternly instructed the other children to keep the windows cracked for a little air flow in the sweltering heat, but I was mostly worried about their safety. I asked Jenny to hold a bottle in the crying baby's mouth. She looked annoyed. It took almost more than I had in me to plaster on a calm and unperturbed face, which was a total deception right down to my shoes and socks. It was the kind of propaganda mothers are good at dishing out, especially when it's a misrepresentation they must sell in order to not scare the heck out of their children. This was one of those times, times ten. I will be back right away, I promised with an air of detachment and a wave of my hand. Just sit tight. Don't worry. This won't take long. They all looked terrified, in spite of my prevarication. I smiled faintly one last time. I took David's hand tightly in my own and began to trudge down the extremely long off-ramp. The sun was just receding below the western mountains, and twilight was swiftly approaching. The stress, the heat, the exhaustion, and the fear for my children alone in the car on the side of the freeway in the sizzling heat, began to press in on me like a hot anvil. The anxiety and weariness bubbled into my throat, and all of the sudden I felt the weight of many difficult days heaving me like an avalanche down a mountainside. I was being mowed down in its path. Unbidden tears sprung from my eyes, but like a dam with too many holes to plug, I couldn't hold them back. First, I began to sob. Then my body began to shake, and my voice become a wail. It was really more of a howl. Everything had been bottled up so long. This march down the freeway ramp served as the proverbial last straw. All I could do at this moment was let it overflow like pot of boiling water. I yowled loudly for about thirty full seconds.

As I continued the outburst, I happened to glance down at my ten-year-old David's upturned ashen face. His hand was still locked to mine. His expression was one of astonishment and terror. His blue eyes were as large as saucers, ablaze with horror and other unfathomable emotions. His full pouty lips were quivering. Oh, my goodness, what in heaven's name am I doing? It was as if someone suddenly and swiftly hit me in the head with a paddle and caused me to regain consciousness. I shut off the tears like a running faucet and turned off the sounds emanating from my throat as if turning a dial on a radio. I wiped my eyes quickly with my clammy hands, brushed them across my old brown and white dress, and stared down at him. There were a thousand questions in his innocent young face. I pursed my lips together tightly, attempted and sort of accomplished, a convincing smile, and just kept walking.

When we reached the road below the off-ramp, I fortuitously spotted a Chevron gas station on the corner a block up the street. Just seeing it made my legs feel lighter and the heat less oppressive. The sixth baby in my belly was heavy and tipping me forward. The station's facade of blue striping and red and blue chevrons had never seemed so welcoming. I quickly noticed a pay phone and headed straight for it. I knew I had no money, but I dug through my wallet to see if, by chance, I had one last dime. Thankfully, there was one swimming around in the bottom of my purse. But just one. I knew I was not thinking things through. Not being prepared was becoming my standard these days. When my husband traveled, I often had no cash or change. There were times I felt like the kids really needed and deserved some sort of treat to brighten up the austerity of our days. Our Wednesday evening ritual had long consisted of going to the library, where each child was allowed to choose ten books to check out and take home. We'd finish off the night with ice cream. We had been skipping the ice cream part for a long time. Nowadays, I usually took them home and mixed up a couple quarts of Kool-Aid instead.

Now feeling relief trickle down my neck instead of just sweat, I started to stick the dime into the slot. I paused a few seconds to consider and then took the leap. I dialed my father-in-law, who lived a couple of cities to the south. Their phone rang and rang, and just as I was about to hang up and retrieve my dime, he answered groggily. When I explained the situation as resolutely as I could, and as humbly, he paused to do his own considering. Then a little gruffly, he said they had retired early, he was sorry, and would I mind terribly calling someone else this time. I swallowed down my disappointment, offense, and annoyance, and forced myself to be polite. "Of course. Not a problem." I slammed the receiver down a little too quickly and loudly, hoping to send the message that this was about his own grandchildren, not to mention my ridiculous predicament. I must admit, my irritation lingered a long time afterwards, and I never totally forgave him.

Now my dime had vanished, and I wondered what my options were. I thought about the children back in the sweltering car. I looked over at David, standing close by. He was distracted, watching the customers pump gas. He looked much less anxious now, but I could only imagine his ten-year-old apprehension. For the moment, he was distracted and calm, and I knew the reason was that he trusted his mother to solve the problem. Resolutely, I strode up to a couple of men and women standing near the storefront. I forced a determined smile and cheerily asked if anyone had a dime I might borrow to make a call. Appraising my bulging belly and glancing at David as he fiddled with his sweaty T-shirt, they smiled back. They were kind and pleasant, and I succeeded in appropriating another dime. This time I called a friendly neighbor, who happily came to retrieve our parched and wilted little brood from the scorching August interstate.

40

Ella

One chilly October afternoon, there was a brisk double knock at the front door. Tap, tap, quiet, tap, tap. Offhandedly, I opened it, expecting the unwelcome face of a solicitor or random child asking to play. I was a little surprised to be standing face to face with a tall, large-boned woman bundled up in a gray tweed coat. There was a short burgundy plaid scarf knotted around her throat. She was not exactly pretty, but rather, handsome. I looked beyond to observe a conservative gray compact car hugging the curb. The forty-something woman stood erect and rigid. A Mona Lisa smile was pasted upon her face like a kitschy campaign button. She paused a few seconds, tilting her head analytically. She attempted to hide the fact with a casual scratch to her neck with a knuckle. She asked for me by name, so I ushered her into the house, where she stood auspiciously just inside the door. She made no attempt to advance further and seemed reticent to identify herself directly. I couldn't help but notice that she was perusing the entire scope of the living room and kitchen, her eyes succinctly spanning the detail. Finally, she turned to face me. I'm certain she didn't miss the fact that my own eyebrows were lifted, and my own head querulously cocked. Finally, she identified herself. Rather icily, she explained that she was a representative from Child Protective Services and was here because of a complaint, one she was obliged to address. A rather serious one, she indicated. She went on to reveal that a neighbor had phoned their office out of kindest concern. The complaint, she recounted, was that my small boy was wandering the streets unattended, likely resulting in accident or jeopardy. He was, the neighbor reported, trudging up and down the street morning and afternoon, unsupervised. The upstanding citizen was expressly concerned for his safety, and also alarmed at his mother's negligence. This unnamed person intimated there were so many children under this roof that the single mother possibly was not able to pay proper attention. I took a breath, and let that sink in. Titanic angry heat began to rise to my cheeks from some spontaneously ignited fire inside. I was also extremely embarrassed. My face felt like it was flashing on and off like a neon sign. How dare she? I'm not sure why I surmised she, not he. Probably a nosy, snooty, high-minded Stepford mother with only one or two manageable children. How noble and courageous of her! This is beyond belief, I thought indignantly! I am nothing if not a good and attentive mother, and my son was not, and had never been, in danger. But I said nothing yet, as I was frantically assembling my arsenal. I was slso infuriated that this kindly, unnamed, self-righteous person had not simply come to me personally, but rather, had the audacity to call the government to come scold me.

With my eyebrows now furled and my mouth pinched, I calmly asked the woman to sit. I motioned to an apple green, somewhat threadbare wingback facing the sofa. She smoothed her rough-textured skirt, closing her knees tightly. She placed her sturdy black-shoed feet flatly upon the carpet. I also sat down. I plopped myself a little heavily on the sofa across from her, my hands laced defiantly in my lap. I took a deep breath and proceeded judiciously to consider my words. I knew better than to display hostility or indignation. After all, this was serious business and there could be terrible ramifications if I lost this battle.

Obviously, the woman would be expecting excuses and justifications. She probably heard them all day long. I realized it was critical that I gather myself enough to speak carefully and evenly. I must be persuasive enough to present a defensible case.

It was not difficult to look directly into her piercing black eyes. I did not blink or look away. I suspected this was a bit unexpected and disorienting. It was exactly my intent. I spoke quietly but confidently. I gazed off into the distance and began my long, drawn-out story, beginning with Andrew's birth. I detailed the early ear infections, reciting in detail the two years with the neurosurgeon, the hearing deficiency, and the growing concerns about his attention span. I went on to describe the process of speech therapy, the hearing aid fiasco, and I ended dramatically with the resulting correctional surgery for his hearing. Then it was my turn to reiterate my sensitivity for Andrew's need to get out and explore his world, thus freely admitting the episodes of escape and wandering. I reiterated my hypervigilance in regard to his safety.

"Miss," I said emphatically, as I looked straight into her hooded eyes, "my child has special needs, yes. Of course, he has. But I am inordinately capable and confident enough to address and deal with them. He is my priority. My ear is always attuned to the sound of a door closing, my eye is constantly trained to span the view of the street, and on innumerable occasions, I have literally run out to gather up my little boy. Never at any time has he been in any danger. And besides, who could you ever find that would love him more than I do?" I am certain the woman could see my hands shaking and hear my voice quivering. But I think, too, she could see that it was not out of weakness. It was passion and strength.

The woman sat very still. It appeared that her knees and feet were glued together. She studied my firm expression and resolute posture. Her demeanor seemed to have shifted, but I was still too off balance to guess which way. Once again, she scanned the rooms in her periphery quite unambiguously, and then stared down at her lap for what seemed five minutes, yet was probably much less. She looked up at me, and when she did her countenance had dramatically eased. The corners of her mouth were relaxed, her eyes were soft and earnest. She spoke kindly, "You do understand that these visits are not entertainment for me. They are my job and they must be done. For every well-managed home I encounter, I find three that are not adequate or are downright unhealthy. There are some very dire situations out there, but this, thankfully, is not one of them. I see and understand your dilemma with Andrew, and I also think it would be a tragedy for you both if he were to be removed from your care. I have ascertained that your household is very much in order and positively conducive to Andrew's special needs." Then she caught me off guard. "Keep up the good work and try to not be overly concerned with the opinions of others who have not had the experience to empathize. Thank you for allowing me into your home. I believe there will be no need for further visits." She stood up quickly, pulled her already secure scarf a bit tighter around her sturdy neck, and smoothed her coat.

"Wait," I stammered. "Could you possibly tell me who it was that called your office? It's important to me, and I would like to know."

The woman looked at the floor, then back to me, and said quickly, "It was one of the neighbors at the end of this circle. That's more than I should say. But as I said before, don't worry about it. They don't understand." With that, she walked briskly out to her little gray getaway car at the curb. In an instant she was gone. I stood in the open doorway watching her drive down the block, and I felt my muscles slacken as if I had reached the finish line of a marathon. I turned to look at the end of the circle where we lived. It was immediately apparent which neighbor had called the dogs on me. Of course, it was the pretty blonde woman about my age who had righteously given birth to only two perfectly behaved children – a beautiful blonde boy and a tiny perfectly dressed girl. It was "my friend," who held her ponytailed head high and spoke condescendingly to me at church or in the grocery store.

41

Ella

Being on my own wasn't much of an adjustment. It was akin to shaking tepid bathwater off my hands and plunging them into lukewarm dishwater. Same temperature, different basins. In reality, I had already felt solitary after the first few days of marriage. I had often gone to sleep at night and woken in the morning feeling I had slept in the bed alone. There was no one ever rapping on the door of my inner sanctum. In good times, we had waltzed around each other as if the furniture might be knocked over if we weren't careful.

There were many confrontations, and to be honest, I initiated the majority of them. We fought about anything I could think of to get his attention. I suppose I wanted some – no, any – real communication. It was as if he wasn't interested enough in me or our family to be present. Provoking him wasn't really effective, of course. Truthfully, even when we fought, we didn't connect. At the time, the dissention wasn't deliberate and it wasn't the aim, but I now realize that I instigated arguments for the express purpose of making contact. Arguing was a form of intimacy, however ineffectual. When I goaded him into a squabble, his usual mode was to take the high road and ignore me, which apparently is the more adult way to behave. Admittedly, I did start the fights. He would roll his eyes, walk away, or not react at all, which triggered more anger and confrontation on my part, not less. I felt irrelevant, and that seemed intolerable. It also served to spotlight me as the inferior person or the one with a problem. In the end, it was futile to engage anyway; there was still no connection. It was like fighting with a phantom.

Our marriage hadn't really been what you'd call a partnership. It was more of a corporation. Our unspoken contractual agreement dictated that he bring home the bacon, which he did until things got sticky at work, and I manage the day-to-day parenting, caretaking, and nurturing. Interesting how couples cull the roles and then stick to them as if they are etched in blood, even if they are not what they really want or need. I became accustomed to carrying the load of the family, physically and emotionally. No matter what balls were in the air, my position on the field was quarterback. Except occasionally, the complications were mine to deal with; illness, injury, upset, scheduling, school, homework, or activities. I was the allocated but willing sentinel. It became a lonely and demanding post.

I felt compelled to conduct the orchestra, and yet felt guilty about it. It was like taking the credit and the bows while he stood on the sidelines playing the tambourine. Things were off balance. From the outside, it would appear that I was excluding him from the symphony; but from my conductor vantage point, he often didn't enter the auditorium. I continually stressed that it was my fault things were out of sync. Based on my limited experience, I tried to hypothesize. Was I modeling a father who never knew a father? Or my grandmother, who didn't have a husband? Was I endeavoring not to be my mother? Or was it what I observed to be his mother's indulgence or his father's business-like indifference? Was I too controlling? Most likely. Control was part of my nature, not his, yet someone had to steer the family ship away from icebergs. Was he too laid back, or did I take too much space? If I had expected more or insisted on his participation, would it have made a difference? I could never quite orient myself to the root. Then again, when two people are like oil and water, isn't it quite predictable there will not be amalgamation?

In the end, I knew I'd been grasping. On a deep visceral level, I had always known where the real problem lay. After only a month of marriage, I had run home to my dad and tearfully disclosed that I could not endure the union. The disconnect had been there from the very beginning, even without household and children. Being who he was, instead of counseling or comforting, my father put his head in his hands, elbows on the table. He was quiet for what seemed an eternity. Then he firmly told me to accept what was a "done deal" and he sent me home.

It took being divorced to realize that from the first day or two of marriage we had not fused, united, or aggregated on any substantive level. We had little physical or emotional intimacy. We were, in essence, trapped solo. In my heart, I knew this was the real glitch, and that if it could have been repaired, we might have remedied the other problems. Without early effectual professional help, the dagger was plunged too deep to ever wrench out. But who really knows for certain? Assuredly, not I.

I do know that life's obstinate and relentless days repeat, no matter what tragedy has occurred in the previous one. The sun comes up and goes down, and those twenty-four hours either don't know or care. The shadows still move across the streets and the houses where people eat their granola, brush their teeth, and move ahead with their daily routines – sometimes in a daze, sometimes in frantic percussion.

I kept the house pretty immaculate, made peanut butter sandwiches by the truckload, took the children to the library every Wednesday evening, and read bedtime stories. I foggily adhered to my routines as if they were what kept us all alive. They became the ordinances which redirected me from things I might regret. From the hot cocoa I savored every morning to washing the countertops and bleaching the wash, the small steps of my life marched in the same direction with little or no change. I was grateful for the grind. I usually slept as if drugged. I had no fear of being the only adult in the house, day or night. The sacrosanct rituals kept my world from tipping off its axis.

I was surprised, and also relieved, that the children were not flummoxed by the divorce, or seemed not to be. I waited tenuously for an earthquake or hurricane, but they did not come. There was flow, but no ebb. Like mine, the children's routines rolled along predictably, steadily, and smoothly. I was astonished at the fluidity of moving from two parents to one. Perhaps it would come later, I worried. You hear such horror stories. Yet for now, they seemed to be thriving. School, activities, and church. If they were floundering, I did not perceive it. I kept watch vigilantly. I wondered if when they grew up and turned thirty, they would suddenly fall into a deep dark crevasse and never emerge, or decide not to speak to me again. My crystal ball was murky, but thankfully, for the time being, the tumult was at bay. The busyness of life seemed to keep everyone upright and looking forward. There were friends, plays, book reports, church camps, and night games on the lawn. If they were missing important beats, it was not apparent. Order, my necessary companion, upon which I relied to remain vertical, seemed to attend to me as a wounded child. One task, then another, and then one more. It produced quiet, purpose, and a modicum of peace. I fell into bed as if I had donated blood every day.

42

Andy

A ndy often drives NBA teams to and from their games. If they play the Jazz in Salt Lake City, he'll pick them up in their own cities and bring them to Utah, and then take them back home again. Andy considers it to be a very special privilege. He knows that not every driver in the company is trusted to chauffeur the opposing teams for the Jazz. Most of all, he knows he's one of the few to be entrusted with their safety, but he also knows that he is also counted on to be kind, respectful, and friendly. It isn't so much about being a basketball fan; he is and he isn't. He fondly remembers playing in the Junior Jazz program as a boy, which his mother always signed him up for. His oldest brother, David, used to play a lot, and even went to state in high school. Everyone thought he was so good, and Andy recalls wanting to be just like him. Everyone thought he was such a stud. Andy was much smaller, but he knew there were plenty of smaller forwards and guards who played well because of their agility and speed. Mom and Dad used to love seeing David play. Mom got so out of control with her excitement and her pride in David's skills. And Dad was so proud, you'd think he'd burst his buttons. For many years, it was almost all they talked about at dinner, and they went to at least a couple games every week. Andy really wanted to play, too, and had a great time dribbling the ball back and forth down the court. He knew he was pretty coordinated, and could move quickly. His excitement was relatively short-lived, though. The trouble wasn't in his prowess but in his ability to remember the rules. It was especially difficult to remember which basket was the one he should dribble to. He remembers Dad yelling, "No, no, Andy. Not that way!" It was a lot of fun, anyhow.

Nowadays, he loves chauffeuring these famous players from their home states and back again, to and from their hotel rooms, to their practice courts, and to the games. He has sat in many stadiums watching the very players who ride on his bus as passengers, while the crowds go crazy. The irony of this makes him almost laugh out loud. As they saunter back up into the bus, often having to duck their heads to get in, they remind him of a mysterious master race. But these are the guys who sleep slumped in their seats, eat snacks noisily and messily, drink and joke around, laugh and talk, and occasionally cuss and swear. Really not so different than the high school kids he drives around. Enigmas, he thinks. That's a word he read easily on a page but had to ask his mother the meaning. He's heard her use it from time to time. Some of them are very friendly and nice, and others keep their distance and never look him in the eye. He knows he's invisible to most. He's not a bit bothered by this. It's just the way it is. He knows they make millions, though he can't fathom what that would look like. Whoever could spend that kind of money? It's downright unfathomable. To Andy, these guys are just passengers on his bus. Different from the others, yes, but passengers just the same. He wants to take care of them, make them happy and comfortable, and most of all, keep them safe. He must admit there's an almost palpable excitement that follows them wherever they go, and he enjoys feeling the electricity they seem to generate. It makes him feel like he's part of the important thing they add to many people's lives. So many lives seem to revolve around the games they are paid to play. He smiles when he thinks of not remembering which side of the court to throw the ball through the hoop in as a kid. He wonders if any of these guys ever did that. He knows it's doubtful.

This week's trip is shepherding the Clippers from Los Angeles to Jazz territory for a game. He's made the trip more than a few times, and always enjoys the drive. He doesn't mind the Death Valley lap to Barstow, and he actually enjoys the rest of the trip to L.A. It's nice to be out on the open road, especially when he's alone in the bus. It feels like having a roaming luxury hotel room all to himself. There's something very relaxing and soothing in steering down the freeways solo. Not that he doesn't enjoy the bus filled up as well; he always does, but this part of the trip really belongs to him.

After so many trips across the country, this is just a short jaunt. After picking up the players in their hometown, they begin the drive back to Salt Lake City. Today there's a lot of chatter among them, and Andy's ears are tuned. He tries never to eavesdrop. He has been told how rude that is but finds it next to impossible not to listen to the back-and-forth conversations, especially when it's obviously not intended to be private. They don't seem to ever whisper. Today the majority of the prattle concerns scuttlebutt about Gordon Hayward leaving the Utah team. He's become a hot commodity for the state in the last few years, and the Jazz are desperate to hang on to him at almost any cost. The whole country is watching expectantly, and every guy on the bus has been placing bets on who he will sign with. They don't seem to think he will end up with their own team, but some are ambivalent about the prospect of who might take him. Where he chooses to play will be crucial to their own competitions. There are many opinions and much talk, and not all of it is positive. Andy supposes that's a natural thing. Heck, that kind of talk isn't off limits in his own family, let alone an NBA team family. He finds it all pretty interesting. Not that he follows any of them very closely, but with such intimate contact with many of the players and teams, he's got his ear plastered to the ground. Probably because it's so much fun to actually hear what's going on from the whole herd of horses' mouths. He loves to report all these goings on to his friends and family at home. Sometimes he can't even believe he's privy to what's really happening, while the national media would give their eyeteeth to know. It's amazing how many people are obsessed with these teams. And Andy is part of it all, in a very first-hand way.

The players seem to enjoy being in Jazz territory. Andy is required to stay in the Grand Hotel with them, which is very luxurious compared to most hotels he stays in. He keeps staring at the opulence of his room, and tries to memorize the furnishings. Elaborate, ornate chandeliers, wide moldings in detailed shapes of leaves and flowers entwined around the edges of the ceilings, nice paintings hung over the beds. He thinks as he looks around that his mom would not have believed this place. She wouldn't believe that her little boy is lying on top of this hoity-toity, gold-fringed white bedspread fully dressed, with his work shoes on. He'd love her to see that every inch of the bathroom is covered in real marble. Even the walls, for heaven's sake. He only knows this because his mother loves it. The bathroom is also bedazzled with brass fixtures, including the toilet paper holder. And to push it all over the top, there are actual cloth hand towels ironed and folded carefully over the countertop to wipe your grimy hands on. He is a little nervous about what the hotel staff might think if they could see the grease he is wiping on them. Andy also gets to eat at the main restaurant here. Pretty snazzy fare.

He remains ready at all times to be called for duty. His job is to be close by to attend to any driving needs the players may have. Oftentimes he is awakened in the middle of the night if one of them has a hankering for something. Sometimes he drives them around town during the day to go shopping or to eat at a nice restaurant. He always waits patiently and quietly in the bus until they re-embark.

Today, a couple of the players call him to drive them around to see the city. He, of course, is quick to oblige. He wheels the bus around with as much agility as these players maneuver around their basketball courts. They don't seem to notice his agility. That's okay. One or two want to stop at Starbucks for coffee, so he easily accommodates them. He wheels the bus right up to the front curb in a single maneuver, and they dash off. Andy is caught a little off guard when out of his periphery, he sees one player lingering in the aisle. He looks up questioningly, and with a servient smile asks, "Can I be of help?" He looks up, and when you look at almost any of these players, it's straight up and up. He sees a giant friendly smile on a kind and affable face. He's gotta be six feet ten or eleven, at least, he thinks. Built like a muscled panther standing on two legs. A mass of thick dark hair, a well-clipped beard, and lots of teeth. "What can I get you, buddy?" the player asks. Oh, my gosh, it's Danilo Gallinari. Andy has been told to keep his distance and not be forward, fawning, or ingratiating, so he tries to not gawk. Although he isn't a super avid basketball fan, he's driven these guys around long enough to understand how famous they are. He's also sat in the bleachers enough to hear the fans roar. He knows how special they are to so many.

He begins to stammer. "Uh, uh, nothing. I'm good." At that, Gallinari leaps out the door, missing two steps, as if the bus was a toy, and quickly disappears into Starbucks. Andy is surprised. It's very rare that he's even acknowledged, not to mention spoken to by any of these guys. He knows his place. Andy feels a grin spreading widely across his face. It's a good day, he thinks. But when the players return to the bus, Gallinari is carrying not one, but two large Caramel Frappuccino's in his enormous hands. He smiles broadly and pushes one of them towards Andy. Andy grins from ear to ear. He thinks this has been more than just a good day. It's been spectacular.

43

Ella

I met my next husband at church. How ironic is that, I wondered? Sometimes I was convinced that I had messed up my life so much that to receive tender mercies from behind the big curtain was beyond expectation. No matter how right it had seemed, I had failed at my marriage. No one could argue with that. The collateral damage was that I took my children's father away.

One summer morning, about a month before my divorce was finalized, I attended a different church venue with a friend of a friend. She had come from out of state and didn't want to go alone. I had no expectations except to be temporarily helpful. My children were my entire focus and kept me more than busy; not to mention, my track record with men had been less than stellar. Yet it was here that I met Sam. He was standing in front of a Sunday school class trying to teach some random doctrine. His long, sturdy fingers were dusted with yellow chalk. Scriptures in hand, he was smiling, but I couldn't help but notice how inordinately serious he was about the topic of discussion. When he turned around to write one point or another on the chalkboard, I glimpsed him from the back for the first time. The snapshot remains clear and distinct in my mind. Tall, elegantly lank, strawberry hair, freckles, eyes a bit too close together, he was wearing a crisply starched, light blue cotton button-down shirt. Somehow, the specific blue of the shirt, a lot like the sky on a clear clean summer day, and the autumn glint of his hair flashed in my mind like a tiny swift meteor across dark skies. It was déjà vu or the emergence of a familiar memory. I had never seen him before, but the impression was that I had been shown this picture before. I couldn't remotely put a finger on where or when, but throughout the years, the spark of recognition I felt that moment has stayed with me, reappearing from time to time.

Up to this point, I had often felt like a victim. It's not that I chose to frame it that way, but I had felt stuck, trapped, and hedged in – by my childhood, poverty, immature choices, my own not-so-small weaknesses, my problems, and all the situations surrounding the marriage and children. Meeting Sam cast a startlingly different light on providence. Was our meeting serendipitous or was it a distinct blessing? I had always tried to sustain my faith and hope, and yet I had not been able to fit the puzzle pieces of my life into the big picture laid out on the board. Most often, I felt responsible for the misshapen fragments that could not be pressed to fit. Life as an adult had flown by at such a frantic pace – college, marriage, pregnancy, children, divorce – one sizable thing after another to keep a grasp of, and I hadn't had the time or the focus to consider the syncope.

I often wonder how much of a role divine destiny plays into our crazy, mixed-up, random lives, and if it does, why are the evidences so vague to be almost imperceptible? Can we expect only to recognize it by looking in the rearview mirror? Or is it like a mirage on the highway, or sentinel on a distant hill? Are the details of our journeys necessarily obscured except sporadically, with tiny intuitions or flickers here and there? Else, perhaps, life would become too easy and predictable, and inhibit our sovereign wanderings?

Meeting Sam alluded to the probability that mortal roads might very well intersect with heavenly ones, and that the two might be inexorably and continually intertwined. Without crystal balls, we must try to guess or simply have faith.

Sam was unexpected, unannounced, and seemingly plopped down right in front of my nose. There was hardly time to pull back, feel insecure, or cocoon myself in a protective blanket of fear. He was thirty-seven, never married, and unencumbered. I was stunned that he wanted to be with me all the time, even with my six little inextricable appendages. When we met on the day he was wearing his blue oxford shirt, he slyly and casually asked how many children I had, obviously hoping to uncover a feasible number. I blatantly dodged, saying they were from ten months to twelve years. He gave me an amused and knowing smirk but didn't back away. To my incredulity he did not, in fact, even stop to consider the children at all. From the beginning, they were part of a package deal, one he apparently thought he could handle. He was positively undaunted. When he picked me up for the first date, he met each one of them, and my heart sank in resignation. How could he not be overwhelmed with six young children who lived in a house supported by a welfare check? Yet, without apparent hesitation, he took them in his stride, went to great lengths to get to know each one individually, and began to mentor and champion them. I was cautious and suspicious at first, but Sam was steadfast in his courting. He courted me and each of my children. After a few initial dates, he came consistently every night from work, ate dinner, did dishes, and read bedtime stories. The children took to him like hummingbirds to a syrup-filled feeder, which did much to calm my fears. There wasn't one of them who wasn't eager to get to know him. None were reticent in any sense. They were drawn to him and anxious to impress him. They accepted him as much as he did them.

As for me, I was immediately charmed. More importantly, I felt deep in my mind and heart that he was a consistent and good person, someone who would have integrity in our lives. I thought it highly likely he would love the children and share in their care. It was this certain heartbeat of solace, which led me to venture into what I had heretofore vowed to never do again: after six months of dating, I married him.

The first week we were married, Sam got up on Saturday morning and told me he would be off for a few hours. While we were dating,

I had been amused to notice his bachelor routines. He worked very hard all week, but on Saturdays he got up later, washed his car, rode his bike or played tennis, and hung out with his trusted friend and long-time business partner. This particular morning, he said he'd like to wash his still-new car, chat with his partner, play a little tennis, and hang out, etc. I didn't want to be a new prickly thorn in his side, but I had been giving much thought to our new life as a family, and his as a father. When he broached the subject of this new activity – or perhaps it was the old one he was comfortable with, I forced myself to smile pleasantly. I didn't object or even speak. I simply took Andrew and Jed-die by the hand, both still in diapers, handed Sam the diaper bag, and ushered them all out to the spiffy little gold car with the round blue and white emblem on the front. Sam stopped in his tracks, studied the up-turned anxious faces of the excited little boys, and turned back to me. I wish I had the words to describe the look on his face. Was it shock, agitation, or comprehension? In any case, he kissed me lightly on the mouth, grabbed the diaper bag, buckled the boys in the back seat, waved, and drove away. I waved back and smiled at my small duplici-tous victory and wondered how long before they would return. It wasn't long at all.

At his age and experience, Sam was no stranger to the finer points of divorce protocol. He lost no time in asking my ex-husband point blank if he would be taking the children every other weekend, as he assumed was customary. This was actually something Sam and I had not negoti-ated, and I realized he just supposed the proprieties to be normal pro-cedure. My ex-husband calmly but firmly told Sam that for expediency's sake, it would not be possible, and that he would let us know when he wanted visitation, which in the divorce decree, he was obliged to have. I wondered if Sam was disappointed, as our new marriage was so crammed full of warm bodies every single moment, but he didn't say much. After a few months, he even told me he had decided this was a good thing, and better for the kids not to have to pack a bag or negoti-ate two households. Soon the pattern was set, and our family model had not been altered from the way it had been before Sam came upon the scene. There were random short visits from their father every two or three months, but no phone calls, no birthday wishes or gifts, no back-to-school conferences or doctor's appointments, just a Christmas party every year and a few days' trip to the Canyonlands in the summer. It worked out well for everyone; in fact, everyone seemed quite content with the schedule. But then again, where children are concerned, I've learned it's all in what they are used to. They only know what they have had experience with.

Sam continued to nurse his fledgling business one day at a time, and money was extremely tight. It was as if we had gone from a welfare check to a budget not much different. It was such a relief, however, not to be dependent upon the government. At length, it became necessary for him to put his bachelor's condominium and luxury sedan on the market. He hung up his bicycle, his skis, and his tennis racket to better provide for our family. It was more than clear Sam's partner and his other single friends thought Sam was totally out of his mind, and I felt bad about that. I hoped he wouldn't come to resent his sacrifice. Years later, Sam admitted that during those first weeks of courtship, which had been pretty wonderful, he went home every night from our house with a palpable knot in his chest, so much so that he wondered if a heart attack might be imminent.

He taped a for-sale sign in the window of his shiny BMW, and it made me sad. Cars had been Sam's thing since junior high school. I had heard him rave on about the remarkable Blaupunkt radio, which he had installed in the car aftermarket. It was plain that this had been a bachelor's dream car. One afternoon, I couldn't locate Andrew and Jeddie for a little while and my search led me to the carport, where I found them both locked in Sam's car. The ashtray had been chock full of pennies, which Andrew had carefully and methodically slipped into the cassette slot of that radio. I was uneasy about how Sam would react, but even though I could see he was disturbed by it, he took it in his stride, even though the radio was clearly and soundly destroyed. I was amazed every day at his consistent patience with our little crew. He passed every single test he was given with flying colors, proving that I had not made another dismal mistake.

We took a few modest family vacations to drive-to destinations, worked on our house and yard, and mostly herded kids through school, church, and sports. Every penny Sam brought home went to feeding, housing, clothing, and raising this brood. He never once complained, but when I grew weary or tired, he rather sharply admonished me to open my eyes to see how lucky we were. We have a real life, he said with authority, and he said knew that by having been single so long. He said he'd had plenty of time to focus on selfish things, which never brought any real satisfaction. I used to roll my eyes and throw up my hands in mock frustration; but I'd smile furtively and mentally raise my outstretched arms to the sky.

It was apparent after more than two years of marriage that Sam had more than proved his commitment to each of the children and, without question, loved them as his own. Jenny was his heart – he adored her and took pride in her strong character and quick wit. He mentored David as his little best friend, and protected Beth tenderly from her own fearfulness and anxiety. Luke had claimed him with both little fists, hopping onto his lap every night after work and not letting go until bedtime stories had been read. Andrew and Jed were the little ones he watched over and herded carefully with the loving care of a father bear. He continued to work long hours tirelessly and diligently to build his business. He spent every spare hour being a faithful and unswerving father and husband.

When Sam proposed, I let him know quite obdurately that with six children, I would not be giving birth to any more. I asked him to earnestly consider the magnitude of not having his own children. It was important to me that he enter into the marriage with clear expectations. I had gone through six pregnancies and could not face another. I had struggled with babies, toddlers, and now budding teenagers and everything that goes along with them. I explained to him very frankly that my mind was made up. I was finished with that chapter of my life, mentally and physically. The cribs and baby clothes had been given away, and along with them my desire for more. I realized how unfair it was to ask him to give up the prospect and was adamant that he would consider the long-term complicated consequences. I said I clearly understood if he wanted to move on. Sam was just beginning to bond with the children, and without a hint of hesitation, he reassured me that the six would be quite enough for him. And at the time, I surmised that he really meant more than quite enough.

A few months after the marriage, we moved into a little fixer upper, one that had belonged to my parents. However, it was a substantial step down in size from where we had lived. After my father's disorderly renters had been relocated, we were forced to rip out every carpet, curtain, floor, and surface. We worked side by side for two full months to make certain the smaller home would comfortably suit the eight of us. We rolled up our shirt sleeves and slathered thirty gallons of paint on every single wall. We resurfaced every dismally dirty room in the house. Every day after Sam went to work, I took Jed and Andrew with me to spend the day at the house. Sam joined me after work and we scrubbed away dirt, painted, laid floors, fixed faucets, patched holes, and grouted tile until we literally could not stand up. There were three occupiable bedrooms. The master, obviously, was for us. Jenny and Beth took another, which we painted a cheerful sky blue. We put the bunkbeds in the third for David and Luke, leaving no place at all for the two younger boys. Sam adroitly built two beds into the wall of a closet-sized nook for Andrew and Jed. I took scraps of navy and plaid fabric and sewed two colorful quits for the beds, and then painted a second-hand dresser dark blue to match. The whole family was finally squeezed into the little house comfortably and cozily. Our aim had been to make it our own and give the children a place to call home again. It turned out to be a successful and happy move for all, especially as it had the familiarity of their grandparents' home. The children melded into the new old house, neighborhood, and schools with ease.

From time to time, as I began to feel more relaxed in my new life, I reluctantly recognized some unbidden thoughts mischievously swirling around in my brain. They concerned the extremely remote possibility of perhaps, really only perhaps, having one more baby. I admired Sam's unwavering sacrifice of time, resources, and mostly his heart to our formerly destitute little family, and something began to blossom inside me, like the little bean plant Beth had been growing in the plastic cup on the windowsill. First, I felt he probably deserved the experience, and second, I suspected it might cement our family even further. That was my biggest hope and dream. Within weeks of making the decision, I was pregnant with little Elizabeth, whom we quickly began to call Lizzie.

The outcome of having a new baby seemed successful on both counts, even more so than I had hoped. Sam seemed to bask in the experience of the pregnancy as well as in the adventure of raising an infant. To make things even better, the other kids were delighted to welcome little Lizzie into the family. She looked a lot like Sam's mother, which pleased him immensely. She had fuzzy blonde hair, an up-turned nose, and a little too close-together blue eyes, which darted back and forth happily to every person in the room. The children carted her around like a cherished new puppy. I now felt content with my burgeoning family, and it seemed I had succeeded in completing my particular mission for Sam, or so I thought.

A little more than a year later I dolefully realized I was unexpectedly expecting again. This time we welcomed baby Joe into our now over-stuffed household.

44

Ella

A ndrew was old enough to start kindergarten in the fall. I had never considered holding a child back in school, but Andrew was, of course, an exception. His illnesses, hearing loss, language deficit, propensity to wander, and immaturity notwithstanding, I desperately wanted him to be "normal." I wanted him to go to school, have good buddies, read and write his name, learn the ABCs, enjoy play time, nap time, snack time, and recess. He would absolutely be enthralled with recess. I was determined that he must have the opportunity to move through life in a predictable pattern and feel normal doing it. Sometimes I actually wondered if sending him to school would be the thing that would make him normal. I reasoned that he would catch up, glide along with his classmates, and the gaps would begin to close. I was certain of it. I felt it in my gut, if not my heart.

He was so happy, enthusiastic, and determined to be like everyone else that it made my heart hurt to think he might feel like he was lacking in something. I refused to accept that. I wanted so many good things for this small boy whom I adored and who had had a less than perfect beginning. Sometimes I wondered, and I suppose this is not unusual, that perhaps his problems were my fault. Maybe I had not carried him quite properly during pregnancy. Did I do something I was unaware of during those months, which had inadvertently injured him? I spent a lot of time analyzing every possible aberrant situation and wondered if that was the day something went awry. Was it when I used spray paint on the new nursery cabinet for church without adequate ventilation? Did I forget to take my prenatal vitamins at a critical moment, or not eat enough leafy green vegetables? Did I run too fast, exercise too hard, or not enough? Perhaps every mother wonders if her child's imperfections are her fault. Yet I could not begin to tolerate the thought that it could have been prevented and wasn't. I wanted the world for this eager-eyed little boy, and I was probably more fearful that he would fail and not get it. I didn't want him to become discouraged, feel different, or not fit in. I debated for weeks about keeping him back. I prayed and deliberated about what would be best for Andrew at this juncture.

In the end, I did keep him home an extra year. It was obvious he wasn't ready. I enrolled him in a little preschool that I told him was called "Andrew's special school" instead of kindergarten. I hoped it would prepare him for the real thing later. I wasn't terribly worried, but there was an anxious pit in my stomach, as he never quite caught up in many areas. He was happy and anxious to go to his special school and didn't seem to realize he was not going to the regular school with the others his age. Age by number wasn't really something he was aware of.

He was talking a blue streak now; he'd made great strides in his lingual dexterity. It was if his brain was trying to make up for lost time. We'd ride in the car, and no matter how far we went, Andrew would sit behind Sam and ask a million questions. Not so abnormal, I thought. All kids ask questions. But Andrew asked one right after another so fast I often thought Sam might give him an elbow over the seat. It was frustrating. What's this, what's that? Why this, why that? Who's this, who's that? Sam, by nature, was very patient and usually tried to answer until his own brain wouldn't cooperate, and then he'd just drive in cadence with the never-ending questions.

After a time, Sam became apparent of something Andrew was doing, which was a little out of the ordinary. One day, Sam asked me to pay more attention and listen carefully to Andrew. Andrew began to pick out the makes and models of almost every car on the road. He knew a Camaro from a Mustang, a Jaguar from a Volvo. He could spot a BMW a mile away and tell you what specific model number it was. He began to recognize Chevy, Oldsmobile, Ford, Dodge, Toyota, and Honda as well. He was so proud to tell you the name of the specific model of each general brand, and he was almost never wrong. It was uncanny and a little disconcerting. Going for a ride, anywhere, anytime, became something Andrew looked forward to like Christmas. He'd watch furtively to see if someone was venturing near the key hooks on the wall. He was beginning to sense he had a special ability that no one else in the family had; a real gift, something that set him apart and made him special. I knew if anyone deserved a special gift, it was Andrew.

One day Sam thought it would be fun to bring home a few Matchbox cars for Andrew. He hoped it would encourage his newfound preoccupation, as well as foster his penchant for memorization, which was another peculiar strength we had discovered. Andrew was in absolute heaven. Cars of his own! He'd lie on his stomach and study them closely for long periods of time, memorizing each little detail of each model. He'd pick out his favorites, wash them in the bathroom sink, and polish them with the bottom of his tee shirt. He'd line them up on the floor by the side of his bed at night and go to sleep gazing down at them in what appeared to be rapture. After that, every time Sam or I went to the store, he'd beg for one. Then two or three. It was difficult to refuse him, as they cost so little one or two at a time. It wasn't long before Andrew had collected close to 100 matchbox cars, and the number just kept increasing. I suspected some of Jed's cars were disappearing into Andrew's box as well. Fighting erupted over whose were whose. Jed and Andrew played cars together, but Jed usually lost interest after a half hour or so, unlike his brother. I finally purchased a big blue plastic bucket to hold them all. Andrew sat in the dirt on the side of the house for hours on end, running them back and forth, lining them up end-to-end, making little ramps for them, and pushing them off. Sam had given the boys a very large magnifying glass, which had belonged to him as a child. Magnifying became one of their favorite pastimes. At first, they used it to examine all sorts of objects, but soon they took to burning leaves, sticks, and then, to my horror, insects. The foul scent was unmistakable. Now and then, I noticed Andrew melting the tires on some of the little cars and attempting to liquefy the metal.

The boys' bedroom was on the second floor, and one afternoon I stood outside the doorway and watched. He had the window open and was racing a hundred cars, one right after the other, rapid-fire, off the slope of the roof and onto the asphalt below. His face was lit up like a Christmas tree. To this day, I cannot bear to throw away a couple of little bent or charred cars that I occasionally find buried in the dirt somewhere in the yard. I trophy them in a spot where I can study them and remember those cherished years.

As soon as Andrew began public school, life became a whole lot more complicated. He was a friendly, open, and agreeable little guy in class, but he simply could not focus. His mind darted like a dragonfly and landed on anything in the room but the lessons. When it did, he began to wiggle, stand up, or scoot along on the floor. He'd poke his neighbor, chat incessantly with anyone who'd listen, or just badger someone into playing with him. Some of the teachers strictly and un-yieldingly set his desk in the corner, others reproached him harshly in front of his peers. A few were downright exasperatedly demanding, and treated him as if he was pugnacious and simply belligerent. Those teachers were the most difficult to deal with. I knew he only wanted to fit in, and mostly he wanted to please. I understood, as well, that the actions and attitudes of these particular teachers confused him terribly and tore at the fragile fabric of his self-esteem. He had no idea what he was doing wrong, nor did he know what he should do right.

Nothing seemed to help. At times, he tried to listen open-eyed and willing, trying desperately to please the teacher, but that usually only lasted a couple minutes. It became apparent to him that he must be doing something to dissatisfy her, and he was anxious to resolve the situation. After a note or a phone call from the teacher, and there were dozens, I sat him down, carefully attempting to explain the gravity of the situation by cajoling or reasoning. In the end, I resorted to threats or bribes. Truthfully, if that had helped in any way, I'd have bought every candy bar or Matchbox car on the shelf without any guilt whatsoever.

Andrew simply could not do what everyone expected of him. Heaven knows he tried. One of his most endearing characteristics was that of trying to please the people around him. His language skills were now excellent, and his reading was above average, though his retention was almost nonexistent. As we observed before, he could memorize long lists of words and recite them quite easily, though he could not contextualize them. The positive particulars thoroughly confused the teachers and threw many of them totally off track. In those days, the logistic trailways of elementary education were very narrow and bumpy. Most teachers were convinced that one and one had to equal two. Those who thought him lazy or uncooperative thought so even more when he got all of his spelling words correct. Something wasn't tracking, and no one knew why or had the time to figure it out. His performance was incongruent. Many teachers surmised he was intentionally disruptive or inordinately stubborn. Some of the more open-minded were convinced he had Attention Deficit Disorder or ADHD, and insisted he be put on conventional medication immediately. After no improvement at all and disciplinary threats on every side, I cried "uncle" and put in a call to our pediatrician. I was frantically willing to try every avenue to make things better for him. As with the candy and the cars, I had no real qualms about medication if it actually helped him be more successful.

I gave him the prescribed pills for about three weeks before I flushed them down the toilet. It didn't take rocket science to realize they were making the child I knew literally disappear. He'd come home from school, sit on his bed, and stare out the window or lazily fiddle with a couple of his cars. He seemed distant and sad, dark and lethargic, and not remotely his usual active, jovial, and interested self. I decided it was too high a price to pay and perhaps downright cruel. I would not throw away this child for everyone else's convenience. I threw up my hands and declared that we would all just have to put up with a rambunctious, unfocused, annoying, but happy little boy. This did not endear me to his teachers in the least. It also made my enclave of support smaller, as I could now see that few were interested in more than their own convenience, although I suppose I understood. The teachers were unhappy with me for not giving Andrew the medication, but I didn't care. It gave me back my little boy.

Andrew and I cozied up on the sofa almost every day after school. He read to me for at least a half hour, and I could see he was as proficient as the other children had been. Of course, the real problem lay in the comprehension, but I was at a loss as to how to help him with that. He read like the wind but couldn't tell me what he had just read, no matter how many times I quizzed him. It was as if the words were like expertly shuffled cards moving rapidly from his head, landing into a box with a hole in the bottom. His attention span was short, usually only minutes.

Some of the teachers were patient and understanding, others insisted his weaknesses were insurmountable and gave up. In some classes, he was ignored and left to his own devices to wander and play, and in others, punished or reprimanded. The poor kid couldn't figure out what was going on or who expected what, in what class. He was constantly confused and disheartened, but as was usual, the befuddled feelings didn't last too long. Getting home to his pets and his cars seemed to temporarily erase all the bad spirits. I was surprised, also, that he hardly ever tried to get out of going to school. He got up, got dressed, ate his breakfast, and trotted off happily. Feigning sick was normal intermittent behavior for most of our other children, who, on a fairly regular basis, were hit with terrible stomach bugs or sore throats just to take a decent break. He rarely, if ever, seemed depressed or downcast. For the most part, Andrew just took life as it came at face value. He looked forward and forgot the past. Every day posed new possibilities, and the memories of the day before simply lost their intensity when the sun rose. Knowing how to let go was just a part of Andrew's nature and his disability. Perhaps, rather, it was part of his ability. More than a few times, I find myself envious of that.

I must acknowledge and appreciate the few excellent and compassionate teachers along the way, determined to be part of the solution. They are out there. Miss Blackburn was one of a rare breed. She immediately perceived Andrew's behavior and lack of focus as absolutely unintentional. Rather, his problems became something she would make her mission to remedy, at least in part. Just being in her presence made the load I carried on my shoulders lighter, and I felt a little stronger. What a relief to actually have an ally, or at least someone who tried to sincerely understand. Andrew and I were not alone that year. She was our superhero. Her kindness and determination to find solutions that did not include medication, punishment, corner desks, or ostriching the whole problem, was noble and inspirational. She had no stock in our family business, campaigned for no medals, and was not looking to be an example. She simply and sincerely wanted Andrew to find a larger opening into the doorway to his education. She was a rare angel.

Miss Blackburn began by petitioning the district for a sound system which consisted of a microphone, which was to be secured around a teacher's neck. The sound was wirelessly transmitted to a pair of headphones connected directly into Andrew's ears. She felt if the words were not vaporizing into the noise of the room, there was a good chance he could absorb them directly into his brain, or at least have a better chance of doing so. I was excited about the prospect, and happily hopeful. Some days seemed more efficacious, but certainly not categorically. The experiment, however, ended abruptly and prematurely when Andrew grew weary of the hassle, not to mention being the only child in the room who had to wear these blatant contraptions. He was beginning to determine that anything that made him seem different would not remain on the agenda. He began to ditch the earpieces regularly and finally in a hiding place which even he could not remember. The honchos at the district were furious and quickly invoiced us for a thousand-dollar replacement. At that point, Sam and I decided to forgo the experiment, and dear Miss Blackburn agreed.

Andrew continued to be sweet and loving even if school and friends were elusive and complicated. He continued to embody many positive as well as negative attributes. One of the most palpable positives was his joyfulness. His unadulterated gladness for living, along with his startling and refreshing vulnerability, attracted many. Yet, it was clear to me that he could not sustain sadness for long. While that may seem like a good thing, it was becoming very clear that because of that, he did not have the tools to sort through life's difficult conundrums. One must maintain discomfort at least long enough to want change or look for solutions. He wasn't able to be downhearted long enough to realize there were options which could affect him for good or bad. That is something we couldn't teach him, no matter how hard we tried. It wasn't that he lacked the ability to be sympathetic. He cared genuinely about everyone he met. He was quick to tear up if someone else was feeling sad. His countenance was expectant, his demeanor was unguarded. If someone else was hurting, he wanted to help, not in an empathetic way, but in a cheerful "I'm sure I can help, but I'm not sure how" magic wand sort of way. I suspected he had come that way from heaven. At the same time, I was saddened to realize that most people would not recognize it.

Though inclined to normal boyish mischief or fun, Andrew was never conniving or mean. He got into trouble because he simply could not see consequences coming down the road, even a few minutes beforehand. He looked for the best in people and trusted everyone without question, often to his own detriment and disappointment. He could not comprehend someone being cruel or discriminatory, so it was difficult for him to be cognizant of it at all. He believed what everyone said, though he often bent the truth to his own advantage. Sam often made the observation that Andrew's lies were so natural to his well-being that they just rolled off his tongue, becoming gospel truth the second they hit the air. Then the challenge for us was to make him see that they were not. We tried again and again but usually failed. He was pure and literal in his immaturity and lacked the ability to recognize evil, scheming, or deceitfulness. He was often disappointed, but he did not have the depth to feel disillusionment. He was simply blind to what was not remotely a part of himself.

That wasn't to say Andrew was always well behaved; he wasn't – far from it. He took the easiest and least complicated path towards fun and satisfaction. He was terribly and utterly impulsive but not manipulative or devious. If it felt good and didn't hurt anyone else, in his mind, it must not be wrong, or at least it might be right. He was simply too simple to weigh consequences. He just acted. He was a lively, rowdy, active, happy-go-lucky little wild man, one who naturally wanted all his wants and needs filled without reservation. Not out of malice or selfishness, just out of living his life one moment at a time.

45

Ella

We rented my parents' home for four years before purchasing a beautiful secluded lot. It was at the end of a long winding road leading to the mouth of a little box canyon. It was on a whole acre of beautiful trees and had a stream running through the front yard. It was necessary, of course, to pay the lot off first, but in time we built a house on it, which was an interesting, pleasant, and harried experience all at the same time. Neither of us were strangers to the design process, so it was a personal endeavor that bound us together even more. We budgeted and scrimped, but it was a satisfying experience; one that the entire family enjoyed. My only lingering fear was that we would lose this lovely new home.

We lived out our days pleasantly, if not frenetically, in this new, beautiful, albeit busy beehive, trying to maintain the integrity of the hive while supporting and encouraging the exuberant bees as they swarmed in a hundred different directions. It seemed as if each individual was flourishing while darting and flying this way and that in their pursuit of school, hobbies, friends, and various interests. We did our best to juggle and keep up, sometimes not well enough. We usually fell into bed like zombies into caskets, but it was a sweet and good exhaustion. We were certain our plan was worthy, and our motives lofty, and we worked happily side by side in everything. We considered this the only way to rear a family, and though hectic and exhausting, it was not remotely boring.

David was devoted to basketball, was always a gifted athlete, and was usually first string on his teams. We carved out time for hundreds of practices and games. For a time, it became our most time-consuming, demanding, and interesting pastime. We were lucky to procure a small, old, run-down pea-green Datsun sedan, which had belonged to my father. It was tiny and rusted all over, but David was grateful to be able to chauffeur himself around.

He drove himself to his practices in the wee hours of the morning and after school. He worked very hard to hone his abilities and was successful. He was also determined to overcome his natural unaggressive tendencies and endeavored to become a voracious team player. Sam always felt it was good for David to focus on sports and saw many benefits for discipline, teamwork, and hard work.

I recall the night after a frustrating loss to an opposing team. We had been there to cheer David on and directly returned home afterwards to get the rest of the kids settled in. A little later, David drove in exhausted and discouraged, having pounded out every ounce of his energy on the basketball court after practice and a full day of classes. As he stepped from his little car in our icy, snowy driveway, his muscles spasmed and constricted, and he knew he was in trouble. He couldn't stand or walk and could do nothing but slip down onto the frigid asphalt and lie flat on his back in the snow. Luckily, we had heard the clickety-clack of his old engine. Of course, I felt alarm, but I felt something much more, as I watched Sam run to him, gather him up like a baby, and hoist his substantial 6-foot, 6-inch frame onto his own back and lug him into the house. That was just Sam. Always there to rescue any child in our household who needed him, emotionally or physically. I was ever in awe of his selflessness and his ability to sweep us all up in his capable arms and put us first.

Sam was determined that each of the boys have a similar opportunity to excel. He pushed them to pick a sport – any sport – and then he facilitated and supported each practice and game. He bought expensive basketball shoes, which we really could not afford, signed them up for training camps, and chauffeured them to sign-ups. Some of them put up a fuss but eventually made their own decisions.

Several times after we had shuttled Luke to soccer, he sat on the sidelines and literally refused to walk out onto the field with his teammates. I'll never forget Sam picking Luke up in his arms and depositing him directly onto the soccer field, after insisting fervidly that he give it just one more try. Luke would simply sit down and pick the grass defiantly. After a whole season of insisting, Sam relented and signed him up for Little League, which went a whole lot smoother, at least for a couple of seasons. The younger boys tried soccer, basketball, and baseball as well, but never got much of a foothold in any of them. I think now, it was somewhat disconcerting for Sam that he hadn't been able to succeed in giving each of them a positive outlet like David had. He felt it was he who had failed, though we have learned that they made their own choices.

As for Andrew, he was wiry and strong, and naturally athletic. He, unlike some of his brothers, was extremely enthusiastic about playing sports. He wanted to play basketball and soccer so badly, and in truth, he was quick, agile, and blessed with natural abilities. Of course, Sam made certain he had a spot on several teams. The problem lay in Andrew's lack of comprehension for rules or patterns. We always cheered for him wildly as he dashed up and down the field adeptly but felt so sad when he repeatedly scored goals for the other team while screaming jubilantly. Or he'd dribble in the wrong direction or tip the ball to the opposite team. When he did these things, his teammates would be angry and downright disparaging. He'd cock his head, look up to us in the stands, and appear to be terribly confused. Sam would gently and quietly pull him aside at the first opportunity, and repeatedly show him which basket was his teams at each quarter, but it did not help. He continued to have a good time playing and exhibited good physical skills, but when the coaches began to bench him for no apparent reason, at least in Andrew's estimation, Sam let him quit.

Sam brought home wood scraps from work and built a treehouse. He provided Luke with building materials for his many and varied projects. He went to scout camps and church activities, never uttering a word of resentment or showing any sign of feeling it, for that matter. He adored the girls, but I could see he was never quite certain what would be appropriate physical closeness with them. They were warm and solicitous, always seeking his approval and advice, but sadly, I saw him hold back just a bit, and I knew he was only being cautious. Granted, it was a complicated mix being a stepfather, but I was grateful for his willingness to be a part of every single drama. I never once saw him retreat, even when things were difficult. I was never on my own. He was serious and focused on the family, and if for nothing else, I was eternally grateful to Sam for that.

It felt like my life sentence of loneliness and single parenting had been commuted, and I hoped the stay would last. But truth be told, my past had caused me to be distrustful or suspicious of good fortune. When I felt vulnerable, I tended to go looking for trouble. When I felt exposed, and I'm not proud to admit it, I goaded Sam into disappointing me, fighting with me, or even accusing him of wanting to leave me. He, however, knew exactly what my vulnerabilities were and would never give in to my insecurities even by pretending to be fed up. He was often impatient and frustrated, yes, but never daunted. It took years, actually, for me not to expect the worst and to realize he was not going away. If we had words, which, of course we did, they were usually centered in my lack of trust, no matter how unjustified it was.

My considerable weakness was feeling like the rug was going to be pulled out from under me when I least expected. To me, it was not a matter of if but when. I couldn't shake the notion that many things really are too good to be true. I thought if my life were going to implode, which I believed it likely would, then getting it over with would be the best for everyone. But it didn't happen; Sam proved every day he was in it for the long haul. His steadfastness was not just for me but also for each of the children. Commitment was paramount to Sam, and I finally learned that it was something he could not let go of, even if at times he might want to. It was not only that he had no inclination, but it was that honor and integrity were integral to his core. Somewhere along the line, it had been woven into the fabric of his being. My grandmother in Levan described such a man as "a prince of a fellow," and after enough time passed, I could not deny it was true of Sam. I had to remember that in reality, his character was the reason I had chosen him in the first place. Not only did I have a full partner, but I had a true and reliable confidant. I could drop my troubles at his feet and he would not only try to understand, but would attempt to talk everything through so thoroughly that I'd get too tired to continue and give in. He was tender and kind, thoughtful and sensitive. We had what I had never experienced in my first marriage, nor seen in my own parents'. I didn't feel the loneliness or isolation I had for so many years. We had intimacy, trust, and understanding on many levels. I felt like I had reached a cool blue oasis after trudging a hundred miles under an unrelenting and scorching desert sun. Whatever Sam couldn't do – and of course he had his faults like everyone else – was made up for in all he did do. I often felt like heaven had reached its reluctant hand down through the clouds and handed me a conciliatory gift, which I had thirstily received. For many years, a part of me would still wonder if it was too good to be true. I also wondered when it would end.

46

Ella

Like many special needs children, Andrew had a penchant for animals. He could not survive without a dog and a cat, and he would have preferred to have a gerbil, guinea pig, rabbit, and parakeet as well. So, we always had a dog. And a cat. Good ones, sweet ones, annoying ones, barky ones, and peeing ones. If one didn't work, we'd get another. Andrew loved them all like brothers and sisters, or more so. I could hear him out on the porch before bedtime holding Cassandra, the ornery Siamese, in his arms like a baby, singing lullabies to her. He let the mean dog we named Sophie sleep at his feet every night, although she growled and bit him whenever he turned over. He'd snuggle them, kiss them, talk to them, and pamper them. He'd sneak food out of the refrigerator for them. As for their part of the bargain, I realized they were the intimate friends he didn't have. They were the constants in his life. They gave the unconditional love we all speak about but never really see given. They welcomed him home every day after school. They were the siblings who did not criticize or make fun, and were there continually with wagging tails, open-mouthed smiles, and slobbery kisses. They were the ones who, no matter how much trouble he was in, were just happy to see him come home.

As an adult, Andrew is charming, good-looking, and clear-eyed. Because of his open, friendly, and talkative nature, and because his language skills are well developed, people are immediately drawn to him. He is simply an open book. He holds nothing back because he wouldn't have the slightest notion of how to do so. He is guileless, interested, polite, and so unreserved that one who hasn't engaged in a conversation lasting longer than ten minutes with Andrew would have no idea he even has disabilities. Those who have, quickly grow fatigued with the circular conversation centering mostly upon one myopic recent task or subject, most likely a towing or driving experience. I watch his brothers and sisters avoid him because they feel they can't escape. He's also developed a tendency toward patting or shoulder rubbing, which can be very annoying. Sadly, it has continued into adulthood. His siblings love him but don't engage.

In the past, if I ever confided my difficulties to a fairly dissociate acquaintance, or if I alluded to his differences or disability to even those we knew fairly well, they simply could not see it. Many times, I was subtly reproved or occasionally angrily reprimanded for being harsh or critical of my own child. I was also accused of being insensitive or unkind. These confrontations really stung. I was shocked and hurt by the repercussions of divulging a personal anxiety. For his sake and mine, I resorted to allowing people to believe as they were comfortable doing. I remember, however, being surprised and offended when a woman with a manifestly handicapped boy about Andrew's age pulled me aside, and told me I was making an enormous mistake by mainstreaming him. The boys had had several play dates in the past. Her son had not done well in public school, so she accessed several other avenues of education, which I had also done in regard to Andrew. Had I opted, I could have enrolled him in one of several schools for children with special needs. I admit it was always a dilemma. I went back and forth, but it never felt right. He had too many strengths within the average parameters. I also knew he would have felt out of place and would not have totally fit in. The woman self-righteously pointed out the repercussions of not giving "these kids" the resources they needed and deserved. How could I, she demanded? She shook her finger angrily in my face. It was a poignant reminder that only a mother who lives with an atypical child tends to recognize the real complexities, and only a mother who does can make the judgment as to where he really belongs.

Sam and I took Andrew to be evaluated by professionals numerous times. Medical doctors, behavioral therapists, psychologists. We were continually trying to reassure ourselves that we were doing right by him or were attempting to dig up new pieces of the puzzle. It's difficult enough to take care of a child when you know definitively what the diagnosis is, but when your child struggles and it's not at all clear as to why, you hope against hope there is a new development lurking around the corner that will fix things, or at the very least, help you to understand why you cannot. I often wondered if the real reason I kept searching was to make me better, not him. To help me settle down and accept what was, as well as to be able to free myself from some sort of guilt for not being able to give him a typical life. Especially when he had some obvious strengths. Nowadays, I have substantially more clarity. I have quit wanting to make him normal. I realize now that he is good enough the way he came, in fact, he is wonderful exactly the way he is, and always will be – at least in this particular realm. No, not much was normal, but then again, I have learned that not much ever is. Back then, I just couldn't let it be. I was compelled to keep trying something new or different – a new doctor, a new medication, a new technique. I longed to find anything which would help me feel like a more successful parent. Now I realize I was looking for a new me, not a new Andrew.

When he was about seven, a highly trained professional in neuropsychiatry examined him thoroughly and told us pretty bluntly that it may well have been easier to raise him if he had been diagnosed with a specific disorder or disability, even if one was more severe. At least, he said, there would be a clearer course to steer him through – an actual prognosis or predictability. He told us Andrew would very likely get lost in the system, as there were so many parts of his brain working very normally. Yes, there were damaged parts as well, but he would be very capable of bobbing and weaving – those were his words – and quickly find a way to adapt to what people expected. This would help him conform but also push him further away from the learning process. His prediction was that Andrew would keep everybody on edge – us, the teachers, even the doctors. He would most likely fall through the cracks of a system that does not understand how to help him. He might well develop above-average abilities in a few areas, while retaining great weaknesses in others. As I look back, I believe this was the most correct prognosis ever given us. But as in most experiences of life, I'm not sure I allowed it to sink in until well after the rollicking storms had already subsided.

The circuitous days lengthened into meandering years. At the top of the agenda every school year was to visit with every teacher, try to explain, and plead humbly and cordially for leeway and mercy. In a way, I was asking that they be patient with him, and that they help us smooth the path by giving him the benefit of the doubt as to his intent. So many teachers immediately jumped to the conclusion that he was just incorrigible, not deficit. As discomfiting and patronizing as this was, I learned that technique usually made things better than they would have been. So, that was the recurring drill for elementary, then junior high, and lastly, high school. There were resource classes or tutored subjects available for those who qualified, and Andrew was registered for most of them. In this way, he was receiving every opportunity he could get within the mainstream school system. Several times, a teacher or other parent suggested alternative special schools, but I know now that Andrew would not have fit in there, either. It may have crushed him. He would have felt substantially more out of place there than where he was.

In the middle of Andrew's senior year, it became apparent that he was starting to become bored and out of sync. His whole body narrated the story. He slunk down the hill to the bus stop, often not even taking his book bag, and dragged himself around the house, saying he didn't feel well. He had an upset stomach, his throat was sore, and so on. This was a phase we had not heretofore encountered. I was finally notified by the school that he had been regularly cutting classes. Where he went during the day remained a mystery. Andrew was never one to get into trouble, and we were certain he wasn't falling prey to addictions or bad habits. He was consistently a great kid, kind and polite as a rule, so we knew he was letting us know he was unhappy at school.

He left and returned on the bus at the appointed times, acting as if he couldn't figure out why the school had marked him absent. He had feigned innocence down to a science these days. He was maturing in different ways than we were accustomed to. In order to reach our goal of graduation, Sam and I put our feet down rather hard. We threatened to ground him and assumed we had authoritatively made our point, yet the school reported continued absence. One day, instead of going to work as he always did, Sam drove to the school, watched Andrew get off the bus and then sauntered casually up behind him. "Well, Andrew," he said, nonchalantly, "I think it's going to be a good day at school today – what do you think?" Andrew looked at him questioningly, then glaringly, then angrily as the obvious began to dawn. He scowled menacingly at Sam and stormed ahead, looking over his shoulder as if he could kill him with a glance, but Sam followed closely behind, never leaving him more than ten paces ahead all day long. From one class to another, to the lavatory, to the lunchroom, Sam stood back just far enough to make sure Andrew knew he was still there. He sat in the back of the classrooms, while Andrew either sat stubbornly with his face to the front or turning and glowering at him with contempt. At the end of the day, Andrew pleaded, begged, and ranted. He was humiliated and angry. Yet the day following went exactly the same, with Sam trailing Andrew persistently. Finally, the point was made; Andrew didn't miss class for the rest of the year.

I recall clearly the moment I realized it. I was sitting on the front porch one soggy, cloudy day watching the raindrops plop onto the sidewalk like bullet points emphasizing the conflicts in my mind. As I sat there stewing, it was as if the dark skies opened up for an instant, and a shaft of sunlight stabbed through to the ground like lightning. Just one flash. It was there and then gone. And it was there and then I decided distinctly and firmly, that against all odds Andrew would absolutely receive his high school diploma, no matter what. I knew he would need it to survive in this world of academia and worldly successes. At least he would be able to show, as well as know, that he had made it through high school. I decided that if I had to pull strings, throw fits, beg teachers with tears running down my cheeks, or even bribe principals, I would do it. I would do whatever it took. That was the least I could do for my boy, spuriously or not.

Andrew graduated with his class in June, and I was a very proud mother. When I look back, I feel like we pulled him through a knothole by the toes. But we, emphasis on "we" – Sam and I together – had done it. I admit to finishing many of his essays, working many of his math problems, and actually going to the lab to throw his last pottery and ceramic projects. The teachers, at least most of them at that point, kindly looked the other way. I felt certain they were as happy as I that he was finally getting his diploma, as well as getting out of their hair.

47

Ella

Ironically, it was during this period of chaos I decided to try my hand at a little design business of my own. It was downright frightening, but something whispered to me that I might succeed. I designed, gardened, organized, and styled my own domain naturally and passionately. It was just how I was wired. I didn't think it was special or extraordinary, and in fact, I considered it a bit eccentric, odd, or a touch flawed. Often, it was embarrassing. I was always surprised when someone was complimentary about what I considered normal, or perhaps a bit abnormal. I followed what came naturally to me, but I didn't choose it. I always felt those attributes had chosen me, not I them. Yes, it was my nature and admittedly my passion, but I never thought much about it, except that it might be a little strange. On several occasions as a girl, I had heard my mother chattily tell people, not unkindly, but in a way that emphasized what sounded to me like peculiarity, that I had been different from the womb. She seemed to enjoy recounting the days, rolling her eyes a little as she did, when I was only eight or nine and decided that I simply could not live without making the bedroom I shared with a younger sister pretty and clean. I begged my father to paint the walls and the little brown metal dresser the same shade of lavender and pestered him until he took me to Sears to buy inexpensive lilac floral curtains. Then she'd say, almost clucking with amusement, "And she kept it neat as a pin," which sounded to my ears like "the poor little odd creature."

Friends, relatives, and neighbors began to come to me often to ask for my expertise or help. Sam asked why not keep doing it, and make a little money at the same time? We could certainly use it, he said, accurately. One morning I gathered all the courage I could muster and drove downtown to apply for a business license. It was one of the scariest days of my life, though it really wasn't so difficult. I proceeded to jump through the other necessary business-building hoops. I even ordered a stack of inexpensive business cards and printed my own letterhead on the computer. No one was more shocked than I to see clients come pouring in, one after another, especially since my business was strictly word of mouth. I did many residential jobs, and after that, quite a few commercial ones. For several years, I was the in-house designer for a well-known corporation. I designed the interiors for several large buildings from start to finish, working with the architects. I tried to venture out of my comfort zone and try different styles, even those I had come to believe I didn't like or couldn't relate to. What I learned was that good design was good design, no matter what style it was, and if it was good, it could always hold its own. I worked with quite a few contractors, and a few hired me to work for their businesses, or in their own homes. All of which led to more jobs. I did houses for several Parade of Home venues, sometimes interviewing for the newspaper or appearing in short television spots. I designed and decorated a few storefront windows and helped Sam with projects he had been hired to do. I made proposals to important companies and won a few of those contracts. Who'd have thought, I always asked myself incredulously.

I thrived on the creativity of the work and enjoyed most of the client relationships. Most of all, I absolutely adored having a little money jangling around in my pockets or a few extra dollars tucked away in my own bank account. I paid for the sprinkler system in the yard, for lovely wooden garage doors with windows, and even took the whole family to

California for an entire week on my own dime. Sam indulged me by not questioning what I chose to spend "my" money on, and more importantly, he was my most enthusiastic cheerleader. He told me I was a natural, and I desperately wanted to believe him, though I never quite could.

I worked from home, putting together my vision boards on the kitchen counter while little kids ran around my feet. But to be perfectly honest, I always felt like a major fraud. Sometimes after a long hard day, I would reiterate to Sam that I was just fooling too many people and that I could not continue to keep it up. He just shook his head and laughed when I said this, and told me that if I would really get serious, he was certain the sky would be the limit. He was encouraging and proud.

Perhaps it was remnants of a tiny cockroach-infested house, eating lunch alone in the school cafeteria, or sitting in the corner of a run-down apartment building that caused me to question my abilities. I wondered if my clients knew what a dog and pony show I felt I was putting on for them. I wondered if they thought I was only telling them what they wanted to hear because I had learned to do it authoritatively, or if they really suspected that I had no real education or expertise. There were times I found it downright difficult to keep my mouth zipped and not blurt this out to a vice president or television producer, as I had several opportunities to present proposals to companies or television stations. I came close sometimes to proclaiming that I was, in truth, only an unsophisticated mother with a trainload of children – one who cleaned bathrooms, wiped noses, and cooked spaghetti for dinner.

48

Ella

The hive was humming along at different pitches, busily and progressively. My routine consisted of cleaning, cooking for ten, washing for ten, driving carpools, shepherding homework, going to doctors' appointments, attending various school functions, chauffeuring to soccer and basketball practice and games, preparing for various camps, and attending parent-teacher conferences. The lesser chores were French-braiding hair, shopping for school clothes, or making sure the clothes were clean and ironed for church every week. I really had very few complaints. After all, everyone was fairly happy and healthy. Even Andrew was making his way, if not a bit tentatively. Jenny was attending the university up north, and was engrossed in dating and activities. David finished an illustrious school basketball career, and was planning a mission for our church. Beth constantly complained about the move to the new house because all her friends lived in the old neighborhood. Sam unflinchingly took to driving her back and forth almost every day. Luke was intently fixing up an old motorcycle, which he discovered in the classifieds, and was taking it for endless spins up the canyon near our house. Jed was in the fifth grade, had many friends, and was doing well. Lizzie was knee-deep in kindergarten, enjoying every minute, and Joe was my endearing little sidekick.

Autumn had languished by lazily with its bushels of burnished leaves, my absolute favorite time of year. The Thanksgiving turkey was all gobbled up, and Christmas was pounding at the door again. I thought I had learned to take Christmas in stride these days – heaven knows I'd had a lot of practice. The children were alternately unmanageable and excitedly mesmerized. The frantic preparations this year were coming along.

The Christmases of my childhood were so simple compared to those raising my own children, or so I thought. As with many things, we don't recognize the work our own mothers put in to make the silver bells ring so sweetly and the magic sweep by so fluidly. It was an illusion, to be sure. I have been surprised to learn that when you raise little people who are programmed to think Christmas is their personal Disneyland, there's so much to live up to. I'd like to revisit my mother and tell her I finally get it, and that I'm sorry I took all her hard work for granted. I think like most mothers, I feel obliged to not disappoint my precious offspring and try to fulfill at least a portion of their sweet and childish, innocently bedazzled expectations of the prodigious holiday. Yet I continue to be wound up like a yoyo on a string before the Thanksgiving dishes are dried and put away. I write copious lists at the end of each November and endeavor to stick to a rigid, serious plan. For me it is the only way to succeed, or rather, not to fail.

Number one on my list was to decorate the house as elaborately as I could afford. And if that was a problem, which it always was, I'd begin to tear "inspiration" pages from magazines and create my own. I sewed rickrack on two dozen fabric hearts from scraps and fashioned bread dough ornaments into snowmen, soldiers, dolls, or miniature stars – I literally spent days meticulously painting their clothes and colors. I'd gather every pinecone I could beg or borrow and immerse them in glossy white paint, bathe them lavishly in glitter, and then try to get all the mess off the garage floor a few days later when it had hardened into fifteen-degree epoxy. Or I'd make little horses out of painted wooden clothespins, adding mops of white yarn hair and tails, pin-dotting them all over with white, and hang them from tiny red ribbons. Or I might cut sugar cookies into stars or bells, then bake and paint them with runny transparent red and green icing, while praying mightily that the toddlers wouldn't eat the entire bottom branches clean before Christmas Eve. The children would jump up and down as we spread out the burgeoning Christmas village on the hall table and cover it in itchy spun glass to look like mounds of new snow. Some days, I admit I felt like a superhero, but that was when I wasn't totally exhausted. Sometimes we'd cut out dozens of white snowflakes from typing paper and tape them to the windows, or we'd spray canned snow in the corners as if it had drifted in the wind. That effect was immediately tracked with a dozen little finger paths.

I always went way over budget even while shopping the bargains and canvasing the dollar stores. It was definitely quantity over quality in those days, because everyone knows children equate better with more. To make things worse, I'd become overwhelmed with the work of it all, and at one point, I awoke to the startling realization that all the red and green bric-a-brac in every corner of the house was making me stir crazy. It was usually a lose-win-lose situation at best.

The pressure to have the picture-perfect little tree sprinkled with colored lights and a perfect star was immense. Before we even drove into the tree lot, I could picture the children spreading out their blankets under it before bedtime, the proverbial sugarplums dancing mystically in their heads. I could imagine their bright, stupefied little faces mesmerized by the magic, and their little flannel-pajamaed bodies cozily nestled under the tree of their dreams. I was convinced these memories would seep into their consciousness and block out any bad thing I may have been responsible for, thus positively reshaping their entire futures.

There were also the traditional Danish Christmas cookies of my mother's heritage, which were, by necessity, tied meticulously, and often sloppily, into knots and baptized in boiling hot grease that spattered the counters and ended up in small puddles all over the floor, which the children and dogs skated around in gleefully.

I must not forget the pressure of needing to be the mom who could bake a million-dollar gingerbread house – and one more elaborate and gorgeous, of course, every year. I designed, cut, baked, and assembled English cottages or French country manors, complete with golden hardened-syrup windows to fit. And we won't even describe the process of five or six children lined up to decorate them with a bucketful of assorted candy, most of which didn't make it past their sticky fingers or mouths.

I should mention parties, programs, and church dinners, which I always felt obligated to cook or decorate for, school plays with memorized parts to be learned by several children, nativities where every child in the family needed some sort of spot-on costume, or Christmas caroling around the block with friends and neighbors. Did I mention the additional adult Christmas parties I had to cook and decorate for, in order not to feel like a recluse or a snob in my neighborhood?

The point of all this recounting? It was a long time before I realized that my blanket of energy simply could not cover everything I felt I wanted or needed to do. There was, also, the jacket of guilt, which was usually thrown on at the onset of cold weather and augmented by the media coverage of homelessness and poverty we don't suffer, no matter how thinly our own finances are stretched. Because of this particular self-reproach, for a few years I began to take on the additional Christmas gifts for an inner-city family across town, somehow convinced it would exterminate a sliver of the guilt, and if not, be a good example for the children.

As wonderful as Christmas is, and of course it always is – with its gigantic doses of sentiment, good will, charity, emotional overload, and expectations all rolled together in one short month, it is enough to make the best of mothers – even mothers with only one or two small children – begin to sputter, choke, and give out. Oh, and I think I forgot to include the mandatory trip to the mall for each child to see and sit on Santa's lap. That little excursion by itself is a very long day in a life. And did I lament the time and pressure, physically, mentally, and financially, of shopping for adequate gifts, while making sure to include a few of the ones asked for? Or the hiding and the never-ending wrapping, which was usually not begun until ten-thirty or eleven on Christmas Eve, or finished up until around three in the morning? Of course I did.

49

Andy

A ndy was just finishing up a trip to the Million Dollar Highway with a busload of Korean passengers. He always enjoyed
having them on his bus, as they were unusually very polite
and easy to please. They were genuinely excited to see so many frontier
sights, as they called them. He enjoyed watching them as they carefully
and neatly arranged their belongings to settle in. They were a peculiar
and marvelous people, he thought. He wondered about their lives in
their own country.

They were a pretty quiet group for the most part, and he ascertained
the reason was that most of them spoke little or no English. However,
they seemed to be up on the best American tours and were extremely
anxious to see the sights. Andy was relieved that for this particular
tour, the home office had provided a translator to ride with them who
not only answered questions and conversed with the passengers, but
could explain the particulars of the tourist attractions.

Andy couldn't understand a word being spoken in their language,
and on this treacherous trip, he was relieved for the freedom to painstakingly navigate the road without questions or distractions. This was
probably the most hazardous trip he ever made, but notably one of the
most spectacular and breathtaking drives in the whole United States.

He had never really seen all the beauty himself, as he rarely took his attention from the road. Thankfully, he didn't have to drive this trip very often. Even with his confidence and skill, he knew he must concentrate on every small curvature and bump in the road. It was one of his preeminent proficiencies.

The winding Highway 550 runs from New Mexico to Colorado, connecting Ouray and Silverton. It is marked with hairpin turns and narrow lanes cut directly into the sides of the mountain. Andy's knuckles were always white while gripping his wheel tightly, maneuvering to keep the black monster tight to the inside of the road. Sometimes he slowed it to a crawl, to keep it safely on the path. Andy knew it was critical to be on the lookout for any aberrant obstacle or unforeseen consequence. This was one trip he would admit to not totally enjoying.

Of course, it was magnificent for his passengers. They had no idea of impending danger. Andy always checked the weather patterns carefully. Even though the drive was not much more than twenty-five miles, the steep climb and hair-raising terrain made it seem three times that long. At times, the roads were shut down without warning for various reasons. This possibility was Andy's greatest anxiety, because the last thing he wanted was to be stranded on this mountain without a decent place to turn the bus around; and there were many such stretches of this precarious but glorious road.

The Koreans were awestruck with everything outside their windows. He heard gasps as they looked down into the extremely deep ravines on the sides. The drop-offs were frighteningly sheer and dramatic. One little lady about four rows back on the left, with straight shiny hair cut into a blunt black triangle around her slightly lined face, was hovering in her seat with her jacket over her head, as if it might shield her from danger. She sat straight-backed against her chair at intervals, refusing to totally give in to her fear. Andy smiled; he thought she was brave and could relate to her concerns. Another man, probably in his early seventies, sat a couple rows behind her, his camera still securely anchored around his neck. He wore khaki Bermuda shorts that displayed thin, crinkly skin stretched tightly over small, knobby kneecaps, which reminded Andy of small round doorknobs protruding from his thighs. He had on what looked like one of Andy's dad's Tommy Bahama shirts in leafy green and white cotton, not tucked in. His hair was neatly slicked back, salt and peppered, but still heavy and thick. He was literally sitting forward and on the edge of his seat the entire time, apparently determined not to miss a moment. His vacant facial expression was difficult to read. Andy couldn't tell if he was frightened, awestruck, or bored. Most likely not bored.

These trips usually went well. The odds were actually very much in their favor, as there was no history of accident or mishap. The bus company would never take a risk with their customers, of course, but Andy knew there was always the off chance of some peril around any bend, and he felt the familiar tightness constricting his chest. It was a grave responsibility to hold so many lives in his hands.

These were the San Juan Mountains, home to many animals and birds. He knew his clients would be anxious to catch a glimpse of anything – eagles, falcon, deer, elk, mountain goats, and even black bears. A few vultures always seemed to be ominously circling high in the bright blue skies. The roads were also dotted with ghost towns and abandoned mining villages. Andy was always on the lookout for a possible area to stop, not only to let the passengers get a better view or look at an old town, but to rest his mind, walk around, and shake out his arms, which got stiff with tension. After all, these roads had been originally carved out for stagecoaches and horses, not behemoth buses. He was always on the lookout for falling rocks or ice chunks on the road, which was a distinct possibility.

Some of the altitudes of these passes were so high, he had heard of an occasional eardrum rupture, not just the usual popping that goes along with such heights. The Red Mountain Pass in particular, is a staggering eleven-thousand-foot altitude, and the Molas and Coal Bank Passes are not so different. Andy expertly wheeled the bus to the outlook area, where his people could get off and see a beautiful view of the Animas River Gorge and the twenty-five-acre Molas Lake.

Andy gingerly ascended the peaks, always reminding himself what he had learned about this highway. Built in 1883, it had been redone in the 2020s. The big question on everyone's minds was why it is called the Million Dollar Highway. He's heard several possible reasons. One was that each mile of the road cost one million dollars to build because it is so treacherous, or that the land itself probably cost that much. Another guess was that the surrounding mines are so rich in gold and silver, that the gravel taken from them to pave it cost over one million dollars. Andy's favorite theory was that many travelers experience so much vertigo on this high, winding road that they declare they wouldn't make this trip again for a million dollars.

The trip was, of course, uneventful, and his group had been enthralled to see the 285-foot Box Canyon Falls in Ouray, typically the impressive finale to the journey. He also introduced them to the famous Maggie's Diner in the town. They served quite possibly the best hamburgers on the entire planet, and Andy considered eating one his merit badge for finishing the journey without issue. There were smiles, pictures, and a few heartfelt but ill-at-ease hugs, except for the timid little lady in the fourth row. She hugged him around the waist and buried her face in his embroidered pocket, making him feel like a bona fide giant for once in his life. He then deposited them into the safety and security of a nice hotel for the night. He would be relieved by another bus driver and rig for the remainder of the trip. Gratefully, he was headed home for a few days.

50

Ella

I had thrown together a large pasta salad for dinner. It filled the big yellow Tupperware bowl to the brim. I called for everyone to come. Kids began to seep from the house like ants from a hill. The salad was made with bow-tie pasta, tomatoes, olives, zucchini, cucumbers, and chicken, slathered generously in creamy ranch dressing, and sprinkled with parsley and shredded cheese. It was large and hearty enough to fill the hungry stomachs of the whole crew, which is the prerequisite for feeding my army. The sun was scorching hot, the air was heavy, and the concrete sizzled on bare feet. Little kids jumped back and forth from cement to lawn and back, trying to avoid the burn. It was one of those days when everyone felt as wilted as the grey-green grass that was always begging to be watered. The little kids smelled like wet dogs after playing outside all day, and the sweat beaded on my own forehead and dripped down my neck.

Sam was just getting home from work, and his sleeves were rolled up past his elbows. We all brought the dishes and the food to the wooden picnic table on the deck in the back of the little house. They were just starting to dig in when I heard the rat-tat-tat of helicopter blades spinning overhead across the swelteringly clear blue skies. Its red and white thorax identified it as a medical rescue. There was something about the mixture of the baking heat, the sight of the helicopter, and the texture of the pasta in my mouth that sparked an ominous alert in my brain. Within ten minutes the phone began ringing off the hook.

The next snatches of time are divided into bullet points in my memory. I wonder if other painful memories are erased or merely stored selectively in microscopic vaults inside the brain cells, locked so tightly we will never be able to retrieve them. I intuit this is nature's way of protecting the most vulnerable parts of the soul, so it can continue in this realm without exploding and ruining everything indefinitely.

I recall vividly the winding car ride up the hillside of Salt Lake City to the hospital. It seemed to take hours instead of minutes. The exerting climb to Machu Picchu comes to mind. The hike up the steep rocky stone paths, which wind tediously up to the ancient city, was always something I hoped never to have the opportunity to do. This evening's trip up the city hillside, though in the car instead of walking, was heavy with dread, yet delicately laced with a tiny grapevine of hope. Upon arrival, the hospital staff was extremely encouraging and optimistic. "She was awake, alert, and asking about her babies. It's a good sign. She's in surgery with two broken femurs. Serious, but fixable," they assured me. For some odd reason, Sam and I were the first to arrive at the hospital. I would later wonder if that was just another assignment given to me as the oldest child.

My baby sister, Grace, had jumped into her car to drive the short couple of miles from her house to the grocery store to procure hamburger for tacos. She had buckled her babies carefully in the back seat. While driving, she turned for an instant to check on them and plowed headlong into the No. 71 Syracuse bus. An ambulance quickly arrived on the scene to convey the two little ones to the children's hospital on the east side of the city. A red medical helicopter landed in the middle of the road like a giant insect to transport my sister to another hospital on the other side of town. They released her from the mangled car with the "jaws of life."

As my parents and other sisters were ushered in, I took up the baton of being reassuring, positive, and even mock cheerful. I'm not certain it made any difference, but I began to formulate a tentative plan for our roles in Grace's recovery. I felt, as in the past, like a parent, not a child.

I recall cringing at the long, cavernous hallways, painted in a dreary off-white, with stark, white florescent lights blazing overhead. We trudged along them in zombie-like fashion, moving towards what we hoped was a place of refuge. They led us all to a conference room with a large oval table surrounded by metal chairs, which felt cool through my jeans in the summer heat. I watched the wall adjacent to the large window. The light was streaming through the blinds casting shadows on the dismal wall, striping them with rows of gray.

I was surprised to note that in an instant, my father transformed from his usual talkative, teaching self into his own mother, my grand-mother. He was completely composed, forthright, positive, though a bit grim, but uncharacteristically void of words. Without announce-ment, he powerfully assumed, without fanfare or hesitation, his role as patriarch of this bedraggled bunch, which was an enormous relief to me, the big sister. Taking a big sigh of relief, I let my role in this drama exit the stage gratefully. He didn't preach hope or certainty; he simply stood at the head of the table stoically, calmly, and silently. Finally, he asked us all to kneel down around the table, which we did, and he led us in fervent prayer and supplication.

An hour or so later, a disheveled but kindly surgeon appeared in the doorway of our makeshift chapel. No one quite remembers what he looked like, except that his shoulders were sloped and stooped, and his pale blue scrubs were wrinkled and blood spattered. His flat blue paper hat was tilted a little to one side of his head, and his matching face-mask was dangling from a breast pocket. It was easy to see he had not stopped to gather himself but had marched directly in to us, as to put the ponderous duty behind him without procrastination. He said calmly but firmly that though they had done all they could possibly do, they had not been successful in saving her. He was extremely sorry. No one doubted his words.

I remember the moment very clearly, but not as if I was part of it. It was more like standing back and watching a horror film on a black and white screen. Two of my sisters slumped to the floor as if someone had entered the room with a gun and shot them at point blank. The image of a rifle always comes to mind as I look back on these moments. These sisters were sprawled in puddles on the green marbled linoleum floor. Others, including me, were plastered against the walls as if the room was spinning so fast the centrifugal force kept us upright. My poor mother sagged in her chair leaning over the table, her shoulders shaking, her face buried in her hands. I heard a dreadful sound erupting from her throat. My father sat silently upright in his chair, but his hands were gripping its arms forcefully. His knuckles were as white as chalk. Yet I remember clearly that he did not cry a tear, at least not then. The rest of the room began to fill up with baleful noise. Sobbing, retching, and bawling; tears seemed to be streaming in every direction.

No one paid any more attention to the surgeon, but he obviously had been frozen beneath the doorframe of the horrific scene. He interrupted the mayhem with a startling question. "Does anyone wish to see her and say goodbye?" I saw jaws dropping around the room. He spoke tentatively and softly, as if he was obliged to offer us the option. All the hemorrhaging eyes in the room moved from face to face, and all heads nodded from side to side horizontally in perfect rhythm. Of course not. No. Then silence. Then my father, still strangling the arms of his chair, pulled himself to his feet as sluggishly as if he weighed four hundred pounds. "Yes," he said. "I would like to see her." My heart rotated in my chest like a three-cornered stone. *No, Dad, no*, I thought. My next thought was that he had protected me my entire life. At this moment, I realized, with great dismay, that the time had come for me to have his back. Resolutely, I told the surgeon that I would like to go, too. Sam looked at us both with great dread and a glance that yelled, *For heaven sakes, what's wrong with you two?* But because I said yes, because my dad said yes, and because Sam had my back as well, he stated simply that he wanted to go, too.

The scene in the operating room was predictably gruesome. It is the last clear picture I can conjure of my little sister when I think of that day. That and one of her as a very small girl, toddling around with white polished baby shoes and lacy anklets, a pink ruffled dress, chubby little legs, a wide-open toothy grin, and light reddish curls. Sam has understandably blanked from his mind the operating room scene, but I will never forget the buckets of blood pooling on the floor under the operating table, a coiled plastic tube snaking from Grace's mouth, a face much puffier than in life, and dark, clotting, burgundy blood matted in her long, beautiful strawberry hair.

I do not recall more than a few nuances of the funeral, but I will always remember the splendorous spray of baby pink and ultra-white roses cascading and spilling like a fountain gracefully over the sides of the rose-colored metallic casket. My thought was that the flowers were the very epitome of Grace. I do remember the dark pant legs and feet of the pallbearers moving in lock step lugubriously from the chapel to the somber black hearse parked outside. I recall the sun beating hard upon the hot blacktopped roads as the procession made its way through town. I still see the bowing heads of the tall, leggy sunflowers growing willy-nilly on the sides of the road as we turned down the narrow lanes of the cemetery. I also remember weeping uncontrollably at the sight of the small, rectangular, pale granite headstone lying level on the ground, its face looking ethereally upwards to the sun. It is etched with a lovely open-faced daisy trailing around and across its surface. In my mind, it is as clean, innocent, and simple as the soul it will shelter under the deep, dark, dry ground. It declares poignantly, but with a whisper, the fleeting dates of her brief mortality here on earth. And it proclaims tenderly her felicitous sweet name.

51

Ella

Life is nothing like I imagined. Nothing like I thought it would be if I were a good girl and tried to do what I was taught was right. I tried to keep the rules. It's as if a gigantic jigsaw puzzle was tossed into the air and my individual pieces fell like jagged rocks in slow motion, landing every which way in the mud and rocks. I thought if I could gather them all up and fit them together carefully, then my little corner of the larger puzzle would make a good picture, even if humble or small. It would lay out, go together, and make sense. I need things to make sense. I didn't know I would gaze at the other parts of the puzzle that don't belong to me and wish I had them instead.

And yes, I do see that I have some pretty darn good pieces to work with. Great ones, even. It's just that nothing fits together neatly or the way I planned or hoped. Yes, there are downright lovely fragments here and there, even miraculously perfect ones, but there are always jagged edges and gaping holes. So many blanks that never get filled. The puzzle seems wrong or incomplete.

Certainly, there are the pieces with faces I couldn't live without, places I thought never to see, beauty I could never imagine, and dreams that actually do come true. Really nice pieces I never thought to collect in a million years. But scattered among them are the heartaches I cannot bear, the injustices I cannot tolerate, the pain too searing to abide, and the sorrow too deep to get past.

Yet sometimes in the stillness, I imagine hearing just a breath of a whisper. "Do you not realize it is the holes that keep you seeking, dreaming, focused, and searching. It's the sad, lonely, and empty gaps that lead you to enlarge the borders while canvasing for pieces that fit. It is not what is there, but what is lacking that causes you to move further out than you would. When you move, there are new experiences, new landscapes, new fortes, and new faces. The substance of the puzzle defines you less than the work of putting it together. Without the holes you would not keep moving."

52

Ella

Three months after burying Grace, my parents left for an eighteen-month church mission to Denmark. My mother was born there, as well as many of my father's progenitors. It was the realization of a dream for them to visit there. I was very happy for them but had mixed emotions about their leaving, especially so soon after Grace's passing. It was a time when the family would most sharply miss them, especially the leadership and mooring of our father's influence. He'd always been a phone call away if I needed him, and even if I didn't see him for weeks on end, it was a comfort to know he was accessible. After Sam, he had been the touchstone and anchor of my life. He continued to keep me balanced when I was shaken, corrected me when necessary, and praised me generously for good choices. This was the pattern I had relied upon for as long as I could remember. He was the voice of comfort and reason from the moment I entered this world. His continual, though oftentimes incredibly verbose commentary about this, that, and everything was pivotal to keeping me grounded. He understood me as well as anyone in the world could. Dad was ever the teacher. He seemed to have the ability to see all around a situation. Occasionally even Sam went to him for advice. In the initial stages of our marriage, Sam was a little querulous as to why he would pop over on a hectic Saturday morning with an armload of vegetables from his garden or a big striped watermelon in hand and expect us to sit and visit on the porch for an hour or so. Sam had quickly been won over. We spent quite a bit of time with my parents, and we were genuinely happy for their new adventure. Heaven knows they deserved a little change of pace, a little fun and relaxation; but I would be lying if I said it wasn't an angst to have them so far away.

My parents fell in love with their new circumstances, and it was great fun for them to share. My father's letters were rich, descriptive, and informative about the country, the language, the food, the flowers, and the people. They were working hard, thriving, and having the time of their lives. We wrote back and forth almost every week. They detailed their adventures, and I kept them up on each child, family activities, and our new house in the canyon. They left before the house was completed, and I was anxious to show my father all my hard work in the garden and in the house. He would have loved to be a part of it all, as he was my harshest critic and most ardent supporter. He was generous with praise but much too forthright to withhold criticism, which made him a valued sounding board. I missed him terribly and looked forward to the day they would return.

They were gone fourteen of the eighteen months. There were only four months remaining, and yes, I always counted down. It was December again, the upside-down month of Christmas, which, as I have said, has always had a diversified effect on my equilibrium. The weather had been drifting from mildly uncomfortable to biting and frigid. It was the time of year that could not quite commit to anything.

One morning I awoke to the sound of the phone ringing. Sam had already gone to work, and I would shortly be up and shepherding the children through breakfast, morning chores, carpools, and school. I lay there lazily and let it ring a few more times before reaching over the side of the bed and fumbling with the receiver. Almost knocking it on the floor, I sleepily and annoyingly greeted the caller. I was aware that my voice sounded like wrinkled sandpaper, but I couldn't have cared less.

The alarm hadn't even gone off. It was probably just some silly kid in the neighborhood begging a ride to school. I tried to conceal my annoyance.

After saying hello, I didn't hear anyone at the other end of the line, only a peculiar buzzing sound in the receiver. I held the phone away from my ear and then back. After an inordinately long pause, there was another couple of beeps. Then I heard my mother's voice speaking softly from a million miles away. I listened intently for a few minutes to what she had to say before dropping the receiver on the floor with a clank.

All I remember is grabbing a pair of knee-length cotton pants and a long tee. I spied my flip-flops in the corner of the closet and mindlessly slid my feet into them. I half skidded down the stairway, hearing the clacking of my heels. I ambled blindly through the cold, dark kitchen. None of the children had yet begun to stir. I wrung my hands and stuck them into my pockets. Then I took them out again and ran them absentmindedly through my disheveled hair, smoothing it down to where it just grazed my collarbones. Why, I thought? Why am I bothering to straighten my hair? Ridiculous. I was outwardly calm and composed, but my emotions were like soup just starting to simmer. I glanced around my pristine kitchen. The pale morning light was cleverly trying to coax everything to wake up. It was painting soft blush-colored shadows on the windowsills, and faint light bounced playfully off the toaster and oven. It cast an eerie pink glow on the chrome faucet handles directly below the windows. I couldn't believe I was even noticing that. I whisked past the bathroom, threw open the door to the garage, and bounded outside. I was careful to close it softly, though, so no one would awaken. Company was the last thing I wanted.

I dashed up the driveway, which was slathered in mushy dirty slush, already melting in chunky rows, revealing blacktop between the striping. I was unable to form clear thoughts, yet I noticed the smallest of details. Incongruent. As I reached the gate, I began to pick up speed. I almost ran to the mouth of the canyon, about twenty yards above the house. The road is narrow and unpaved, and the washboard-like ridges of hardened dirt were now frozen solid, ice-crusted, and bumpy. The uneven surface was difficult to negotiate in my floppy rubber-soled shoes. I trudged forward, my heels sliding in and out every few feet. I could feel the sting of freezing snow beating bitterly on my head, face, and shoulders, and didn't care a whit. Dad was gone.

The dreadful realization of what my mother had told me from Copenhagen just minutes before was beginning to fully dawn, like the shafts of sunlight striking through the naked maples.

Strangely and without context, my thoughts flashed to an image of a darkened stage where I was standing. The lights simply went dark. It was as if I was forced to walk off without finishing the most important lines of my life. I was being cast aside and renounced in the middle of the second act. Over and done with, the concluding scenes would never be played out. Prematurely, the final curtain dropped with a thud. The play was over, my part in it as well. The word *disappointment* seemed anemic, and *despair*, insipid. Alone. Adrift. Drowning. Better words for what I was feeling. I was as exposed as my bare feet in the stinging snow. I couldn't fathom going forward to portray my life's character, nor did I want to, if it meant that my father was not going to be there to observe. The act was shattered, and with it, a large chunk of my heart.

I continued to trudge up the road to steeper trails. At the moment, I was emotionally unequipped to return to a warm house. An icy stream meandered down the center of the path and my ankles were immersed in frigid water. When I stepped to the sides to get out of it, I stepped on and through thin transparent crusts of ice. At the higher terrain, the trees were heavily laden with snow and were bowing closer and closer to the ground as if they, too, were succumbing to defeat. Oddly, there were no sounds emerging from my throat. Only silent tears surging from a bottomless well. As they splashed down my cheeks, some froze in my nostrils and on my chin. As they passed my open mouth, I tasted salt. It had been my understanding that life passing before one's eyes was an experience exclusive to death, yet there were pieces of mine flying willy-nilly all around like bats. In no orderly fashion, memories scuttled to the surface. Hurt, hardship, loss, children, sadness, anger, grief, and shards of fear. I was afraid that if I glanced back over my shoulder, I might see my house and everything in it burning to the ground.

Another disjointed thought sauntered unbidden onto my jumbled mental landscape. I pictured perfectly the clear sunny June day that I helped my next-door neighbor plant flowers in her front yard. The poor disintegrating and suffering woman was holding the flats of bright purple and yellow pansies in her arms while looking utterly and cheerfully hopeful. Convincingly hopeful. But on the third day of July, just three weeks later, pansies thriving cheerfully in front of the stoop, she passed away.

I had been a believer in happy endings. No matter how difficult life became, I counted on deliverance, justice, and mercy as the counterweights. I believed that compensation for sacrifice was some sort of decreed, leveling, universal law. This morning, those illusions were dashed like snowflakes melting on pine needles. First Grace, now Dad. Exhaustion had been stealthily leaching into my bones, and I felt no momentum to move in any direction. I tried to remember how long I'd been ankle-deep in snow. I felt gusts of ice whipping against my bare calves, leaving red welts like stinging bees. My toes were thick and numb, and blood was trickling across the foot-bed of one of my flip-flops. Yet, I felt like wrapping myself up in the soft snowy white blankets spread benignly all around me, and lying down on this icy trail like the weary snow-burdened branches.

My frosty brain was cold but on fire, and I couldn't think clearly. Dad. How could you do this? How could you leave us? Leave me? You were always the marrow in my bones. Now I am hollow. I will surely not stand.

Instead of sitting down, I decided to lean against a thick brown maple. Dad always said they were one of the hardest of woods. The snow sloughed off the branches above my head and splatted onto my shoulders in snowball-sized clumps. As I slumped against the tree in the calm, white silence, I suddenly had the sensation that someone or something was close by. I looked around carefully in every direction, in case there was an animal approaching, but I couldn't see anything. Yet the feeling persisted as if there were eyes watching my every move. I listened carefully but could hear nothing but my own breathing. The impression seemed very real but also vague. It was akin to straining for a closer look at a dim star in the darkness or watching a single leaf quiver on a branch while wondering where the wind was coming from. I rubbed my hand up and down my bare wet arm.

I was feeling calmer now, my breathing was slow and even. I continued to listen and began to think more clearly. If perhaps by chance, someone could be nearby, what would they wish to convey? Would they gently remind me that indeed, I had always relied too much on my father? On his life, wisdom, point of view, spirituality, steadfastness, and strength? Now that he was gone, would I have enough skin of my own to protect the vital parts? I didn't have to consider very long. The answers were flying through my consciousness rapidly, and I had no choice but to acknowledge the truth in them. It was like a gunshot piercing the quiet. It cut through the frosty air like an icicle to my heart.

The thoughts, though staggering, were, in an odd way, very soothing. I eased my body away from the tree trunk and brushed the snow from my shoulders. I was surprised at how far I had climbed. My intent had only been a wild compulsion to flee. From life, from pain, and from the appalling reality of my father's death.

I was able to think with clarity for the first time since the phone call. A distinct picture of Sam leaped to mind. I pictured my children nestled in their beds needing to get up and off to school. I pictured their sleepy, innocent, and vulnerable faces, and their soon-to-be-hungry tummies. For the first time that day, I began to worry about someone else's grief besides my own. I must hurry back to pour the juice and put the cereal in the bowls before I break the disheartening news about their grandfather. I must get myself down this hill. I pressed my bleeding toes firmly into the flip-flops, squished them together to hold them in place, and staggered downward. The tears did not stop. They continued to sheet onto my shirt, yet I could see clearly. Even though I was not blinded by them now, I knew it was likely I would continue to shed tears for a very long time.

I continued to notice the bite of the wind and the arctic sleet pounding my body. I retraced my steps and made my way back to the gate. I descended the driveway and twisted the doorknob into the house. The kitchen remained empty and silent.

The light was now streaming through the windows, and I heard quiet noises coming from the bedrooms. I wiped my face with the back of my stiff crimson fingers and grabbed the bottom of my shirt to clear the frozen snot from my face. I smoothed down my hair for the second time this morning. This time it was drenched and matted, but there was not a thing I could do about it right now. I reached into the cupboard and pulled out glasses and bowls.

53

Ella

I never felt victimized. I never thought I was unusual or alone in my motherly anxieties or pressures, but it took me much too long to see that the skittish, erratic heart beating in my chest could not carry me the entire distance I felt compelled to go. It is no wonder the scarlet fever of my early childhood finally caught up with me on a snowy Christmas Eve.

The evening in question included a Christmas Eve party brewing in the kitchen. The house pulsated with pre-Santa fever, along with the usual ensuing hysterics. My mother, Sam's parents, the newlyweds Jenny and Evan, and the rest of the children were talking, laughing, and dancing to Christmas carols. It wasn't only the little ones who were on a perpetual sugar high these days. The evening was a culmination of an extraordinarily hectic season and the precursor to a very merry Christmas.

The tree was especially beautiful and magical, the snow village everyone loved was lit up and sparkling on the mantel. There were, of course, colored lights on the eaves of the house and white icicle lights draped along the front fence posts. There were even actual ethereal snowflakes fluttering down from the dark skies just like the powdered sugar dusting our perfect sugar cookies – at least a few of them were.

In fact, everything was quite perfect. At least as perfect as it was going to get. There was an aroma of honey-glazed ham and scalloped potatoes wafting through the air, making all the mouths water. There was the traditional and favorite twelve-layered Jell-O salad in red, green, white repeated in between layers of cream cheese. There was a green salad put together by my mother and frosted gingerbread snowmen baked by Sam's. I spent the morning making my famous and now traditional crème brûlée, complete with burnt sugar topping. It was all set in individual fluted ceramic ramekins. I had run around all morning trying to scour up what I could find at the dollar stores in two adjacent cities. I had been collecting them for a few years now, and there were never quite enough. "I Saw Mommy Kissing Santa Claus," "Silver Bells," and "Grandma Got Run Over by a Reindeer" blasted from the radio, while the little ones jingled and jangled every which way.

Everything was on schedule and there was definitely a celebratory "night before Christmas" magic permeating the air. I smiled as I caught a peripheral glance of Sam's mother and mine, holding hands, laughing, and twirling to the music in a most inelegant fashion, but it made my heart happy. I must admit to feeling contentment. My work was almost done, but not quite, and I felt more than just weary. I was drained, but not much more than I was used to being. I pursed my lips and smiled, happy to have almost made it to the end, and in such style, I thought not so very humbly. I remembered a bit frantically that there were just a couple more gifts to wrap. So I asked Lizzie and Beth to join me upstairs to help with the last exchange gifts for the night's grand finale.

Lizzie and Beth sat cross-legged on the floor, dutifully immersed in their wrapping, fighting over scissors and Scotch tape while I knelt next to the long table adjacent to the window. I was exhausted but calm. I ceased my frantic wrapping for just a moment to catch my breath and to examine the feathery white flakes floating ghostly as dandelion seed puffs in the soft northerly wind. I took a moment to study them as they touched the warm windows and melted, almost as if they were taking a last bow while showing off their lovely crystalline silhouettes. It was so peaceful, so pretty. I am almost to the finish line of this year's Christmas marathon, I thought with satisfaction. I have run the race pretty darn nicely, I thought. A really good effort, if I do say so myself. Yes, I'm always saying so myself – one of my many faults, I think. I stopped just for a speck of quiet pleasure while anticipating the joyful gathering of my family. All the kids seemed happy and content, excited and anxious. That made all the stress and craziness worth it. Yet another successful run, I thought again. As I watched my daughters contentedly wrapping, they seemed to be craning their ears to the merriment on the floor below. I took a deep breath and went back to my own package.

I looked around for a paring of paper to wrap the last tiny box. I spied a bit of silver foil lying on the floor by the table leg. Perfect, I thought. Yes, just the exact size for the tube of pink lip gloss I had for Jenny. I bent forward to retrieve it. As I arose from my knees I felt a rush of lightheadedness – just a momentary burst of dog-tired dizziness, I remember thinking. Then my head began to spin like a small planet, and everything simply went blank behind my eyelids. That was all. I disappeared into the blackness.

I learned later that Lizzie and Beth had barely noticed. At first, they thought I was playing a trick or joking around. They reported much later that my throat had rattled noisily and that my eyes had rolled back into my head. They chided me to stop playing but went on with their wrapping. In a few minutes or so – that's what everyone speculated – I was up on my feet again, no worse for the wear. I shook off some confusion. There was an immediate, strange, and very fresh recollection in the forefront of my mind. I was absolutely certain I had just left an enormous hall, or perhaps a ballroom. Some sort of gathering place, one with a massive and highly polished floor. I remember studying it but don't remember if it was made of stone or some other gleaming material. Curious. I was certain I had just been standing in the center of a large group of people, each nodding their heads, smiling, and giving me instruction, but no content I could now recall. How strange, indeed. The memory was so vivid I shook my head back and forth to make it disappear. Lizzie and Beth were looking at me quizzically. I quickly came to my senses and heard the laughter coming from downstairs. We shuffled our gifts to the closet and returned to the party.

The evening went ahead as planned. Several times throughout the evening, I pondered the peculiar incident. I had no doubt that I had lost consciousness, but whatever it was and why, it was over and done with now. It was, after all, Christmas Eve. There was no time for alarm or for doctors, although I knew I must tell Sam as soon as things settled down. Christmas Eve was its own kind of cataclysm, and for now, the show must go on, especially when eight children were involved. So, for now I kept the disturbing event to myself. Everyone had a wonderful time, and when it was over, they were all nestled snugly in their beds for a long winter's nap. I fell exhaustedly into my own bed and into a coma-like slumber.

After Christmas was over, the decorations loaded back into their labeled boxes, the tree taken down, and I might add after the house was back in pretty good order, I called the doctor. I had a premonition that when I did, things would dramatically change, so I decided to attend to the order of the household first. I wasn't wrong. When I called and reported what I labeled my "spell," I was surprised at the doctor's reaction. He told me with alarm that it was exactly what he had been dreading for years. It was my heart, but of course, he had not needed to tell me that. Several doctors throughout the years had postulated with certainty that the scarlet fever of my childhood had wreaked havoc with the electrical wiring of my heart. There was no genetic malfunction, but the potential for a dangerous event was highly possible. Though structurally healthy, it became apparent that my heart could lapse into a dangerous rhythm with no warning. Because it had not happened in all these years, except in testing, they had decided to watch and wait. Therefore, the current doctor was not surprised when I suffered what they termed a cardiac death. He was only surprised that it had not occurred earlier. Even in all my pregnancies, there had not been a serious problem. "At the very least, you're lucky to be alive," he said emphatically. He told me he would call the specialists and to wait for their instructions. I knew I was caught and would be forced to be submissive. Not my strong suit.

Sam drove me to the hospital to see the specified cardiac expert for a simple battery of tests. It wasn't that I was fearful, I was quite calm. It was my nature to feel infallible, and though I braced for a change, I marched forward easily. Nothing too serious, I was certain. Whatever it was, I knew I would take it in my stride. I was willing to swallow whatever medicine was prescribed. Heavens, I am the mother of eight – I have too many irons in the fire to be thrown off kilter for too long. They'll figure it out. Sam, of course, insisted on going in with me, but I knew he was needed at work, so I brusquely hurried him off. He protested, but I convinced him I would be fine and that I'd call when I needed a ride home. "An hour or two at best, you'll see." But that wasn't the way it went at all. I did call, but only after I had been corralled into a bed and admitted to the hospital. The specifics of the next month or so were a blur of sorts, but certainly, it was a living nightmare.

What transpired that afternoon was that I arrested during the very first test, and they had been forced to use the defibrillator paddles to revive me. Formerly buoyant, tough, and stoic, within a few short minutes I was a molten mess. They certified it a miracle that I had picked myself off the floor on Christmas Eve at all. A couple of them even voiced the opinion that it must not have been my time to go. I was immediately shuffled off to a cubicle on the cardiac floor, which became my hotel room for the next five weeks.

The most predictable diagnosis was "damage to the electrical system of the heart due to the ravages of scarlet fever as a young child." Not definitively, because of the extensive passage of time, but most likely. More tests would be necessary to be certain. The impairment was, however, a typical latent symptom of the diagnosis. I thought back to the obvious apprehension of the doctors when I was a child. So,

I thought with a little irony and morbid humor – this is what my heart has been muttering about all these years. I had vague recollections of my mother's fervent admonitions to stay in bed, to be quiet, and not to run around. But I was so small, and three-year-olds are difficult to keep tied to a bed for two weeks, so it was what it was. I was incredulous that all this damage could have been inflicted by one little microscopic virus.

In the beginning, I resorted to being calm and collected, hopeful and patient. David's mission open house had a hundred or so people invited and was approaching in a week. Certainly, they would find the underlying cause of this annoying disturbance very quickly. I needed to get home to prepare David and the household. I also really needed to be with David in these last days and weeks, physically and emotionally. He was leaving our family for two full years, and I wasn't quite ready to let him go.

It seemed the doctors knew more than they were letting on. Their adamant protectiveness was all I could go on. The monitor, whose cord was snaking from my hospital gown, told them a lot, but they were waiting for more evidential testing. The nurses were attentive but discernibly anxious. They hovered around me like I was a cracked and broken porcelain doll. In and out of my room night and day, just making sure, they said. Others looked in at me with piteous expressions, as if they were afraid to cough loudly or scare me. One young male nurse rushed in one morning blurting out his surprise and pleasure that I was still alive. It was disconcerting and baffling at first, but the magnitude of the situation began to dawn on me.

I could see after the fact that the players in this horrific drama had begun to practice for the grand finale – not death, but an extremely difficult fix, which was hopefully a last resort. I learned that there was a specific protocol which must be followed before going straight to the worst-case scenario. Obviously, they knew what must be done if the drug treatments didn't work, but they saw no benefit to informing me if it wasn't necessary. So we proceeded along the prescribed path. First,

they administered an antiarrhythmic drug via IV for three days in a
row. After that, a pleasant, but adolescent orderly would wheel me to
the catheter lab, where they would cut a tiny slit into my groin and
snake a threadlike length of tubing up and directly into my heart. At
that point, the doctors, who reminded me of mischievous children fiddling with their electrical erector sets, excitedly attempted to stimulate
another arrest. I was given absolutely no sedative to calm or settle me.
I was painfully and frightfully aware of everything happening around
me. To make it more surreal and distressing, they spoke to each other
as if I wasn't even in the room. They played music, they laughed at each
other's jokes, and spoke of recent vacations. The results of each drug
tested were being checked off day by day as if on a gigantic flow chart.
If the current drug administered kept the dreaded arrest at bay, I would
happily be in the clear. That, of course, was the objective. If not, I
would end up dying – at least suddenly and for a few seconds – until
the cardiac paddles were banged into my chest again to shock the life
back into me. It was more than a nightmare. The catheter lab became
my literal Frankenstein's torture chamber.

The horrendous drills continued without success. After three more
appointed days, the wheelchair-pushing teenager arrived on his skate-
board (it seemed) to escort me to the lab, and in the end, to more
Frankenstein-ian shocks with the dreaded paddles. Yes, they did thoughtfully apply protective pads to my chest and back, but soon there were
bruises and small burns anyway.

I was extremely frightened and terribly afraid of dying, but also
equally afraid of the therapy that would spare me from death. I quickly
began to untether. I prayed, I cried, I pleaded, I shook, lost my appetite, and then I cried some more. I felt trapped in a terrible time machine or in my personal Groundhog Day. Even the doctor approaching
my bedside brought terror. It was impossible not to associate him with
the torture. Just his appearance in my room caused me to quake and
to neurotically begin moving my bed up and down repeatedly. No matter what he said to me – even if it was just "Good morning" – I felt

horror. For the first time in my life, I understood the phrase "She's a real basket case."

There was no effective drug thus far, therefore, no reprieve from the drills or the hospital stay. My children were taken in by various relatives and friends. I obsessed and worried about each of them constantly. I imagined with distress little Joey's fears. I hoped someone was paying attention to the stress and bewilderment of having his mommy suddenly taken away. I knew he couldn't understand. I was terrified that little Lizzie wouldn't get to kindergarten and back safely, or that no one would fix her hair properly. I stewed over Jed and his emotional well-being, about Luke taking too many liberties, about Andrew staying on track at school, and a million other particulars concerning them. I desperately needed to break out of this prison and go home to mother my children. They were my reason for being, and I now had no control over anything. It became almost more than I could handle. It felt like my very life depended upon getting out of this joint and back to them. That impediment, in and of itself, was a different nightmare, unrelated to my physical state, but just as critical. The whole predicament was not one I could have imagined in a thousand years. It was so not wrong. It was unfathomable. Yet, the hospital doors were sealed shut to me, and everyone seemed convinced it was for my own good. Thus, the three-day drug testing rituals went on, but in the end, it was to no avail. There were no drugs on the market effective enough to guarantee I would stay alive.

David's farewell party was going forward as scheduled. I cringed at being strapped to my miserable bed, missing his talk at church, and not being there to participate in his monumental life juncture. I was overcome with exasperation and anguish to be told the night before the gathering that little Lizzie and Joe had come down with a severe case of the stomach flu and were throwing up everywhere. Poor David was the only one there to take care of them, and I knew he was preoccupied with the uncharted two-year trip abroad, the packing and planning, his talk at the pulpit, and the big gathering to follow. This had to be very difficult for him without his mother in the house to buffer things. As for Lizzie and Joe, I knew they weren't being comforted as only I could, and I knew no one was cleaning up the messes as I would have done. Months later I found dried vomit still caked on the walls and carpets behind their beds.

It seemed as if the terrible, no good, very bad was being made more horrible every passing day. It seemed there would be no reprieve for my misery. I was sick to my stomach at the thought of a hundred or so people congregating inside my home on a snowy, slushy day, trudging mud onto my immaculate floors, overrunning my pristine kitchen with food to feed an army, and forty-two children running rampant around my clean house. I sobbed all that afternoon and evening, and when Sam made his daily supportive visits, I wept bitterly again.

After all the drugs had been tested and had failed, the predetermined last resort was put in place. There would be an internal defibrillator surgically implanted into my abdomen. A thoracotomy to open my ribs, pads sewn directly to my ventricles, and other intense wiring snaking down into my abdomen, attaching to the device. It would be the only safe solution, they asserted. The unfortunate problem was that they were awaiting the imminent arrival of a small device, which could be placed directly in the chest wall. It was so close, they said, but obviously not close enough to benefit me. How propitious, I thought cynically. We would find out that within a year, one was indeed approved.

One day, in the middle of a fairly calm afternoon, as far as hospital prisons go, I was trying desperately to stay anesthetized by the television above my bed. A man of around seventy-five or so came drifting into my room. I looked at him quizzically and shut off the TV. He just stood there and looked at me for a minute or two as if he had no idea how to begin. My first thought was that he was lost or disoriented, and I thought to redirect him. He was not tall, but old and wrinkled, his skin tan and leathery. He looked like he'd had a rough lifelong ride on a horse somewhere out on the range. He had scratchy gray scruff on his chin, and his matching hair was combed over his balding head in long thin strands. Quickly, I ascertained that he was not necessarily well spoken. His conversation wandered here and there, and he seemed to be trying his best to put me at ease, but was failing miserably. My anxiety level was on the rise just trying to listen to him. Finally, he seemed to give up on the prologue altogether. He simply stopped midsentence and unbuckled his old leather belt while unbuttoning his dark trousers. He pulled down the front of his pants far enough to display a large bulging pouch in his bare, white, dimpled abdomen. Finally, he said simply that my doctor had asked him to stop by and show me what my newly implanted defibrillator would look like. A loud gasp escaped my throat. Now I understood what he had been trying to say without saying it. He then buttoned up his pants and buckled his belt, tucking the long pointed raggedy end into his waistband. He shrugged his sagging shoulders as if to say he was sorry. Then he smiled at me embarrassedly and congenially, turned, and disappeared from my room.

My brain couldn't register what it had just seen. It was totally incongruous with anything sensitive or kind. It lacked any semblance of gentle instruction for what was about to happen to me. I felt nauseated, appalled, and dismayed at what I had just witnessed. It was freakishly unsavory, not to mention out-of-the-park frightening. No one else entered my room, so I buried my head in my hands and sobbed until Sam came to visit a couple hours later.

The surgery was scheduled without fanfare for early morning. There were no more questions or discussions. They put a new IV in one arm, and in the other, a different sort of arterial port. As they wheeled me into the operating room, I counted backward from one hundred, as they had told me to do, but I don't remember even getting to ninety-eight. I went to sleep, and the procedure was completed without my being aware of anything. I look back and cannot believe the complicated things they did to me while I slumbered. I suppose that's the one and only beauty about surgery. When I did awake, I could hear them conversing casually about this and that, once again, and playing music. Again, I felt like a nice piece of luggage on a rack that everyone was examining. But I felt like I was being strangled. I coughed and struggled with my breathing and realized I was being suffocated by a large tube coursing down my throat. Panicked, I looked at them in desperation. They told me to cough again, and gently pulled it from my throat and windpipe a little at a time. The first thing I saw when I calmed down was Sam standing at my bedside. There was unmistakable pity in his green eyes. His hand was grasping mine tightly, and he looked at me expectantly. "It's over," he said, "Everything's going to be okay."

It soon became apparent that they had sliced me open from stem to stern. The incision went from under my armpit across to my breastbone. They had opened my chest, pried open a couple of ribs, breaking a couple in the process, and sewed small electrical patches onto my ventricles. The connections were then snaked down to a bundle of wires leading down my left side and into my abdomen.

There was a large incision there as well. Staples and stitches were everywhere; now I really did resemble Frankenstein. When I dared to get a good look at my abdomen, I could see the new appendage clearly. It was impossible not to see. It was a large rectangle-shaped box sticking out abruptly from my belly. It looked exactly like the old man's when he so abruptly and obtrusively barged into my room a few days before. It reminded me of an old Sony Walkman we once had. It looked as if I had stolen it and hidden it under my skin. The corners stuck out bluntly underneath the thin casing and were blatantly obvious and obtrusive. The outline of the box was startling. There was a large rubber tube about as big as my thumb sticking out from my side. It had reddish liquid running from it into a bag near the floor. There were tubes everywhere, and alarms went off eerily every now and again. They kept commanding that I "breathe." I was wheeled into the ICU for a few days, where I felt as if even a small cough would bring a nurse running. Finally, I was wheeled back to my old familiar room, which by comparison seemed like a three-star hotel.

I never felt so ill in my entire life, nor had I ever been in so much pain. The morphine, of course, was a boon, but when it wore off even a little, the pain returned. There was pain in my chest, my abdomen, and down my left side. I could barely breathe because my ribs hurt so much. I felt I had been drained of all my blood, though of course, I wasn't. I was totally incapacitated. Any former robustness had disappeared, and I felt like a delicate empty shell. I felt weak, vulnerable, and afraid to move even the unaffected parts of my body.

I had entered the hospital a whole and independent woman. A mother and a wife. Now I was an altered mutant. I tried to be grateful, tried to be relieved, but for those emotions to become remotely real, it would take a lot more time. All I longed to do now was go home. Go home and do mundane things. I craved to vacuum. I used to hate vacuuming. Now I was anxious to do dishes, clean a toilet, or make a big pot of spaghetti and clean up the mess. Most of all, I desperately wanted to tuck each of my children into their beds, give them a kiss, and tell them I loved them and that I would never ever leave them. And I wanted to tell them, too, that everything would be all right and that things would return to normal. I knew I was kidding myself. It's funny how stepping off a ledge into an entirely different sphere can change absolutely everything. All the things you thought were boring, tedious, unimportant, or not exciting become the finest and most coveted things in the world once they're gone.

I was confused about all my unanswered prayers. I had literally prayed twenty or more times a day since entering the hospital weeks ago. I had begged, bargained, pleaded, cried, and demanded, as well as bowed my head humbly and asked. I had been certain to remind heaven of my long-term faith and a dozen other self-righteous attributes I thought I had acquired, but to no avail. My prayers had simply not been acknowledged in any way. If they had been, I presumed, the answer must have been a resounding "no." As I languished prisoner-like in my mechanical bed with the sliding side tray stocked regularly with a plastic mug of tepid water, bland food, lip balm, generic tissues, plastic bedpan, and Styrofoam cup of ice chips, I gave much thought to God's apparent silence. I did realize that my pain was only adding to my burgeoning disillusionment.

Does the God I've believed in, and been loyal to my entire life, care one little whit about my suffering? Have I been deluding myself all these years? Is the truth really that we just drift with the random winds and are subject only to the tides? Do we foolishly cower on the shoulder of the road with our thumbs out, hoping we aren't mowed down? And if we happen to be spared, is it merely the luck of the draw? Has my faith been juvenile and silly? Has that faith served me at the most critical time of my life? Just look at this broken body, this flailing, crazily beating heart, and now this hideous protruding box on my belly. Have I been one of the sheep, blindly bumbling along behind the blindfolded flock? Have sweet fables pacified me through the lesser storms? Have I idiotically banked on impertinent principles? If so, then now what? Do I join the ranks of the questioners, the cynics, or the sit-back-and-waiters that I have always disdained?

54

Ella

I could see a little light seeping through a crack in the hospital doors. It seemed there might be a way to finally get through them and back into the real world. I felt like an injured cougar with a slim but possible chance of being sprung from her cage. My survival instincts were heightened and attuned. The paperwork was ordered and signed, and I was feeling the enormity of the huge event dangling like a carrot over my head. The morning of my scheduled reprieve, Sam went to bring the car around to the front of the sprawling factory doors to rescue me. I had packed my meager belongings into a large white, hospital-logoed, string-tied plastic bag. There were only the clothes I had come in with the month or so before, a couple of books, and a few toiletries Sam had brought. I cannot tell you how excited I was to leave this prison. I was feeling as close to hope and excitement as I had in many weeks.

I was watching for Sam as expected, but instead, it was my doctor who strolled into my room. The electrophysiologist. The torturous savior. I felt the hairs on the back of my neck begin to rise. He had, indeed, saved my life with his vast stores of knowledge, significant skills, and extensive lab tests. He was also the expert who had never really treated me like a human being with fears and feelings, but more like his fortuitous little lab rat. He strode through the door quickly as if he was making a short and annoying stop before heading out to eat his lunch. He quickly advised me that the orderly would be down any minute to wheel me back to the catheter lab one last time for an angiogram, and obviously, one more shock. "Why? What for?" I asked him timidly, with alarm.

"Well, to test out your new defibrillator, of course," he said impatiently with a smidge of an eyeroll.

"But, why?" I was getting worked up now.

"Because, it's my protocol, and I cannot let you leave the hospital without the test."

I felt a sinister storm erupting precipitously through my whole body beginning at my toes and moving rapidly up into my chest. The deluge of tears began to flood down onto my blue and white chevron patterned hospital gown. I tried to cough back the sobs bursting from my throat but was unsuccessful. "I can't do it," I pleaded. "I just can't." The tears fell in torrents now.

He pointed an elegantly tapered finger at me and shook his head in high-minded disgust. "I'm sorry. That's the deal."

I could hear my own pathetic sobbing now as if it were coming from somewhere else in the room. It sounded like a feral cat in the early stages of howling. I was feeling and acting like a prisoner all over again, and I knew that he meant business. I knew there would be no way out except through his personal tunnel. I continued to sob.

At that very moment, however, providence made a surprise visit to my room, waving its erratic, yet merciful hand. The surgeon who had performed the complicated handiwork at the other doctor's bidding just happened to pass by the open doorway. He stopped in the hall, paused, walked in, eyed the doctor circumspectly, and glanced over at me weeping uncontrollably in my bed. "What in heaven's name is going on in here?" he asked, with not a small measure of annoyance. The other doctor totally missed the nuance of annoyance and appeared to be high-handedly pleased with himself.

"I just stopped in to let her know that we will be testing the device one last time before she goes home. That's it."

The kindly surgeon looked back at me crying and cowering in my covers. He paused another few seconds, looking perturbed. "No, we will not be," he said sharply with even more superiority, obviously due to his higher rank and stature in the hospital hierarchy. "Let the poor girl go home. I tested that device nine times in the operating room, and it works like a charm." He waved his hand dismissively. The first doctor looked as if someone had poked a large stick into his abdomen and the air was slowly seeping out like in a bloated cow. He shook his head in disbelief and offence, but he did not retort. He looked icily in my direction, turned on his heels, and left the room without a word.

I traded in my austere hospital room and mechanical bed for my lovely and comfortable bedroom at home. My broken ribs hurt almost all the time, as did the incisions in my chest and abdomen. It was difficult to breathe in and out without wincing. But I was immensely grateful to be home. For the first while, I didn't let myself think about the future. I settled into my bed, limping in and out of the bathroom when necessary. The children frolicked about the house, in and out of my room, obviously very happy to have their mother alive and home, even if she could not go too far or do much. The rumors around the close community had been rampant, and the poor children had heard them all.

Sam catered to my every need, staying home from work as long as he could afford. My mother came three times a week for a couple of hours to do the laundry. A neighbor picked up Lizzie after kindergarten on the front porch of a neighbor's house where the school bus deposited her. It was nearly a mile down the hill from our home, and I could picture my little girl bundled up in her little green coat hugging her yellow Big Bird backpack, while hovering on the cold cement porch steps waiting patiently. Every minute she was late I worried. Neighbors brought in dinner for a few weeks, which was helpful to Sam, and a relief to the children. However, it had been drilled into me from childhood that one must be independent, do your own work, and not expect others to do what you can do for yourself. If nothing else, the pre-divorce poverty had reinforced the ABCs of that independence. Obviously now, we needed this charity, and this was an exception to the rule. But it grated on my nerves when the doorbell rang around six o'clock, and I could hear sweetly channeled, cheerful voices in the entry. After a week, I wanted to pull the covers over my head and hide. After that, no one came inside anymore but simply dropped off the assigned food and left. I began to feel like a project.

Sweet baby Joe was only three, and he was most jubilant about my return. It was as if his own life and well-being had been restored after having them snatched away suddenly. With great despair, I had continually pictured his terror at my sudden and lengthy departure. Of course, it was difficult for me to be separated from him as well, but toddlers don't do well without mothers. They have no ability to reason the future. He frolicked joyfully around my bed all day long, playing with his toys, climbing up and down and around me, letting his little legs dangle from the footboard, and crawling back and forth under the box springs. I was heartsick that he had suffered such a trauma, and worried about possible future outcomes. Silly as it was, I felt tremendous guilt about it, but there was nothing to be done now except hope he would not suffer long-term anxiety or worse. I reveled in his seemingly renewed contentment.

I stayed tethered to my bed for the better part of six months. In the first week or two, I felt as helpless and exposed as a naked baby robin whose scrawny body had been blown from its nest onto the cold hard pavement. My limbs felt as spindly as the robin's neck might appear. My strength had been drained gradually, not only from the surgery, but also from being restrained to a bed for so long.

The bundle of wires running down my left side under the skin and into the device in my abdomen were the most difficult to heal. All I had to do was move or turn, and the newly formed scar tissue began to tear away. It was seemingly impossible to be still enough in any position to allow the tissue to reconnect. My insides felt like they were continually on fire. I paced the floor weeping and hunting for a comfortable spot to land. When I could not bear it, I gave in and called the doctor. He didn't return my call for several days, and when he did, he arrogantly intimated that if I wasn't willing to listen to him in the hospital on that last day, then why should he waste his breath now? Needless to say, he wasn't helpful. When I did start to feel well enough to move about, it was difficult to walk up and down the stairs. I was winded at the fourth step. I knew it would be a long, slow road to becoming my old self again, if I ever did. I had been, heretofore, a young, energetic woman. Now I felt like a freak. I felt damaged and altered, not to mention unappealing. My sense of self was murky and distorted. When I stood before the mirror, the large box with sharp corners protruded from my emaciated body like a forty-eight-count crayon box just below the skin. I couldn't imagine how a pair of pants or a skirt could hide it. It didn't make me feel any better that Sam displayed no reaction. He would never be disparaging, even if he were inclined.

I spent most days nestled in my comfortable bed – frustrated at times, peaceful at others. The biggest part of me was still so happy to be home and alive. I endeavored to accept the inevitable sustained recovery. My life had been sharply revised, however, and I was acutely aware that there was no way to change it back. Like most people, I thought something like this would never happen to me, even though I had been aware of the arrhythmia most of my life. We all witness horrors on the news happening to others, but we're certain that it's never going to happen to us. There are many things more terrible than this, of course, and yet here I was, astounded at my misfortune. It was dawning that I had much to come to terms with, and I began to realize I would need to start reckoning with it.

I often studied the pretty blue and yellow flowered quilt draped over the rail of my footboard. It was pieced in triangles like the Flying Geese pattern I used to see at my grandmother's quilting bees. The blue was gentle like the rain in midsummer, and the yellow was soft and creamy like smooth lemon ice cream. I stared out the windowpanes. The wintery skies were usually cement or charcoal, and the dark bones of the bare trees stood out stoically. They were faithful sentinels guarding my castle dungeon. I watched the snow drift softly or in sheets, depending upon the day and the direction of the wind. Translucent icicles either grew fat and long or shrank quickly, dripping water droplets from their sword-like points. If I couldn't sleep, I stood at the same panes of glass and studied the tree shadows crisscrossing the snow like latticework or roping down the hills like thick black snakes. In the morning, the sun shone brightly through the glass, throwing brilliant shards of light across my bed. I tried to chase away the boredom by reading books or watching television.

After a while, I grew accustomed, even comfortable, with being bedridden, and it actually became easier to enjoy as the days slipped by. I did much reflecting, fiddling with theories or reorganizing thoughts. I did this instead of purging the cupboards and drawers like I usually like to do in the winter months.

I never stopped praying, but in the first weeks, regular bouts of "why do I bother" crept in. I kept up the praying, and one day it dawned on me that my prayers were becoming extremely deliberate, not just out of expediency or habit as in the past. Yes, anger had blazed an acidic pathway through my veins and brain, but now I was seeing that my fury had not really been directed at God at all. It took some time for me to realize that it had mostly been borne of deep disappointment and the disquieting and frantic fear of leaving my children behind like my little sister had done. My world had been toppled and my core of certainty had been raggedly dislodged. A new bearing would require resettling and reassessing. Thankfully, I had the time.

I did much reflecting on my grandmother's austere life. I went over and over her heart-wrenching losses and, more importantly, her reaction to them. I thought about Levan and the excruciatingly lonely and long life she had lived. My mind held a clear black and white snapshot of her standing stoically at the little window of the front door of the tiny old house, watching the snow falling in the darkness, winter after long winter. I considered her deep disappointments and how different they were from my own. They had been substantially harsher in most respects. How did her faith not waver in all the long years of yearning, isolation, and sorrow? What propelled her to keep going and keep plodding through her unremittingly mundane and humble routines? Was it simply survival or something much more? I had known her well enough to know she was as firmly planted in her beliefs as the stubbornly rooted peony bulbs buried deep in her yard. She remained steadfast to her convictions until the day she died, though crippled, in pain, and debilitated. In her silent, taciturn way, she had made the declaration that she would rather endure with unswerving resolution than be ground down like a dainty wildflower beneath the heel of a shoe. I reasoned that had she not so declared, no one would have ever faulted her.

I also spent some time reexamining my father's life. It had not exactly been a cakewalk or ride on the fast train for him either. He was raised in poverty in a blink-and-miss-it little farming town without a father. He had been given no leg up by anyone. He left his high school position as student body president to serve his country in a grave and critical world war. He pinched pennies and worked two or three jobs to achieve a college degree. Yet he struggled and worked relentlessly his entire life for things he simply could not hold on to. He strained to support his large family on a meager schoolteacher's salary while janitoring at church buildings after school and on Saturdays to make ends meet. I remember when he pumped gas at a little station on the outskirts of town to pay the mortgage. Later, he labored arduously from dawn to dusk in a hot, dank dry-cleaning business which he purchased with his last dime, and which never amounted to more than just sustenance. Yet I never heard him whine or complain about unfairness. He never lay down but just kept on working as hard as he could. I can sit and all but hear his easy laughter and positive opining sermons, and I can't help but smile. He lost his beautiful red-haired youngest daughter to death prematurely, he let go of his own dreams, and he gave the last days of his life serving a mission for his church in a far-off country. Yet he clung firmly to his principles as if they were grafted to a rod of steel. He did it through an itty bit of feast and a whole lot of famine. He, too, simply chose to keep believing.

For a time, I was in the habit of endlessly asking the "why" question. It would have been extremely helpful if someone had actually showed up beside my bedside in the middle of the night to hold my hand tenderly while patiently explaining the plan to me in black and white terms. Disconcertingly, it took a lot longer than it should have for me to realize that my prayers had not been ignored or denied. The miracle I had desperately pleaded for turned out not to be dodging a life-changing event but waking up to finish the party on Christmas Eve. It had been to get the medical help necessary to go on living and raising my children, as I so frantically desired. How miraculous were those things? When I was sufficiently malleable and humbled, it was very clear that the reply to my pleading and demanding had not only been given freely, but had begun long before I had even recognized that I needed to ask.

Nowadays if I'm clear-headed, which is only part of the time, my thoughts wander to the light behind the clouds on a spring afternoon and the ominous grinding of boulders moving in the rushing creek bed in front of our house. I recall the hefty cobalt bluebirds wobbling precariously on the little feeder while chubby squirrels scurry to clean up underneath. I think about the deer families crisscrossing the backyard beneath the majestic silver pines. I think about icy blue delphiniums and silky coral roses crawling up and around the arbor, always astonishing in their prettiness. I remember waking on a clear spring morning to spy waxen white snowdrops poking their bright heads through layers of freezing snow, heralding the subsequent arrival of the lush peonies and lilacs. Higher hints and broader promises. I like to think that if God created such a vast and lovely world for his children, he must love them dearly, in spite of the difficult things He must allow them to learn.

I am learning from my own mothering that because you love your children more than your own life, you would do anything to give them happiness. But because you love them so much, you don't give them everything they want in the very way they want it. Despite the heartbreak, you try to give them what they need. Even if they come to hate or discard you.

So, I continued my prayers, and they were, perhaps, more plaintive and less demanding. I am gradually learning to ask for answers, not outcomes, though I don't always do that. I need to ask for understanding and patience, not just relief. I endeavor to ask for strength instead of liberation. I would like to be able to ask for comfort in pain and perseverance in anguish. I'm not always successful, of course, but I am attempting to be more yielding and cognizant of blessings. That's always a good place to start.

55

Ella

For Sam and me, Andrew's path was not remotely clear. Personally, I was hoping for a harbinger or sign. College was the natural progression for most of the children, and the one thing quite clear to us both, was that Andrew would have neither a penchant nor aptitude for higher education. No doubt, university is not for everyone. Many have no opportunity and just as many have no inclination, but Andrew was suspended in a subcategory all his own. It was a dilemma. He had his diploma, but we didn't have the foggiest idea where it would lead or what good it would do. We often talked long into the night debating what to do for him. We had always felt, since he had been a toddler throwing his hearing aids into the street, that we had a great responsibility to him. The years had showed us he was very good at bobbing and weaving, and falling through any cracks in any system. Now that we didn't have to herd him through school, we were at a loss as to what we could do to further his progression. It was much harder now than making sure he got to school and stayed there.

Sam finally resorted to taking Andrew to work at his exhibiting business. They designed and fabricated trade show and museum exhibits, and coordinated large company events. Each of the children, at one point, worked there as teenagers. Jenny had kept the books, and David was an excellent runner – "gophering" here and there as needed. Beth was a proficient receptionist. Luke had done several different jobs and was showing interest in following Sam indefinitely. Andrew was now hired to be a runner as well. He was a proficient driver, but as usual, lost focus easily. He would be given an assignment to deliver an item or obtain one and wouldn't come back for hours. He chatted endlessly with the vendors, losing track of all time, and wandered through the city happily taking in the sites. There was no malice or mischief, just impulsivity, but obviously, the job didn't last long.

The next employment opportunity for Andrew was working at a gas station in town. As he loved and understood all vehicles, it was right up his alley, I thought. It seemed to go well enough as long as he didn't have to work the cash register, which he simply could not do. He was very good at pumping gas, cleaning windshields, and being helpful and friendly with the customers. In the end, unfortunately, he was let go for giving friends and family "good deals" on car parts. He simply misinterpreted the concept of what belonged to the business owner and why there were not automatic discounts for relatives. He also couldn't comprehend the importance or purpose of inventory. He assumed that because the parts were on the shelves, they were only part of the general services, and that it was of no consequence how they came or went. He seemed genuinely shocked and hurt to be in enough trouble to lose his job. He truly thought he was being helpful by giving everyone what they needed, and for a good deal. Again, it was his aim in life to serve and be helpful, and I had always known that his first choice was to become a police officer. I knew, also, that if he could pass the academy exams, he would serve well. Yet, I was realistic enough to know he could never cross that line to find out.

As much and Sam and I stressed about further job options for him, Andrew made a surprising choice for himself. Without informing or consulting with us, he simply drove down to a local towing company, approached the counter, flashed his brilliant grin, and asked for a job. Of course, he could drive a tow truck, he told them. He wasn't stretching the truth about that. He knew large vehicles, always had. He knew he would be good at it, and I have no idea how he knew it. He said it would be no problem to drive a large vehicle, a C-class, he said knowingly. It was, of course, something we had not remotely considered. We were quite surprised, and I remember laughing out loud when he told us. But the last thing we wanted was to discourage him. In truth, I was relieved and hopeful, proud and encouraging.

He now had somewhere to go and a way to make a little money. We were a bit intrepid about his success at this new job after what had occurred with the others. The last thing I wanted was for him to try so hard and fail again. And if so, what would his options be? Would he survive another blow? I needn't have worried. He did very well. He put in the necessary time to train, did the job proficiently, and proudly brought home his paychecks. He had soon honed the necessary skills to wheel the tow truck around with ease and self-confidence, expertly rescuing every stranded vehicle assigned to his care. He made friends everywhere he went, and was well liked by his employers and coworkers alike.

He talked to everyone about anything and everything. He made fast friendships with the police officers who attended the accident scenes. His congeniality made the job a perfect fit. Shooting the breeze was something he could have had an advanced degree in. Best of all, he was happy. He was, actually, exuberant. He was overjoyed to put on his uniform and go to work every day, and he came home to dinner just as happy, prattling on and on about his daily escapades. Of course, he liked literally every person he met. He was rarely inclined to judgment. The benefit of the doubt came as naturally as breathing. My only fear where that was concerned was that he could be taken advantage of.

Andrew began to go out on dates a little here and there, nothing more serious than a few movies or Cokes. But one day he met Muriel, a mud-faced little waif of a girl with stringy dishwater hair and small blue eyes. She latched onto him like a magnet to his tow truck bumper. I didn't worry too much about them. I was thrilled he had someone who seemed genuinely to care for him. Fitting in had always been a problem. He hadn't dated or even attended the prom during high school. He was affable, so he always had a few friends, but no one he could relate to for very long.

When he turned nineteen, it was decided by Sam and me, not Andrew, that he would serve a two-year mission for our church, as the other boys had done. He didn't object, and actually, he seemed excited about the prospect. We were certain it would be good for him on several counts. It would give him a bit of structure, time to gain a little maturity, and a way to strengthen his interpersonal abilities, not to mention it was the traditional way young men of our background learned to serve. Andrew seemed anxious to follow in his brothers' footsteps, and was enthusiastic about the adventure. He was called to serve in a nice sunny spot of California, and he was pleased as punch. With the usual tight family budget, the suits, white shirts, ties, and sturdy shoes were purchased, along with the many other necessities for the two years' travel. The launch was on schedule, though I dreaded every passing day. I worried and stewed; and for good reason, it turned out.

He gave the customary pre-mission speech in church the week before, reading proficiently from the script he and I wrote together out on the back deck one summer evening, me with a flat stone lolling in my chest. I don't think anyone who listened to the talk knew that he understood only a fraction of what he was preaching so fervidly. His reading skills had always been so good. When it was over, he was pounded on the back appreciatively and hugged adoringly by almost the whole congregation. I was proud of him.

In truth, I had a hundred emotions fluttering from my brain to my stomach that day. Is it too late to back out? Will he be terribly homesick? The thought terrified me. I recalled the many nights in his childhood when he would awaken and need a drink of water or go to the bathroom, but also need to be soothed and calmed from his nightmares. I rationalized that he would be relatively far away, but not so far that I couldn't rescue him if I had to. He was all grown up but still so very vulnerable, and I suspected that part might never change. I worried that he might never be totally self-sufficient. I wondered if those he encountered in his new world would appreciate his sweetness and sensitivity. Or would they expect more than he could give, simply ignore him, or brush him aside. Would they give him the leeway to bob and weave and get lost in the fray? Would they perceive his kind heart or be critical of his circular conversational ability? Would they cut him some slack, and not judge him as being simple or slow? Would they find a niche for him to serve with a little confidence? I wasn't certain of anything at this point, and yet as his mother, I knew I must open my arms enough to let him venture out into this big scary world. He needed to try. He had always wanted to try.

I had flashbacks to the hospital days with the neurosurgeon when he was only two. He always had a big smile on his little chubby face and looked expectantly at me as if to say, "Am I doing what I'm supposed to do? Are you happy with me?" I felt sad even then as I held him in my arms a little tighter. How did we get here from all the way back there? It wasn't going to be easy to let him go, but I could see he was pushing outward, as he saw others do. He wanted so badly to be normal.

I hugged and kissed him good-bye at the airport, clutching his navy-blue suited shoulders as tightly as I dared. He clenched his carry-on satchel with both hands, and his missionary badge hung crookedly on his lapel.

What I desperately wanted was to tug him back, tell him this was a big mistake, take him home, and lock him in a drawer forever. Of course, I did not do that. As he left the gate to board the plane, there was so much trepidation palpitating through my chest I thought I might not be able to go through with it. I felt poised to fly towards him at the slightest variation in his countenance. Yet, when I saw the gigantic grin plastered upon his childlike face and felt flooded with excitement, pride, and hope, I swallowed back the tears and bit my cheek until it began to bleed. I simply stood still, hands glued to my sides, and let him go.

I had spent all the days of his life worrying, manipulating, and shepherding. Now I must mark this bittersweet milestone and let him march through that gate. I had to allow him the freedom to fly through the air to somewhere completely foreign. My head told me it was a hurdle worth the jump, but my heart said it would be very difficult for him, and perhaps more so for me. I desperately hoped that the mission machine, which would receive him shortly, would be proficient and kind. I prayed they would take good care of him.

Yes, we had come so very far, but I sensed that the dreaded unknown was skulking around the bend, ready to enfold and snatch him. Little did I know that my last sliver of imagined control would evaporate like the exhaust of the plane he was flying away on.

I counted the days until his first letter arrived. It was upbeat and cheerful, and I was comforted because I knew that Andrew had no idea how to "put on a good face." If he said he was happy, then he was happy. It seems he had taken to the mission with fervor – not so much for the work and not for the premise of purpose, but for the fun and the friends he was making. Obviously, his performance was not rooted in expertise or aplomb. He did try very hard to do what he was told, which was all I ever hoped for. He loved and embraced every person he met and made many new acquaintances, which is what always kept him interested. Under the circumstances and against the norm, the mission president called me quite regularly to report. I realize now with great appreciation that his instinct was to reassure me. He was kindly, understanding, and supportive, and he clearly had a real affection for Andrew. He didn't expect too much but encouraged and loved him. What more could a mother have asked? He reported that everyone was drawn to him, always a positive thing, and that they were happy to have him. Yes, he affirmed, he's not the sharpest tool in the drawer, but we are enjoying him. His words were not meant to be critical or unkind, and I completely understood. All I cared about was that he was doing fine.

I cannot find the words to describe the relief I felt. My days sailed by easier now knowing someone else was firmly holding the reins. The reins, which had left permanent calluses on my palms and on my heart-strings.

56

Ella

A ndrew was the fourth child in the family to serve a mission, so the routine was not new to us, but the uncertainty of his success made it nerve wracking. Several months into his mission, life at home was moseying along at a pretty smooth clip. The weather had a familiar crisp bite to it and all the trees shed their beautiful leaves like tattered orange and yellow jackets. We had a pleasant Thanksgiving, and were beginning to make plans for December. I should have known that with Christmas approaching, impediments and difficulties always tagged along behind, holding the holiday's hand like naughty children.

About ten one evening, just before retiring to my bed, I received a phone call from Andrew's mission office. I felt a nervous twitch in my face as I put the receiver to my ear. After exchanging a few pleasantries with the kindly mission president, I waited for the punchline of his call. I heard, as well as felt, the ear-splitting thud of the first shoe dropping. He told me gently and carefully, that Muriel had been writing to Andrew, and much too often. That came as no surprise, as I had expected as much. He said, however, that Muriel had begun to write detailed letters detailing the sexual abuse meted out by her stepfather. Oh, no, I thought with alarm, well aware of Andrew's caring disposition regarding injured animals and humans alike. I suppose I should have felt a pinch of sympathy for Muriel, but I did not. I was furious that she would burden Andrew with her poison, trumped up or not, and I immediately had suspicions about that. Andrew had been trying so hard to succeed in a new circumstance, and I felt automatic misgivings about her entire story. The president went on to say that this had been terribly disconcerting to Andrew, of course, and revealed that he had confided tearfully, asking for council. Muriel wanted, no, she had begged him to come home. After much discussion, the president was chagrined to report the crucial outcome of the situation. Andrew had impulsively purchased a bus ticket, and without an inkling that he should probably try to hide the fact, he openly declared his plans to return home. The president gave me the necessary details. He told me the name of the bus company, the bus number, and the time Andrew would be arriving. He also said that under these unusual circumstances, he would gladly welcome his return to the mission field, if we were of the mind to facilitate it. In that moment, my heart stopped its crazy, arrhythmic beating and stood still. I started to breathe in through my nose and out through my mouth.

The next morning at three-thirty, Sam and I drove an hour south to meet the bus, which was scheduled to arrive around five. It was still dark when we entered at the back of the tiny bus depot, where we waited and watched in silence. The darkness echoed and amplified my dismal mood. I wept at intervals, attempting to get control of my irrepressible emotions. I knew it wouldn't help for me to be undone. Conversely, I had to steel my nerves for the ensuing encounter. Dim streetlights poured small dreary ponds of light over and around the lumpy black asphalt, casting shadows everywhere. Mists of fine rain shimmered under the domed hooded lights. It was frigid inside and out, and we kept the motor running to stay a little warmer. We didn't speak because there were no words to express. My heart felt like a cold, stale potato – bland, pallid, and mushy. It was obvious to both of us that we had failed in our endeavors to help our son. How foolish of us to have sent him on such an indeterminate journey. It was no surprise he would be such a naive and willing victim to Muriel's devious plans. We knew without question why he had fallen prey to them. We also knew full well that she did not need saving, least of all by Andrew, who was the real victim in this drama.

We saw large round lights coming towards us like hollow eyes in the darkness, and the big silver bus glided in like a gargantuan loaf of bread on a moving platter. It slowed to a stop not ten feet in front of our car. The instant the door opened the lights inside blinked on. It felt a bit voyeuristic, like peeping into a room you shouldn't be. The passengers were putting on coats and gloves, chatting, picking up luggage and packages, and filing towards the front. Most looked bedraggled and tired from driving the entire night. One by one, they descended the stairs and dispersed to their different ways. We quietly watched the lighted room on wheels, trying to catch a glimpse of our boy. Finally, when the bus was almost emptied, we saw his slight frame making its way through the aisle to the doorway, absolutely clueless that someone was waiting to heave a roadblock at his heroic objective. Seeing him after so many months felt surreal, and I was drenched to the bone in sadness and homesickness. A memory leapt to my mind from many years before when Andrew was only ten or eleven. As I comforted him from his regular night terrors, he told me sobbingly about a recurring dream he was having. When I coaxed him to relate it, thinking it would calm him, I see now I was less worried than I should have been. He told me he often dreamed that he was alone on a bus driving to somewhere far away from our family and home. Wiping his eyes and sniveling, he told me how sad he felt to leave us and hoped that it would never happen. I put my arms around his little shoulders and rocked him, saying it was just a nightmare, and that everybody has them. I assured him that the dream would never, never come true. I promise. You will always be our boy.

Andrew gathered his meager belongings, his coat draped through one arm, and moseyed down the bus stairs, unknowingly walking towards us. He was studying the diminishing pile of suitcases that had been removed from the bus's outside compartment, piled on the black-top to be retrieved. It was only then that I saw it, and I had to catch my breath when I did. The sight of it caused me to literally sag in despair and futility, and the tears again began to pour from the wellspring behind my eyes. Seeing it was almost more than I could bear. I knew of Andrew's passion for saving anything living or breathing, and at that moment I knew that this mission, along with our dreams for its benefit to Andrew, was likely over and done with. I know Sam felt the same way. I heard the sound of air being sucked hard and fast from his throat. What we saw was clutched tightly in Andrew's right hand, the one without the coat and the bag. The disturbing "it" was a long-stemmed plastic red rose. As I looked more carefully, I was stunned to see that it was lit up in the center of the bloom. It was a plastic, battery-powered, glowing red rose, the gaudiest thing I had ever seen. Obviously, a gallant gesture for poor unattractive and insipid little Muriel.

To say he was surprised would be understatement. He was also confused and angry. As gently and kindly as we could, because it was not easy to muster the necessary magnanimity, we gathered up our son and placed his belongings in the trunk of our car. We drove straight to his brother's home nearby for a family pow-wow. He didn't say a word the whole way.

Once at David's house, we telephoned the mission president. He counseled us, and he cajoled Andrew. Jenny and her husband arrived to buffer the blow, and Luke and his wife came shortly as well. The children were sensitive and kind.

They knew Sam and I were vulnerable in our own way, and they did their best to support Andrew and us. As we look back on that dismal dark morning, the one bright spot we remember is the tenderness and the scaffolding of our other children. We have rarely felt so loved.

In turn, each presented the logical arguments to Andrew: This will not work. Muriel will be okay. Legal help can be obtained. You will be happier if you go back to finish your obligation. Quitting is not the right thing to do. You made a commitment. You must live up to it, and if you do not, you will always regret it. They persistently pledged their support and devotion to their brother and to the cause. Andrew was discouraged, defiant, and dubious for a little while, but also cheered and warmed by his family's affection. He finally agreed it would be better to return to the mission field. He even began to echo their arguments. Yes, he could be insolent and stubborn, but usually Andrew was carried along with the sweep of enthusiasm, no matter which way it was headed. Without giving him time to change his mind, all the men in the family – Sam, Jenny's husband, David, and Luke – shepherded Andrew and his luggage out to one of the larger cars and headed for California. I've been told it was a joyous journey, enjoyed by all. Plenty of laughter, fifty shredded beef tacos, and gallons of soda. Once back at the mission office, Andrew was happily welcomed by his kindly president and glad-handed genially by his compatriots. Father and brothers hugged and applauded Andrew's decision and promptly and uneventfully returned home.

I felt like a sandbag of sharp rocks had been lifted from my sagging shoulders. Now, maybe, I could start planning for Christmas. Back to safe harbor. But a small nugget of something in the outer reaches of my mind suggested that this save had been much too easy.

A week after Christmas, there was one more call. This time the mission president, with kindhearted sympathy in a large booming voice, told me that Andrew was AWOL again. This time he had no idea as to arrival time. All he could tell me was that Muriel's mother had sent Andrew a plane ticket, and he was winging his way back home.

I was too devastated to formulate a plan. We waited every day for some word from him, but it never came. After a week or two, we heard through the grapevine that he was living with Muriel and her parents just a couple miles down the road. I couldn't believe he wouldn't call or come home, even momentarily. I couldn't fathom how he could be so close yet be a million miles away. I was angry, devastated, and disoriented. We discussed what it would look like to storm over there and make various demands, but at this point, it was out of our control. We also knew that his need to save Muriel was greater than his need for us right now. He was in love and deemed himself Sir Lancelot. Andrew was making all his own decisions now, decisions I never thought he would be inclined or have the disposition to make. So, for good or for bad, and for all our blustering, our opinions would be like spitting into the wind. So, we hunkered down and went on. At least that's what we did physically. Emotionally, there was no peace for Sam and me. It's all we talked about, thought about, and what filled many of our dreams, day in and day out. I cried myself to sleep most nights. I really do not know how we got through those months. Those are the days you unconsciously wade through, hoping you wake up to see the next. Your body just keeps on breathing. The other children were needful and busy, and again, I couldn't just lie down and stop. It was another choice I didn't have the luxury of making.

The aftershock of Andrew stealing home like a thief in the night to live with Muriel's family was that my equilibrium was upside down. It took about five months before I felt I was making progress. Andrew was always in the foreground of my thoughts, but I had ceased to retch or cry except on occasion. I resumed my routine without being on autopilot. I was starting to relax and move on as best I could. After all, there wasn't much I could do. The hole in my heart was beginning to grow a thick protective scab.

57

Ella

ndrew had been living with Muriel and her parents now for about eight months. Ironically, the daily grind was the thing that kept us plodding forward. Often you are not aware of the blessing of continuing to do what must be done. It was a time in our lives when every dollar was allocated. In fact, it was not much different, in that regard, from most years. The paychecks were deposited into the bank like clockwork. I kept an organized and strictly updated check register, as well as a detailed budget sheet, which I checked and re-checked. It was not a choice; it was a necessity. The kids used to hate coming home from school on bill-paying day, which amounted to once every couple of weeks. I would be hunched over my checkbook, enve-lopes, and invoices, tapping away on my little calculator for an hour or two. My mood was always impatient, sharp, irritable, and frazzled, and the kids sped past the office from the back door without stopping, to avoid the penny-pinching tigress on the loose. There were piano les-sons, school lunches, mortgage payments, utility bills, car payments, and many other household expenses, which made counting the money a necessity.

My history rendered me either hypervigilant or downright crazy, in increments. I have been a nuisance to many close to me because of my fear of losing control of the finances, which means losing control of our entire well-being, which is a place I just cannot revisit. It was also the reason I religiously went to the bank on those afternoons to deposit the paycheck and mail all the stamped invoice envelopes.

Bill paying commenced as usual one day, but for reasons I cannot recall, I had uncharacteristically forgotten to deposit the paycheck at the bank, which had become, actually, more important than making dinner. It was a warm spring evening about nine o'clock, and the sun was just setting. When I realized my mistake, instead of waiting until the next morning like most levelheaded human beings, I leapt into the car and sped to the bank like my hair might catch fire if I didn't.

I circled around the back of the building, so I could be heading in the right direction for the automatic teller. As I circled around, I passed a couple of police cars behind the building. There were several officers surrounding a young man in the center. His shoulders were sagging, and he was clutching a large ripped brown paper grocery bag in both arms. I remember thinking he looked bedraggled and defeated. As I drove past, I remember feeling sadness for whatever trouble the young man was in. I got almost to the ATM machine when it registered like a brick to the head. Andrew! It was Andrew. It couldn't be, but it had to be. The stance and body language of a child is emblazoned in the memory banks of a mother's brain. It was the first time I had laid eyes on him since the day he got off that awful bus with that dreadful plastic rose in his hand.

With no thought of depositing the check, I threw the car into reverse and backed up, stopping adjacent to the police cars. I got out and looked from Andrew to the police, hands on my hips. "What in heaven's name is going on here," I demanded angrily, as if I were the detective in charge. They looked at me like I was a wacky indigent lady bent on interfering. Andrew saw me and reflexively dropped his chin and eyes in apparent shame. Asking about my interest – in other words, this is none of your business, lady – I told them I was his mother. Their demeanors softened immediately, and they informed me that there was a warrant out for his arrest. Muriel's mother had reported Andrew for beating up her other daughter, and they had no choice but to pick him up. However, they were familiar with him from the towing business, and admitted they knew him enough to know he wouldn't hurt a fly. They were right about that. There was no question in my mind that the allegations were trumped up to get rid of Andrew, because they now had a clearer picture of his incapabilities. The police conferred for only a moment, and said if I would take him with me, they'd look the other way. With that, Andrew stuffed his raggedy sack in the back seat of my car, and we drove away.

Some miracles you beg for, many of which you never get, and others are just handed to you on a platter even when you don't ask.

It was wonderful to see him. He hugged me, he cried and said he was sorry. We went home to Sam and his siblings for a belated and somewhat guarded reunion. It was difficult to be angry with Andrew for very long, under the circumstance of his gullibility. For the moment, I was just happy to have him home.

He settled in quite nicely, resuming family life, and seemed to be taking things in his stride. He was pretty much his happy-go-lucky self. He still worked at the towing company, and I was hopeful that he would stay on an even keel for a season. Things did go smoothly for a time, but before we could blink, Muriel beckoned. He was like a moth to a flame, and before we could get our bearings, he was in the wind again.

After six additional months of being together again, and seemingly out of the blue, Muriel changed her mind once more. Surprise, surprise. This time I wasn't certain if it was her choice or her mother's, but she said needed time, space, and freedom. This time Andrew was outright heartbroken, but he seemed to quickly accept what he was learning to be the inevitable with her. If it had been up to him, he'd have married her, purchased a double-wide trailer, had a passel of kids, and settled in until the cows came home. He didn't want, need, or expect ideal or complicated. His only dream was to marry Muriel, love and be good to her, work hard, and life a simple life. But again, no. This time

Andrew moved in with a coworker because he couldn't abide our constant shepherding. He still pined for Muriel and hoped for a slight crack in the door so he could be with her again. He knew we would put up a fight about that. I had learned not to expect things to run smoothly for Andrew. They never had, they never would. He, on the other hand, never blamed Muriel for anything and was understanding of her so-called needs. He kept in touch with us, even spending some time at the house on a regular basis – eating, chatting, or relaxing. It was kind of wonderful to have a relationship with him, no matter how disappointing it was that his life wasn't tracking in a straighter direction like we had hoped.

What would happen to him? Would my boy ever be happy? Would he find someone who could sincerely love him? He seemed destined to float along merrily day-by-day, head in the clouds. He couldn't see very far ahead. For now, he was relishing his towing escapades and enjoying the blue skies and ice cream flavor of the week. Life for Andrew was as it had always been, minute by minute. It was not sad or unsatisfying, it was just wherever the wind blew him. Usually, he found some sort of silver lining in every cloud. For that, I was both happy and sad. Happy he was happy, sad that he didn't have a clue. We worried about his finances and occasionally we'd suggest a budget or even a check register, which he, of course couldn't fathom the need for or the concept of, not to mention doing the math involved. I worried he wasn't paying his bills on time or being current with the rent. Occasionally, he complained about the effects of not keeping up and angering someone or another because of it, but in the wake of calamity, he always seemed to be able to charm the socks off his friends or coworkers and be given one more chance. I tried to keep my despair tucked into the back of my mind, clipped, of course, to a long dangling thread, hoping harder and praying longer every day for his well-being. Many times in life, that's the only thing left to do.

58

Ella

One day while we were vacationing in California with several of the children and grandchildren, I got a call from Andrew. Between Disneyland and the beach, he insisted that he really needed to talk to us. After first asking sincerely and politely about the trip and each of his beloved nieces and nephews, he began, "Mom ... I wanted you and Dad to be the first to hear the good news!"

"News, Andrew?" I replied. I couldn't fathom any good news coming from his direction just now.

"Yeah ... well ... [long pause] I'm getting married!" There was jubilation in his voice.

"Come again? Married?" I asked incredulously. I hadn't even heard that he was dating.

"Yeah, Mom, I met this awesome girl. You'll just love her! She's the best! Her name is Maya."

"Where did you meet her?" I asked with a carefully contrived calm. It took every ounce of control I had not to shriek.

"Oh," he said matter-of-factly, "at a party. It's just one of those things that is meant to be."

"And just how long have you known her, Andrew?"

"Not too long, but when you know, you know," he said sagaciously.

"Where does she live and what's her story?"

"Oh, Mom, you'll meet her soon enough. She's great. Like I said, you'll just love her. She's so pretty. Long blonde hair, blue eyes. Soooo cute. Much prettier than Muriel. Anyhow, we're getting married in two weeks."

I felt the blood rush to my head. "Two weeks! Andrew! Why two weeks? We haven't even met her! Heavens, I didn't even know you were dating again."

"I don't know, Mom. We just want to, so we are. Why wait? It's all planned. Her mom has been so nice to help us get it all set up. She's super happy about it."

"Andrew, before you even think of marriage, we first need to meet her. I mean it, we need to get acquainted with her before you make serious plans like that!"

"Well, like I said, her mom is with us right now and wants to know if you'll bring the meat," he said without a hint of reservation or pause.

"The meat? The meat for what?"

"The wedding, of course! She has about three hundred relatives coming in from Wyoming and Colorado, and we're having the wedding and then a dinner at the church. So, can you bring it? Please? They're counting on us."

Sam had been standing close by and listening in. He grabbed the phone from my hand and all but screeched at Andrew. After being told the exact same story in the same plaintive repetitive tones, Sam got himself under control. He vehemently but thoughtfully told him he should take a little more time for such a monumental life decision. Andrew, in his easygoing, trying-hard-to-please-everyone way, just repeated back to Sam the same sentences he had used on me. It was, of course, something we had gotten used to, especially when there was a little push back. Sam firmly, but calmly now, reiterated that when we returned home in a few days, he must bring her to the house to meet us right away. "I will, Dad, for sure, I will." Sam and I hung up the phone and just stared silently at one another, shrugging our shoulders and rolling our eyes.

In the following days, we called Andrew numerous times and made several firm appointments to meet Maya, but when the time for each appointment arrived, they never showed up. Andrew began not to answer his phone. The days flew by and I decided I must, for everyone's sake, come to terms with the unfortunate facts of the matter. It took every ounce of incentive I could muster to begin to gather up the "meat." I asked all the daughters and daughters-in-law to pitch in. I purchased and sliced copious amounts of roast beef, chicken, and ham. It was difficult not to picture a hundred cowboy hats and silver belt buckles as I prepared.

The day of the wedding came like a hurricane barreling across the ocean towards our coasts, and I had a million jumbled and erratic emotions threatening to erupt and heave me into the roiling waters. But I did have a countertop chock full of meat. It was all wrapped, sliced, and sitting there like silent lumpy heads judging me harshly as I passed them. Or rounded headstones sticking morosely out of the granite while insinuating that I rest in peace.

The wedding was scheduled for six o'clock in the evening. The day dragged on most unbearably. I felt like I had been dragged up a cliff backwards. My arms and legs felt sapped, and my crazy-horse heart was kicking up a storm. That was my physical state. Emotionally, I was sad, depressed, apprehensive, and too weary for words. At intervals, I felt numb and zombie-like, but also ready to weep. I carried a Kleenex around in my pocket to dab regularly at my nose and red eyes. At three o'clock, I lay down on the sofa to prepare for the upcoming catastrophe, which was causing such quaking and trembling.

59

Ella

The phone rang, and I jumped up from the sofa to answer it quickly, hoping it was Andrew saying the whole wedding thing had been a nonsensical hoax after all. But it wasn't. I was greeted with an unexpected sniveling voice that could only belong to Muriel. After feeling initial shock and disbelief, I felt a rising antipathy. My initial inclination was to screech any number of nasty expletives into the phone. I slid my head and voice into manual gear and steeled myself. Control is often a deeply unsatisfying attribute. I had not let go of my hard feelings for Muriel, even slightly. I had every intention of giving them up eventually, but up to now I had been too busy to give her the time of day, let alone space in my thoughts.

"Ella?" she asked in her insipid blubbering little voice. "Yes, Muriel, what is it?" I asked with a modicum of restraint. In my head, the dialogue was quite different. It went more like, "What could you possibly want today, for heaven's sakes, you crazy little bitch?" I succeeded in keeping my voice inflexible and low.

She stated the obvious, insipidly and coolly – much too coolly – "Andy is getting married tonight."

I could almost feel the tepid temperature and limpness to the dishwatery cadence of her simpering little voice. "I know that, Muriel, I said icily. "And what is that to you?"

"Well," she said condescendingly, "that's just it. He can't. He can't marry Maya."

"Can't?" I countered every bit as condescendingly.

"No," she came back, volleying the serve brutally into my court. "He can't marry Maya, she said, pausing for effect. "*I'm* pregnant."

The ball racketed right into my flank like a chunk of cement. Any retort I may have conjured was jammed in my throat like a putrid old sock. Absolutely stunned, I couldn't come up with anything coherent to smash back with, so I slammed the phone down onto its cradle. I screamed for Sam.

After he ascertained that I wasn't dying on the spot, Sam immediately called Andrew, who was busily setting up chairs in the church cultural hall in preparation for the upcoming joyous occasion. He was chatting chirpily back and forth with someone in close proximity, making a joke of some sort, and wasn't paying close attention to Sam. "Andrew!" Sam barked.

"Yeah, Dad? You guys will be here pretty soon with the meat, right?"

"Andrew!" Sam repeated, and he was roaring this time. "Listen to me. Stop whatever you're doing and just listen!" Silence, finally. "Muriel just called your mother and told her that she's pregnant. Can this possibly be true, or is she lying as usual?" There was deafening silence on the other end of the line. "Andrew? Are you hearing me?" More silence.

"Well … yeah, Dad."

"Tell me how this happened?" Sam commanded, and not in a compassionate way.

"Well … she asks me to stay with her from time to time."

"Oh, Andrew. Seriously? When was the last time?"

"Well … I think maybe … last night?" His answer was positioned somewhere between honesty, cluelessness, and stupidity.

"Oh, Andrew! What in heaven's name are you thinking?" Of course, Sam knew it was a rhetorical question Andrew wouldn't have the foggiest notion how to answer.

"You realize, don't you, that you cannot marry Maya under these circumstances?"

More silence. "Well, yeah, Dad, I guess so. But what am I supposed to do now? Everybody is counting on it."

"Well, Andrew!" Sam was still yelling. "You've got to put a stop to this wedding this very instant!"

"But, Dad … I don't think I can." Deathly silence, some choking up, and more silence on Sam's end.

I was standing there just listening like a statue. It seems I had no power to speak or intervene. What I really wanted to do was head to the bathroom and run some really warm water for a bath. It felt like five full minutes of space between the pushing of the red button on a bomb detonator and the impending explosion itself. Although everything felt like it was in slow motion, I was preparing for total devastation. I was finally bracing for the walls to start crumbling. In reality, only a few seconds had elapsed. Then I heard Sam choke back a deep gravelly sigh, which was somewhere between a sob and a groan. It sounded as if it was being sucked from his ankles through an invisible vacuum hose clear up into his throat. It wailed like a growl swirling around in his gullet. Then his demeanor simply softened. His chest heaved, and he sighed deeply. "Do you need help with that, son?" he asked plaintively.

"Yes, Dad."

"Okay, meet us in ten minutes at the towing company, and we'll follow you to Maya's house. Oh, Andrew …" he trailed, the sob collapsing flatly inside his chest.

60

Ella

Sam and I drove mutely to the towing garages on the outskirts of town. The little car itself seemed empathetically weighted down as we roiled along the crunchy snow-packed roads. The skies were a congested putty gray with drunken snowflakes drifting chaotically in several different directions. I felt numb, deflated, and overcome at this disturbing development. As if the whole circumstance of this insane wedding hadn't been bad enough. Amazingly, all I could let my mind linger upon were the heaps of cooked, packaged, and sliced animal flesh splayed out on my counters waiting to be delivered to the ill-fated wedding dinner. My heart was thumping in a disturbingly regular rhythm, extremely unusual for this kind of stress. That alone seemed precipitously incongruent and threatening. As we pulled up, we saw Andrew's blue compact car idling at the curb. He was hunched over the steering wheel as if he were protecting it from imminent danger. I wondered if he was cold or, perhaps, crying. As we approached, I could see it was neither. He waved widely but without the usual smile, motioning us to follow.

We wound through several small neighborhoods whose humble homes were hunkered down and blanketed in mounds of snow. Andrew stopped in front of an unassuming split-level with a long, narrow cement porch anchored to its roof by unproportioned diminutive posts. We meandered along the snowbanks and knocked at the front door. Even though my heartbeat was unusually steady for such a crazy circumstance, my legs felt weak and rubbery. My breathing was rapid and shallow. The image of a brown paper bag used to breathe in and out popped into my head. Sam took the lead and placed his hand firmly on Andrew's shoulder. The door opened slowly.

To my surprise, two small children, a boy and a girl, answered the door. I would have guessed they were about two and four years old. "Andy, Andy," they cried gleefully. Without hesitation, Andrew bent down and hugged them both. Then it hit me like a ton of bricks. Those children belong to Maya. Oh, terrific. I had no idea, of course. That revelation alone made me want to turn tail and run back to the car. All I needed were more disturbing details to augment the whole dog and pony show. The children flung open the door and we stepped into a small living room adjacent to a dingy little kitchen.

Two young women, apparently in their late teens, stood there picking at chocolate chip cookies on a tray on the stovetop. At first glance, they reminded me of a set of Barbie dolls dressed up for a pretend prom. One was blonde and the other brunette. Same curvy bodies and slender waists. Their faces were caked with makeup – vivid blue eyeshadow, black eyeliner, false lashes, and vivid shades of pink and coral lipstick. They looked as if they'd been digging through the dress-up box I used to keep for my girls under the stairs when they were little. Both wore long pastel gowns, but both still had tennis shoes sticking out underneath. I think I recall a pale apple green and a peachy organdy, or perhaps satin, which I probably conveniently manufactured to fill in the gaps of the picture. Both girls' hair was upswept in curls and curlicues, dotted with flowers and sparkly plastic baubles attached to gold bobby pins. I avoided looking directly into their faces or taking in the details of the little house. I was disoriented and detached, and I resisted forming any sort of familiarity with anything there. The kitchen seemed drab and empty, but that could well have been my mood. I avoided the children, having no desire to connect with them in any way. Physically, I could barely stay on my feet, and I had to concentrate to do that. I felt stiff and robotic. I don't think my face offered up even a hint of a smile. I had no inkling of being cordial, and I simply didn't care enough to pretend to be interested.

Andrew was frolicking with the children, tickling and teasing them single-mindedly and openly, as I'd seen him do a thousand times with any child in his proximity. Kids and dogs were Andy's sweet weaknesses. At least they were if you knew you didn't have to worry about his impulsive fourteen-year-old maturity level and the possible consequences of it. As I've often said, it's tough to remain angry with Andrew. He's pretty harmless. He's so darn innocent and well intentioned. However, today I wasn't feeling so generous. I felt like slapping and shaking him. Didn't he realize what dangerous territory he had wandered into with Maya and her poor little children?

As for me, I was at a breaking point with this damned wedding anyway, and I knew we had arrived at the "enough is over-the-top enough" moment. The breaking point hovered perilously just above my head and was poised to smash me in the face. I felt like puddling into the worn-out brown shag carpet, but at the same time, I felt like opening my mouth and screaming murder at the rafters. I did neither. I commanded quietly, but as imposingly as I could, that the children march up the stairs to ask their mother to come down. They jumped up and down, and sing-songingly recited what they had obviously been told earlier. "No! Andrew can't see Mommy in her wedding dress before the wedding! Bad luck, bad luck," they twittered in unison. I could almost feel the steam escaping from my ears and the fire flaming from my eyes as I scooted them up the stairs. I demanded sternly that they bring her down immediately. They lowered their little heads and scowled at me in silence, as if I were the Grinch himself who had come to steal their Christmas. But they trotted up to get her.

It seemed like thirty minutes before the entourage descended, but it couldn't have been more than a minute or two. Maya and her mother,

who looked to be about my age, trod down the stairs cautiously. The
mother was a pleasant-looking sort of woman in faded snug black
polyester pants and a long-sleeved, striped T-shirt. She appeared to be
quite athletic. Her hair was dyed bright auburn and was ratted to the
size of a large bird's nest, which framed her jovial but attractive square
jaw like a shroud. She had minimal but deftly applied makeup. Somehow, she wasn't anything like I imagined her to be. I had pictured her
as trashy, imposing, irrelevant, and militant. She looked at us and then
back at Andrew quizzically but congenially, smiling widely, and showing rows of straight white teeth. Her demeanor was annoyingly friendly
and agreeable. I wanted desperately to be put off by her enough to give
her a piece of my mind. But she continued to smile widely. Then, without missing a beat or modifying her countenance in the least, she proceeded to shock the pants off us all. She motioned to Andrew gracefully
with her hand, as if she were the conductor of the entire situational
orchestra. Then she looked at him straight in the eyes, and without
blinking or missing a beat in this absurd musical concerto, she casually
asked Andrew if this visit was about Muriel. I almost fell on my face. I
sucked in my breath loudly, as did Sam. Andrew immediately looked
down at the floor, pursed his lips, and scuffed a black boot mark across
the linoleum. He said nothing for a few lengthy seconds but finally
nodded his head up and down affirmatively. "Oh, I thought so," she
said, almost insouciantly. Again, I was absolutely stunned. At this astonishing turn of events, I shifted my attention to the young woman
who could be no one else but Maya. I had scarcely had a chance to look
at her, as her mother had been deftly stealing the stage. For the first
time, I turned toward the object of Andrew's affection with real focus.
Who was this girl anyway, and what did she have in mind for Andrew?

She was a couple inches taller than he was, but I could see that she
was wearing ivory satin pumps. Above the sockless pumps were cuffed
light faded blue jeans with a couple of rips at the knees. She, too, was
wearing a T-shirt. It was striped like her mother's, but it had some sort
of juvenile pink ice cream graphic across the front. It said, "It's always

ice cream o'clock somewhere." I unconsciously rolled my eyes and turned my investigation to the top of her head. Her light hair was shockingly beautiful. It was the color of spun honey and was upswept like her bridesmaids'. It was adorned with small tendrils dripping here and there, curling like silken ropes just over her ears and above her collarbone. There were decent facsimiles of pearls dotting the entire hairdo, and it brought to mind pages in a popular bridal magazine. Reluctantly, I had to give her mother points there. Her ears were threaded with long delicate golden chains, one end of each cuddling a single teardrop of bright clear blue glass. They were the only things she wore which looked to be a little pricey. My eyes moved from them to her face, and my first thought was that it didn't quite fit with her mass of flaxen hair. She wasn't nearly as plain as Muriel, but she was not really a beauty, either. Her features were not unattractive, they were just squished together a little too closely. The result was a bit cherubic. She was flamboyantly made up like the others, which further shortened the distance between her already compacted features. Her mouth was painted bright rose pink in a small perfect bow. Her thick false lashes batted back and forth as if they weighed too much to keep her eyes open. They reminded me of black caterpillars clinging to her eyelids. Beneath them, though, her eyes were clear and blue like the glass in her pretty earrings, but they reflected not even a speck of appreciation for us to be standing there in her house.

With her mother's lightning-bolt to-the-point comment about Muriel, Maya's lash-laden eyes darted across the room, and her attention was riveted upon Andrew's face. Yet she didn't flinch or make a sound. She didn't shift her weight towards him even slightly, as if her feet were cemented to the floor, and she remained glued to her mother's side. She was obviously more comfortable letting her handle this mess. She didn't react in any way. She also disregarded the rest of us as if we were completely irrelevant. The mother spoke again, still kindly, but more poignantly and firmly now. "Andrew." She punched his name solidly. "What about Muriel? What is this about? What is going on here?"

Then, there it was. "Is Muriel pregnant?" The last sentence was more of an acknowledgement of fact than a question. There was also no surprise or alarm in her tone. Just an open vocal assertion of what most likely was reality. Now the blood began to drain quickly from Andrew's face, and he began to look as if he'd seen a ghost or was one. He fleetingly scanned Maya's mother's face. He caught her eye directly and quickly glanced down to the floor.

Bewilderingly, my heart was still not beating wildly but rather steadily, and I wondered why this was the case now. Much lesser drama usually sent it galloping to the races. Yet, it was only my thoughts which were racing. Back and forth. To Andrew and back to the mother, and then to Maya. What in heaven's name is going on? I couldn't allow myself to cogitate, much less be rational. Andrew looked at Maya's mother again for an instant but never even glanced at Maya, as if she were not present. He simply dropped his shoulders, shrugged them ex-aggeratingly, and in an almost inaudible voice, said, "Yes." The word bounced across the room like a stone skipping across a pond. Though it came out in a whisper, we all heard it like a gunshot. To my further shock and dismay, and before anyone else could respond, he sprinted towards the front door like an antelope escaping the wolves, threw it open, hopped over a three-foot bank of snow at the porch, and dashed to his car at the curb. We all just stood there and watched wordlessly as he put the car into gear and drove away. Run, rabbit, run. In unison, Maya's mother raised her eyebrows and lifted her shoulders, as if to say, "That's the way the cookie crumbles, folks." She turned to Sam and me and thrust her hand sweepingly towards Maya. She said, much too matter-of-factly and without a hint of cynicism, "She's pregnant, too, you know." It rather felt like she was letting me down gently.

When Andrew's car rounded the bend, I just fell apart and let it all go. I couldn't see straight. I couldn't think straight. My mind was play-ing tricks, and I pictured rows and rows of rabbit hutches. My shoul-ders heaved, my head pounded, and my tears fell in torrents. Sam put his arm around me as if to keep me from dropping to the floor. I could see water silently escaping the corners of his eyes as well. For Sam, that was an exceptional occurrence, especially in public.

Maya's mother deftly moved to my other side, grabbing my elbow supportively and with a bit of momentum. She looked genuinely sympathetic now. "It will be okay, honey. Really, it will. We'll all get through this just fine. This is not my first rodeo, so I do know what you're going through. You'll be okay – you've got this." She actually smiled sweetly and kindly, with no pretense of annoyance. I felt only pure unadulterated empathy. She patted my shoulder gently and unceasingly until I began to get my bearings. Then in her totally unflappable way, she said, "Of course, there will not be a wedding tonight. But you understand that I've got family arriving shortly. Many of them have traveled long distances and will need to stay and eat dinner. Will you still be bringing the meat?" she asked expectantly.

Sam and I made our way to our car holding on to each other like parallel guardrails along a steep and dangerous ravine. We didn't even consider contacting Andrew. No point. There are times in life when you simply recognize that what is, is, and that it's enough of a burden to just put a period at the end of it for a while. We drove home with not a lot of time to spare and began to gather up the predatory spoils into the back of our car. Luke called, we told him the disheartening news of the day, and he sympathetically insisted on meeting us at the specified celebratory hall to help. Luke has always been the child who feels obliged to be supportive of his parents no matter what his disposition or how busy his life is spinning. I think it hearkens back to when Sam rescued him as a five-year-old from being fatherless. I also think it stems from the endless bedtime stories Sam used to tell him at the side of the top bunk every single night. Luke has always been the one in the family to mitigate the storms. We called him the lightning rod. The three of us lugged the substantial spread into the back door of the church. We were greeted with smiles and full-on bear hugs from Maya's extended family – quite a magnanimity, I think, as I look back. Maya's mother ushered us into the flamboyantly but tackily decorated cultural hall.

There were two three-foot gilded, fat, cement gray cherubs, albeit badly chipped, heralding the entrance. There were crimson theater ropes, their poles topped with small battery-powered plastic lanterns, lining the pathway, beckoning us to come in further. One of the first things to catch my eye was the enormous white plastic lattice arbor, though blaringly vacant, hovering piteously over the celebratory area. Obviously, it was the location where the formerly happy couple would have been greeting their gleeful guests. It was about eight feet tall and five feet wide and was stationed under a fraying and grimy basketball hoop. The arbor was draped lavishly with red and orange plastic roses and tulips and garnished generously with different colored varieties of ivy (some teal blue from being left outside in the sun). The greenery webbed in and out of the latticework, and you could see the rubbery junctions of the plastic plants poking out clumsily here and there throughout. It looked extremely festive, very garish, but mostly sad. Even I was feeling sad now. The shockwaves were beginning to dissipate, and my mind was desperately attempting to fit all the pieces together. In repetitive surges, I felt stabbing jabs of disappointment, anger, embarrassment, sorrow, and pity, along with bouts of self-flagellation.

My eyes searched for Maya, and I spotted her loitering at a large watering station with, I suspected, a half a dozen of her cousins. There was a huge punchbowl constructed of yellowed plastic, filled with what appeared to be orange fizzy punch. It was definitely color coordinated to match some of the flowers lying everywhere. There was another punchbowl which practically everyone was partial to, filled to the brim with something clear and obviously alcoholic. Couldn't blame them a bit. I wanted to tear right over there myself, rip out the orange and red fake flowers from an adjacent vase, fill it to the brim, and gulp it down.

Maya was still in her jeans and T-shirt but had traded in her satin pumps for some well-worn tennis shoes. Her hair was still done up stunningly, and her lovely long blue earrings were swaying as she moved.

Her makeup had a bit of smudging and streaking at the corners of her startlingly blue eyes, and she kept raising and lowering her eyebrows as if they were holding up her face to keep it from crumbling. She was absent-mindedly tugging at a long tendril at her left ear, twirling it like the corner of a security blanket. She didn't appear to be sad or destroyed, as I might have imagined, but she was pensive. She was dragging an invisible cloak of melancholy upon her thin shoulders, and it seemed to have rocks sewed into its hem. She was obviously putting on a good face for her cousins. Her pretense was an attempt to communicate that she was cool with everything. Pity floated through my sorrowing soul like a ghost, and it pierced me suddenly that Andrew and I were not alone in our confusion and sadness. Life. Forrest Gump chocolates. Just plain crap. My head was pounding to a beating drum, and I wasn't certain I would last the evening in the upright position.

I needn't have worried about standing. Maya's mother ushered us merrily to the paper plates, cups, and utensils, and urged us to dig in. She motioned to one of the long church tables and folding chairs. The tables were covered in white butcher paper with scraps of masking tape keeping it securely in place. The centers were laced with more plastic red and orange flowers, and embellished with the multicolored plastic greenery. I was alarmed to notice the flat unframed black and white photos of Andrew and Maya in various poses of blissful optimism. They were lying lugubriously here and there among the plastic foliage. Sam and I looked at each other, raising our eyebrows wearily. Luke just turned the palms of his hands up and shrugged.

We each took a plate and plastic fork and began to fill our plates. I felt nauseous but piled mine uncharacteristically high. Macaroni, potato salad, and Jell-O. Green salad, carrots, string beans, pickled beets, cheese, and of course, meat. Mounds of meat from my own kitchen. All kinds of meat. Our meat. It felt like sacrificial flesh. We sat at the appointed table, which, thankfully, was not filled with chatty relatives. Though they were courteous and overly friendly to us, you couldn't blame them for avoiding us. We were the reason for the tumbledown party. We sat there morosely for as long as seemed respectful. We had a bird's-eye view of the rest of the group, so we watched silently as we picked at our plates. I'm not sure I really ate anything. As I scanned the hallway, I was surprised, but not really, to spot my ex-husband and his wife peeking around the partition and into the gym. Oh. But of course. They hadn't heard. I felt a small sly smile track automatically across my face. It took only a few seconds for them to ascertain there was no wedding going on here. They bolted across the doorway and vanished. Some things never change.

We didn't need a consensus as to when to leave. We simply set aside our plastic forks, pushed our chairs away from the table, and dumped our plates into the large plastic garbage can positioned at the head of one of the tables. No one seemed to notice as we made our way out the back door and to the car. We had spoken earlier with David, and we drove straight to his house. One by one the other children arrived, as if obliged to attend an empty wake. We all sat in David's living room until it was late enough to go home to bed. It was consoling for me to be with them, and I knew they were well aware of that. The brothers and sisters joked and laughed in an uncomfortable, awkward sort of way. It got pretty unkind. "How perfectly Andrew this is! Can't he ever be anything but stupid?" Beth complained.

"How can he keep embarrassing himself, not to mention the entire family?" Jenny moaned.

"Well, what kind of people were they anyway?" David asked sincerely, trying to understand the breadth of the situation.

"You should have seen that weird place," Luke told them. "It was bizarre! Her mother was acting like it was a perfectly normal thing, chattering to everyone as if she was throwing a cool party or something. Mom and Dad and I felt ridiculous, trying to sit there and spoon food into our mouths while talking to all those redneck relatives," describing everything and everyone in detail.

I suppose it was a natural way for them to let off a little steam while orienting themselves to the crazy drama. As for me, I sat there quietly and wept enough silent tears to fill a decent-sized cereal bowl. The front of my dress was soaked through, but I was determined not to make more of a scene by letting any pitiful sounds escape from my throat. I kept brushing my cheeks with the back of my hand and pretending to listen. I wasn't. I just needed the day to be over.

61

Ella

I have a recurring dream of being about ten years old and at a canyon campground with my parents on a sunny summer afternoon. They are sitting at an old rough-hewn, paint-chipped wooden picnic table in a pretty grove of tall trees, eating potato chips and watermelon, while conversing nonchalantly. I don't remember seeing my siblings. The weather is bright, clear, and cool. My father and mother are not picking at each other as usual but are getting along and smiling. In the dream, I feel safe and happy. I am in the foreground running like the wind. I zigzag across rocks, weeds, and wildflowers, back and forth to where my parents are sitting. I run to the top of a gentle ridge and look down over a beautiful verdant valley in the distance below, and I pretend I am the princess of it all. My red Keds are comfortably broken in, dotted with a couple of holes here and there, and my feet are winged. My torso and limbs are nimble, and nothing can stop me. My lungs fill with clean fresh air and I am not fatigued.

Only a couple of years ago I used to look forward to putting on my running shorts and Nikes to run on the boulevard. I'll never forget how freeing it was, and I will miss it until the day I die. Not so much because I was out of the house without children hanging on my skirts, which was admittedly a pleasure, but I miss the wind blowing through my hair and the warmth of the sun on my shoulders. I had a little time to breathe. Yes, it was a workout, and I was glad when it was over, but I felt I was accomplishing something, along with carving a bit of time for myself. Though I didn't register it at the time, I felt invincible. I felt strong, healthy, and independent. And powerful.

Now, though I was gaining strength quickly, I mistakenly assumed that because my body had healed, my heart had healed as well. One day after taking a leisurely stroll on the boulevard, determined to get back into some sort of shape and exercise regimen, I finished and returned to the back door of the garage. I was bending to untie the shoelaces of the brand-new, blue-swished Nikes Sam bought me as a carrot to entice me forward. Out of the blue, I was hit with the first shock from my newly internally wired transmission system. Ironically, I had been feeling much like a car newly repaired at the shop. The pain was substantial, not unlike an unannounced horse kick to the chest. It was not unfamiliar after the episodes in the hospital, but it was more than a whack to the chest. I had experienced that. This was a sharp slap and rude awakening that things were never going to be normal, or perhaps even okay. A wave of nausea washed over me, and I could barely breathe. I didn't dare shift my weight from side to side for fear of another wave. It was all I could do to toss my shoes on the floor, shuffle into the house, and flop down in a chair.

The episode abruptly ended my ambitions to exercise, as I assumed that the walk had been the root cause of the shock. Yet in a week or so, another happened while I was just swinging my legs over the edge of my bed. The pattern continued to be illogical and random. At times, there would be a few months' respite, and I would slowly begin to relax, only to have a flurry more in a few weeks' time. The fear they generated was much worse than the shock itself. I began to look at the device as my personal sniper, one I perceived was holding a rifle and following close behind me, wherever I went and whatever I did. I could never predict when there would be a bullet in the chamber, and the possibility stopped me dead in my tracks. I tried to do as the doctor admonished and go about my business, feeling, as he said condescendingly, very fortunate and protected by the amazing internal electric paddles embedded beneath my ribcage. He even suggested that I continue to walk on the boulevard, and if I happened to sustain a shock, simply sit down on the curb and let it pass. Seriously? Did he think me a robot without emotion? It was clinical and logical, I suppose, but not comforting or therapeutic.

I did everything in my power to avoid getting another shock. I would have slept on the front lawn in the nude if I had thought it would help. I employed unreasonable and illogical defenses. I crept from room to room slowly like a lame old horse, or I'd unwrap several sticks of gum and chew until my jaws ached. I would avoid bending over quickly or simply stop short in any given spot to breathe deeply through my nose and blow it out through my mouth, as someone had suggested for anxiety relief. As I said, there was no rhyme or reason to any of it. The length of time between the shocks varied inconsistently, so I had no barometer. Sometimes I went without one for long periods, and I was hopeful that I'd outgrown them like an old pair of shoes.

One morning while naked and wet from the shower, I received two shocks in a row. In those long minutes, I believed my time on earth had come to an end. It wasn't long before the monkey of terror I carried on my back turned into a full-grown gorilla. The fear seemed to take a form as real as the problem that precipitated it. It wasn't long before I learned that these accompanying episodes were panic attacks. When the attacks appeared, apparently out of nowhere and without warning, my heart would pound and I began to breathe like a sobbing child – shallow and quick. I frantically paced around the house or yard, or run for cover to the car from any given place – restaurants, malls, or bleachers. Each time, until the attack abated, there was absolute certainty that I would surely die.

One day while doing errands in the car, I began to feel my heart once again pounding erratically in my chest. I pulled to the side of the road and looked down. I was certain the small rose pattern on my blouse was jumping, though it probably was not. Between the bank and the post office, I was positively convinced that a heart attack was imminent, so I frantically drove directly to the emergency room of the hospital. I parked in front of the entrance. It was at that moment that I realized I was between a rock and a hard spot. I absolutely could not bring myself to even approach the door of the hospital, let alone walk down the corridors as I had in the months previous. Yet at the same time, I knew if I didn't, I was sure to die in my car. As I sobbed, I laid my elbows across the steering wheel and put my head over them. I forced myself to be still. I sat like that for half an hour. Then with a large deep sigh, I simply started the engine and drove home.

This pattern continued. There were days I awoke with fear grinding like boulders in a stream, and other days went smoothly without incident. I navigated through my days balancing the need to be a mother and a wife with being what my doctors called a "cardiac cripple." I knew that giving up and taking to my bed indefinitely would not solve anything; so, I kept trying, if only for the sake of the children. The smallest occurrences began to set off the anxiety. They were sporadic and unpredictable, such as waiting a long time for a table at a pizza place, or watching the kids run back and forth across the soccer field. It took everything I had to keep shuttling the kids here and there, and I forced myself to continue doing what needed to be done. But when the attacks manifested themselves, I'd simply flee. I'd run away to no specific destination, just to what seemed like might be a safe spot. There, I'd wait for the terror to pass.

Several times, I went to the grocery store, filled my basket to the brim, and then got caught off-guard by some small fixation. As illogical as it seems, the multiple colors or labels on the wall-to-wall store shelves seemed to trigger some sort of shift in my brain, and the anxiety cycle began to spin up. One day when this occurred, I bolted to find an empty spot on the floor between the Cream of Wheat and the Maxwell House Coffee, where I sat miserably, avoiding eye contact with anyone who might be wondering if I'd had too many cocktails for lunch. A few times I just fled the store altogether, abandoning my basket. I'd go sit by the

Redbox machine in the front of the store and wait for Sam to come save me or take me home. The groceries became irrelevant. I felt sorry that Sam had to go back to the store, find my abandoned basket, and pay for the needed groceries. But he never complained.

I became weary of the endless shocks and anxiety, but I couldn't face more hospitals or doctors. I felt as forlorn as the croquet mallet I could see tossed in the grass across the yard. The days zigzagged in crooked paths like the snail trails I noticed here and there on the hot cement. Translucent, narrow, and aimless. Life was monochrome. I cooked, cleaned, and managed the children robotically. I'd often plop into my wingback and stare out the window as long I could get away with it. I could see the pink geraniums, stuffed and overflowing their baskets, craning their necks towards the sun. The waxy yellow buttercups I transplanted years ago from my grandmother's garden preened their baby heads towards the sky, but now they seemed faded and dingy. The beautiful things I had enjoyed for years were washed with a dull film. I had no concern for the dandelions encroaching on the flowers, nor was I interested in the needed deadheading. I just didn't care. It was a challenge to braid hair, fold towels, or dry the dishes. I quit bothering to say little things like "Don't eat the dirty snow" or "Be sure to wash your hands before dinner." It was difficult to look at my reflection in the mirror, much less apply makeup. It was a chore to pull the brush through my hair or scrub another across my teeth. Because of the fear of a shock or panic attack, it was difficult to get into the car. Fear lodged in the back of my throat like a large steel marble, bobbing around enough to let in a little air.

One afternoon I dropped off Joe at the back door of the junior high and watched his gangly frame amble in. He was wagging his long thin arms, his blonde hair was brushed up in front, and with a crooked grin, he glanced back hopefully. I had two powerful and opposing thoughts. First, I wondered sadly if I would live to see him go to high school, and second, I thought it might just be easier not to have to worry about that at all.

I recall watching a young deer on the hill behind our house dragging a skinny wounded leg across the narrow trail. He was traversing alone. He looked a bit like I felt. As I watched him limp away, it suddenly felt important to make a connection, so that he'd know I knew he was there. That he was alive. I tried to look at his face, but he kept his head to the trail, his concentration navigating the rocks and ridges. I wondered why he bothered. If he just stopped looking for food, it would solve all his problems.

I had no one to share my burdens with except Sam. He had too much to lose if I faltered. I avoided others not close to me because it felt like constructing an important protective edifice with a box of toothpicks. It was just too effortful to fill the myriad of complicated blanks with a casual acquaintance, no matter how esteemed or kind. It was my own fault I had no friends. I was too busy, too aloof, too private, too proud, etc. And when I really needed someone, it seemed pointless to begin to build a bridge from the middle point.

One day I decided, with equal parts guilt and self-pity that I had had quite enough. I couldn't drag myself much further. I never had morbid thoughts or plans – I had simply run out of options. One night before bed, I told Sam that my feet felt like they were chained to cement blocks. There was sadness and pity in his soft green eyes. "Oh, Ella. I get it. I understand. This is a terrible time, absolutely, and you have every right to be down. But you don't mean that. I know you don't. We'll get through this, I promise. I need you. We need you. Hang on. Things will get better."

He hugged my shoulders while my arms dangled limply at my sides. I managed a weak smile to placate him. He tried so hard to take care of me. He was decent, open-handed, and self-sacrificing. I sighed deeply, feeling as trapped as I had in the hospital room a couple years back. I didn't say more because there was nothing to say. I just looked at him and shrugged. I pulled my nightgown down over my messy brown hair and fell into my nest of pillows. My eyes clamped shut like vaults. I slept like the dead, too exhausted to let even a dream slip through.

62

Ella

The dream which unbiddenly invaded my sleep was a simple visit from two men. A casual friendly sort of visit, not unlike two guests stopping by for a leisurely chat on a run-of-the-mill slow-moving afternoon. They could have been coming for tea, or cookies and milk. It was that kind of unhurried visit. I invited them into my living room to sit down. It was some time before I had the startling realization that one of the gentlemen was my own father. My deceased father. My dead father. Even in the dream, I knew full well he had been gone for several years. He passed when he was sixty-two. But in this easy, gentle encounter, he appeared more like the father I had known when I was thirteen. He wore an open-necked plaid shirt with the sleeves rolled to the elbow and a marled grey sweater vest, much like one he had favored in life. He looked almost exactly as he had when he was teaching junior high school. He was lithe and fit. His hair was not thin, stringy, and graying, but dark brown, course, and a bit unruly. His skin was ruddy and taut.

His hands were strong, muscular, and a bit meaty, as I remembered them as a girl. Realizing who he was, I was overjoyed. I almost laughed out loud to see him sitting on my sofa. I was so happy, in fact, that I could scarcely believe my amazingly good fortune.

He greeted me jovially and warmly, every bit the father I had known and loved. It was like every Christmas I had ever known rolled into one. How could this possibly be? I angled my head towards the unfamiliar man accompanying him. They seemed apparent comrades or close companions. They were about the same age, and I wondered if they had been long-time friends. The other man was an inch or two taller than my dad, but more stoutly built, and his shoulders were a bit broader. It was his full and fleshy face that caught my attention. He was quite handsome with his almond-shaped navy eyes and heavy eyebrows matching the color of his thick brown hair. His eyes were deeply set, making the lids almost invisible. The texture of his hair was a lot like my father's. Course and thick, but slicked back off his face with some sort of pomade. He wore a dark suit and a white shirt and tie, but the collar of his shirt was curious. It was high, wide, deep, and pointed. Very old fashioned, I thought. The most distinctive thing about it was that it seemed to pinch the flesh at the base of his neck, accentuating his fleshy jowls. A flash of remembrance bolted across my mind, and I recalled an old tintype photograph I had studied at my grandmother's house. I think the photo was of her husband, my grandfather. Oh, my goodness. This has to be the grandfather I had heard about who passed away and left his wife and three small boys sadly and prematurely. As I looked back and forth at the two men, I became rather certain of the fact. He looked quite different in real life than in the photo, but I further observed an uncanny resemblance to Beth and also to David. Absolutely astounding, I thought. My dead father and his dead father have come to pay me a visit.

We laughed and talked for quite some time, even making a few jokes. We chatted and conversed convivially about many things. They were pleasant and interested. Clearly, they loved me. It was as enjoyable a visit as I have ever had. After a while, they wished me well and got up to leave.

At the very moment they arose from their seats to be on their way, I jarringly awoke. My room was still dark. I was deflated and disappointed to realize it had only been a dream. It was disheartening to be alone again. It had seemed so real. Of course, that was highly unlikely. I settled back into my pillows, rehearsing the particulars. I postulated that because they had simply vanished into thin air, it was not reality. At that bleak realization, I felt sorrow envelope me like a scratchy blanket. I had found them only to lose them again, especially my father. I felt tears trickling down my face and on to my pillow. I pinched my eyes shut and forced myself back to sleep.

The night seemed like three compressed into one. I finally opened my eyes to the morning light. There were no little kids bouncing on my bed urging me to get up. I languished, glancing around my room. Images of the visitors were still vividly clear. As I remembered the pleasant encounter, dream or not, I perceived a tiny tack hammer of hope rapping ever so gently on my consciousness, begging to be let in. It felt like the earth had shifted just a hair on its axis.

The sun poured through the windows like butterscotch, dripping through the panes like golden honey. It cast prisms through the chandelier, and they fluttered around the room like tiny yellow and blue butterflies. The leaves on the trees effervesced translucently, sparkling like emeralds in the sunlight. I squinted my eyes. The cloudless skies were cerulean. Somehow, and I hadn't a clue as to how or why, it was as if someone had entered with a clean cloth to polish the lenses of my eyes. My spirits were immediately brighter, and my resolve sported an oversized Band-Aid. Oh my. What has happened? I soaked up the unexpected relief.

I was perplexed that as lucid as the vision was, I couldn't recall one single word of the exchange. The particulars of our pleasantries had been completely erased. Whether or not there is a possibility that my father and grandfather are actually aware of my life was not at issue that morning. For the first time in a very long while, I had the overwhelming, all-encompassing sense that I was not alone. Perhaps there was more to my struggle than I thought. I let the surprising idea penetrate. Strangely, it was all I needed for the moment.

I spent a few more minutes under my covers before deciding I should probably get up and get going. I threw my legs over the edge of the bed and glanced at my grandmother's old dresser, remembering nights and mornings spent with her. Then I pictured the little noses that needed to be wiped and eggs that needed to be scrambled. I actually smiled. *I think I might be okay. At least for today. Besides, what choice do I have?*

I had the sense that someone had spotted my little white flag. It was just a week or two later, early in the morning hours, that I sustained six – yes, six – shocks from the defibrillator, in just four minutes. I was utterly terrified, and again, believed my life to be over. Yet again, it was not. In a couple of days, a brand-new doctor decided enough was enough and performed a cardiac ablation, which is a procedure that scars some of the tissues in the heart to block abnormal electrical signals, It worked immediately and miraculously, and in record time, the same good Samaritan MD scheduled an appointment with a psychiatrist, who kindly and expertly began to comb through the tangles of my post-traumatic stress disorder. He asserted that I was almost exactly like his Vietnam vets, except that my personal sniper was following in real time. Things were looking up in a big way. This time I didn't quibble about which answers to which prayers. I knew mine had been heard, loud and clear. Even if not in the time-frame I would have thought prudent.

63

Ella

We didn't hear from Andrew for a couple of months. Not a word, and I must say it was no surprise. When he did surface, it was business as usual. Cheerfulness and positivity. Look forward, don't look back. No matter how often we supported him or tried to catch him from falling headlong into cement, he would get up and keep moving in his predictable Andrew sort of way. I was used to it. His actions weren't personal, unthoughtful, or begrudging in any sense. He was simply Andrew on autopilot. There wouldn't have been much self-consternation, guilt, sadness, or even reflection about the road that had led up to the recent debacle. Brush off the past, full steam ahead. Don't sweat the large stuff, or for that matter, the small stuff. Some days, I was a little jealous of his ability not to think things into oblivion or to be regretful. To not feel destroyed or deeply hurt. He did not seem to know how to wallow in the depths of emotion that seem to slosh over and around my world at the first raindrop plop. Yes, in many ways, Andrew can navigate whatever comes to him and not be sidelined, and I believe it's because of this inability to study things close up. Live in the present, be happy, be kind, be good, work hard, and move on when you must. It was true. I didn't begrudge Andrew his inability to feel. In fact, I have always been a "titch" jealous.

Andrew brushed himself off and went along his merry way, now turning his attention to Muriel. As history would prove, she never focused nearly so much on him. I waited to see signs of an upcoming marriage, obviously because of her pregnancy. Months went by without a hint of announcement or even the smallest alteration in her figure, as Andrew reported after running into her at the carwash. After a time, it became very clear that she had not ever been pregnant.

One day Andrew dropped by to make a sandwich in the middle of the day, and I nonchalantly asked about upcoming plans. He dropped the knife he was spreading choke cherry jam with and looked at me wide-eyed. "Oh," he said, just about as dispassionately as he had asked about the kind of jam I had in the fridge. "Did I forget to tell you? She isn't pregnant after all." I tried to swallow down the astonishment with my spoonful of peanut butter and turned to look out the window towards the bleakly empty road.

"Really, Andrew? What happened? Did she miscarry?"

Again, he stared at me blankly. "Oh, no, Mom. Nothing like that. It turns out she was never pregnant in the first place. She just couldn't bear to see me marry Maya," he said with a smile. He spit out the words smoothly as if it was the most logical explanation in the world. Clearly, he had taken it in his stride or was flattered by it. I felt like choking on my peanut-tasting, sticky, and thickening tongue. At that moment, I felt like wadding up the dishrag on the countertop and throwing it hard at his face. I didn't. I coughed and sputtered a few times, turned on the faucet, and gulped down a full glass of lukewarm water. I felt my hands shaking with a surge of anger, so I grabbed both sides of the sink and stood there until I could calm myself enough to speak without fury. Before I could say a word to him, however, my thoughts leapt unbidden to the baby in Maya's belly. My grandchild. The child I would never get to cradle or watch grow up. I counted the months backwards in my head and quickly calculated that he or she would probably be born any day now. I had no idea if Andrew even knew the sex of his own child. I was becoming crazy with rage. Rage at

Andrew for being so clueless and simple. Rage at Muriel for being so selfish and malicious, and rage at Maya for being so insipid and stupid, to let herself get pregnant again after having two other children out of wedlock.

Andrew picked up his peanut butter and jam sandwich, not unlike the millions I had made over the course of years in my self-righteous acts of mothering, and bit off a large portion. He picked up his generous glass of milk to wash it down with and stuffed a few potato chips into his mouth. I saw absolutely no sign of emotion in his face. For some reason, that infuriated me. Why? Why? Why did Andrew's problems have to bleed into so many other areas of our lives? Wasn't it enough that his life was always and forever part circus? Raising him had been one thing, but how would the ripples affect his children and my grandchildren? I could not speak. I had no words. So, I grabbed a couple of chips and began stuffing them into my mouth as fast as I could.

About three weeks later, Andrew came by the house again. This time he didn't come in but motioned me outside to his car. In the back seat, I spotted an infant carrier strapped securely and adeptly into the correct position. Inside it, there was a little blue cotton blanket barely lapping over a tiny face. A sweet little face on a head about the size of a naval orange. His skin was the palest shade of apricot and his soft downy cheeks were dusted with the colors of a sunset, powdered and bottled. His eyes were closed, his dark lashes were feathery, he was very still, and his little pink bow mouth was forming a perfect O. I could see his tiny chest rising and falling with his dreaming. There were fine strands of blonde hair kissing the sides of his tiny head.

Andrew gazed down at him protectively, and said a little too sunnily, "Mom, meet Jackson, your new grandson." I gazed at this little bitty bundle and swallowed down a golf-ball-sized lump of acid. He was simply and completely mesmerizing in his perfection. It was like looking at a velvety new white rosebud in the garden for the first time. Fresh, clean, innocent, and breathtakingly flawless. I felt a rising protectiveness along with a gigantic swell of devotion. They were tapping miniature cracks into my carefully guarded heart cage, not unlike as with my own little bundles. The following emotion was a more reasonable and profound sadness. It was as poignant as the first wave of wonder had been. It went about immediately sealing up the new expansions of my heart, and was sending roots of gloom straight through my body and down into the cement I was standing upon. If everything went as it usually did with Andrew, there was a high likelihood that I would never gaze upon this little prince again. I never did. It was the only glimpse I ever had of little Jackson. Maya quickly married a new man, and Andrew magnanimously gave up his parental rights. Of course, he did. It wouldn't have taken much to manipulate him into thinking it was in the child's best interest. He lives in the moment and cannot visualize more than one day and its problems.

It was a whole year later when Andrew broke the news of his upcoming nuptials to Muriel. I can't say I was very surprised, and I was pretty numbed to the prospect. My guess was that it would probably fall through, and that he'd be heartbroken again. At least his poor sappy heart tended to mend quickly. Andrew and Muriel's saga seemed to be a never-ending one, equally cursed and blessed. In my opinion, Andrew was the one who felt blessed whenever Muriel condescended to pay him any attention at all. I think he really did love her, or thought he did. As for her, I believe he was just a hard habit to break. Her options, knowing her as I did, would most likely be few and far between. She was not at all what you'd call a "catch." She was only an empty barbed hook on the end of a dark line, I mused.

They did marry, however, and with surprising fanfare. I had to give her points for pulling off the whole white dress with a train thing. Her white flower crown was balanced a little crookedly on her head in a deceptively sweet fashion, even if none of our family was buying it. They were married in a charming old park chapel by a justice of the peace, which I thought was ironically undeserved. We all perched on short wooden pews like extras in a movie scene. Our role was to pretend to be enraptured and enchanted. But we weren't. I wasn't. It was all I could do to keep a dour and disgusted look from sticking to my face.

Clearly, Muriel had sustained her fill of our family as well. As she trounced herself up the short aisle to the front of the chapel for the ceremony, she didn't even grace us with a glance, and she never spoke directly to me the entire evening. There were no pleasantries, even fluffy ones, whatsoever. To her, we were unintended and unpleasant consequences. Acknowledging us would mean she would have had to own up to any unsavory antics of the past. I looked at Andrew's openly adoring and happy face and tried to be a little bit happy for my boy. It was difficult.

He was wearing a snow-white tuxedo that looked too tight, too short, and a little bit plastic. On the other hand, his rented patent leather shoes looked a couple sizes too large. He reminded me of the tin man in the Wizard of Oz. His neck looked a little pinched, and I wondered if his hot pink striped tie was a clip-on. He had a matching wide pink cummerbund wrapped around his waist like a cheap ribbon thrown around a package. His face was beaming, seemingly proclaiming, "This is the day I have waited for my whole life. You all must see that it is an acceptable and normal step for me to take, and I'm so glad you are all here to see how well things have turned out." Several emotions spilled out of my brain like green goop. I felt guilty for not being happier and more accepting. I felt happy to see him happy. I felt repulsed by Muriel's charades. I felt with absolute certainty that he would sustain inevitable heartbreak, which led to a sharp pang of sorrow. I felt dread once again for his future. Lastly, I felt just a tiny pinch of what I knew to be ridiculous hope. What if, by some far-fetched chance, they ended up being happy, had a few children, and grew old together? But that dream was just too out there to even be reasonable.

They did settle down for a season, set up a household, and had a baby girl named Carly. She was beautiful and smart. She looked a lot like Andrew and acted a lot like Muriel. She was easy to love, but Muriel saw to it that we had precious little time to get to know her. I can count on one hand the times they came to our house, and we were never welcomed into theirs. In another year and a half or so, they brought little Joshua into the world, but by the time she gave birth to him, her tolerance for Andrew had worn palpably thin. The cards were now face up on the table for all to read. I hand stitched a beautiful periwinkle quilt, and when Josh was a day old, Sam and I thought we'd surprise them with it at the hospital. I took flowers and chocolate as well. Andrew greeted us in the lobby and said as sincerely as he could that Muriel was exhausted and was not up to seeing us. His head dropped to his chest, and he didn't dare look us in the eye. My heart ached for him. "But I made a quilt for the baby," I wheedled. "We can be very quick and peek at the little guy for just a minute. We promise not to stay."

Poor Andrew did not have the stomach or the courage to turn us away, so he slunk back into Muriel's room to plead our case. I knew it was only for show. Less than a minute later, he came out and took the quilt, the flowers, and the candy from my arms, while shaking his head timidly. "She said no. I'm sorry, Mom and Dad. You can see him after we go home." I rolled my eyes, gave him a quick hung, and we left.

We probably saw little Josh only two or three times before Muriel was finished with the marriage. Again, there was no standing up to Muriel. She tossed Andrew aside like a soiled bedsheet. He was on his own again, but this time all but chump change of his income went to his family. He drove a sad little scraped-up Corolla and lived in a dark basement studio apartment. Occasionally he came by for a sandwich because he didn't have money for food. Every so often, Sam and I gave him what we called "lunch money." As per classic Andrew, he took everything in his stride. He didn't moan, groan, or criticize Muriel. He just got back in his little boat and began to row as hard as he knew how. The one constant for Andrew was working hard, no matter what the job was. He'd put on his tow truck uniform and put in his eight hours.

He yearned to see Carly and Josh as much as he possibly could. It was part of the custody agreement. At first it was on and off, here and there, but after a time, after he'd driven the forty miles to pick them up, there would be no one home. Muriel would later say that she forgot or imply that he was the one who was mistaken. It hurt my heart to hear that he would sit for an hour at a time by himself on her front porch waiting for them to show up before giving up and going home. Paying child support was never an issue for Andrew. Supporting his children was at the top of his list. He had the payments automatically deducted from his paycheck, so that they were always on time. In the end, it was determined that he had actually overpaid several thousand dollars, and the court informed him he didn't need to pay for a time. Muriel stubbornly kept to her plan of not letting him see them, except for rare occasions. He hired a lawyer friend and appeared in court trying to make the visitation viable, especially since child support was not an issue. But the whole legal system was so intimidating and confusing, not to mention expensive, that he just couldn't keep up. He also didn't have the wherewithal to explicate in his own behalf. He felt tongue-tied, overwhelmed, and subjugated. It wasn't long before he owed the lawyer more money than he could possibly ever pay back, so he simply gave up.

One Christmas Eve, I encouraged him to urge Muriel to allow the kids to come to our family party. Surprisingly, she gave in, and the trio arrived at the appointed time. It was so wonderful to see them, even though it was obvious they didn't know the other cousins and were not really sure who Sam and I were. They clung timidly to Andrew's pant leg. On the way back to Muriel's, Andrew spotted flashing lights in his rearview mirror and dutifully pulled to the side of the road. After frisking him, the police informed him that Muriel had reported him taking the children without permission. After questioning him at length, and somewhat satisfied that this was not a legitimate kidnapping, they deposited the children into the patrol car and left poor Andrew scratching his head at the side of the road. Perplexed, upset, and in tears, he called us.

Muriel continued to use every trick in the book to intimidate him and keep the children from him. Sadly, after several years of not being allowed to see them at all, Muriel urged him to give up his parental rights so that her current husband could legally adopt them. Discouraged and resigned, he knew that the children who had become estranged to him would need some sort of constant father in their young lives. True to form, Andrew was not selfishly or egotistically cleaving to his valid paternal rights, but rather, was thinking about his children and what would be best for them. He was also clear about Muriel's tenacity and cunning, as well as his own inability to stand up to her. One day he gloomily asked my opinion, thinking, perhaps, that I would stiffen his resolve to deny the request. I actually surprised myself by saying I thought it was probably the most kind and loving thing he could do for them under the hopeless circumstances presented. He spoke of writing them a heartfelt letter explaining that it wasn't ever his desire or choice and about how much he loved them. He agreed that Muriel would never let them lay eyes upon such an epistle. I suggested he write it, have it notarized, and hide it to give them when they came of age and needed some clarity. He agreed. The thought seemed to soothe him a bit. He hung up and I shed more tears for my own child.

64

Ella

A couple of years winged by without a single earthquake. Just when we were becoming accustomed to the fluidity of a regular breathing pattern, Andrew met Dixie, the next woman of his dreams. This time, Sam and I had heard all about her through the grapevine, along with a few disconcerting details, but we decided to withhold judgment until we could meet her face to face. Unluckily, the meeting venue was that of my mother's viewing. I had spent some long, drawn-out weeks with her through the burdensome, tedious, and complicated business of dying, and was admittedly not my best self. My store of discretion and control had been raggedly depleted. We were centered and consumed in the age-old procedure of greeting friends and relatives around an open casket. Out of my periphery, I spotted Andrew sauntering towards us with the new girl in tow. I subtly stepped a few giant steps away from the rose-colored, rose-laden casket to deal with this questionably cordial summit. He excitedly proffered the introductions.

I should say that past experience with Andrew's girlfriends had not left me with high expectations, but whatever I had come to expect, I was always caught off guard. Dixie was short, round, and solidly situated on fat little bowling pin legs further extended by sharp pointed sky-high black stilettos. They seemed to have more height than her tibias. She was unabashedly made up with drawn-on, sweeping black eyebrows, which danced precariously above her dark cat-lined eyes. She was, it appeared, a fan of heavily caked pale foundation, bright red lipstick, and chandelier earrings. Her face was obviously a canvas for her outlandish artwork, so I couldn't really tell if she was as unattractive as she appeared. She was swathed in a slinky wraparound dress cut from an enormous black and white palm-leafed print, which further served to accentuate her generous curves and blooming décolletage. The open skin areas were decorated with tattoos, and there were numerous piercings peppering her body in what I imagined were outlandish places. Like so many others nowadays, it seemed that she had taken some comic book images to her tattoo artist and haphazardly picked out a few favorites for him to scrawl upon her. Trendy but permanent, tattoos are something I have a hard time relating to in the first place. Her short, spiky black hair was striped with shocks of platinum and blended perfectly with her ensemble. She reminded me of a well-fed skunk I had seen waddling across our driveway. As rude as it may be, it declared that Andrew was getting desperate. Dixie would not look me in the eye as she clung protectively to Andrew's suit coat. Her painted feline eyes darted this way and that. She dragged Andrew away from us like a heavy piece of luggage as soon as she could get away. I knew instantly that he was in trouble, though understandably and obviously, he craved female attention. As disconcerting as it was that night, we didn't see them again for a few months. It wasn't long after we heard through the same grapevine that Dixie was pregnant. The crazy thing is we almost took it in stride.

Heaven knows, Sam had spent hours over the years coaxing and schooling Andrew as to the moral and the pragmatic. We taught our children abstinence as a rule, not birth control, as it was in keeping with our religious principles. A case in point, on one Thanksgiving evening when Andrew was about seventeen, and before any of his children had come into the world, Sam reiterated what we had preached too many times to count. After the festivities were over and everyone had gone home or retired to their rooms, he asked Andrew to take a seat in the living room. Usually not a good sign unless one didn't mind confrontation. Andrew was generally unintuitive about such things, but this time he sensed Sam's impatience and urgency. "Andrew, Sam said calmly, "You can't bring precious babies into this world to unstable homes or to no home at all."

"I won't, Dad. You know I would never do that!" Andrew protested sincerely. Sam went on.

"I realize this may be awkward. I wish I didn't have to keep admonishing you about these things over and over. But it's for your own good." Andrew kept his head down and became uncharacteristically silent. "You must realize there are dire consequences to premarital sex. If you don't do it for yourself, please think of the innocent unborn and the consequences to them." Then Sam's tone became much more firm and his attitude less intense. His jaw was clenched and his hands were clasped so tightly in his lap that his knuckles were alabaster. "I know you don't understand anything but how you feel at any given moment. But you must try to think things through! Obviously, you are not practicing a smidgeon of self-control! I'm going to say something I never thought I'd say to one of my boys. It just hasn't been necessary up until now. Either keep your pants zipped or use a condom, for heaven's sake!"

The truth is, Andrew's impulsiveness had always gotten the best of him, but his attraction to the opposite sex had been out of control for a while. We didn't have specifics, but parents usually know what's up. Sadly, we were becoming numbed and resigned to his behaviors and were starting, by necessity, to brace ourselves for the inevitable. We had known for many years that Andrew had no real control over his emotions and his impulses. We'd seen it so many times in so many situations that we were not ever surprised.

The more I learned about Dixie, the more concerned I became. She and her ex-husband were addicts, though she said she was now clean. He was still in prison, and she had been recently released after being his partner dealing drugs. Her mother had been awarded legal custody of her other two children – surprise, surprise – and, of course, Andrew and Dixie were living with her as well.

When the darling little red-headed bouncing baby boy was born – luckily during Dixie's short run of being drug free – Andrew brought him home several times to visit us. He looked almost exactly like Andrew as an infant, except for the red hair. He was plump, happy, and sweet, and without reservation, he bounced on everyone's knee with a big grin on his dimpled face. Yet it wasn't long before Dixie relapsed into her previous puddle of addiction and left Andrew and the baby high and dry. Andrew couldn't work and cope with a newborn, so before anyone could do anything about it, Dixie's mother whisked him away to live with her other daughter in a neighboring state. Again, Andrew was heartbroken, if only for a season. This time, I couldn't get the fat little face, bright blue eyes, and ginger tufts of hair out of my mind. I obsessed continually as to his well-being and probable bleak future. I began to search in earnest for a family to adopt him. I knew it was futile to expect Andrew to step up to care for a baby and highly impractical even if he had the wherewithal to do so. I actually found two different amazing couples who showed great interest, even to consulting their lawyers. But in the end, I couldn't talk Andrew into pursuing his parental rights long enough to retrieve him from the next state, even with our help. By now, he was so intimidated and crushed by the legal system that he couldn't even think about it, no matter how I cajoled, reasoned, and made promises of assistance.

I have never seen that sweet baby again and have absolutely no hopes of it. As with the others, I have become quite good at pushing him from my thoughts.

Andrew forged ahead again. He's still the same congenial, kind, and friendly boy that I love. He tries to keep in touch with us, depending upon his work and the disposition of the female he is entangled with at the moment. He lived with and then married a surprisingly good and kindhearted woman. I like her very much. She seems, actually, too good to be true. Apparently, she accepts and embraces him for who he is. And let's not forget who he is – a hard worker, a good man, and a loyal partner. He has become a real father to her sweet young daughter. If Andrew has the opportunity to be trustworthy and steady, he will never disappoint. This time I genuinely feel positivity about this union and am hoping against hope that it will somehow stick. When they did decide to tie the knot, they zip-lined it down to Las Vegas to stand in front of a minister in Elvis attire. We were not invited. I was relieved, and not remotely insulted.

He called out of the blue the other day after no word for several months, which has become the new normal. He pleasantly asked if we could help them move some furniture with our truck. When we showed up to help, the sun was high and scorching, and we were all anxious to get it loaded up and be on our way.

But Andrew lingered by the door of our open truck, reclining his head on my shoulder for what seemed an uncomfortably long time. He said something to the effect that he never realized he was such a momma's boy, but that apparently, he was. His vocabulary was one thing that had always been surprisingly proficient. Everyone else watched and waited, a little annoyed and impatient. I, on the other hand, rubbed his coarse newly razored hair with the back of my hand, breathing in the scent of sticky hair product on his dark, irregular head. His thick, full beard was carefully trimmed around his full cheeks. For a quick moment, I was conveyed back to the days when his little head was covered in fine blonde clumps, smelling like freshly mown grass on a summer day. Or stringy, damp, and fusty like wet dog fur on a humid afternoon. The words to the song I used to sing to him decades earlier while bouncing him on my knee interloped unexpectedly into my head. "There's sunshine in my boy, there's sunshine in my boy …." My heart strained in its hidden cage and a single renegade tear meandered across the bridge of my nose. I plastered on my best poker face as I gently patted him on the cheek. He stood up, grinned, and we went our ways.

65

Andy

He usually ambled down Highway 160 through Colorado and then cut across the corner of New Mexico into Arizona before heading back up through Utah. He liked the ease of the drive home after finishing the Million Dollar Highway tour. His shoulders were relaxing nicely, and he cranked his head back and forth to loosen up his neck muscles. The air outside was stiflingly hot and dry now, but within the walls of the bus, it was always cool and comfortable. It felt like his own little upscale hotel. He had pulled over at a large Chevron station parking lot for his requisite ten hours of rest and was now plodding down the road again.

First light was just arcing over the horizon, and all of a sudden, a hearty breakfast sounded really appealing. His stomach began to make rumbling noises. He wheeled the bus into the parking lot of a small diner, one he hadn't really noticed on previous trips. Its blue neon sign was still ablaze, winking and blinking at intervals, at least the few letters that weren't burned out. Those remaining were only empty white tubing. He carefully locked the bus and headed through the doorway into the little restaurant.

He glanced at the decor and grinned. Mom would get a big kick out of this. Decidedly a Western motif, there were a few felt cowboy hats tacked haphazardly to the walls, several old saddles hoisted over a rail, two dozen or so spurs nailed in crooked rows a foot below the ceiling, and numerous fake potted philodendrons hanging in painted tin cans on literally every blank wall. The walls were quite expertly papered in a predominantly brown bucking bronco rodeo theme. He made his way to a red faux leather booth near the middle aisle. It was embellished with star-shaped nail heads on the back and sides, and there were cowboys on horses imprinted in the backs. The seat he landed on had been slashed jaggedly in several places, obviously with a sharp utensil, but the green and white buffalo check plastic tablecloth had been wiped clean. He glanced at the menu only a few seconds before ordering a stack of buttered blueberry pancakes, maple syrup, a side of bacon and sausage, juice, and two scrambled eggs. His mouth was already watering. As much as he enjoyed being with his passengers, the concluding solitude was pretty nice. He glanced around and could see only two or three other customers.

The front door swung open with a grating sound, and Andy turned to watch an Arizona Highway Patrolman striding to the counter. The officer began to study the overhead menu. It took only a second for Andy to react. He knew without even blinking what he was going to do next. He slid from his torn bench and walked directly to the officer's side. The man was a full head taller than Andy and half again as broad. His dark beige shirt was clean and pressed; the collar looked starched. His pants matched and were tucked into tall polished black boots. His wide black belt held the tip of his black tie, as well as a leather-holstered gun. On his head was a large flat-brimmed hat, rounded like a bowling ball at the top and rimmed in black. It showed off a large gold metallic emblem in the middle. He had another emblem on his shoulder that Andy had seen many times before. Uniforms were his thing, of course, especially those belonging to law enforcement officers. The Arizona Highway Patrol emblem patch on his right shoulder was distinctive. It declared the name of the state and its department, and it had a sizable red and yellow, fanned phoenix in the middle. Andy was sufficiently impressed. Just something about those guys, no matter which state or branch they represent. It was the same as encountering celebrities or rock stars to other people. His heart welled up in his chest and he felt genuine reverence overtaking him. He'd felt that same feeling sometimes when he went to church.

He reached out his hand for the officer to shake it. The patrolman revolved on one foot slightly. He smiled crisply but a little quizzically before cordially extending his hand to Andy. "Sir," Andy said with genuine awe and admiration, "I'd like to thank you for all you do. It's a real privilege to meet you. And ... I'd like to buy your breakfast."

A bit taken aback, the man's mouth softened into a smile and he said, "That's right nice of you, son. But I've got my little lady out in the car with me this morning and I need to buy her something to eat, too."

Andy's face was as bright as the working neon letters hanging in front of the diner. He grinned widely. "No problem, sir. I would be honored to buy both of you breakfast!" Thank heaven he had some extra tip money rattling around in his trouser pockets.

66

Ella

L ife was full and satisfying but galloping at a pace as to throw one off the horse if the feet weren't tied to the stirrups, and I felt mine were.

Where had the time gone? Jenny worked long and hard to receive her bachelor's degree in accounting. We were so proud of her. She was now marrying her handsome high school skateboarding heartthrob. We were equally thrilled about that. The reception was to be held in our beautiful canyon yard. I was so excited, but it took so much effort that I thought I'd collapse before it was ready. We laid sod, wheelbarrowed dirt here and there, dug and set a big area in brick pavers, planted perennials (my favorite thing to do), and popped a hundred or more bright-colored annuals into borders and pots. It wasn't that money wasn't tight, it was extremely constricted. But everything seemed justifiable for this momentous occasion. Our first daughter's marriage. What could be more important than that? Everything was looking pretty magical, if I did say so myself. In addition to my button-busting gardens, we tied bunches of pink and ivory roses with white ribbon, added snowy baby's breath and three shades of pink peonies. We trailed them down the driveway and across the front porch. It looked like the pathway to Neverland, along with the hundred maples, boxelder trees, and river birches, which were an integral part of the landscape.

Jenny was absolutely radiant in her new satin gown. It was exactly the color and texture of melted strawberry and vanilla ice cream swirled together. I hand-tied a lovely white daisy crown for her beautiful blonde head. We chose a frosted, creamy pink three-layered fondant cake, which was made by a friend. Fresh flowers spilled over the layers, which perfectly matched her bridal bouquet of roses, lily of the valley, and pink peonies. I begged and borrowed as many tablecloths, vases, and glass lanterns as I could. We served slices of beautiful cake and plenty of pink lemonade. I charged the credit card with abandon, avoiding mentioning the specific numbers to Sam. It was pretty much perfect and worth it, I kept thinking. I talked myself out of any residual guilt. I was proud and excited, and I thought Jenny had never looked so beautiful. Clearly, Evan was the love of her life, and Sam and I adored him. He was funny, smart, kind, and ambitious. What more could you ask for your oldest daughter?

Evan worked hard at the university, as did Jenny by his side, and he began a prolific career in physical therapy. I watched her grow into a sensitive and good mother, and loving wife. Her babies came like clockwork. I had obviously not been a good example of raising a small, manageable family, but it was wonderful to watch them bloom and thrive. Five rambunctious boys and one sweet little girl. It made my heart burst to watch them, and it almost made me feel more successful at my own mothering, thinking I just may have set an example for Jenny. Of course, there were the occasional ups and downs as in every burgeoning family, but they were gliding along happily and proficiently, and definitely in the right direction.

Then came the unthinkable. The unimaginable, inconceivable, and implausible. One calm, clear, blue-skied summer evening, when all of life appeared sunny and bright, Jenny's second son and my grandson died suddenly in a violent car crash while on his way to the movies with friends. Seven teenagers had packed into a car without seatbelts, and several sustained serious injury, but there were no other deaths.

I have come to believe that the death of a loved one is a fifty on a pain scale of one-to-ten. We learn to expect trials, of course. We know there will be plenty to go around. We see them everywhere and have regular doses along the way. Difficult, even excruciating episodes when we must strap in by the skin of our teeth, hang on, and just get through. But when the loss is unfathomable? When a loved one evaporates into thin air without warning, one whose roots have entwined themselves in and throughout the flesh of our hearts and embedded themselves into our very souls? How do we tolerate the thought of being without them, let alone the dreadful reality of life going on? These particular losses have to be the deepest wellsprings of mortal suffering and the highest pinnacles of pain. I cannot say with certainty that the younger the person, the more excruciating the loss, but I think it's a fair assumption.

When David called me with the news, I was, ironically, walking out the front door of a hospital after visiting Jed's wife, whose water had broken just twenty-four weeks into her pregnancy. She was destined to remain there for the duration of her pregnancy, or as long as they could keep her labor from progressing. We were very worried and were making arrangements to help them. As I listened to the unfathomable words coming from the other end of the line, I felt I was being boxed soundly and senselessly to the head, to the point of tumbling, or should I say slumping over a rock wall and right into a rose garden at the building's entrance. I felt as if I had been run over by a car. I couldn't think, I couldn't comprehend, I couldn't speak. I knew I would probably sit in that garden forever, brushing up against the most beautiful flowers known to man, with their sharp thorns tearing at my flesh. I wouldn't have the strength to get up and out of the dirt. Ever. As the tears gushed, I pushed my hands and fingers into the moist soil around me and pictured my daughter's face. The girl I began my own career of motherhood with, the girl who I had shared most of my life with, not to mention my body.

As much as I was hurting, I knew that a gigantic lightning bolt had just leveled Jenny to the ground to writhe in agony. I felt sparks of that electricity reaching across the vast skies to surge through my own body. It was more than I could physically endure. It was a pain I could not have prepared for. When I finally mustered the courage to climb out of that flowerbed, mud and thorn blood on my skirt and legs, we ran to be by her side. Where else in the world could we possibly go?

Reaching her house seemed to take hours, not minutes. It was worse than I ever imagined. Cars moving towards her house lined the streets like ants flocking to an evil picnic. It was dreadful. The living room was already crowded, and the air itself felt thick with gloom, as if it were a substance all its own. The house seemed darker than it probably was. I looked through a sea of people to find Jenny. She was floating around like a ghost, flitting here and there, and finding no place to light. It wasn't long before I sensed that she was in shock and was actually retreating inside herself. I wanted to run and wrap my arms around her and protect her like I had so many times when she was little, but she wouldn't stand still. And worse, it became apparent that she didn't want me to. Though understanding of this, I felt like a cold metal barrier had been thrown up between us, forcing me to stand back and watch in horror. Though I could never see through her eyes, I understood intuitively what it must feel like to have life and reality forever altered.

The roots entwined in and around her heart had not only been severed but slashed so deeply that the profuse bleeding threatened to drain her own life. I felt frantic for her safety. My most commanding fear at the moment was that her pain might take her own life. Or worse, ruin it forever. I stood back and realized that I had become invisible. Though it was not about me in any sense, the pain of that realization was worse than anything physical I had yet suffered in my life.

I had endured loss through death, yes, but I found that being forced to stand on the sidelines to watch my own child walking the dreadful path of grief alone was a whole different level of suffering. I was being imprisoned by the plodding, death-defying, self-imposed personal walls she was throwing up to shield her vulnerable core. Not being able to mother her at this moment was as distressing as anything I had ever experienced. Clearly, she was incapacitated, devastated. But I knew she simply did not have the capability to let me come in to comfort her. I felt ripped in half, like she must feel on a different level. It was akin to having my spirit leave my body to never be allowed back in. It was becoming evident that I would not be allowed to share her desolate emptiness. It was like beating on the glass outside of an enclosed room and getting no one's attention. I sensed that my own child was being drained of the will to live, and I wanted to scream my lungs out.

I felt hatred for the flocks of friends and neighbors who seemed to be able to slightly pierce her bubble of anguish, real or pretended. Jenny's life's work had just been stolen unfinished, woefully incomplete. Her own precious child had vanished into thin air. Now for the first time since giving birth to her, I was helpless to help. I felt shackled to the point of desperation. Yet I wouldn't have dreamt of even whispering the thought, knowing her suffering will always dwarf my own.

I've learned a lot about the process of death and dying. My fear was that it could be long, excruciating, and hellish. I could picture the process of choosing the casket. I could visualize the roses and the daisies they would order but never actually see through blurred and swollen eyes. I knew about purchasing a burial plot and fretfully ordering the headstone. I could picture the ridiculously torturous viewing with its masses of flowers and innumerous vacant smiles, cardboard handshakes, and empty platitudes. There would be a gazillion hugs they would have no choice but to stiffly endure. Then there's the funeral. I could picture the stoic hour and a half of listening to precious personal anecdotes about their own child blared across a whole chapel full of strangers, even if most were friends. It would be an ineffable encroachment they would never in a million years think they'd have to steel for. I wept as I pictured piles of earth heaped around a casket buttressed over a gaping black hole. I could almost smell the sickeningly sweet stench of a thousand flowers. Last of all, I visualized the long nights of playbacks, what ifs, and the "did we do enough" scenarios over the long course of forever.

One of the random crazy thoughts I began to obsess over was the morning cereal Jenny always looked forward to and relished since babyhood, but now would have to gag down just to stay alive. I never thought I would or could beg to suffer for another, for I am generally too selfish. I'm too much a coward. But at this moment, I would have given all the money or worldly goods I would ever have, maybe even my right arm or left leg to take her place. She will never know this, because her own pain will always eclipse mine. I understand this as well.

After the funeral fiasco was over, we tried to be there for them. We needed to be there for us as well as for them. They were polite and cordial, but no more so than to the lines of strangers darkening their doorstep. They cocooned themselves very quickly in an armored covering that protected and girdled them from everyone else. After a time, the covering became a hard, brittle shell protecting their vulnerable underbellies for a future time when they might actually care to survive. To me, Jenny was simply not Jenny any longer. I hardly recognized her. She was now only a mother to five children who mercifully needed her to get out of bed and take care of them. At least that kept her alive. As for my son-in-law, he wore his grief like a heavy, leaded overcoat, which constantly tried to wrestle him to the ground. His shoulders sagged, and his poor eyes were vacant. I winced as I heard him say there were "no good days." I knew he was doing the best he could, but I also knew that he was telling the truth.

When you lose a child, it's a safe bet that you've hit the bell with your mallet on the carnival pole and flung the puck clear off the top and twenty-five miles across the park. Though I never lost a child to death, it was always my greatest fear as well as my greatest relief. I watched my parents lose my little sister, and I thought I knew a thing or two about subterranean grief. But nothing could have prepared me for the horror of witnessing my own child losing her fifteen-year-old boy. Though I never lost her to death, I lost her. Though she still breathes and walks the earth, I lost the part of her I always loved the most and fear I'll never have again. Some tragedies bring a torrent of mudslides in their wake that sweep the most carefully built and precious of edifices off their foundations, never to be rebuilt. Tragically, there are some things one never gets past.

67

Ella

I sit on the porch in one of my treasured vintage wicker chairs. They are labeled "Palecek" on the back. I ran across them one day at a garage sale. I drag my fingers over the chipped white wicker. The early east light is peeping over the mountain and dances across the yard like lords a-leaping. I study the 150-year-old stump in the distance, sliced level and covered with many metal pots of lush pink geraniums. My grandmother's favorite geraniums were red, but mine are pink. They make a dramatic splash as they preen their lavish and bulbous heads in the sunlight, the heavy blooms compressing together to create a huge single bouquet large enough to fill a whole dining room table, which of course, the stump is. I watch as the sun kisses the tops of them, bathing the petal edges in a blushing glow. At the end of the porch, a gluttonous brown squirrel stuffs his bulging cheeks with seeds that have fallen from the feeder hanging above him. He is pretty endearing, I think, though when I picture him without all his heavy fur and tail, I see only a regular rodent. His simple nervous system provides for only short jerky movements, and he turns his head in quick mime-like action to survey me, surveying him. Apparently, he knows whom the seeds belong to but resumes his gleaning anyway, taking no more notice of me. "Silly little creature, but delightful," I say out loud. My little puddle of white fluffy dog, Evie, sits contentedly at my feet, her fur suffused in sunlight, appearing like fresh snow. My breathing is smooth and slow, and my mind hums with contentment if only for the moment, mimicking my dog's constant disposition.

Who would have thought that I, of all people, would ever have an acre of lush canyon land to work, plant, nurture, and enjoy? Digging in the centuries-old, rich, black soil has become one of the seemliest of pleasures nowadays, and I love filling each square inch with plants, flowers, or groundcover. After so many years, I have them in abundance. It is as if providence resolved, for some odd reason, to open its smiling mouth into a big gaping grin and spill out wonderful gifts into my open lap.

I often sit by the creek in the afternoons listening to the mesmerizing sounds of water rushing downhill. No matter where you go on earth, creek sounds are almost identical. They sing in their constant and ancient gravelly voices, probably a soothing white-noise lullaby orchestrated by the creator Himself. The afternoon light fans across the maples, highlighting only portions of the leaves.

Some are left deep green and opaque, and others, even adjacent, are rendered translucent and apple green. They are so different in the light it's as if one tree consists of several different species. The leaves lit up are naked, or you can peer right through their flimsy clothes. Their secret and delicate parts run up and down, their inner spines exposed.

Sam and I can usually be found on the front porch on summer evenings, surveying the beauty of the long curving driveway across the wonderful noisy creek. The bends are bordered in arching rock walls. The mint-green, wrought-iron, leaf-covered arch at the opening of the drive sparkles in white fairy lights, as if glitter has been shaken on top. It was a Mother's Day gift one year from Sam.

We chat easily about the nuances of our days, politics, or current events. We debate the particulars of this or that, the children, the grandchildren, or the never-ending problems that remain stubbornly glued to our large family. We can't see the sunset, as it is miles down the hill and out of our view, but we watch the skies turn from gold to pink with a smattering of coral and sometimes a splash of lavender, as it creeps stealthily across the tree line, spreading onto the mountaintops. Perhaps not quite as good as a regular sunset, but just as peaceful and sustaining. When the darkness bleeds through the leaves to the branches, Sam always says it's time to go in.

68

Ella

More musing. I've decided life may be a lot like eating a prickly pear. The fruit is sweet and delicious, not to mention nutritious. Also, the entire plant is edible.

But in order to get to what you want from it, you must put on heavy gloves, yank out the spiny thorns with pliers, and run the skin over an open flame to remove the stinging hairs upon its skin. There's always a price, always complexity, and forever compromises to taste the sweetness. It's unpredictable and downright uncomfortable unless you learn to accept the realities.

If only I could have realized in those disorienting, aggravating, and stressful years of trying to shepherd Andrew, that having him be born to me would be such a gift. I didn't dream I would learn so much more than I could have without him. He opened my world, and I am the better for it. The experience has let in more light than I would have ever imagined, and allowed me to hear sounds not normally in my range. When we pass to the eternal phase, and I know we will, perhaps the most frustrating, painful, and difficult incidents we experience in this realm will be the most precious and appreciated to look back on. The badges of courage, the forced learning, the stretching beyond the comfortable.

Nowadays when Andrew calls, I put the phone on speaker and just try to listen. He tells me all about the bus trips, the people he meets, the sights and sounds of his days. I love listening. As usual, most of all, he tells me, in great detail, about the bus itself. It's his trusted friend, partner, and ally. His only complaint about bus driving is being gone so much, but at the same time he enjoys sights and sounds most of us never get to experience, and meets more interesting people than most of us could ever dream of meeting.

Of course, he repeats himself as usual, but he is a joy to listen to. He is, as always, full of exuberance and positivity. I have come to love his circuitousness. Often, we don't get everything on the first pass, anyway.

It is, of course, highly gratifying to observe the other children work at the business of life as well. I take pride in their achievements, their charity, their parenting, the running of their businesses, the teaching, or other praiseworthy pursuits. I appreciate the successes, the citizenry, the productivity, and the dutifulness. It warms my heart to see them prosper and flourish, and admittedly, it adds a smidgen of smugness to my own parenting.

At the same time, I have come to realize that Andrew is the child who is likely the happiest from moment to moment. He is rarely discontent and expends little energy longing for more. He is not annoyed with others, but rather looks for the best in them and inevitably finds it. He enjoys the simple sights and sounds of life every hour. He takes his days in stride and looks forward to each new adventure, slowing down only briefly for the disappointments.

I could never have envisioned this in the earlier years but have come to see Andrew as one of my most successful children. Of course he struggles. My goodness, he has struggled. But really on a different level than the others. He finds attainment in his own way and time and scatters good everywhere he goes. He doesn't carry huge expectations, so he is not easily disappointed. He is honest, kind, considerate, interested, and has practically no disposition for evil. He loves animals, children, and most people who are reasonably decent. He thrives on hard work, no matter how mundane or simple, and feels no need to compete or win. He sincerely wishes everyone the opportunity to triumph.

Life is brief, and there are so many ways success can be measured. It will be startling, I think, to discover the complexity of the measuring stick. When it all shakes out, the Andrews of the world will take their rightful places among the honorable, illustrious, and the very best of God's children. Of my children, too, I think.

69

Ella

On a brisk fall day, Andrew called for an afternoon chat. If I remember correctly, he was driving a thoroughfare along the Oregon coast. He could identify each mile marker and how it denoted his progress. I happened to be painting doorframes in the basement. I set the phone to speaker, laid it on a folding chair, and continued to brush. He began to fill me in on the adventures on his recent trip. As usual, he was happy and full of detail and description. I smiled as I dipped, painted, and dripped on the carpet. I wiped a dab of paint across my forearm and cleaned it with my shirt. What a character he is, I thought happily, for the thousandth time.

He recounted the trip with three dozen exuberant high school students as they made their way across the country performing with their marching band. He had taken them several times before because the faculty always requested him, having proved his reliability, kindness, attentiveness, and harmlessness. He told me he knew every student's name. He recounted in rather painful detail anecdote after anecdote. He related how he playfully joked around with them each time they got on and off the bus. He even rented what he called a large plastic bumper body ball and cavorted in it with them around a football field, bouncing and falling over to their delight and to his genuine enjoyment.

After the rehearsing trip particulars, he went on to recite, for the fiftieth time, what he calls his "bus rules," as he usually does every other time he calls. Keep the bus shiny and polished at all times, make certain the windows are clean inside and out. Wipe the seats down and sweep the floors. Polish the rail and fixtures, and make sure the bathroom is spotless. Always keep plenty of water for thirsty guests. Make certain the secondary mirror is positioned just right so the back area and patrons can be viewed clearly. Check the tire pressure and always do a thorough safety check of all systems before heading out. He reiterates how he keeps the bus from weaving even the slightest bit on the road by holding the steering wheel in one spot with both hands. He says it makes for a much smoother ride.

I am now able to be calmer, and I have learned to listen. I try to picture the execution of all of these procedures one by one, as my boy carefully takes stock of his very large Matchbox car. For a split second, I can vividly see them sailing off the hot black asphalt roof from his open bedroom window, landing in the pile of dirt below.

Andrew has taught me to adjust my mental periscope and paint with a broader brush. What I used to accept as right and wrong, black and white, and good and evil has not been altered much. Surprisingly, I haven't needed to adjust my foundation, my principles, or my views. But I do think I see a little farther through the narrow windows out into the distance. I have learned that life cannot be controlled, though admittedly, I do my darndest to try. I realize I'm not in charge, but I suspect I am definitely responsible for managing what I've been given.

I have come to believe people hit the ground running with a specific set of individualized gifts, inclinations, strengths, and weaknesses — traits that were part of them before birth. If this is true, they will have ample freedom and responsibility here to become who they will, without too much meddling on anyone else's part. We would do well to settle down, teach as many correct principles as we have time for, then sit back, acknowledge, and enjoy the differences. That's been the learning curve for me.

Observing Andrew has also taught me to cut myself a little slack. I have my own perplexing set of attributes, my own inherent peculiar packaging. I usually measure my own success or failure by comparing them with others', thus spending inordinate amounts of time feeling inadequate (and sadly, at times superior).

Andrew has taught me many unexpected things, which I would never give for an easier path. He has taught me to focus on the horizon, as his gaze is always upward and out.

The suggestion has surfaced from watching Andrew that being good is less about following a set of rules than it is the decency embedded in an imperfect heart. Also, that there is never only one right path or even a few acceptable roads to follow.

I have come to believe that although good intentions, in and of themselves, rarely make for a smooth-running life, they do earn a decent allocation for forgiveness. I have come to think charity is more about good intent than good deeds. It's the desire to help, even without capacity or resource to do so. It's less about being right than wanting to do right.

Another very important lesson Andrew has taught me is that human beings should only be judged by the principles they can grasp and comprehend, and that it's almost impossible for the rest of us to discern which for whom.

Life is about striving. It's less about winning than staying in the race. Victory is not about intellect, talent, or getting to the head of the class as much as it is about putting one wobbly foot in front of the other. Obviously, life is about crossing the finish line, but it's not about getting there in one swift straight line. Zigzagging is just another way to get home, if you get there as well and as soon as you are able. What counts is that you cross the finish line better than when the starting gun went off.

I like to play around with a somewhat childish metaphor about life. I compare it to that of putting on a coat. A very particular coat that an adoring parent carefully and individually made for each of us. It's never the one we would pull off the rack. The cut is often unappealing, the fit a bit uncomfortable, and the color and fabric less than stunning. Yet it is the coat we are handed, obliged to keep, and constrained to wear for the entire span of taking breaths.

Each coat has big, deep pockets filled to the brim with fascinating possibilities and strict certitudes, although the mix seems random, haphazard, or serendipitous. They are jammed with gifts, challenges, pain, and surprises. Again, often not the ones we would choose or long for. We wistfully long for those we see others wearing. The resources inside the pockets are plentiful as well, but they are not measured in desired increments. We can pluck out experiences, relationships, journeys, wonders, and knowledge. Everyone is gifted with one passion or twenty, and not a few storms to weather. Unfortunately, mingled among the gifts or hidden in the seams are razor blades, dry sticks, sharp stones, poisonous snakes, and the occasional lightning bolt.

Each coat is open enough to allow exposure to harsh weather in the form of fear, anxiety, pain, suffering, sadness, disappointment, disillusionment, envy, offense, and sorrow. But in the breast pocket of each (nearest the heart) is a small trove of treasures that is never depleted. This compensatory compartment is lined with silver and stuffed with things like sunsets, rainbows, rivers, stars, cool breezes, and sweet-smelling roses.

For better or worse, the coat remains upon us, though we constantly ask why. He who chooses our coat is the only one who knows. He understands us better than we could ever discern ourselves. He knows which coat will shelter, expose, and protect as necessary. He knows which coat will be roomy enough for growth but snug enough for striving. It will be durable enough to last until the journey's end, which is different for each as well. Happily, we all get a coat generous enough for do-overs and second chances. And no matter how much we wish we'd gotten a different one, we must acknowledge that without this tailor-made gift from an omniscient parent, we wouldn't have a coat (or life) in the first place.

Ella

After wrapping up his account of the week's bus adventures, Andrew went on to ask about the plans for Sam's upcoming seventieth birthday. There was a dust storm beginning to brew in his head. He grabbed at each swirling puzzle piece as if they were flying willy-nilly in the air, and threw out several possibilities. He offered some pretty crazy ideas, most of which I politely ignored. Then a plan hit him like a brick, catching him off guard. He began to get more and more excited, and I quickly caught his vision and grabbed hold of his ideas, acknowledging they just might work. He began to lay out viable plots one at a time, being as thorough and methodical as Andrew could be, taking pleasure in every detail. It was as if he was anticipating the pleasure of his elderly bus passengers or cherished high school students.

He arranged for me to rent his beloved toy, his bus, for an evening – at a reduced rate, of course, as his employers were quick to reward their easy, affable, and extremely valued employee. His idea was to park it in the Home Depot parking lot at six o'clock sharp, adjacent to a restaurant I knew I could get Sam to agree to. It was easy to enlist the help of all the kids and grandkids, and we surreptitiously group-texted Andrew's scheme into motion. On the appointed day and time, Sam and I drove to the preplanned dinner destination. The entire family was quietly hidden away inside the darkened gray and black monster. It looked almost sinister crouching between the fence and the curb under the streetlight in the big parking lot. One of its massive headlights appeared to be winking under its painted black eyeliner.

Someone had volunteered to decorate the interior of the luxury liner with streamers, a massive collection of balloons, and some very happy signage. Someone else planned impromptu speeches and silly songs, and another made reservations at Sam's favorite Mexican restaurant downtown. I baked six dozen yellow cupcakes with dark chocolate frosting, also Sam's favorite, and bought sixty frosted eclairs, his other preference. I stashed them under the stairs in the basement, hoping the mice wouldn't discover them before the big day.

It was more difficult to manipulate my husband than I had hoped. He wanted to park and run directly into the restaurant, as he thought Joe was the only family member who could meet us for dinner. He had been mildly annoyed with me for being a little late, and I believe more than a little disappointed at the meager line-up for the celebration, though he would never have admitted it. Just before we spotted a parking place, I pretended to notice the bus out of the corner of my eye and begged him to drive over closer for just a minute to see if it might be one of Andrew's. After a bit of fussing and wrangling, he grumpily gave in. As we approached, Andrew imperially dismounted the bus in his freshly cleaned and ironed gray and black uniform with the stitched logo over the breast pocket. His cap was straight, and his tie hung neatly from his buttoned collar. He seemed jubilant. More like an airline pilot greeting his passengers. I leapt up the bus steps feigning playfulness, and Sam slowly but reluctantly followed. At that moment, the lights flashed on inside, and it sounded like a hundred gypsies yelling and screaming "Surprise!" Sam was flabbergasted and enormously pleased, to say the least. I smiled as I watched a huge grin spread over his previously sullen face.

Andrew climbed into his captain's chair and ceremoniously started the engine. It sounded like a roar. He glanced up through the mirrors to the back, scrutinizing his beloved patrons. The beast glided smoothly and deftly away from the curb. As we drove away, Luke came through the front aisle and began with an emotionally tearful birthday speech honoring his dad, while utilizing Andrew's infamous cordless microphone. Many of the others followed suit in presenting warm familial toasts. There was much joking, singing, and laughter, but the big bus did not weave, tip, or rock. With Andrew at the helm, it resolutely kept its trajectory. Through all the chaos, I noticed Andrew's hands expertly gripping the wheel in his two-way position, and his clear eyes staying glued to the road. He was adroitly steering us to our destination in safety and in style. The night was an important milestone for Sam, of course, and a pinnacle one for our family.

Affectionately, I observed Andrew throughout the evening as he played his important role in our family event. With a burgeoning lump in my throat, I realized that he was clearly and proudly in his element. Until the last stanza of the birthday anthem faded, and a hundred hugs had been happily meted out, he remained stoically "in bus driver mode," serving proficiently and professionally. His shoulders were squared, his blue eyes were gleaming, and his head was just the right tilt of high. Without question, Andrew's plan and his beloved bus had rendered the evening an enormous success. Undoubtedly, I mused, he is a masterful bus driver, but in his mother's eyes, he is much more. In his own arena, he stands a champion. No, I cannot recall seeing him look so pleased.